44 IRISH SHORT STORIES

44 IRISH
Short Stories

An Anthology of Irish Short Fiction
from Yeats to Frank O'Connor

❋

Edited by Devin A. Garrity

THE DEVIN-ADAIR COMPANY
Old Greenwich, Connecticut

The Devin-Adair Company, Inc.
143 Sound Beach Ave.
Old Greenwich, Conn. 06870

*or from the following publishers and persons controlling
copyrights of stories.*

Brandt & Brandt for permission to reprint "Come Back My Love" by Maurice Walsh, from TAKE YOUR CHOICE, J. B. Lippincott Co.; copyright 1953 by The Curtis Publishing Co.

Paul Vincent Carroll and Richard J. Madden Play Co., for permission to reprint "She Went By Gently," from *Irish Writing.*

Desmond Clarke for permission to reprint "The Islandman," from the *Dublin Magazine.*

Maurice Crain and the author for permission to reprint "The World Outside" by Val Mulkerns, from *Irish Writing.*

Eric Cross for permission to reprint "Saint Bakeoven," from *Irish Writing.*

Curtis Brown, Ltd., for permission to reprint "Bell Wethers" by Jim Phelan, from BOG BLOSSOM STORIES, Sidgwick & Jackson, Ltd.; and "Persecution Mania," by Sean O'Faolain, from *The Bell*, November, 1952.

The Devin-Adair Co., for permission to reprint "The Awakening" and "The Return" by Daniel Corkery, from THE WAGER AND OTHER STORIES, copyright 1950 by The Devin-Adair Co.; "The Kith of the Elk-folk" by Lord Dunsany, from THE SWORD OF WELLERAN, copyright 1954 by Lord Dunsany; "Weep for Our Pride" by James Plunkett; from THE TRUSTING AND THE MAIMED, copyright 1955 by James Plunkett; "Father Christmas" and "The Wild Duck's Nest" by Michael McLaverty, from THE GAME COCK AND OTHER STORIES, copyright 1947 by The Devin-Adair Co.; "Teresa," by Sean O'Faolain, from THE MAN WHO INVENTED SIN, copyright 1948 by The Devin-Adair Co.; "The Hawk" and "The Tent," by Liam O'Flaherty, from THE SHORT STORIES OF LIAM O'FLAHERTY, copyright 1955 by Liam O'Flaherty.

Doubleday & Co., Inc. and Harold Matson for permission to reprint "The Lady on the Grey" by John Collier, from FANCIES AND GOODNIGHTS, Doubleday, 1951; copyright 1951 by *The New Yorker.*

Introduction

The Irish have always had a way with words. Long ago they took on a language not their own and learned to rework it into pure magic. Nowhere is this magic more in evidence than in their short stories—stories that combine lyricism, humor and tragedy with rare imagination set in simple backgrounds, without resort to props.

The seemingly effortless art of the best Irish writers has an appeal that is naive and highly sophisticated at the same time; the disarming simplicity with which the tales are spun being somewhat misleading at first reading.

The stories in this collection should be read for enjoyment rather than for critical evaluation. No attempt has been made to comb the output of the twentieth-century Irish writers for 44 "best." That would be a most difficult task; for almost everyone in Ireland writes a poem or two, a play and a short story, at one time or another. And while the poems and plays have received considerable attention in recent years, the Irish stories, by and large, have not. Many fine examples can still be found buried in the pages of the "little" magazines which appear in Ireland periodically and as quickly disappear, never having broken the Irish barrier. *Irish Writing*, edited by David Marcus; Seumas O'Sullivan's *Dublin Magazine; Envoy*, and *The Bell*, edited by Sean O'Faolain and later by Peadar O'Donnell, gave many of the young writers their start.

More than half the stories, 23 to be precise, are published here for the first time in America. They have been collected over the past decade and reread at intervals to see if they retained their peculiar magic. Each of the present 44 has stood that test well.

"Irish genius," someone has said, "works best, if not solely, in short explosions." But even in short bursts, variety is desirable and an effort has been made to avoid sameness—a quality which can be as boring in a gathering of the elect as among any other group.

Some of these stories are not stories at all, but sketches—and in one original instance by Bryan MacMahon, a recording of conversation in an English pub. The inclusion of John Collier is by way of contrast, to show the difference between an Irish story written by a talented Englishman and the real thing. The comical vaudeville-Irish story and the overly sentimental tale have been studiously avoided.

Devin A. Garrity

Contents

Contents

44 IRISH SHORT STORIES

PAUL VINCENT CARROLL

She Went by Gently

❊

It was close on three when the knock came in the night.
She was out of bed on the instant in her old flannelette
nightgown, with her silver-grey hair tossed down her back.
The night-light was flickering quietly as, in the shadows
by the elm tree outside, she discerned Manahan's un-
shaven face under the battered hat.

"The pains is bad on the girl," came his voice. "I think
maybe it's surely her time."

"Go before me fast and have plenty of hot water," she
answered. "I'll be at your heels with Frank."

She heard his foot in the night hurrying off as she
drew on her heavy dress over the nightgown. Himself
stirred and put his beard irascibly outside the blankets.

"You'll go none," he snapped. "A slut like that, that
gets her child outside of priest and law. Four miles uphill
on a mountain road and the mists swarmin'."

"I'll go," she said quietly, and crossing, she ruffled

From *Irish Writing*.

Frank's unruly hair on the little camp bed. "Be risin', Frank, and let you carry the lantern for me to Manahan's."

"If there was just a drop o' tay before we'd start, ma," he protested sleepily.

"There's no time, son."

"A grand pass we've come to, in this country," grumbled himself. "Encouragin' the huzzies and the sluts to be shameless. I'd let her suffer. A good bellyful o' sufferin' would keep her from doin' it again."

He moved coughingly into the deep warm hollow she had vacated in the bed. The strictures of his uncharitable piety followed her into the silver and ebony of the mountainy night. She went gently . . . her feet almost noiseless. There was an inward grace in her that spilt out and over her physical lineaments, lending them a strange litheness and beauty of movement. Frank was a little ahead of her, swinging the storm lantern. He was munching a currant scone plastered with butter. His sturdy little legs took the steep sharp-pebbled incline with careless grace. Now and again, he mannishly kicked a stone from his path and whistled in the dark.

"Careful now, Frank, in case you'd slip over the bank in the dark," she admonished.

"Och, ma," he protested, "the way you talk! You'd think I wasn't grew up. It makes little of a fella."

She smiled and watched him lovingly in the silver dark. He was her youngest. The others had all followed the swallows into the mighty world. Martin was in America, Annie in England, Matthew in Glasgow, Paddy in the Navy, Mary Kate a nursemaid in Canada, Michael was at rest somewhere in Italy. His C.O. had said in a letter that he had died well. If that meant that he had had the priest in his last hours, then God be praised, for he was her wayward one. She preferred him dying full of grace to dying full of glory. . . . But Frank was still with her. He had her eyes and gentleness and the winning tilt of the head. It would be good to have him to close her weary eyes at the end of all . . .

They had now crossed the cockeyed little bridge over a dashing tawny stream and the mountains came near her and about her like mighty elephants gathered in a mystic circle for some high purpose. Everywhere in the vast silvery empire of the dark there was the deep silence of the eternal, except for the rebellious chattering of the mountain streams racing with madcap abandon to the lough below. They were the *enfants terribles* of the mighty house, keeping it awake and uneasy. Now and again a cottage lifted a sleepy eye out of its feathery thatch, smiled at her knowingly and slumbered again. All of them knew her . . . knew of her heroism, her quiet skilled hands, her chiding, coaxing voice in the moments of peril. . . . In each of them she had been the leading actress in the great primitive drama of birth.

The climb was now gruelling and Frank took her arm pantingly. The lantern threw its yellow ray merrily ahead. All would be well.

She ruffled his hair playfully, and smiled secretively under the black mask of the night.

At a mischievous bend on the mountain path, the Manahan cottage suddenly jumped out of the mist like a sheep dog and welcomed them with a blaze of wild, flowering creepers. Inside, the middle-aged labourer was bending over a dark deep chimney nook. A turf fire burned underneath on the floor. From a sooty hook far up, a rude chain hung down and supported a large pot of boiling water. She nodded approvingly and donning her overalls moved away in the direction of the highly-pitched cries from an inner room.

"If there's anythin' else I can do . . ." he called, half-shyly, after her.

"Keep a saucepan of gruel thin and hot," she answered. "And put the bottle of olive oil on the hob in case we'd need it. Play about, Frank, and behave yourself till I call you."

She went smilingly to the bed and looked down at the flushed tearful face, the big bloodshot eyes and the glossy

3

tossed hair of the girl. No more than eighteen, she
thought, but a well-developed little lass with a full luscious
mouth and firm shapely breasts. Jim Cleary who skipped
to England in time had had a conquest worth his while.
. . . The little rebel, caught in the ruthless trap of Nature, grabbed her hands beseechingly, held on to them hysterically and yelled.

"Oh, Maura, ma'am, please, please, please . . ." she
sobbed.

Maura chaffed her hands, soothed her gently, clacked
her tongue admonishingly and pretended to be very disappointed at her behaviour.

"Now, now, now, Sadie," she reproved her. "A fine
soldier *you* are! When I was here at *your* comin', your
mother, God rest her, bit her lip hard and said no word at
all. Come on now, and be your mother's daughter."

"Ah, sure how could I be like me poor dead mother,
and me like this, and all agin me?" sobbed Sadie.

"Am *I* agin ye, child?" soothed Maura, "and I after
walkin' four miles of darkness to be with you!"

The tears came now but silently, as Maura's skilful
hands warmed to her work . . .

Frank remained in the kitchen at a loss until suddenly
the door opened and a large nanny goat sailed in with perfect equanimity and balefully contemplated this stranger
on home ground. Frank looked askance at her full-length
beard and her formidable pair of horns, but this was of
small consequence to the goat which advanced on Frank
and in the wink of an eye had whipped his handkerchief out
of his top pocket and stuffed it in her mouth. Frank's protest brought an assurance from Manahan who was stooped
over the fire bringing the gruel to the boil.

"She'll not touch you," he said without turning his
head.

"But she has me handkerchief," protested Frank.

"Ah, sure isn't she only playing with you!" returned
Manahan heedlessly.

But by this time the goat had consumed the handkerchief with terrific relish, and was about to make a direct attack on the sleeve of his jersey. Frank dashed for the door with the goat after him. In the little yard he dived behind the water barrel that caught the rain-water from the roof. The goat snuffed past him in the darkness, and Frank hastily retraced his steps to the kitchen and barred the door.

He was just in time to see his mother put a generous spoonful of butter into a bowl of thin steaming gruel.

"Go in and feed this to your daughter, and coax her to take it," she directed Manahan. "She's quiet and aisy now and all will be well." He obeyed her shyly and without a word.

"You must be a big grown-up fella tonight and help your ma, Frank," she said.

"Anythin' you say, ma," he answered. "What is it?"

The baby had come forth without a cry. It was limp and devoid of any sign of life. She carried it quickly but calmly to the open peat fire, as close to the grimy chain as the heat would allow. It was naked and upside down. Frank, under her calm directions, held it firmly by its miniature ankles.

"Be a good son now and don't let it fall," she warned him, and plastering her own hands with the warm olive oil, she started to work methodically on the tiny body. Up, down and across the little chest, lungs and buttocks went the skilful fingers rhythmically until the newborn skin glistened like a silver-wrought piece of gossamer. The long minutes went by heavily. The oil lamp flickered and went out, leaving the dancing rays and shadows of the fire to light this crude drama with its eternal theme. Five minutes, seven, ten . . . without fruit or the promise of fruit. . . . But the moving fingers went on with rhythmic ruthlessness, searching for the spark that must surely be hidden there in a fold of the descending darkness. Frank's face was flushed, his eyes gathered up with the pain of exertion, his breath coming in spasms. On his mother's forehead beads of sweat gathered, rivuletted down the gray gentle face and flowed on to the newborn body to be ruthlessly merged in the hot oily waves of her massaging.

Then suddenly, as the tension had reached almost to the unbearable, a thin, highly-pitched cry came from the tiny spume-filled lips. She seized the baby, pushed Frank from her, turned it upright, grabbed a chipped, handleless cup of cold water and even as the fluttering life hesitated on the miniature features for one solitary second to receive its divine passport and the symbol of its eternal heritage, she poured a little of the water on the tiny skull and said, "I baptise you, in the Name of the Father and of the Son and of the Holy Ghost."

She wrapped the little corpse in the remnant of a torn sheet, without tear or trace of any sentiment, placed it in a drawer she took from the crazy wardrobe, and having made the Sign of the Cross over it gave it no further attention.

When she saw that the bowl was almost empty of gruel, she chased Manahan out with a gesture and settled the little mother comfortably. She was adjusting her wet, tearstained hair over her pillow when suddenly she felt Sadie's arms tightly about her neck. Her big eyes were quiet now and the pain and the travail were gone, but the tears came rushing from them again as Maura kissed and soothed her.

"I wish I had me mother," she sobbed. "Maura, ma'am, I'm goin' to be a good girl from now on."

"You have never been a bad one, darlin'," coaxed Maura, tucking the faded bedclothes into her back. "A wee bit foolish maybe, but the world and the years will learn ye. Sleep now and I'll see you tonight."

She re-donned her old black cloak in the kitchen.

"I'll tell Maloney to bring you up a white box," she said to Manahan. "It will save you the journey down."

On the mountain path she went noiselessly, with Frank a little ahead, carrying the extinguished lantern. The dawn greeted her from the heights with far-flung banners of amber and amethyst. The heights themselves ceased from their eternal brooding for a brief moment of time and gave her a series of benign obeisances. The racing rivulets tossed her name from one to the other on the Lord's commendation. The sun himself, new-risen and generous, sent a very special ray of light that caught up her tossed hair and rolled it in priceless silver.

"Why do men lie prone in their beds," she murmured, "and the great glory of God washin' the hills with holy fire?"

Shamus Dunne was taking in his two nanny goats for the milking as she passed his cottage.

"The blessin' o' God light on ye, woman," he said, touching his wind-swept hat.

"And on yourself too, Shamus," she answered. "How is the little fella now?"

"Ah, sure isn't he over a stone weight already. Ah, woman-oh, wasn't it the near thing that night? Ah, sure only for yourself, wasn't me whole world lost?"

"Arrah, men always think the worst at such times," she answered smilingly. "Sure, there was never any great fear of the worst that night! Herself, within, is much too good a soldier for that!"

Frank had now discovered a salmon tin and was kicking it vigorously before him. She took out her rosary at the bend where the path dips perilously between two ageless boulders, and as she trudged along, she began counting the beads effortlessly. There on the heights at dawn, caught between the gold and the deepening blue of day, she might have been a pilgrim out of a Europe that has long since vanished, or maybe a Ruth garnering the lost and discredited straws of the age-old Christian thought.

Frank had now lobbed his salmon tin on the lofty fork of a tree, and when she caught up with him, he took her arm undemonstratively. Himself would be up now, she thought, with his braces hanging, and maybe a hole in his sock that she had overlooked. He wouldn't be able to find the soap and the towel even if they were both staring at him, and of course if he blew the fire, even with a thousand breaths, it would never light for him. . . . But no matter now. Thanks be to God, there was an egg left in the cracked bowl that would do his breakfast. If the little white pullet in the barn laid in the old butter box, Frank would have one, too, with the help o' God. . . . When the cock himself laid an egg, Glory be, *she'd* get one all to herself!

They crossed the rickety bridge, as the dawn was losing its virgin colour. Frank saw a squirrel and rushed ahead of her. She paused for a moment and contemplated the restless waters. They took to her like a rich tawny wine poured out of some capacious barrel by some high ruthless hand who had suddenly discovered the futility of all riches. A May blossom rushed under the incongruous arch and emerged to get caught between a moss-covered stone and a jagged piece of rock. There was a turmoil and pain for a moment, and then it freed itself and rushed on. She wondered if it was the little soul she had lately saved, rushing on in a virgin panic to the eternal waters. . . . Maybe it was. . . . Maybe she was just an imaginative old fool. . . . Ah, sure what harm anyway to be guessing at infinite mysteries, and she so small on a mountain road?

Himself met her in the stone-floored kitchen. Indeed, yes, he was trailing his braces, and the sulky fire was just giving a last gasp before expiring.

"I suppose you saved the slut's bastard," he commented acidly.

She bent on her knees to blow the fire aflame again.

"I saved him," she answered, and a flame leaped suddenly upwards and made a sweet and unforgettable picture of her face.

DESMOND CLARKE

The Islandman

✳

The Islandman came zig-zagging down the mountain from his shelter high on Craughan, a shelter built of thick sods of earth and grass, roofed over with two sheets of galvanised tin, and bedded, deep and thick, with bracken and mountain moss.

He was a tall thin angular man, young and loose-limbed. His face, firm and unsmiling, was bronzed a deep brown and weather-beaten; a tousled mass of black curly hair waved in the breeze like the unclipped mane of a young filly.

He was dressed like a fisherman in a thick loose-fitting jersey of navy blue with a high collar reaching to his chin, and long sleeves doubled over his wrists. He wore rough grey homespun trousers, the seams thick, like pieces of rope. The pampooties on his feet were wet with the morning dew.

He came to the pier sheltering the small unused har-

From *The Dublin Magazine*.

bour at the foot of the mountain, a pier jutting out to the sea shaped like a large crooked L. He stood still for a while, shading his eyes against the bright glare of the early morning sun thinly suspended over the distant blue water, and watched the cork markers of his line bob gently up and down.

The morning was very quiet and still; the little village across the bay was asleep. As yet no smoke poured from the blackened chimneys of the cottages huddled closely together. Along the beach upturned curraghs lay, their black bottoms to the sky like a line of giant beetles asleep.

Quite suddenly he jerked his head to one side, and screwed his eyes tightly together, for the noisy agitated flight of a flock of gulls disturbed the calm peace of the morning. He watched the gulls pour from the cliffs in a great stream and wheel excitedly over the sea. He followed their flight to where they wheeled and gathered in a mass, and then he saw a moving patch of sea bubble up like a boiling pot. The gulls wheeled and circled over it, and screaming loudly dived, one after another, into the water.

The mackerel shoal moved quickly round the rocky head. The young man watched the sea and gulls for a while longer then he nodded his head thoughtfully up and down, a faint sarcastic smile gathering at the corners of his tight mouth. He turned and looked over at the sleepy village, then at the upturned curraghs on the beach, and the long nets hanging from upright poles.

He dropped lightly from the pier and walked across the shingle, his long arms swinging loosely by his side. His small curragh lay in a bed of stones close to the water's edge. Deftly he turned it over and dragged it into the sea, the water swilling about the end of his trousers and covering his feet. Carefully he manoeuvred round the end of the pier out into the shafts of golden light that cut deeply through the water revealing the rocky weed-covered bottom.

A quarter of a mile out, the row of corks bobbed gracefully up and down in line. The Islandman slew the curragh round in a wide sweep and brought it to the end of the line. Very carefully he reached over the side and drew the first pot into the boat. There were a few lobsters in it and he emptied them into the bottom of the curragh, returning the pot to the sea. The curragh drifted slowly along the line as he played it through his hand stopping just to take each pot and empty it.

The Islandman then rowed shore-wise. His face had grown softer, and he whistled quietly to himself. There was a fair heap of milling lobsters disentangling themselves in the bottom of his curragh. He stopped whistling and counted them roughly. Close on four dozen lobsters he had. They'd be worth at least sixpence apiece, maybe more, for the fishermen reckoned it was a poor season, and blamed everybody and everything for it, everybody and everything but their own innate laziness.

The curragh grated once more on the shingle and the Islandman dragged it gently to its bed of stones. He gathered the lobsters into a sack, leaving aside those he considered too small and immature.

Across the bay the cluster of white cottages came to life. Smoke curled thickly from all the chimneys. The women were raking out the dead ashes, uncovering the still glowing embers and building a fresh fire for the day. Children had gathered about the open kitchen doors, and two young girls were milking tethered goats by the gable end of a cottage.

The young Islandman wiped his forehead on the back of his hand, and gathering his sack of lobsters over his shoulder he climbed in a slow zig-zag fashion up the mountainside. Outside his sod-built cabin he made a fire of brushwood and dead bracken and brewed a can of strong tea. He ate a thick chunk of dry bread, washing it down with hot unmilked tea. Then he rested.

The sun had moved round in the heavens when he came down the mountain again. There was plenty of movement in the village like an uncovered ants' nest. Only

a few curraghs still lay on the beach, the sun glinting
brightly on their black bottoms. Many more were at sea
moving quickly towards the shore, whilst far out a few
were riding motionlessly like small specks on a polished
board.

The Islandman, his sack slung across his shoulder,
crossed the beach running by the village. The station, a
dingy low-sized shed, lay further round and was slightly
obscured by the cottages. The young man walked on, his
head down. He looked neither to the left nor right, neither
did he bid the time of the day to the men and women who
watched him with cold unblinking eyes. He could feel the
cold eyes on him and in his ears he could hear what they
were saying about him; he could only partly understand
them but he sensed their feelings deeply. He was an Islandman from Innishcloghan, and the sea, the sea that
washed their shores, was their sea, their very own.

Yes, he was a foreigner to them, an outsider, a strange,
unspoken, deep sort of fellow who lived for a few months
each year in a sod-built shelter on the mountainside, snug
in a hollow against the wind, with a bed of brushwood and
dry moss to lie upon.

At the station gossiping fishermen hung about, their
legs dangling from stacked empty mackerel cases. They
were smoking and spitting and talking in loud deep voices.
The Islandman walked past them and entered the low
dark building smelling strongly of fish and brine.

The agent was in his shirt sleeves, standing at a desk,
and writing with a stub of a pencil which he wet every now
and then with his tongue. He was a big chested man, red
faced and almost bald; he had a big belly held in with a
thick leather belt, hole-punched every inch or so. He
turned his head. " 'Morrow," he said gruffly, and then
"What have ye got to-day?"

The Islandman told him, and planted his sack on the
wet concrete floor. He rubbed his numbed hand up and
down the course seam of his trouser. He stood painfully at

ease whilst the agent opened the mouth of the sack and poked amongst the lobsters with a piece of stick.

"Not bad, not bad at all," he muttered to himself. Then he straightened up with a grunt and crooked his thumbs in the broad belt across his belly. "How d'ye manage it at all?" he asked queerly, and he looked hard at the Islandman.

The young man grinned foolishly, not quite understanding. The agent took the piece of pencil from behind his ear and sucked it for a moment or two.

"What are ye askin' for them?" he said, his eyes narrowing shrewdly, and his lips sucked into his mouth.

"Sixpence apiece," the Islandman told him.

The agent grunted and frowned a little.

"The lot for a pound—twenty shillings," the Islandman said.

"A tidy lot for lobsters, son. A tidy lot."

Three or four fishermen came in. They nodded in a friendly way to the agent. "What's he got?" one of them asked.

"A handy case of lobsters," the agent said.

The fishermen were silent then and stood about with their hands deep in their pockets.

The Islandman felt uneasy; he bent down and gathered the neck of the sack in his hands. "D'ye want them, mister?" he asked simply.

The agent took the sack from him. "Sure. Of course I want them. But, son, your price isn't reasonable, ye're askin' a bit much, aren't ye?"

The Islandman shook his head. For a moment he was at a loss for a word then he said, "They're scarce, very scarce."

The fishermen laughed loudly and one of them said in a hard voice, "Not so scarce with you, lad, eh?"

The agent was grunting and mumbling to himself. "A tanner apiece son? It's a bit steep, isn't it?"

The Islandman shook his head blankly.

One of the fishermen detached himself from the group and opened the sack. He poked a thick tobacco stained finger amongst the lobsters. The Islandman looked at him, his brow darkening and his mouth twisting to one side. The fisherman was grinning and looking at the agent. "Not worth a tanner apiece, Johnny. They're smalls," he said.

The other fishermen gathered round and mumbled together in deep voices. The Islandman, his face flushed, pushed them aside and gathered up the neck of the sack. "They're mine," he said warningly, and turning towards the agent he asked, "Are *you* taking them, mister?"

The fishermen stood back their eyes fixed darkly on him. "Ye're an uncivil bloody man," one of them said, and another said he should go back to the island he came from.

"Are ye takin' them, mister?" the young man asked again, and he dragged the sack towards himself.

The agent nodded. "I'll take them. A quid for the lot, an' if ye ask me anything it's a divil of a lot of money to be handin' out."

The Islandman hauled the sack across the shed and tipped the lobsters into a box. He could hear the fishermen whispering and mumbling among themselves, and he knew they were talking about him.

The agent handed him a pound note, crumpled and dirty, which the Islandman folded and placed in a small leather purse.

"Ye gave too much for them lobsters, too bloody much," he heard one of the fishermen say as he went out.

"I'd like to know where he gets them," another said.

"Don't we all know," a third said in a loud voice.

The young man stopped, and turned and faced the men in the shed. For a moment he stared them hard, his eyes bright and burning like small red coals, he was thinking out the words he wanted to say. "I catch them honest," he cried. "No one can say I don't. No one! No one!" A lock of hair had fallen curl-wise over his forehead, and he tossed it back with a defiant jerk of his head. "There's plenty, plenty of them, and fish too," he said remembering the shoal of mackerel passing round the head when the village slept under the morning sun. "Plenty, be God!" he cried. The men were grinning at him so he turned around and went out.

The sun was just a bright red ball with a blunted side, resting on the distant sea, when the Islandman pulled his curragh out to the row of corks, resting peacefully on a flaccid sea, a sea stained with gold and purple stripes. Leisurely, as though it were a pleasant easy task, the young man drew in each pot, examined it carefully, and then baited it liberally.

In the same leisurely way, with long slow strokes, he pulled his curragh to the shore, dragging it lightly over the shingle, deftly up-ending it, and then placing large stones against the gunwale to hold it in place for the night.

He was thinking all the time, thinking in a slow unhappy kind of way. He sat down beside the curragh; his eyes narrowed slightly as he fixed them on the dimly-dark outline of the island, a ragged and discordant rent in the unbroken skyline like a great tear. Gradually the broad expanse seemed to narrow, the sea between the shore and the rocky island faded to a thin line like a road between.

A feeling of loneliness surged about him and then swept over him like a great encompassing wave. A choking lump tightened in his throat and his mouth felt dry. He swallowed hard, and then buried his face in his hands. His island home never seemed so near and yet, yet a sea swept between them.

For an instant he thought of the upturned curragh beside him, and how easy it would be—O so easy—to draw it out to sea and row swiftly steadily homewards to warmth and friendliness and . . . He set his face hard against the temptation, after all a few months lobster catching, even from an inhospitable shore, was all he had. A few months to earn enough to sustain him through a winter, to roof the half-built stone cottage on a rock-strewn acre from which a few unwilling potatoes grew, and where there was only sparse feeding for his goat. A few pounds to complete and furnish the cottage, and then pay the priest for making Maireadh his wife.

Maireadh! Maireadh of the curling jet black hair, of the creamy complexion, and the fresh young breasts rising firm and enticing from her body like ripe apples. His thoughts dwelt pleasurably on Maireadh, on the rough stone cottage in the shielding of Ballyvoggy Head. His thoughts were satisfying, like a pleasant dream, and he was happy. Then grating footsteps on the shingle disturbed him and he turned his head sharply, startled like one awakening suddenly.

There was a woman standing close by him. A tall, thin wizen creature with torn unlaced boots, a torn shawl about her head and clutched tightly against her scrawny breasts. Her black skirt was badly torn and frayed all round the end. She leaned heavily on a hobbly stick, bent and gnarled like herself.

"God and Mary bless ye," she croaked a greeting in Gaelic.

The young Islandman was frowning but his face softened, and he stared the strange creature wide-eyed. Nobody on the mainland had ever addressed him in the tongue of his island home. He returned the old hag's greeting.

"You're a stranger here, *avico*," she said, eyeing him closely.

He nodded.

"You sleep on the hill beyant?" she jerked her stick towards the mountain.

"Yes."

"Your home is there, there on the island beyant, eh?"

"Yes, over there," he told her, pointing to the blurred mass fading into the darkening sky.

"Innishcloghan, *avico*, Innishcloghan," she cried in a

high squeaky voice, and she nodded her head. "Sure I know it, know it well, *avico*."

He jumped quickly to his feet and stood close to the withered old woman, lank and lean like a hungry scarecrow. "Dhia!" he cried like one reunited to an old friend.

"Aye, I know it, *avico*," the old woman croaked, "but 'tis many the year since I set foot there, many and many the year long before you were borned, *avico*. I've travelled a bit since then, many a lane, many a road, aye and many a land, but sure 'tis on'y a cross, cantankerous woman I am, an old bothered woman of the roads with ne'er a roof over me head, an' ne'er the chick or child to offer one, but . . ."

"You can have my cabin for the night," he interrupted quickly, adding apologetically. "It's not much, woman, but 'tis warm an' dry."

She laughed loudly, harshly, her whole frame shaking, her hobbly stick dancing on the stones. The Islandman stared her, a puzzled expression clouding his face.

She stopped laughing and touched him with a cold hand. "You've the generous warm heart of an islandman, *avico*, a kind good heart, but . . ." she wagged her head from side to side and laughed again, not so loud though.

"What are ye laughin' at?" he asked.

"Yerrah 'tis the innocent ye are," she said, her voice harsh, "the innocent without eyes to see, without ears to hear. What d'ye think they'd be sayin' across the bay there? Aye, what would they be sayin'?"

He was amazed at the harshness of her voice, a harshness with venom pouring from a toothless mouth and thin indrawn lips.

"Aye, I know what they'd be sayin'. Aye, I know for I've ears that hear and eyes that see. Liz, mad Liz, sleepin' in the stealer's shack, the stealer from the island who takes our lobsters from our pots, and . . ."

"A stealer! A stealer!" the young man cried, his face ugly with anger. He turned his head and looked across the bay to the village growing dark and hazy in the fading light, then he turned on the old hag gripping her roughly by the shoulders.

She shook herself free. "Don't heed them, *avico*, don't heed them, for they're a hard bitter people," she said in a voice that was acid with hate. She shook her head from side to side. "They talk to me, me," she said, "for they don't mind me. Hi. Hi. I'm just Liz, a harmless bothered old woman of the road. Duine le Dhia, moryah! A woman of God. But 'tis me that knows them, knows what they say, an' what they think, knows the schemes they plan deep down in their hard hearts. Ye're not the first man they broke, son. There are them that went before ye, *avico*. Aye, them that went before ye," she said, in a quiet faraway voice like one recalling a memory dimmed with the forgetfulness of years. Then the venom poured from her thin drawn lips again and she pointed a scrawny finger to the cottages. " 'Tis the badness in them, the badness in their hearts, and, *avico*, they'll come in the night, an' you high in the mountain there, an' cut the pots from the line, an' lay them adrift."

"Why should they, woman?" the young man cried, his face close to hers. "Why should they? What have I done? What?" he cried, his dark eyes ablaze deep in his head.

He looked hard at the ugly line-seamed face of the old woman whose eyes were screwed up into tight little knots. She's mad, mad, he told himself.

"A stealer, a thief from the island, that is what they say," she told him, pouring the words out close to his ear. "Ye take the lobsters from their pots, the mackerel from their nets, the herrin's and plaice from their lines, the . . ."

The Islandman drew back and laughed loudly, a harsh forced laugh. For an instant the absurdity of it struck him as funny, but then very slowly he began to understand. She was not mad, she spoke the truth, didn't they always look at him with strange sidelong glances, didn't they whisper and mumble to one another, didn't they interfere with him, come between him and the agent and make fun of his catch. He turned on her, his mind bitter. "It's a lie! A lie!" he cried. "When did I ever have herrin's, mackerel, plaice? When? When?"

"Easy, *avico*. Easy," she said, a strange gentleness creeping into her croaking voice.

"I've only lobsters, lobsters," the young man told her. "I have them because . . . because . . ."

He sighed deeply and turned away.

It had grown dark. The sun had slipped far down beyond the rim of the sea, leaving a faint halo of crimson and purple like the last red embers of a great fire. On the earth's edge the sea was still alight burning softly, and high overhead small dark clouds chased one another unguided by a single star. On the sky-merged island a long beam of light moved round in a great circle tearing a long bright gash across the calm water.

The Islandman turned his head. "Good-night, woman," he said. "God and Mary be with you on your way."

"God and Mary and Patrick bless ye," she said, and he heard her stick grate on the stones as she walked into the night.

The sun was lying low in the east, pale and watery, and across the bay the white cottages were huddled coldly in a grey mist.

The Islandman picked his steps slowly and carefully down the mountain. The water from the wet bracken seeped into his pampooties, and he made a loud squelching noise as the weight of his body came down on each foot; the thick upturned ends of his trousers were wet and heavy.

He stood for a while by his curragh, one hand resting on the bottom. He looked out over the grey sea, undecided. The tide was flowing strongly, a turbulent undercurrent agitating it somewhat. A cold shiver passed through his body as the damp air gathered thickly in minute blobs on his jersey.

He brushed a recalcitrant lock of hair back from his forehead, and then dragged the curragh roughly into the water, pushing himself out with an oar. The water was fairly calm in the shielding of the pier, but beyond that the sea was rough, and beat noisily against the wall of stone.

The Islandman bent his back and pulled strongly to the line of corks bobbing frantically ahead of him, straining hard from their mooring. The curragh danced and reared violently so that he had to dip and hold his oars tightly to steady the frail craft. With a knowledge born of experience he pulled the line in on the tip of his oar carrying it across his bow.

His face grimly set, his lips drawn tightly together, he gathered the line in his hand and drew in each pot. He did not empty them for he was thinking of Mad Liz and the fishermen in the row of cottages by the beach. There were lobsters aplenty in the pots, large greedy fellows locked together, but the Islandman tried not to see them. Instead he piled the pots in a neat heap in his curragh, drew in the line and cut the anchoring stones away.

The young man was tired, and he rested for a while, his oars dug deeply into the water, and gripped against his side. Across from him the row of cottages were blurred in the mist, and away out far where the sun peered blearily from a bank of watery clouds the island was shrouded in a thick curtain of dull grey, cold and forlorn it was like a death visited house.

On the shore in the shelter of the pier Mad Liz clutched her shawl tightly to her shrivelled breast. She peered through rheumy eyes at the bent figure of the young man lying idly on his oars. She saw the curragh drift shore-wise, rising on the crest of one wave, and then disappearing in its slough, but all the time coming nearer and nearer to the shore with the incoming tide.

Then, quite suddenly, life seemed to jump into the

bent body. With a quick strong pull on one oar he turned the curragh round. And as the heavy clouds gathered overhead, and the swell rose along the beach she saw him pull swiftly away.

She clawed the shawl tightly against her breast, and opened her mouth to cry out. The rain started, pouring down heavily. The woman turned towards the Islandman's track up the mountain. Half way up she stopped and looked. The curragh seemed far away, a lone frail thing like a bobbing cork. "God be with ye, young man," she said half aloud, then shaking her clenched fist towards the village she muttered a low curse through her tight bloodless lips.

JOHN COLLIER

The Lady
on the Grey

❄

Ringwood was the last of an Anglo-Irish family that had played the devil in County Clare for a matter of three centuries. At last, all their big houses were sold up, or burned down by the long-suffering Irish, and of their thousands of acres not a single foot remained. Ringwood, however, had a few hundred a year of his own, and if the family estates had vanished, he had at least inherited a family instinct that prompted him to regard all Ireland as his domain and to rejoice in its abundance of horses, foxes, salmon, game, and girls.

In pursuit of these delights, Ringwood ranged and roved from Donegal to Wexford through all the seasons of the year. There were not many hunts he had not led at some time or other on a borrowed mount, or many bridges he had not leaned over through half a May morning, or many inn parlors where he had not snored away a wet winter afternoon in front of the fire.

From *The New Yorker*.

He had an intimate by the name of Bates, who was another of the same breed and the same kidney. Bates was equally long and lean, and equally hard up, and he had the same wind-flushed, bony face, the same shabby arrogance, and the same seignorial approach to the little girls in the cottages and cowsheds.

Neither of these blades ever wrote a letter, but each generally knew where the other was to be found. The ticket collector, respectfully blind as he snipped Ringwood's third-class ticket in a first-class compartment, would mention that Mr. Bates had travelled that way only last Tuesday, stopping off at Killorglin for a week or two after the snipe. The chambermaid, coy in the clammy bedroom of a fishing inn, would find time to tell Bates that Ringwood had gone on up to Lough Corrib for a go at the pike. Policemen, priests, bagmen, gamekeepers, even the tinkers on the roads, would pass on this verbal *patrin*. Then, if it seemed to one that his friend was on to a good thing, the other would pack up his battered kit bag, put rods and guns into their cases, and drift off to join in the sport.

So it happened that one winter afternoon, when Ringwood was strolling back from a singularly blank day on the bog of Ballyneary, he was hailed by a one-eyed horse dealer of his acquaintance, who came trotting by in a gig, as people still do in Ireland. This worthy told our friend that he had just come down from Galway, where he had seen Mr. Bates, who was on his way to a village called Knockderry and had told him very particularly to mention it to Mr. Ringwood if he came across him.

Ringwood turned this message over in his mind and noted that it was a very particular one, and that no mention was made as to whether it was fishing or shooting his friend was engaged in, or whether he had met with some Croesus who had a string of hunters that he was prepared to lend. He certainly would have put a name to it if it were anything of that sort, he thought. I'll bet my life it's a pair of sisters he's got on the track of. It must be!

At this thought, he grinned from the tip of his long nose, like a fox, and he lost no time in packing his bag and setting off for this place Knockderry, which he had never visited before in all his roving up and down the country in pursuit of fur, feather, and girls.

He found it was a long way off the beaten track, and a very quiet place when he got to it. There were the usual low, bleak hills all around, and a river running along the valley, and the usual ruined tower up on a slight rise, girdled with a straggly wood and approached by the remains of an avenue.

The village itself was like many another: a few groups of shabby cottages, a decaying mill, half a dozen beer shops, and one inn, at which a gentleman hardened to rural cookery might conceivably put up.

Ringwood strode in and found the landlady in the kitchen and asked for his friend Mr. Bates.

"Why, sure, Your Honor," said the landlady, "the gentleman's staying here. At least, he is, so to speak, and then, now, he isn't."

"How's that?" asked Ringwood.

"His bag's here," said the landlady, "and his things are here, and my grandest room taken up with them, though I've another every bit as good, and himself staying in the house best part of a week. But the day before yesterday he went out for a bit of a constitutional, and—would you believe it, sir?—we've seen neither hide nor hair of him since."

"Oh, he'll be back," said Ringwood. "Meanwhile, show me a room. I'll stay here and wait for him."

Accordingly, he settled in, and waited all the evening, but Bates failed to appear. However, that sort of thing bothers no one in Ireland, and Ringwood's only impatience was in connection with the pair of sisters, whose acquaintance he was extremely anxious to make.

During the next day or two, Ringwood employed his time in strolling up and down all the lanes and bypaths in the neighborhood, in the hope of discovering these beauties, or else some other. He was not particular as to which it should be, but on the whole he would have preferred a cottage girl, because he had no wish to waste time on elaborate approaches.

On the second afternoon, just as the early dusk was falling, he was about a mile outside the village and he met a straggle of muddy cows coming along the road, and a girl driving them. Our friend took a look at the girl and stopped dead in his tracks, grinning more like a fox than ever.

This girl was still a child in her teens, and her bare legs were spattered with mud and scratched by brambles, but she was so pretty that the seignorial blood of all the Ringwoods boiled in the veins of their last descendant and he felt an overmastering desire for a cup of milk. He therefore waited a minute or two and then followed leisurely along the lane, meaning to turn in as soon as he saw the byre and beg the favor of this innocent refreshment, and perhaps a little conversation into the bargain.

They say, though, that blessings never come singly, any more than misfortunes. As Ringwood followed his charmer, swearing to himself that there couldn't be such another in the whole county, he heard the fall of a horse's hoofs and looked up, and there, approaching him at a walking pace, was a grey horse, which must have turned in from some bypath or other, because there certainly had been no horse in sight a moment before.

A grey horse is no great matter, especially when one is so urgently in pursuit of a cup of milk, but this grey horse differed from all others of its species and color in two respects. First, it was no sort of a horse at all, neither hack nor hunter, and it picked up its feet in a queer way, and yet it had an arch to its neck and a small head and a wide nostril that were not entirely without distinction. And, second—and this distracted Ringwood from all curiosity as to breed and bloodline—this grey horse carried on its back a girl who was obviously and certainly the most beautiful girl he had ever seen in his life.

Ringwood looked at her, and as she came slowly through the dusk, she raised her eyes and looked at Ringwood. He at once forgot the little girl with the cows. In fact, he forgot everything else in the world.

The horse came nearer, and still the girl looked, and Ringwood looked, and it was not a mere exchange of glances; it was wooing and a marriage, all complete and perfect in a mingling of the eyes.

Next moment, the horse had carried her past him, and, quickening its pace a little, it left him standing on the road. He could hardly run after it, or shout; in any case, he was too overcome to do anything but stand and stare.

He watched the horse and rider go on through the wintry twilight, and he saw her turn in at a broken gateway just a little way along the road. Just as she passed through, she turned her head and whistled, and Ringwood noticed that her dog had stopped by him and was sniffing about his legs. For a moment, he thought it was a smallish wolf-hound, but then he saw it was just a tall, lean, hairy lurcher. He watched it run limping after her with its tail down, and it struck him that the poor creature had had an appalling thrashing not so long ago; he had noticed the marks where the hair was thin on its ribs.

However, he had little thought to spare for the dog. As soon as he got over his first excitement, he moved on in the direction of the gateway. The girl was already out of sight when he got there, but he recognized the neglected avenue that led up to the battered tower on the shoulder of the hill.

Ringwood thought that was enough for the day, so made his way back to the inn. Bates was still absent, but that was just as well. Ringwood wanted the evening to himself, in order to work out a plan of campaign.

That horse never cost two ten-pound notes of anybody's money, said he to himself. So she's not so rich. So much the better! Besides, she wasn't dressed up much; I don't know what she had on—a sort of cloak or something. Nothing out of Bond Street, anyway. And lives in that old tower! I should have thought it was all tumbled down. Still, I suppose there's a room or two left at the bottom. Poverty Hall! One of the old school, blue blood and no money, pining away in this godforsaken hole, miles away from everybody. Probably she doesn't see a man from one year's end to another. No wonder she gave me a look. God! If I was sure she was there by herself, I wouldn't need much of an introduction. Still, there might be a father or a brother or somebody. Never mind, I'll manage it.

When the landlady brought in the lamp, "Tell me," said he, "who's the young lady who rides the cobby-looking, old-fashioned-looking grey?"

"A young lady, sir?" said the landlady doubtfully. "On a grey?"

"Yes," said he. "She passed me in the lane up there. She turned in on the old avenue going up to the tower."

"Oh, Mary bless and keep you!" said the good woman. "That's the beautiful Murrough lady you must have seen."

"Murrough?" said he. "Is that the name? Well, well, well! That's a fine old name in the west here."

"It is so, indeed," said the landlady. "For they were kings and queens in Connaught before the Saxon came. And herself, sir, has the face of a queen, they tell me."

"They're right," said Ringwood. "Perhaps you'll bring me in the whiskey and water, Mrs. Doyle, and I shall be comfortable."

He had an impulse to ask if the beautiful Miss Murrough had anything in the shape of a father or a brother at the tower, but his principle was, "Least said, soonest mended," especially in little affairs of this sort. So he sat by the fire, recapturing and savoring the look the girl had given him, and he decided he needed only the barest excuse to present himself at the tower.

Ringwood had never any shortage of excuses, so the next afternoon he spruced himself up and set out in the direction of the old avenue. He turned in at the gate and went along under the forlorn and dripping trees, which were so ivied and overgrown that the darkness was already thickening under them. He looked ahead for a sight of the tower, but the avenue took a turn at the end, and it was still hidden among the clustering trees.

Just as he got to the end, he saw someone standing there, and he looked again, and it was the girl herself, standing as if she were waiting for him.

"Good afternoon, Miss Murrough," said he, as soon as he got into earshot. "Hope I'm not intruding. The fact is I think I had the pleasure of meeting a relation of yours down in Cork, only last month." By this time, he had got close enough to see the look in her eyes again, and all this nonsense died away in his mouth, for this was something beyond any nonsense of that sort.

"I thought you would come," said she.

"My God!" said he. "I had to. Tell me—are you all by yourself here?"

"All by myself," said she, and she put out her hand as if to lead him along with her.

Ringwood, blessing his lucky stars, was about to take it when her lean dog bounded between them and nearly knocked him over.

"Down!" cried she, lifting her hand. "Get back!" The dog cowered and whimpered, and slunk behind her, creeping almost on its belly. "I don't trust him," she said.

"He's all right," said Ringwood. "He looks a knowing old fellow. I like a lurcher. . . . What? Are you trying to talk to me, old boy?" Ringwood always paid a compliment to a lady's dog, and in fact the creature really was whining and whimpering in the most extraordinary fashion.

"Be quiet!" said the girl, raising her hand again, and the dog was silent. "A cur," said she to Ringwood. "You did not come here to flatter a cur." With that, she gave him her eyes again, and he forgot the wretched dog, and she gave him her hand, and this time he took it, and they walked toward the tower.

Ringwood was in the seventh heaven. What luck! thought he. I might at this moment be fondling that little farm wench in some damp and smelly cowshed. And ten to one she'd be snivelling and crying and running home to tell her mammy. This is something different.

At that moment, the girl pushed open a heavy door, and, bidding the dog lie down, she led our friend through a wide, bare stone-flagged hall and into a small vaulted room, which certainly had no resemblance to a cowshed, except perhaps it smelled a little damp and moldy, as these old stone places so often do. All the same, there were logs burning on the open hearth, and a broad, low couch before the fireplace. For the rest, the room was furnished with the greatest simplicity, and very much in the antique style. A touch of the Kathleen ni Houlihan, thought Ringwood. Well, well! Sitting in the Celtic twilight, dreaming of love. She certainly doesn't make much bones about it.

The girl sat down on the couch and drew him down beside her. Neither of them said anything; there was no sound but the wind outside, and the dog scratching and whimpering timidly at the door of the chamber.

At last, the girl spoke. "You are of the Saxon," said she gravely.

"Don't hold it against me," said Ringwood. "My people came here in 1629. Of course, that's yesterday to the Gaelic League, but still I think we can say we have a stake in the country."

"Yes, through its heart," said she.

"Is it politics we're going to talk?" said he, putting an Irish turn to his tongue. "You and I, sitting here in the firelight?"

"Through the hearts, then," said the girl. "Through the hearts of the poor girls of Eire."

"You misjudge me entirely," said Ringwood. "I'm the man to live alone and sorrowful, waiting for the one love, though it seemed something beyond hoping for."

"Yes," said she. "But yesterday you were looking at one of the Connell girls as she drove her kine along the lane."

"Looking at her? I'll go so far as to say I did," said he. "But when I saw you, I altogether forgot her."

"That was my wish," said she, giving him both her hands. "Will you stay with me here?"

"Ah, that I will!" cried he in a rapture.

"Forever?" said she.

"Forever," cried Ringwood, for he felt it better to be guilty of a slight exaggeration than to be lacking in courtesy to a lady. But as he spoke she fixed her eyes on him, looking so much as if she believed him that he positively believed himself. "Ah," he cried. "You bewitch me!" And he took her in his arms.

He pressed his lips to hers, and at once he was over the brink. Usually he prided himself on being a pretty cool hand, but this was an intoxication too strong for him; his mind seemed to dissolve in sweetness and fire, and at last the fire was gone, and his senses went with it. As they failed, he heard her saying "Forever! Forever!" and then everything was gone and he fell asleep.

He must have slept some time. It seemed he was wakened by the heavy opening and closing of a door. For a moment, he was all confused and hardly knew where he was.

The room was now quite dark, and the fire had sunk to a dim glow. He blinked, and shook his ears, trying to shake some sense into his head. Suddenly, he heard Bates talking to him, muttering as if he, too, were half asleep— or half drunk, more likely.

"You *would* come here," said Bates. "I tried hard enough to stop you."

"Hullo!" said Ringwood, thinking he must have dozed off by the fire in the inn parlor. "Bates? God, I must have slept heavy! I feel queer. Damn it—so it was all a dream! Strike a light, old boy. It must be late. I'll yell for supper."

"Don't, for heaven's sake," said Bates, in his altered voice. "Don't yell. She'll thrash us if you do."

"What's that?" said Ringwood. "Thrash us? What the hell are you talking about?"

At that moment, a log rolled on the hearth and a little flame flickered up, and he saw his long and hairy forelegs, and he knew.

DANIEL CORKERY

The Awakening

✳

Ivor O'Donovan knew it was Ted Driscoll had called him: raising himself above the edge of the bunk he was just in time to see him manoeuvring that bear-like body of his through the narrow little hatchway, to see the splintery shutter slap to behind him. At the same moment he heard the Captain clearing his throat. The bunk opposite was his, and now Ivor saw him, all limbs, mounting awkwardly yet carefully over the edge of it. What between the sprawling limbs, the ungainly body and the hovering shadows above them, the place was narrowed to the size of a packing case. The timber work of the cabin had become so dark with the smoke of the stove that neither shadows nor limbs seemed to stir except when their movements were sudden and jerky. Ivor soon heard the Captain gathering his oil-cloths from the floor with one hand while with the other he dragged at the bunk where the cabin boy was

From THE WAGER, New York, The Devin-Adair Co.

sleeping; this Ivor knew, for as he sat up he caught the familiar words:

"Come on, come on; rouse up; they'll be waiting."

The Captain he then saw disappear through the toy-like hatchway.

Ivor O'Donovan himself with a stifled groan descended lifelessly from the bunk to the floor. He drew on his sea boots—they had been his father's—drew his oil-cloths about him and in turn thrust his hand into the warm pile of old coats and sacking in which the sleeping boy was buried. He shook him vigorously: "Come on, come on; they'll be waiting," he said, and then hurried aloft into the drizzling darkness and took his place with the others.

The tightness that he felt on his brain from the moment Ted Driscoll had roused him seemed natural, not unexpected; nevertheless he groaned to recollect the cause of it. Now, however, as he settled down to his night's work, planted in the darkness there at the gunwale, braced against it, facing the Captain, the dripping fish-laden incoming net between them, he noticed that the tightness had somehow slackened, was still loosening its grip of him, so much so that he had some fear that it would again suddenly pounce on him with its first heat and violence.

Ted Driscoll and Tom Mescall were forward at the windlass; beyond them the boy, bending down, was coiling the rope they passed to him.

It was very dark. Everything was huge and shapeless. Anchored as she was, tethered besides, clumsy with the weight of dripping fish-spangled net coming in over the gunwale, the nobby was tossed and slapped about with a violence that surprised him; flakes of wet brightness were being flung everywhere from the one lamp bound firmly to the mast. Yet the night was almost windless, the sea apparently sluggish: there must be, he thought, a stiff swell beneath them. What most surprised him, however, was to find himself thinking about it. That evening coming down the harbour, he would not have noticed it. The whole way out, his back to the sea, he had stood upright, his feet set wide apart, his hands in his belt, glum, silent, gazing at the cabin boy who, sprawled upon the deck, was intent upon the baited line he had flung over the stern. But as far as Ivor was concerned that patch of deck might have been free to the sun: his own anger, his passion, was between him and the world. That afternoon he had waited for Chrissie Collins for two hours. At the very start he knew, he *knew*, so at least he had told himself she would not come. For all that he had gone hot and cold, again and again, while waiting for her. He had broken from the spot impulsively: a moment later he had trailed back again, giving her one more quarter of an hour to make good in. Then when his rage was at the peak, hurrying down to the jetty, he had suddenly caught sight of her, all brightness, stepping briskly up the hillside, the school-master walking beside her, as eager as herself. Her head was bent, her eyes were fixed on her dainty toe-caps, and she was listening complacently to the schoolmaster's blather. Only that he should have to tear through the vil-lage and it filled with the gathering crews, he'd have told her what he thought of her.

With his eyes downwards on the sprawling limbs of the boy, he had indulged, as if it were the only thing for a man to do, the heat of the passion that that one glimpse of her had aroused in him.

Now, ten hours later, braced against the timbers, swaying and balancing, freeing the net, freeing the rope, grabbing at the odd dog fish, the odd blob of seaweed, the tangle of seawrack, flinging them all, as they came, far out, clear of the rising meshes—he was puzzled to contrast his present indifference with his stifling anger of the after-noon. Yet he was not pleased with himself. This calming down of his seemed like a loss of manhood. His mind could not, it appeared, stay fixed on the one thought. He found himself noticing what he had never noticed before —how the mackerel, entangled in the meshes, would catch the light of the worried lamp and appear just like a flight of shining steel-bright daggers hurtling by him from gunwale to hold. Never to have noticed so striking a thing before, how curious! But had the Captain ever noticed it? He glanced shyly at the aged face opposite him and started, for the Captain, he saw, had had his eyes fixed on him, all the time, perhaps! And Ivor recalled, reddening slightly, that also that afternoon while lost in his own passionate thoughts he had caught him observing him with the selfsame silent gravity. Why should he do it? He was Captain. But the boat was his, Ivor's; and one day when he was somewhat older, and when his mother was willing to trust him, he would sail it. But this was unfair, he felt, for the Captain, this Larry Keohane, had been ever and always his father's dearest friend and shipmate, had sailed with him till he was drowned, had indeed been with him that very night; and afterwards he it was who had undertaken the management of the boat for them; and in such a way that not a penny of the fish money had ever gone astray on them. Later on, now two years ago, he had taken Ivor on board as one of the crew, and taught him whatever he now knew of sailoring and deep sea fishing. There was surely plenty of time yet for thinking of playing the Captain. Besides, the selling of the fish was trickier work than the catching of it. His eyes fell on the claw-like hands of the Captain, they were twisted with rheumatism, and a flood of kindly feeling for this grave and faithful friend suddenly swept over him with such power that he found his own hands fumbling at the net without either skill or strength in them. To glance again at the Captain's face he did not dare.

"Up, boys, up!" he impulsively cried to the windlass men as if to encourage them. In the clinging darkness, although the drizzle was becoming lighter and lighter, he could make out only the shapeless bulk of themselves and the windlass: two awkward lumps of manhood rising and falling alternately, their sou'westers and oil-cloths catching some of the flakes of the wet brightness that were flying around everywhere. 'Twas curious work, this fishing. Like a family they were, confined in a tiny space, as far almost from the other boats as they were from the houses on the hills where the real families were now huddled together in sleep. The real families—each of them was different from the others. Tom Mescall's was the most good-for-nothing in the whole place. Others had quite nice houses, clean and well-kept. But most strange of all was it to have him, Ivor, thinking of such things, his head calm and cool (and he thereupon grabbed a huge dog-fish from the passing net and with a gesture deliberately sweeping sent it far out into the splashing darkness).

II

The work went on and on and Ivor could not help all kinds of thoughts from crossing his brain, nor help noticing the onward rush of them. The dragging of the net was done in silence, no one speaking until they each and all were sure that they had had a fairly good catch, and that all the nets were heavy. Ivor then was aware that some dull and lifeless conversation was passing to and fro between the men at the windlass. He was hailed suddenly by one of them, Ted Driscoll: "Look where Leary is, east."

Far off, east, Ivor saw a tiny light. As he watched it the other voice came through the darkness, half speaking, half calling:

"'aith then he wouldn't belong swinging on to the Galley in there."

"Is it Leary, do you think?" Ivor asked the Captain, and he was answered:

"'Tis like the place he'd be."

Ivor then sent his gaze ranging the sea noting the disposition of the boats. They were far off, nearly all of them. Some were miles beyond Galley Head. Others were away towards the west. Here and there a pair of lights seemed to ride close together, only seemed, however, while an odd one, like Leary's, played the hermit in unaccustomed waters. Far to the west the great light of the Fastnet every few moments threw a startling beam on the

waters and, quenching suddenly, would leave a huge blackness suspended before their very eyes, blinding them. He
noticed how, little by little, the timid lamps of the fishing
fleet would in time manage again to glimmer through that
darkness. He bent himself once more on the work, thinking over and over again what a curious way they had of
making a living. On the land at this time of night every
one of the houses was a nest of sleep—chilly walls and
warm bedding. After all Chrissie Collins was a farmer's
daughter, a small hillside farmer, a "sky" farmer. Farm
houses had ways of their own. Fishermen also had ways of
their own. The next time he met her he would hold his
head as high as hers.

The dragging went on and on. The unending clanking of the windlass, the wet mass of the net, the grip of his
feet on the narrow way between gunwale and hold while
the boat tossed and tugged, the sudden flashes of the lamp,
the long silences of them all, the far-off lonely looking
lights of the other anchored nobbies and ketches, the bold
startling blaze of the Fastnet, and above all the stream of
shining daggers sweeping by—for the first time in his life
he reckoned up the features of the fisherman's calling, and
felt some sort of pleasant excitement in doing so, as if he
had heard some good news or come upon some unexpected
treasure. He could not understand it.

When the last of the nets was in they tidied the decks,
pitching the seawrack into the sea. He heard the Captain
say to Driscoll, whose head was bent down on the confused
mass of fish and net in the hold: "Good, and a fair size too.
I'm very glad."

"I'm very glad," repeated Ivor in his mind, wonder-
ingly, yet feeling that the words fitted in. He noticed Driscoll and Mescall, their arms hanging heavily after their
night's work, their sea boots lumping noisily along the
deck, going aft to the little cabin, making down the hatchway without a word. The boy had gone down previously.
The waft of the smell of boiling fish, of boiling potatoes,
that came from the smoke pipe told of his toil below. To

Ivor it was very welcome. He was hungry; and besides they would presently all meet together round the little stove, "I'm very glad," he whispered, not knowing why. And the smoke, he saw, was like a lighted plume rising from the top of the iron pipe.

The Captain drew closer to him. He took the fragment of pipe from his mouth and, smothering the glowing bowl in his fist, pointed sou'west:

" 'Tis Casey that's going in."

"Is it?" Ivor said, also picking out the one craft in all the far-scattered fleet that had got under weigh that—very slowly, for there was scarcely a breath of wind—was making for the land.

"Maybe 'tisn't," the Captain then said.

"I'm sure 'tis him all right," Ivor said, though he was not sure at all.

They stood side by side following with their eyes the distant slow-moving light. There was scarcely a morning that some boat or other did not hoist sail the moment their catch was made and hasten in. There was always some special reason for it. And the other craft, every one of them, would make guesses at the boat, as also at the cause of her lifting anchor in such haste. The others were content to make the pier any time before the buyers had received from other fishing ports and from Dublin itself their morning telegrams fixing the day's prices. Ivor thought how it was nearly always something having to do with the real household, with the real family, that brought a fisherman to break that way from the fishing grounds before the others. Sickness, or the necessity for some early journey, or the emigrating of a son or daughter. "I remember your father, one time we were out, and far out too, south the Galley, ten mile it might be, how he called out and we not ready at all: 'That'll do, boys, we'll make in.' "

The Captain's quiet husky voice stopped, and Ivor wondered if that was all he had to say; but the tale was taken up again:

"That was twenty-two years ago this month."

Ivor was once more astray, he could not find reason in the words.

"Yes," he said, quietly.

"That night he expected a son to be born to him; and he wasn't disappointed."

Ivor knew that he himself was the child that on that night came into the world; but what kept him silent was the Captain's gravity. Such matter among them had always been a cause for laughter. Ivor was nevertheless glad that the Captain had spoken seriously; for all that, fearing to betray his own state of mind, he answered:

"That's not what's taking Casey in anyhow."

The Captain did not seem to hear.

"All night long," he said, "I'm thinking of things that I saw happen out here on these waters for the last fifty-four years."

Ivor raised his head in astonishment. Why should such recollections have set the Captain examining him the whole night long?

"Strange things," the Captain resumed, "strange voices, sad things too, very sad, things that should not happen."

After all, the Captain was in the humour for spinning a yarn, that was all. But, instead of the yarn, the Captain, scanning the sky, merely said:

" 'Tis going south; the day will be fine, very fine."

Ivor too felt a slight stir in the air, and from the hatchway Driscoll called them down.

"With God's help 'twill be a fine day," the Captain said once more, throwing the words over his shoulder as they moved aft, one behind the other, sauntering along in their heavy sea boots.

III

The air in the cabin was reeking with the smell of fish and potatoes, and so thick with fire smoke and tobacco smoke that one could hardly make things out. There was hardly room for the five of them there. The boxes they sat on were very low and the men's knees, on which they held the plates, seemed to fill the whole space. One felt the warmth against one's face like a cushion. Yet Ivor welcomed it all—the heat, the smell of the good food, the close companionship—not alone for the comfort it all wrapped him round with but for the memory it raised in him of those many other nights on which he had experienced it, his body as cold as ice and his fingers unable to move themselves. The others were already eating lustily and noisily.

"Not too bad, not too bad," he cried out cheerily, planting himself between Driscoll and Mescall, just because they were head to head and nose to nose in earnest argument. They took no notice of him, continuing it still across his very face. Driscoll, who was the simplest of them, was showing how Mrs. O'Connor, the shopkeeper who supplied them with all and sundry, had done him out of two and elevenpence, and Mescall, who, in spite of his harum-scarum wife and family, was their merrymaker, was explaining how she had tried the same trick with him and how he had laid a trap for her and caught her—a trap so clever that Driscoll had no idea how it worked or how by using it he could recover his two and elevenpence. The boy was heard plunging vessels in a bucket of water. All the time the Captain held his peace, and Ivor, noticing it, glanced at him, wondering if he were still recalling what he had seen happen on the fishing grounds during his long lifetime upon them.

Leisurely yet ravenously the meal went on, and when they thought of it, or at least so it seemed, first Mescall and then Driscoll, who had had no sleep till then, threw off their sea boots and disappeared into the darkness of the bunks. In the same haphazard way Ivor, the Captain, and the boy returned to the deck.

IV

At last they had her moving: her sails were flapping, coming suddenly between their eyes and the dazzling flood of light outwelling from sea and sky. When they filled,

when she settled down, Ivor heard the Captain say in a
voice that sounded unusual:

"I suppose I may as well go aft."

Unable to account for the words Ivor answered in
mere confusion of mind:

" 'Tis better, I suppose," as if the matter was not
quite clear.

Silently the Captain went aft to the tiller, and Ivor, as
was his custom, threw himself on the pile of rope in the
bow: there was no more to be done. He felt the streaming
sun, into which a benign warmth was beginning to steal,
bathing his body from his hair down. After the work of the
night, after the food, a pleasant lassitude, as thick as his
thick clothing, clung to him. The cabin boy was already
fast asleep on the deck, cuddled up like a dog, his face
buried in his arms. Ivor felt sleepy too, yet before he
yielded to it, he recalled the memory of the handful of
them, cut off from all other company, working silently in
the drizzling darkness, the tossing lamp momentarily flashing in their eyes and lighting up their dripping hands. He
recollected too the rise and fall of the awkward bodies of
the two men at the windlass, the clanking of the axle, and
the uncompanioned boy beyond them working away in
almost total darkness. Clearer than all he recalled the
flight of glittering spear heads sweeping by between himself and the Captain. Then also the group in the smoky
cabin, the hearty faces, the blue and white plates, the boy
plunging the vessels in the water. How different from
what was now before his eyes! The sea was wide; the
air brisk, the seagulls screaming, quarrelling, gathering in
schools, dashing at the transparent crests of the waves or
sweeping in great curves to the east, the west, everywhere,
their high-pitched cries filling the air with a rapture that
opened the heart and at the same time alarmed it. Yes,
very different, yet his pictures of the night time—the
groups silently working in the darkness, the gathering in
the little cabin—these were dearer to him just now than

the bright freshness of the morning. He recalled the unexpected words of the Captain—"I'm very glad."

At last the drowsiness that he would keep from him overpowered him.

He awoke to find the boy's hand timidly unclutching his shoulder:

"Himself wants you."

Rising up he caught the Captain's eyes resting upon him with a calmness that surprised him, that disturbed him. He went aft.

"You're wanting me?"

"Sit down there, Ivor, there's a thing I have to say to you."

Fearing some reference to Chrissie Collins, some questioning, some good advice, Ivor sat down without a word. The Captain blurted out:

"Ivor, boy, 'tis time for you to sail what belongs to you."

As he spoke his hand lifted from the tiller—an instinctive giving up of office. Instantly however it fell upon it again. Ivor perceived the action with his eyes, not with his mind, for the words had sent a thrill of delight through his whole body. Everything he had been noticing that night of nights was in that overwhelming sensation—the darkness, the clanking windlass, the shining fish, the cabin, the seagulls, everywhere—but he caught hold of himself and said:

"But, Lar, why that? Why that?"

"Because 'tis time for you."

"But why so? 'Tisn't how you're going from us; what's after happening?"

"Nothing. Nothing. Only all the night I'm thinking of it. 'Tis the right thing. Herself is at me too. If there's a touch of wind in the night, she don't sleep a wink."

"Oh! If the boat goes we all go."

"You can't talk to them like that. Anyway 'tis right. 'Tis your due. We got on well, Ivor. Them that's gone, they deserved as much. We done our best, all of us."

"Lar, 'tis better wait till my mother hears of it."

"If you wouldn't mind I'd give you Pat to be in my place. He'd be better for you than a stranger."

Again that thrill of delight went through him. He thought at once if the Captain had not offered his son, a stranger would have to be brought into the boat, one of those unlucky creatures perhaps who had given the best of their lives sailoring the wide world over, creatures who were not trustworthy, who had bitter, reckless tongues, who destroyed the spirit of goodwill in any boat they ever got footing in. That danger the Captain had put aside. There was, therefore, a clear way before him, and a boat's crew after his own heart.

"I'm thankful, Lar, and herself will be thankful; but what will you be doing with yourself?"

A little smile grew upon the Captain's face, and both of them raised their eyes to scan the hillsides they were approaching. In the sun which now lay thick upon their brown-green flanks, nestling in the zig-zag ravines they saw the little groups of houses where the fishermen lived. Some of the cottages, snow-white, faced full in the eyes of the morning, sunning themselves. Others were turned aside, still asleep in the shadows, catching a bright ray only on chimney head or gable.

"Wouldn't I want to sit in the sun and smoke my pipe as well as another? That will do, Ivor. Ted's coming up. He's after smelling the land. In the evening I'll fix up with your mother."

v

It was a Saturday morning. That night and the next they would all sleep in their own houses, not in the boats.

In the evening the Captain went to Ivor's house, and, as he said himself, fixed things up with his mother. Then he shook hands with them all, with Mrs. O'Donovan, Ivor, his two sisters, and his young brother, who was only a boy. He then set off up the hill for his home.

Afterwards, standing up before the bit of glass nailed against the wall, Ivor stood shaving himself. His heart was blazing within him, his cheeks burning, for the Captain had been speaking his praises, and all his people had been staring at him.

It had been a day of uninterrupted sunshine, and now a bright heaven, slow to darken itself, although the sun had been a long time sunken, darkened to blackness every ridge, bush, tree clump, roof and gable that stood against it. On the roads and fields it still threw down a persistent glow; and Ivor went in and out of the doorway praying for the dusk to thicken. In the midst of the Captain's praise of him he had felt a burning desire to see his boat once again with his own eyes, to be sure it was still there at the pier, where, with scores of others, it was fastened. He wanted to feel the tiller beneath his right hand —that above all. And yet he would not care to have any of his neighbours see him doing so. Nightfall was never so slow in coming. At last, however, with a yearning look at the still livid sky he set off down the path towards the roadway. He could gambol, he could sing, only that at the same time he had thoughts of the heavy responsibility that in future would rest upon him. He strove to calm himself, to walk with the appearance of one who had no other business than to breathe the cool air of the evening. He knew there would be groups of men still in the public-houses as well as along the sea wall; and these he wished to escape.

Before entering the village he vaulted over the wall, descended the rocks, and made along by the edge of the waters. At a point beyond the farthest house he climbed onto the road again, and, more assured, made towards the deserted pier. At its extreme end, almost, his *Wildwood* was moored. The pier itself, the debris on it, the fish boxes, the ranks of barrels—as well as all the conglomeration of boats along its sheltered side—the whole had become one black mass sharply cut out against the livid waters of the harbour. On a standard at its very end a solitary oil lamp, as warm in colour as the waters were cold, was burning away in loneliness. Towards it, and as quietly, almost as stealth-

ily as if on a guilty errand, he steered his way. He was glad
when the piles of barrels so obstructed the view that no
one could spy him from the road. Doubtless the news was
already abroad; by now the men were surely all speaking
about it; as for himself, it was very strange coming at the
time it did, coming, without expectation, at the tail-end of
the night when for the first time he knew what it was to
be a true fisherman. He was glad Chrissie Collins had her
schoolmaster. It left himself as free as air. And thinking
the thought he breathed in the pleasant coolness of the
night, yet could not, it seemed, gulp down enough of it.
Glad of the darkness, of the loneliness, he suddenly threw
out his two arms wide apart, stretching them from him,
and drew the keen air slowly and deliciously through his
nostrils. And breathing still in the self-same manner went
forward a few steps. Then suddenly, he saw a figure, outlined against the tide, seated on some fish boxes, gazing silently at the nobby for which he himself was making!
He knew it was the Captain. His arms fell and he stood
quite still.

"Oh!" he said, in a sudden stoppage of thought. He
turned stealthily and retraced his steps, fearful of hearing
his name cried out. But nothing was to be heard except his
own careful footfall; and before he reached the road again
he had recovered himself. It surely was a sad thing for
Larry Keohane to have his life drawing to an end. Why
was it that nothing can happen to fill one person with happiness without bringing sadness and pain to somebody
else? Yet the Captain, he remembered, that evening in his
mother's house had been quite cheerful, had told them
how glad he was that they had made quite a good catch on
his last night, and what a peaceful night it had been! And
what a fine boat the *Wildwood* was; and how happy he was
to be leaving her in hands that would not treat her foully;
indeed he could well say that he was flinging all responsibility from his shoulders; and that was a thing he had been
looking forward to for a long time. And saying that, he had
gone from them cheerily and brightly. Yes, yes, but here

surely was the real captain, this seaman staring at his boat.

Ivor waited, sitting on the wall in the darkness, for a long time. At last he heard the slow steps of the old man approaching, saw him pass by—saw him very indistinctly for the darkness, yet knew that he had his hand covering his pipe in his mouth and his head on one side, a way he had when he was thinking to himself. He waited until the footsteps had died away up the hillside; then he rose to resume his own quest towards the nobby. He found he could not bring himself to do so. He did not want to do so.

With slow lingering steps, with stoppings and turnings, at last he too began to make towards his home. His head was flung up, almost flung back. More than once he told himself that he didn't ever remember the sky to have been so full of stars. Somehow he felt like raising his hand towards them.

DANIEL CORKERY

The Return

❄

Where Ankle Lane joins Blarney Street there are four high houses, dark-looking and very old, of that sort lane-dwellers call "fabrics" or "castles." The number of inhabitants varies from day to day: tricky-men in for the races will stay two nights, cattle-drovers only one; in periods of idleness a group of coal-porters sometimes attains to a certain solidarity—the same figures go in and out the doors day after day—but, just as happens in a factory, change sets in with prosperity; new faces come and go; and the next period of idleness sees a new colony, the same in its general characteristics, though made up of quite different individuals, repeat the fortunes of the last.

The largest, the darkest of these four houses was kept by a widow named Tynan; Bonnety Tynan she was called, from a wisp of a bonnet that clung to her scanty hairs; the other lodging-house keepers wore shawls. Her face was crabbed, shut like a fist against craft, reduced to its small-

From THE WAGER, New York, The Devin-Adair Co.

est and toughest by dint of years of hard-dealing. And her bonnet was equally shorn of its beams; this, too, was now not much bigger than a fist, but the legend still held that it was the lodging-house keeper's money-box. Sometimes she would have as many as thirty men under her roof, most of them idle, so her hardness, her aloofness were needed. How else could she have managed them? The Law?—it was too complicated; and besides, she kept too irregular a house to care to invoke it. She had laws and ejectment-processes of her own. Sometimes she conceived suspicion of a lodger; she waited till his back was turned; then she would slap a few buckets of water over his bed; he returned to find it sodden; and she went on with her washing while he stamped and cursed.

In the beginning of winter one evening towards six o'clock, as she shuffled in along the dark hall, she was surprised to see a glare of firelight breaking out towards her from the kitchen; she had been out of the house for some hours and hoped for nothing better than a spark in the bottom of the grate.

Opening the squeaking door she was still more surprised: a great figure, a darkness, sat on a stool before the fire; she noticed the curving width of his back; the huge head bent forward—he was asleep. She went silently up to him, bending to see his face: it was tanned; she glanced at his hands: they were dark with tar, knobby, and had blue rings and flags tattooed on them; but it was the hard, exaggerated-looking creases in his serge clothes that spoke his trade most clearly—these clothes had been folded tightly for weeks, perhaps for months, in the bottom of a seaman's chest. She shook him: "Come on now—wake up, who are 'oo? who are 'oo?"

He growled; then his voice softened; he rose and stretched himself, very much at his ease; a light came into his sea-bleared eyes; he examined the old woman's face with interest, with amusement apparently. "You're not changed a ha'p'orth," he said, "not a ha'p'orth."

She stared up; he was handsome in such a place.

"Sit down," she said, "I can't call to mind what your name is—'tis after escaping me memory."

With a seaman's license he put his great arm about her, drew her towards the glowing fire, and said again:

"You're not changed a ha'p'orth."

"I don't know you," she snapped out, breaking away.

"If you don't there's not a soul in Cork to say who I am—I'm Jim Daunt that was."

A memory or two, quite unimportant, stirred in her brain:

"So you are, so you are; you're welcome; how long will you be staying?"

"Till half-past eleven, anyway," he said.

"Where's the boat—Queenstown?"

"No—the Jetties," he answered, "and I must be aboard for midnight."

II

She treated him well; she gave him a couple of eggs and many rounds of bread; yet for a seaman he made but a scanty meal.

"You're not doing well?" she said.

"If I only had it yesterday," he said, "you'd see the death I'd give it."

She moved about in the silent way of a woman who is accustomed to keep people at a distance. It was he who spoke:

"Isn't this a quare thing," he said, "I was never a bit lonesome wherever I was on sea or land—thousands of miles away—never a bit lonesome till this evening sitting there on that there stool."

She believed him; for she knew these sailormen well; and how any shelter that has the look, or even the name of home, stirs them.

"You were a great long time out," he continued, half complaining.

"How did I know you'd be here?"

"When did you leave the house?"

"Near four, I expect."

"Well, now, look at that," he said. "You mustn't have been well round the corner when I came in; and here I stopped, for I couldn't go away again—couldn't go away. Was I asleep when you came in?"

A lodger they called Brother entered; Mrs. Tynan made the two men known to each other. The sailorman wanted drink to be sent for; Bonnety, however, wouldn't have it: there was plenty of time, and, besides, drink was no food for a man after a day's work. Brother seconded her; Saturday Night would be coming in soon, and he was the best of company; 'twas company a man wanted after being shut up for months in a wind-bag, "Wasn't it, matey?" he said, taking the seaman's hand. A radiance had come into Brother's face: unexpected joy is straight from the hands of the gods: exhausted, heavy in all his limbs from climbing with a laden hod forty-foot ladders from early morning—terrible work—he had hoped for nothing beyond a single drink in Miss Nora's, and lo! the pleasures of a revel were emerging in his imagination.

"Have you enough of it?" he said.

"Of what?"

"The say?"

"God knows an' I have," said the sailor, with unexpected earnestness, "but isn't it a quare thing to say that I was never a bit lonesome till this evening sitting there on that there stool?"

"How so?" said Brother.

And then with lingering detail the sailor told how he had kept watch while Mrs. Tynan was down in Miss Nora's.

III

Saturday Night came in after a few moments; in every feature, in every limb he had become misshapen by dint of combat; his most restful attitude challenged; yet in Brother's words he was the best of company: spirit is spirit.

Brother, introducing the men, mentioned the sailor's

former connection with the house: "There's no house like the old house," he said, and Saturday Night, gripping the sailor's hand, told him that though he had never met him before, he felt they were old friends already: "There's something draws me to you," he said, and the sailor answered: "A fellow don't hear words like them from foreigners."

And three minutes afterwards he told Saturday Night that he had never known what it was to be down-hearted till that evening, sitting on that there stool before the fire. And, indicating Brother, "Himself will tell you," he answered Saturday Night's look of inquiry.

Again he wanted to send out for drink; but again the landlady blanked the proposal: "What hurry was there? wasn't the night long enough? couldn't they wait for Johnny Swaine at least?"

Instead of Johnny Swaine came Katty Sullivan, saying as her first word:

"Isn't Johnny here?"

"Not yet," and they bade her sit down.

"By James, I might as well," she said: the form of swear she had invented herself, and its use seemed to lift her above the common throng; yet she needed no such aid; by nature she was above her surroundings. Strong and happy, with full, firm flesh, her face colored like ripe corn, her eyes blue and bright as the skies that go with it, she was large-hearted, and merry and frank because of her fearlessness, of her consciousness of power.

"Here's a lonely sailorman wouldn't object to a bit of company," said Saturday Night, and " 'tis a thing no wan objects to," she answered, in a tone that had as much daring as pity in it. Her words seemed to take the sailorman off his guard; the impudence in his face withered before her eyes. She had laid her spell on him; but everyone saw that some weakness of spirit denied his rising to it: he looked like a sick sportsman who, on a morning of sunshine, suddenly discovers that he is unable to lift his body from the bed. The moment's unrest was swallowed in a whirl of words, for Katty Sullivan was one they all liked to talk with. She was one of those who, though they might give a man a "wipe" across the mouth, never get on their dignity, an attitude that takes all heart out of a night's merriment. Soon Johnny Swaine came seeking Katty, even as she had been seeking him; and the sailor saw at once that he was her accepted lover, and with the knowledge a touch of daring came back into his look; his eyes; in spite of himself, as it were, would now find themselves resting on Johnny's face. Brother was sent for drink; he returned with two friends; " 'twould go to me heart to refuse them," he explained to the sailor.

The sailor drank nothing but raw whiskey, and it soon appeared that his loneliness had gone from him; so, too, had his hold on himself. He became aggressive; when Brother was telling his champion tale of a sailor who, having deserted, signed on again in the self-same ship under stress of drink, the sailor stopped him half-way, and in his mouth the story from being a mere fill-gap became wild and thrilling. And almost without a pause he went on to tell the story of a parson's daughter of Adelaide, the girl who hid herself in a ship's hold for the sake of a young captain—how she might now be met with in the cities of the South American seaboard, in Buenos Aires or Rio—the sailors speak of her as the Australian Rose. He had seen her himself. His voice became higher and louder; he seemed to be talking against time, and his eyes shifted continually from face to face. He twitted Brother on his powers of drinking; he joked Saturday Night on his wounds; yet somehow his merriment was not contagious; and they all sniffed trouble when he began to raise bad blood between the lovers, for they could see that Katty's eyes were rife for mischief.

Johnny, she said, would have gone sailoring himself only for the wetness of the sea and his love for his mother; anyway, he wouldn't like to be pickled as well as drowned and, by James! she wouldn't care to see him pickled herself; "he'd be a terrible sight!" Then the sailor, with great concern, asked her what would she do if Johnny went off with another girl? She laughed, bent with laughter at the idea, and the whole room laughed uneasily with her. And so Johnny Swaine, made scapegoat for the company, sat by the girl's side, looking with glum eyes at his unfinished drink. But at the end of a bout of merriment the sailor stretched his hand to him saying that a joke was a joke; Johnny would not even look at the proffered hand. "Anyway, fetch us the measure," the sailor continued with some diplomacy; and Swaine, thinking of peace with honor, rose from his place and made for the gallon. Without a sound the sailor sprang into the vacant space at the girl's side, and Johnny, turning, found him there. A roar of laughter addled him, maddened him. He flung the gallon about the floor, squared out, and his voice rose above the jubilee: "Stand up, if you're a man."

"Miss Sullivan," the sailor's voice was heard saying in the sudden, expectant silence, "isn't it lovely weather?"

"Stand up, I say."

"A beautiful night?"

"Will you stand up?"

And the girl's eyes danced to see such spirit in her lover.

"You won't, won't you?" and Johnny's open hand met the sailor's cheek with a ringing blow. In a flash the two men were dancing at each other, the sailor all activity, his voice jerking out the best known of all the chanties:

> *Ranzo was no sailor;*
> *Ranzo, boys, Ranzo.*

And every time he came to "Ranzo" in the refrain—the word on which the rope is dragged as they hoist sail—he struck or rather touched Johnny's face or side or ears: he played with the landsman, dancing round him, tipping him wherever he wished.

Ranzo was no sailor;
Ranzo, boys, Ranzo.
The mate he was a good man;
Ranzo, boys, Ranzo!

The company, seeing that he did not mean to punish his man, let their mirth loose; they began to cry out: "Go it, Johnny, go it, old man." But after some time the sailor became overconfident, became careless; Johnny, on the other hand, had recovered his self-possession. Seeing a chance, he stood statue-still for a moment; then, making a wild charge, struck full in the sailor's face. The sea-blood fired up; song and dance ceased; with swift, careful drives he drove Johnny back, back, almost into the fire-grate. The room had become silent. Both men seemed to be fighting for life. They panted; their feet scraped the floor. Katty stood up: "Sir," she said, in a breathy voice that was scarcely audible, "Sir, sir"; but neither fighters nor onlookers heard her at all.

Suddenly shuffling steps were heard coming in the hall, and "Police," whispered Brother; for policemen walk into such houses in the same manner as factory-inspectors enter factories. At the word the sailor's face went white; he turned half-round from his man towards the room door; and Johnny, who had not perhaps heard Brother's warning, battered him right and left with great will.

"Wait awhile," said the sailor, all confusion, still staring at the door.

"Come on," shouted Johnny, wondering what had happened.

All faces were on the door; some of the men were gripping others by the shoulders. It was old Ned Mulcahy, the mason, who stuck in his head. The next moment the sailor was dancing once more around Johnny.

He gave him five and twenty;
Ranzo, boys, Ranzo.

His terror had lifted; he resumed his antics, and soon he had Johnny hemmed into a corner, where he kept him until he had his nose pumping blood. Then the combatants were separated.

"He's a game fighter, anyway," said the sailor, releasing him; and Katty Sullivan, passing the defeated man a handkerchief, thought in her heart of hearts that she wouldn't give him for all the tanned-faced sailors on the sea.

IV

It was now high time for the sailor to be going if he was to make his ship by midnight; yet he dawdled to hear the end of a story, to turn a joke, to look at Johnny's nose. He lingered too long; for Saturday Night suddenly began to tell the tale he always reserved till he had become quite emotional in his drink. They were unloading the *Cyclamen*, he said, and the first glimmer of dawn was coming on the river and, merciful God! he saw a woman floating down the tide, her golden hair spread out on top of the water. They got her into a boat—the handsomest woman he ever laid eyes on, and he tried to persuade the men to say nothing at all about the matter, only just take the corpse up to Burnt Lane on a shutter and give her a decent wake with candles, and Christian burial in the Gardens; but they wouldn't, they were afraid of the law; and the police came, and the first words the sergeant said were (and Saturday Night wept to repeat them): "What do you know about this *person?*" "What do you know about this *person?*" Saturday Night spoke the words again, turning towards the sailor; and "Was that what he said?" the sailor gasped out, but his voice was so strange that the whole room on the instant forgot the story; the sailor's jaw had become locked, his neck rigid, his head looked as if carved in hardwood, the eyes unskilfully painted—a blank stare. But he lifted himself up, and "I'll be late," he said, in a voice that beseeched them not to question or hinder him; he had broken down; he could not explain himself—at least, this is what they would think.

"Good night," he said, putting out his hand to Katty Sullivan in a sudden, jerky way, his eyes meanwhile turned away from all the faces. She took no notice; she let on to be speaking to Johnny, who was now once more at her side. Without another word the sailor vanished from their midst.

After a pause the old woman spoke in her hardest voice: "Did any of ye see that fellow coming in here?"

No one spoke; in the silence Brother cracked a match on the bowl of his pipe.

"He said he came in here to-day after I wint out."

"And sure he might."

"I'd like to know," the old woman rejoined, and she lit two candles—a signal for them to retire.

"He said he was asleep," she added, "he was no more asleep than I was."

"Holy Mother!" said Katty Sullivan, as she rose to go, "I'm sorry I iver laid eyes on him."

V

Now, I think that the sailor, as he stumbled down the deserted hillside streets towards the river, shook himself and stood still a moment here, stood still a moment elsewhere, saying at every pause: " 'Twill be all right—what a fool I am!"

Anyway, he got to his ship; made to walk up the plank with his head in the air, and—who knows how the end came?

But the next day they brought up two dead bodies from between his ship and the quay-wall; one of them, the second mate it was, had a knife-wound in the right lung and another in the back below the lung; the second body, bearing no signs of struggle on it, was our sailorman, Jim Daunt; and it was proved by the stopping of their watches and otherwise that one body had been a couple of hours longer in the water than the other. Saturday Night says

that as he went up the plank maybe he heard a voice saying "What do you know about this *person?*" but Brother
says that 'tis how he threw himself in, for he saw that the
whole race of men were turning against him—look at how
Katty Sullivan, with no reason at all, *couldn't* shake hands
with him. Johnny Swaine says they all came well out of
it, as if a murderer has evil spirits at his beck and call.

But what brought the sailorman up to Bonnety
Tynan's at all? Was he trying to prove an alibi? Or was it
that the word Home was ringing in his brain?

ERIC CROSS

Saint Bakeoven

✳

I don't pretend to be musical, apart, of course, from know-ing a good tune when I hear it—the sort of thing that a fel-low can whistle in his bath. It does so happen, however, that I was almost responsible for what might have been one of the musical sensations of the century, and, before I forget it, I'd better make some record of it for future gen-erations.

I used to spend a part of each year fishing in Kerry in those days. On one occasion, while I was returning from a mountain lake, I ran into a terrific thunderstorm. Below me in the valley I spotted an isolated farmhouse and I worked my way down to it as quickly as possible. I had barely knocked at the door when it was opened by an old man who ushered me in as though I were the prodigal son returning home. He helped me off with my coat, drew up a chair to the fire for me, and, in general, treated me with

From *Irish Writing*.

58

even more eager hospitality than you usually meet in Kerry.

"You must find it a bit lonely tucked away back here," I suggested, once the preambles of hospitality were settled.

"Yerra—lonely, is it?" replied the old man, whose name, by the way, was Johnny Quill. "The divil a bit lonely am I ever," he went on. "To tell God's truth, 'tis just the other way about."

"How come?" I quite naturally asked, considering the situation of the place.

" 'Tis the fairies," he replied, in a matter of fact way. "Them divils do be at me, pestering and worrying and annoying and bothering me all hours of the day and night. 'Tis only when a Christian, such as yourself, comes along that the sight of him drives them out and I have a bit of peace and ease for myself as it is now. But the moment you'll be gone them divils will be back again with their whispering and their rustling like mice round a corn bin. They have me patience worn out. There should be a law passed against them by those useless people up in Dublin and then put the police onto them. But, oh, no—they're much too busy passing laws to make hens lay eggs by act of Parliament to have the time to do anything useful. I tell you that the fairies are the plaguiest, most pestering and bewildering form of creation that man was ever burdened with."

"Yes," I agreed, for, after all, an old man's fancies break no bones. "I am sure that you must find them a bit of a nuisance."

"Nuisance! Nuisance!" bellowed Johnny. "Why, the divils have me near driven mad. I lambaste them with the handle of a broom. I give them a histe of my boot and a skelp of my tongue, but it's all a waste of energy. A few minutes later and they will be back at their old comether again: whispering hocus pocus; mislaying things and upsetting things on me. There's all classes of them," he continued, "but there is one of them—the plaguiest one of me whole pick of divils, who comes mainly by night. A sort of a foreigner, I'd say he would be, and a damned bad-tempered one at that. There's some of them all mischief, but with this one the game is all music. Whenever he puts his face inside the kitchen, the whole house does be filled with the sound of music as though it was the air of the place. Then he tries to be telling me something, but I can't make head or tail of the queer language he speaks and that only seems to make him madder and he shakes the great head of him and holds the great fists of him in the air, with the fingers spread out like a dealer trying to buy a beast in a fair for ten pounds from a slow witted man.

" 'Saint! Saint! Saint!' he yells. Then 'Bakeoven! Bakeoven! Bakeoven!' and I can't make sense of that at all for the divil a bit does he look like a saint and the divil a bit do I know what he means by his 'Bakeoven' unless it be one of these newfangled fakes that they have in the towns for the lazy women to bake in.

" 'To hell with you and your "bakeoven," I yell at him, 'if it's a "bakeoven" that you are trying to sell me or persuade me to buy. It was on the cake from the bastable pot that I was reared and on the same I'll finish my days. Then the music starts all over again till my head is like a hive of bees ready to swarm with the sound of it.'

"All very interesting," I agreed. "It looks as though the worst of the storm is over. I think that I'll be pushing on." I said goodbye to Johnny and thanked him, and, as far as I was concerned, that would have been the end of the business, for fairies aren't particularly in my line.

It so happened, however, that there was a professor of music johnny, from Oxford, staying in the hotel, collecting 'folk music,' whatever that may be. Naturally he was a difficult subject for conversation and that night I happened to mention the rigmarole Johnny had told me that day, by way of being sociable.

The professor johnny, whose name was Peterson, pricked up his ears almost immediately and showed more signs of life than I had seen so far in him, when I told him the yarn. I went away to bed and naturally had forgotten all about it by the following morning but it seemed that this fellow Peterson had, overnight, made a mountain of the story. He had worked out some crazy notion from it about a German composer called Beethoven, who had composed nine symphonies and died before he had finished his tenth; and he had come back in ghost form to worry poor old Johnny Quill about it.

Peterson had worked out that Johnny's 'Saint' was the German for 'tenth' and his 'Bakeoven' was really 'Beethoven'—the composer's name, and the music Johnny heard, was, of course, the music of the tenth symphony, now finished. It didn't seem to be dripping with sense to me.

I happened to go into the bar before lunch for an appetizer and who should be there but Johnny Quill himself, celebrating a deal in sheep. We had a drink together and I left him to it and went off in search of food. But in the dining room I ran into Peterson, bubbling over with some new brainwave on Johnny's story. In the hope of finishing the matter off, as far as I was concerned, I led him out and introduced him to Johnny himself, the fount of inspiration. But it wasn't my lucky day, for in spite of his knowledge of music he could not make anything of Johnny's accent, no more than Johnny could make of his, so I had to stand in as interpreter.

I opened the ball with the first round of drinks, Peterson having lemonade and going straight into action, instructing me to ask Johnny to describe the appearance of the ghost or fairy or whatever it was, in detail.

"Tell him," said Johnny, "that he is a stout block of a bucko with a great stook of hair on his head as though he is in dispute with the barber—and that might well be, for he has a fierce, bad tempered jowl on him. His clothes? . . . Yerra, he does mostly wear some sort of an ould swally tail coat with an ould choker round his neck and the knee breeches they used to wear in the time of the caroline hats."

"Hm!" snorted Peterson, like the man who had found

the piece of kidney in the pie, when I translated this for him. "Ask him now what language his fairy or whatever it is speaks."

"The divil be from me but how would I know that," replied Johnny. "Tell the man of the lemonade that 'tis neither English nor Irish but some gibberish makeup of his own and that the only words that I can make out at all are his 'Saint' and his 'Bakeoven,' and to hell with him and his 'bakeovens.' I'll stick to me bastable pot."

Peterson was studying Johnny intently as he put him through the third degree. "Ask him now," ordered Peterson, "if anyone else sees this apparition or hears the music."

"Only the divil himself could answer that," snorted Johnny, "but 'tis not likely for ould Bakeoven wouldn't have the time left to be annoying anyone else after all the time that he spends annoying me. He'd scarcely have the time left to wash himself . . . and will you add to that," Johnny continued, "that I will answer no more questions till the gentleman puts away the lemonade and has a glass of whiskey with me like a Christian."

Peterson, in spite of protests, had to yield. Johnny, as the oracle, could call the tune and he called it quickly.

"Would it be possible for me to hear the music and see this ghost if I went along to the house?" was Peterson's next query.

"It might and it might not," was Johnny's answer to this. "But mostly I'd be saying against it for I do notice that when anyone comes into the house to me the music stops and ould Bakeoven goes up the chimney or out of the window. But tell the gentleman that he's welcome anytime and if he can salt the ould divil and take him away with him to foreign parts there will be no man was ever so welcome."

The party spirit was getting into its stride by now. Peterson disappeared for a few minutes and I was hoping that we could adjourn *sine die* but it wasn't to be. He had only been up to his room and he returned with an illustrated history of music. He instructed me to hand it to Johnny and to tell him to look through it and to see if there was a picture in it at all like his 'fairy.'

Johnny licked his thumb and started to turn the pages one by one. I did not translate all his remarks and comments on the pictures of famous composers he saw, though they were amusing. I had doubts if this Peterson fellow had any sense of humor at all.

After thumbing about half way through the book Johnny let out a yell, putting his finger down on a picture of Beethoven.

"The pesky ould divil himself," he whooped. "The living split image of him! Saint Bakeoven and the great ugly puss of him!" At this Peterson went up in the air. He ordered another round of drinks immediately. Even I began to wonder if there might be something in it after all.

"Ask him now," said Peterson, as pleased as Punch, "if he could describe or remember the music he hears."

"Could I remember the music!" exclaimed Johnny. "Indeed, but it would be the day of the greatest aise to me when the day dawns that I disremember every screech of it. As for describing of it," he continued, after some head-scratching, "will you tell him that it would be beyond the powers of the worst poet yet born to put words to it. 'Tis such a roaring and a buzzing and a banging and a beating: such a twirling of trumpets and a tweaking of flutes and a scattering of the scraping of fiddles that the like of it was never heard before in the history of the world. 'Tis like the bellowings of dumb animals in pain and the howling of infants in divilment and the scolding of women in crossness and in the midst of it all there is this ould divil of a queer one, waving his hands up and down and about in the air as though the sound was all running out of the ends of his fingers like porter out of a tap."

"Only once did I hear the match of it in my life and that was in the days of the ould militia in the town of Kenmare when someone had treated the band with decency and the band had treated themselves with equal decency and they marched through the town 'stocious' and every man of them doing his best to outblow the other fellow.''

Johnny now ordered a round and Peterson replied with another question, asking if Johnny could hum or whistle the music or give some actual idea of it. Johnny was now most ready to oblige.

"I'd give you more than an idee of it, with a heart and a half, and good riddance to it," said he, "but that it is a class of music that has no sense at all to it at all at all. 'Tis what you might call a porridge of a music—not like the 'Blackbird' or 'The Coolin'' or 'The Wind that Shakes the Barley' or any of the decent civilized tunes that wake a man's heart and set his feet tapping. But I will do the best I can to accommodate the gentleman for he is turning out to be a better class of a man than my first judgment of him. 'Tis something like this that it goes."

With that Johnny drained his glass, threw back his head, fixed his eyes on a spot on the ceiling and started to screech and to bawl and to roar and to groan until, after a couple of minutes, even Peterson, with all his interest in music, had had enough of Johnny Quill's version of Beethoven's Tenth Symphony. It was a thirst-provoking effort and Peterson thought the game worth while but demanded a *quid* for his *quo*.

"Ask him if there is any musical instrument that he can play, with which he might be able to reproduce some of the music he hears."

After probing into the nature of Johnny's polite accomplishments, the only thing that I could discover was that when he was young—and that was a long time ago—he had been able to play the bagpipes—but not very well. About here the party broke up.

The following morning, when Peterson had recovered after a good night's sleep, he had worked out a plan of campaign, for there wasn't any doubt now in his mind, on the circumstantial evidence so far produced. He was on the verge of the most amazing musical discovery of the cen-

tury. The weather wasn't too good for fishing and as
there wasn't much else to do I continued as *aide de camp*
and the general adviser and interpreter.

The first thing that we did was to visit Johnny's house
and we soon found that we were quite definitely not al-
lergic to fairies. Even Peterson did not hear a note. According to Johnny the moment we entered the house both
the fairy and his music faded away. Naturally Peterson was
a bit hurt about this but he was quite certain that Johnny
was speaking the truth and quite incapable of pulling
Peterson's leg on his home ground, as you might say.

This meant that we had to fall back on Johnny himself as medium, interpreter or what you will. And that
meant that, by hook or crook, he would have to reproduce
what he heard by means of the only musical instrument
he knew—the bagpipes. Peterson wasn't at all in favor of
my suggestion, my quite practical suggestion, of bringing a
band along and letting Johnny conduct it. He even suspected that I was pulling his leg and not treating the matter with sufficient gravity.

So the problem, or rather the practical solution to it,
was narrowed down to bagpipes. Somewhere in the district
there was reputed to be a pair or set or whatever it is of
them but when it came to finding them, they were as elu-
sive as the end of a rainbow, flitting ahead of us from
valley to valley and house to house. At last we caught up
with them. Johnny regarded them carefully, seriously and
ruefully. With all his native gift of courtesy he could find
little good to say about them. There was a whistle or a
tweeter or some such vital part missing. One of the protruding flutes or whatever they were was most obviously
cracked. More apparent still was a great rent in the wind-
bag. But, with optimism, a dash of glue, some twine and
wire, a splash of tar and a bit of an old tire, Johnny
thought that he might be able to make a job of them.

Eventually, with the help of the 'smith and the carpenter and a man who was a great hand at tying a fly and
another man who had an uncle in America who, in his day

had been a famous piper, so that he had claims to being an expert, one place removed, we got the contraption fixed up. As Johnny tactfully described it—"they worked in a kind of a class of a way." Now all that he needed was a few days' practice to get his wind and fingers into trim.

The appointed night arrived and with it rain in sheets and floods and torrents. This seemed to me to be a warning to let well alone and sleeping spirits lie. It seemed just any other kind of night rather than one to set off into the darkness and the wetness of a desolate mountain valley to hear the first performance of a symphony played on bagpipes—or played any way at all for that matter. Peterson's mind, however, was made up and I decided that being in, for a penny I might as well be in for a pound.

We borrowed the hotel proprietor's car. I took along a bottle of whiskey and a couple of rugs. As luggage Peterson had a wad of music paper. Long before we arrived at the concert hall it was obvious, even above the storm, that Johnny had entered into the spirit of the occasion and was already having a preliminary canter. It seems that somehow the fairy or ghost had got an inkling of what was in the wind and had readily co-operated with the notion. In fact they had already a dress rehearsal and come to a common understanding of the procedure to be adopted. Beethoven would conduct a few bars and while they still lingered in Johnny's ears he would have a skirl or whatever the musical term is for a dash at it and so they would progress from bar to bar.

Johnny himself was by this time so taken up with the idea and the possible hope of ridding himself of his musical lodger, that he was taking the matter almost as seriously as Peterson himself. He wouldn't even have a drink before we started. "Only a dart, now and again, of the purest of spring water," he said, pointing to a bottle at his side, "just for the wind's sake, until the gentleman is satisfied."

Still we were not *personae gratae* with fairies and while we were within the kitchen Johnny said there would not be a note of music. When you think of all the trouble that Peterson was giving himself and other people, it did really seem a bit inconsiderate on the part of Beethoven, but judging by the picture of him it was about what you might be led to expect from him. So it meant that we—or rather Peterson—would have to eavesdrop through the window.

I, never having been much of an enthusiast for symphonies or bagpipes, retired to the shelter of the car. I wrapped myself up in the rugs and opened the bottle of whiskey. Unfortunately I was still within earshot of the bedlam which was let loose when the performance started, but as the storm increased the howling of the wind and the lashing rain toned it down somewhat. There would be a squealing and a screeching from the kitchen as though a score of pigs were being slaughtered. There was Peterson huddled up against the window ledge, with the rain cascading over him from the roof, while he scribbled down crotchets and quavers. Now and again he would bawl through the window for a repeat. Now and again there would be a lull in the noise, as Johnny took a swig of the purest spring water for his wind's sake.

Mercifully after a short while I fell into a doze. What woke me wasn't a noise. It was the absence of a noise. I came to, conscious that now there was only the howling of the wind and the roar of the swollen mountain torrents around me. There wasn't a sound from Johnny's kitchen. The door was open and Peterson was missing. I made a dash for the house to find Johnny on the flat of his back on the floor, as he would describe it, 'stocious.' The bottle of the 'finest of spring water' lay smashed beside him and from the trickle which was left in it there came a smell which might be mistaken for whiskey. It is not unknown in Kerry where so many improbable things seem to be possible for 'the finest of spring water' to have such a smell. Beside the fragments of the bottle lay the corpse of the bagpipes in a heap.

"Busht! Busht and be damned!" were Johnny's last

words as he gave himself up to the soundest sleep that ever fell on any man. The description aptly covered all— Johnny, the bottle and the bagpipes. We made Johnny comfortable for the night in his bed. There was nothing more that we could do. The performance was ended. The carriage awaited at the door.

Peterson was quite happy but very wet. There wasn't a doubt now in his mind. It was the true, authentic Beethoven music alright, recognizable even through the medium of bagpipes. A few score nights such as this and he would have the whole thing down in crotchets and quavers. A few months of work on it and it would be ready to astonish the world.

It seemed unfortunate that Peterson developed a high temperature during the night and had to be rushed off to a nursing home the following morning with pneumonia. But all's well that ends well and a few days later Johnny himself had to be taken to the county hospital. The combination of the finest of spring water, the excitement and the strenuous exercises of bagpipe blowing had not been the best treatment for the heart at his age. So, as it turned out, Peterson would not have been able to do anything more, and anyway the bagpipes were quite beyond any further repair.

I had quite a busy time between the two invalids: writing letters for Peterson, when he turned the corner, and doing a few odd things for Johnny. The doctor had advised Johnny to stay on in the hospital and he wasn't at all unwilling. I arranged the settling of his bit of land to a relative so that Johnny would be able to draw the old age pension and so have no further worry.

As soon as Peterson was well enough, I drove him over to see Johnny and, needless to say, Peterson had only one interest in the visit.

"Ould Bakeoven and his music? . . . Yerra, thank God that I have neither sight nor sound of him since the blessed day that I came in here—and good riddance, for at last after all these years I have peace and ease for myself and am able to call my soul my own."

"But, manalive!" almost shrieked Peterson, "don't you remember the music?"

"The divil a note of it," answered Johnny, puffing contentedly away at his pipe. "The divil a note of it have I heard since I came in and the divil a note of it will I hear to the end of my days for I have handed the place and the cow and the sheep to a nephew of mine and I have no mind to budge from here till they carry me out feet foremost. I'll live the rest of my life like a fine civil servant, at the country's expense, taking my aise like a lord, instead of being at the beck and call of a pack of fairies like a boots in an hotel."

Peterson cajoled, bribed, bullied, pleaded, wheedled and argued but Johnny would listen to no argument and no persuasion. The last thing that he said to Peterson when we came to say goodbye was: "If you should happen to see Ould Bakeoven at any time during your travels will you tell him from me that I did him a great harm and a great injustice and that I am sorry for it, for after all he was right. 'Tis the new-fangled 'bakeovens' that they use in this place for their breadmaking and you never in all your life tasted sweeter or grander or nuttier bread."

LORD DUNSANY

The Kith
of the Elf-folk

❄

The North Wind was blowing, and red and golden the
last days of Autumn were streaming hence. Solemn and
cold over the marshes arose the evening.

It became very still.

Then the last pigeon went home to the trees on the
dry land in the distance, whose shapes already had taken
upon themselves a mystery in the haze.

Then all was still again.

As the light faded and the haze deepened, mystery
crept nearer from every side.

Then the green plover came in crying, and all
alighted.

And again it became still, save when one of the plover
arose and flew a little way uttering the cry of the waste. And
hushed and silent became the earth, expecting the first
star. Then the duck came in, and the widgeon, company
by company: and all the light of day faded out of the sky

From The Sword of Welleran, New York, The Devin-Adair Co.

saving one red band of light. Across the light appeared, black and huge, the wings of a flock of geese beating up wind to the marshes. These too went down among the rushes.

Then the stars appeared and shone in the stillness, and there was silence in the great spaces of the night.

Suddenly the bells of the cathedral in the marshes broke out, calling to evensong.

Eight centuries ago, on the edge of the marsh, men had built the huge cathedral, or it may have been seven centuries ago, or perhaps nine; it was all one to the Wild Things.

So evensong was held, and candles lighted, and the lights through the windows shone red and green in the water, and the sound of the organ went roaring over the marshes. But from the deep and perilous places, edged with bright mosses, the Wild Things came leaping up to dance on the reflection of the stars, and over their heads as they danced the marsh-lights rose and fell.

The Wild Things are somewhat human in appearance, only all brown of skin and barely two feet high. Their ears are pointed like the squirrel's, only far larger, and they leap to prodigious heights. They live all day under deep pools in the loneliest marshes, but at night they come up and dance. Each Wild Thing has over its head a marsh-light, which moves as the Wild Thing moves; they have no souls, and cannot die, and are of the kith of the Elf-folk.

All night they dance over the marshes, treading upon the reflection of the stars (for the bare surface of the water will not hold them by itself); but when the stars begin to pale, they sink down one by one into the pools of their home. Or if they tarry longer, sitting upon the rushes, their bodies fade from view as the marsh-fires pale in the light, and by daylight none may see the Wild Things of the kith of the Elf-folk. Neither may any see them even at night unless they were born, as I was, in the hour of dusk, just at the moment when the first star appears.

Now, on the night that I tell of, a little Wild Thing had gone drifting over the waste, till it came right up to the walls of the cathedral and danced upon the images of the colored saints as they lay in the water among the reflection of the stars. And as it leaped in its fantastic dance, it saw through the painted windows to where the people prayed, and heard the organ roaring over the marshes. The sound of the organ roared over the marshes, but the song and prayers of the people streamed up from the cathedral's highest tower like thin gold chains, and reached to Paradise, and up and down them went the angels from Paradise to the people, and from the people to Paradise again.

Then something akin to discontent troubled the Wild Thing for the first time since the making of the marshes; and the soft gray ooze and the chill of the deep water seemed to be not enough, nor the first arrival from northwards of the tumultuous geese, nor the wild rejoicing of the wings of the wildfowl when every feather sings, nor the wonder of the calm ice that comes when the snipe depart and beards the rushes with frost and clothes the hushed waste with a mysterious haze where the sun goes red and low, nor even the dance of the Wild Things in the marvelous night; and the little Wild Thing longed to have a soul, and to go and worship God.

And when evensong was over and the lights were out, it went back crying to its kith.

But on the next night, as soon as the images of the stars appeared in the water, it went leaping away from star to star to the farthest edge of the marshlands, where a great wood grew where dwelt the Oldest of the Wild Things.

And it found the Oldest of Wild Things sitting under a tree, sheltering itself from the moon.

And the little Wild Thing said: "I want to have a soul to worship God, and to know the meaning of music, and to see the inner beauty of the marshlands and to imagine Paradise."

And the Oldest of the Wild Things said to it: "What have we to do with God? We are only Wild Things, and of the kith of the Elf-folk."

But it only answered, "I want to have a soul."

Then the Oldest of the Wild Things said: "I have no soul to give you; but if you got a soul, one day you would have to die, and if you knew the meaning of music you would learn the meaning of sorrow, and it is better to be a Wild Thing and not to die."

So it went weeping away.

But they that were kin to the Elf-folk were sorry for the little Wild Thing; and though the Wild Things cannot sorrow long, having no souls to sorrow with, yet they felt for awhile a soreness where their souls should be, when they saw the grief of their comrade.

So the kith of the Elf-folk went abroad by night to make a soul for the little Wild Thing. And they went over the marshes till they came to the high fields among the flowers and grasses. And there they gathered a large piece of gossamer that the spider had laid by twilight; and the dew was on it.

Into this dew had shone all the lights of the long banks of the ribbed sky, as all the colors changed in the restful spaces of evening. And over it the marvelous night had gleamed with all its stars.

Then the Wild Things went with their dew-bespangled gossamer down to the edge of their home. And there they gathered a piece of the gray mist that lies by night over the marshlands. And into it they put the melody of the waste that is borne up and down the marshes in the evening on the wings of the golden plover. And they put into it too the mournful song that the reeds are compelled to sing before the presence of the arrogant North Wind. Then each of the Wild Things gave some treasured memory of the old marshes, "For we can spare it," they said. And to all this they added a few images of the stars that they gathered out of the water. Still the soul that the kith of the Elf-folk were making had no life.

Then they put into it the low voices of two lovers that went walking in the night, wandering late alone. And after that they waited for the dawn. And the queenly dawn appeared, and the marsh-lights of the Wild Things paled in the glare, and their bodies faded from view; and still they waited by the marsh's edge. And to them waiting came over field and marsh, from the ground and out of the sky, the myriad song of the birds.

This too the Wild Things put into the piece of haze that they had gathered in the marshlands, and wrapped it all up in their dew-bespangled gossamer. Then the soul lived.

And there it lay in the hands of the Wild Things no larger than a hedgehog; and wonderful lights were in it, green and blue; and they changed ceaselessly, going round and round, and in the gray midst of it was a purple flare.

And the next night they came to the little Wild Thing and showed her the gleaming soul. And they said to her: "If you must have a soul and go and worship God, and become a mortal and die, place this to your left breast a little above the heart, and it will enter and you will become a human. But if you take it you can never be rid of it to become immortal again unless you pluck it out and give it to another; and *we* will not take it, and most of the humans have a soul already. And if you cannot find a human without a soul you will one day die, and your soul cannot go to Paradise, because it was only made in the marshes."

Far away the little Wild Thing saw the cathedral windows alight for evensong, and the song of the people mounting up to Paradise, and all the angels going up and down. So it bid farewell with tears and thanks to the Wild Things of the kith of Elf-folk, and went leaping away towards the green dry land, holding the soul in its hands.

And the Wild Things were sorry that it had gone, but could not be sorry long, because they had no souls.

At the marsh's edge the little Wild Thing gazed for some moments over the water to where the marsh-fires were leaping up and down, and then pressed the soul against its left breast a little above the heart.

Instantly it became a young and beautiful woman, who was cold and frightened. She clad herself somehow with bundles of reeds, and went towards the lights of a house that stood close by. And she pushed open the door and entered, and found a farmer and a farmer's wife sitting over their supper.

And the farmer's wife took the little Wild Thing with the soul of the marshes up to her room, and clothed her and braided her hair, and brought her down again, and gave her the first food that she had ever eaten. Then the farmer's wife asked many questions.

"Where have you come from?" she said.

"Over the marshes."

"From what direction?" said the farmer's wife.

"South," said the little Wild Thing with the new soul.

"But none can come over the marshes from the south," said the farmer's wife.

"No, they can't do that," said the farmer.

"I lived in the marshes."

"Who are you?" asked the farmer's wife.

"I am a Wild Thing, and have found a soul in the marshes, and we are kin to the Elf-folk."

Talking it over afterwards, the farmer and his wife agreed that she must be a gipsy who had been lost, and that she was queer with hunger and exposure.

So that night the little Wild Thing slept in the farmer's house, but her new soul stayed awake the whole night long dreaming of the beauty of the marshes.

As soon as dawn came over the waste and shone on the farmer's house, she looked from the window towards the glittering waters, and saw the inner beauty of the marsh. For the Wild Things only love the marsh and know its haunts, but now she perceived the mystery of its distances and the glamor of its perilous pools, with their fair and

75

deadly mosses, and felt the marvel of the North Wind who comes dominant out of unknown icy lands, and the wonder of that ebb and flow of life when the wildfowl whirl in at evening to the marshlands and at dawn pass out to sea. And she knew that over her head above the farmer's house stretched wide Paradise, where perhaps God was now imagining a sunrise while angels played low on lutes, and the sun came rising up on the world below to gladden fields and marsh.

And all that heaven thought, the marsh thought too; for the blue of the marsh was as the blue of heaven, and the great cloud shapes in heaven became the shapes in the marsh, and through each ran momentary rivers of purple, errant between banks of gold. And the stalwart army of reeds appeared out of the gloom with all their pennons waving as far as the eye could see. And from another window she saw the vast cathedral gathering its ponderous strength together, and lifting it up in towers out of the marshlands.

She said, "I will never, never leave the marsh."

An hour later she dressed with great difficulty and went down to eat the second meal of her life. The farmer and his wife were kindly folk, and taught her how to eat.

"I suppose the gipsies don't have knives and forks," one said to the other afterwards.

After breakfast the farmer went and saw the Dean, who lived near his cathedral, and presently returned and brought back to the Dean's house the little Wild Thing with the new soul.

"This is the lady," said the farmer. "This is Dean Murnith." Then he went away.

"Ah," said the Dean, "I understand you were lost the other night in the marshes. It was a terrible night to be lost in the marshes."

"I love the marshes," said the little Wild Thing with the new soul.

"Indeed! How old are you?" said the Dean.

"I don't know," she answered.

"You must know about how old you are," he said.

"Oh, about ninety," she said, "or more."

"Ninety years!" exclaimed the Dean.

"No, ninety centuries," she said; "I am as old as the marshes."

Then she told her story—how she had longed to be a human and go and worship God, and have a soul and see the beauty of the world, and how all the Wild Things had made her a soul of gossamer and mist and music and strange memories.

"But if this is true," said Dean Murnith, "this is very wrong. God cannot have intended you to have a soul.

"What is your name?"

"I have no name," she answered.

"We must find a Christian name and a surname for you. What would you like to be called?"

"Song of the Rushes," she said.

"That won't do at all," said the Dean.

"Then I would like to be called Terrible North Wind, or Star in the Waters," she said.

"No, no, no," said Dean Murnith; "that is quite impossible. We could call you Miss Rush if you like. How would Mary Rush do? Perhaps you had better have another name—say Mary Jane Rush."

So the little Wild Thing with the soul of the marshes took the names that were offered her, and became Mary Jane Rush.

"And we must find something for you to do," said Dean Murnith. "Meanwhile we can give you a room here."

"I don't want to do anything," replied Mary Jane; "I want to worship God in the cathedral and live beside the marshes."

Then Mrs. Murnith came in, and for the rest of that day Mary Jane stayed at the house of the Dean.

And there with her new soul she perceived the beauty of the world; for it came gray and level out of misty distances, and widened into grassy fields and ploughlands

77

right up to the edge of an old gabled town; and solitary in the fields far off an ancient windmill stood, and his honest handmade sails went round and round in the free East Anglian winds. Close by, the gabled houses leaned out over the streets, planted fair upon sturdy timbers that grew in the olden time, all glorying among themselves upon their beauty. And out of them, buttress by buttress, growing and going upwards, aspiring tower by tower, rose the cathedral.

And she saw the people moving in the streets all leisurely and slow, and unseen among them, whispering to each other, unheard by living men and concerned only with bygone things, drifted the ghosts of very long ago. And wherever the streets ran eastwards, wherever were gaps in the houses, always there broke into view the sight of the great marshes, like to some bar of music weird and strange that haunts a melody, arising again and again, played on the violin by one musician only, who plays no other bar, and he is swart and lank about the hair and bearded about the lips, and his mustache droops long and low, and no one knows the land from which he comes.

All these were good things for a new soul to see.

Then the sun set over green fields and ploughland, and the night came up. One by one the merry lights of cheery lamp-lit windows took their stations in the solemn night.

Then the bells rang, far up in a cathedral tower, and their melody fell on the roofs of the old houses and poured over their eaves until the streets were full, and then flooded away over green fields and plough, till it came to the sturdy mill and brought the miller trudging to evensong, and far away eastwards and seawards the sound rang out over the remoter marshes. And it was all as yesterday to the old ghosts in the streets.

Then the Dean's wife took Mary Jane to evening service, and she saw three hundred candles filling all the aisle with light. But sturdy pillars stood there in unlit vastnesses; great colonnades going away into the gloom, where evening and morning, year in year out, they did their work in the dark, holding the cathedral roof aloft. And it was stiller than the marshes are still when the ice has come and the wind that brought it has fallen.

Suddenly into this stillness rushed the sound of the organ, roaring, and presently the people prayed and sang.

No longer could Mary Jane see their prayers ascending like thin gold chains, for that was but an elfin fancy, but she imagined clear in her new soul the seraphs passing in the ways of Paradise, and the angels changing guard to watch the World by night.

When the Dean had finished service, a young curate, Mr. Millings, went up into the pulpit.

He spoke of Abana and Pharpar, rivers of Damascus: and Mary Jane was glad that there were rivers having such names, and heard with wonder of Nineveh, that great city, and many things strange and new.

And the light of the candles shone on the curate's fair hair, and his voice went ringing down the aisle, and Mary Jane rejoiced that he was there.

But when his voice stopped she felt a sudden loneliness, such as she had not felt since the making of the marshes; for the Wild Things never are lonely and never unhappy, but dance all night on the reflection of the stars, and, having no souls, desire nothing more.

After the collection was made, before any one moved to go, Mary Jane walked up the aisle to Mr. Millings.

"I love you," she said.

Nobody sympathized with Mary Jane.

"So unfortunate for Mr. Millings," every one said; "such a promising young man."

Mary Jane was sent away to a great manufacturing city of the Midlands, where work had been found for her in a cloth factory. And there was nothing in that town that was good for a soul to see. For it did not know that beauty was to be desired; so it made many things by machinery, and became hurried in all its ways, and boasted its superiority over other cities and became richer and richer, and there was none to pity it.

In this city Mary Jane had had lodgings found for her near the factory.

At six o'clock on those November mornings, about the time that, far away from the city, the wildfowl rose up out of the calm marshes and passed to the troubled spaces of the sea, at six o'clock the factory uttered a prolonged howl and gathered the workers together, and there they worked, saving two hours for food, the whole of the daylit hours and into the dark till the bells tolled six again.

There Mary Jane worked with other girls in a long dreary room, where giants sat pounding wool into a long thread-like strip with iron, rasping hands. And all day long they roared as they sat at their soulless work. But the work of Mary Jane was not with these, only their roar was ever in her ears as their clattering iron limbs went to and fro.

Her work was to tend a creature smaller, but infinitely more cunning.

It took the strip of wool that the giants had threshed, and whirled it round and round until it had twisted it into hard thin thread. Then it would make a clutch with fingers of steel at the thread that it had gathered, and waddle away about five yards and come back with more.

It had mastered all the subtlety of skilled workers, and had gradually displaced them; one thing only it could not do, it was unable to pick up the ends if a piece of the thread broke, in order to tie them together again. For this a human soul was required, and it was Mary Jane's business to pick up broken ends; and the moment she placed them together the busy soulless creature tied them for itself.

All here was ugly; even the green wool as it whirled round and round was neither the green of the grass nor yet the green of the rushes, but a sorry muddy green that befitted a sullen city under a murky sky.

When she looked out over the roofs of the town, there too was ugliness; and well the houses knew it, for with hideous stucco they aped in grotesque mimicry the pillars and temples of old Greece, pretending to one another to be that which they were not. And emerging from these houses and going in, and seeing the pretense of paint and stucco year after year until it all peeled away, the souls of the poor owners of those houses sought to be other souls until they grew weary of it.

At evening Mary Jane went back to her lodgings. Only then, after the dark had fallen, could the soul of Mary Jane perceive any beauty in that city, when the lamps were lit and here and there a star shone through the smoke. Then she would have gone abroad and beheld the night, but this the old woman to whom she was confided would not let her do. And the days multiplied themselves by seven and became weeks, and the weeks passed by, and all days were the same. And all the while the soul of Mary Jane was crying for beautiful things, and found not one, saving on Sundays, when she went to church, and left it to find the city grayer than before.

One day she decided that it was better to be a Wild Thing in the lovely marshes, than to have a soul that cried for beautiful things and found not one. From that day she determined to be rid of her soul, so she told her story to one of the factory girls, and said to her:

"The other girls are poorly clad and they do soulless work; surely some of them have no souls and would take mine."

But the factory girl said to her: "All the poor have souls. It is all they have."

Then Mary Jane watched the rich whenever she saw them, and vainly sought for some one without a soul.

One day at the hour when the machines rested and the human beings that tended them rested too, the wind being at that time from the direction of the marshlands, the soul of Mary Jane lamented bitterly. Then, as she stood outside the factory gates, the soul irresistibly compelled her to sing, and a wild song came from her lips, hymning the marshlands. And into her song came crying her yearning for home, and for the sound of the shout of the North Wind, masterful and proud, with his lovely lady the Snow; and she sang of tales that the rushes murmured to one another, tales that the teal knew and the watchful heron. And over the crowded streets her song went crying away, the song of waste places and of wild free lands, full of wonder and magic, for she had in her elf-made soul the song of the birds and the roar of the organ in the marshes.

At this moment Signor Thompsoni, the well-known English tenor, happened to go by with a friend. They stopped and listened; every one stopped and listened.

"There has been nothing like this in Europe in my time," said Signor Thompsoni.

So a change came into the life of Mary Jane.

People were written to, and finally it was arranged that she should take a leading part in the Covent Garden Opera in a few weeks.

So she went to London to learn.

London and singing lessons were better than the City of the Midlands and those terrible machines. Yet still Mary Jane was not free to go and live as she liked by the edge of the marshlands, and she was still determined to be rid of her soul, but could find no one that had not a soul of their own.

One day she was told that the English people would not listen to her as Miss Rush, and was asked what more suitable name she would like to be called by.

"I would like to be called Terrible North Wind," said Mary Jane, "or Song of the Rushes."

When she was told that this was impossible and Signorina Maria Russiano was suggested, she acquiesced at once, as she had acquiesced when they took her away from her curate; she knew nothing of the ways of humans.

At last the day of the Opera came round, and it was a cold day of the winter.

And Signorina Russiano appeared on the stage before a crowded house.

And Signorina Russiano sang.

And into the song went all the longing of her soul, the soul that could not go to Paradise, but could only worship God and know the meaning of music, and the longing pervaded that Italian song as the infinite mystery of the hills is borne along the sound of distant sheep-bells. Then in the souls that were in that crowded house arose little memories of a great while since that were quite quite dead, and lived awhile again during that marvelous song.

And a strange chill went into the blood of all that listened, as though they stood on the border of bleak marshes and the North Wind blew.

And some it moved to sorrow and some to regret, and some to an unearthly joy. Then suddenly the song went wailing away, like the winds of the winter from the marshlands when Spring appears from the South.

So it ended. And a great silence fell foglike over all that house, breaking in upon the end of a chatty conversation that a lady was enjoying with a friend.

In the dead hush Signorina Russiano rushed from the stage; she appeared again running among the audience, and dashed up to the lady.

"Take my soul," she said; "it is a beautiful soul. It can worship God, and knows the meaning of music and can imagine Paradise. And if you go to the marshlands with it you will see beautiful things; there is an old town there built of lovely timbers, with ghosts in its streets."

The lady stared. Every one was standing up. "See," said Signorina Russiano, "it is a beautiful soul."

And she clutched at her left breast a little above the heart, and there was the soul shining in her hand, with the green and blue lights going round and round and the purple flare in the midst.

"Take it," she said, "and you will love all that is beautiful, and know the four winds, each one by his name, and the songs of the birds at dawn. I do not want it, be-

LORD DUNSANY

cause I am not free. Put it to your left breast a little above the heart."

Still everybody was standing up, and the lady felt uncomfortable.

"Please offer it to some one else," she said.

"But they all have souls already," said Signorina Russiano.

And everybody went on standing up. And the lady took the soul in her hand.

"Perhaps it is lucky," she said.

She felt that she wanted to pray.

She half-closed her eyes, and said "Unberufen." Then she put the soul to her left breast a little above the heart, and hoped that the people would sit down and the singer go away.

Instantly a heap of clothes collapsed before her. For a moment, in the shadow among the seats, those who were born in the dusk hour might have seen a little brown thing leaping free from the clothes; then it sprang into the bright light of the hall, and became invisible to any human eye.

It dashed about for a little, then found the door, and presently was in the lamplit streets.

To those that were born in the dusk hour it might have been seen leaping rapidly wherever the streets ran northwards and eastwards, disappearing from human sight as it passed under the lamps, and appearing again beyond them with a marsh-light over its head.

Once a dog perceived it and gave chase, and was left far behind.

The cats of London, who are all born in the dusk hour, howled fearfully as it went by.

Presently it came to the meaner streets, where the houses are smaller. Then it went due northeastwards, leaping from roof to roof. And so in a few minutes it came to more open spaces, and then to the desolate lands, where market gardens grow, which are neither town nor country. Till at last the good black trees came into view, with their demoniac shapes in the night, and the grass was cold and wet, and the night-mist floated over it. And a great white owl came by, going up and down in the dark. And at all these things the little Wild Thing rejoiced elvishly.

And it left London far behind it, reddening the sky, and could distinguish no longer its unlovely roar, but heard again the noises of the night.

And now it would come through a hamlet glowing and comfortable in the night; and now to the dark, wet, open fields again; and many an owl it overtook as they drifted through the night, a people friendly to the Elf-folk. Sometimes it crossed wide rivers, leaping from star to star; and, choosing its way as it went, to avoid the hard rough roads, came before midnight to the East Anglian lands.

And it heard there the shout of the North Wind, who was dominant and angry, as he drove southwards his adventurous geese; while the rushes bent before him chaunting plaintively and low, like enslaved rowers of some fabulous trireme, bending and swinging under blows of the lash, and singing all the while a doleful song.

And it felt the good dank air that clothes by night the broad East Anglian lands, and came again to some old perilous pool where the soft green mosses grew, and there plunged downward and downward into the dear dark water, till it felt the homely ooze once more coming up between its toes. Thence, out of the lovely chill that is in the heart of the ooze, it arose renewed and rejoicing to dance upon the image of the stars.

I chanced to stand that night by the marsh's edge, forgetting in my mind the affairs of men; and I saw the marsh-fires come leaping up from all the perilous places. And they came up by flocks the whole night long to the number of a great multitude, and danced away together over the marshes.

And I believe that there was a great rejoicing all that night among the kith of the Elf-folk.

ST. JOHN ERVINE

The Burial

✳

The funeral procession from the girl's home to the grave-yard was due to begin at half-past two, but long before that hour the crowd of mourners began to collect. They stood about the entrance to the lane leading to the churchyard, and waited. The home of the dead girl faced the lane, and the procession, therefore, would reach its journey's end in a few moments from the time when it began to move. Townsmen and neighbours mingled with men from the country and the hills, and fishermen from the bay where the girl was drowned; and each man, as he came up to a group of his acquaintances, spoke of the terribleness of the disaster, and then the talk circled round the affairs of the small town.

John Mawhinney came along the old road to Bally-shannon, and when he was by the lane he hailed James O'Hara.

"How're ye, James?" he said.

James O'Hara, a lean, foxy-looking man, turned at

From EIGHT O'CLOCK AND OTHER STUDIES, Dublin, Maunsel.

the sound of Mawhinney's voice. "Och, I'm just middlin'," he replied, "I've the quare cowl on me! How is yourself?"

"Ah, I'm not so bad. Man-a-dear, this is a tarr'ble sad thing about this young girl!"

"Aye, it is that. Man, I mind her when she was that height, the same wee girl!" He allowed his hand to fall to the level of his knees as he spoke. "An' a smart wee girl she was, too! Aye! She always had an answer for ye, whatever ye said, she was that sharp!"

He looked up as he spoke, and saw John McClurg approaching. "Is that you, John?" he said.

McClurg, a large, moon-faced man, with little, smiling eyes, came puffing up to them.

"It is surely," he replied to O'Hara's greeting.

"I saw ye in the market the fair day," said Mawhinney, "but ye wurn't lukkin', an' ye didden see me. Did ye do well wi' yer cattle?"

"Ah, I didden do so bad. I might 'a' done better, an' I might 'a' done worse!"

"Did ye sell thon wee heifer ye had wi' ye?"

"I did not. I wudden take the price——"

O'Hara tapped him on the arm. "I s'pose ye come to the funer'l?" he said.

John McClurg glanced across the road to the door of the house where the dead girl lay. "Well," he said, "I thought I wud just dander into the town an' show me respect til the dead, God rest her sowl!" The three men raised their hats at his prayer. "What time does it begin?" he asked.

"They wur talkin' about half-after-two," replied Mawhinney, "but I'm thinkin' it'll be later'n that. Sure, the mail train's not in thrum Bilfast yet, an' there's fren's comin' thrum there an' thrum Derry, too, an' they'll be wantin' their denner when they git here. It'll be three o'clock afore iver they stir out o' the dure!"

"Aye, it will that," said James O'Hara, and then he turned and spoke to John McClurg. "Wur ye wantin' much for yer wee heifer?" he asked.

McClurg bit a piece of tobacco off a long twist of dark villainous stuff, and when he had chewed it in his mouth a while, he spat yellow juice over the kerb, and then said: "You might think I was wantin' too much, an' I might think meself I was wantin' too little!"

"I saw her meself," exclaimed Mawhinney, "afore she went intil the sea, laughin' an' jokin' like annythin'! Aw, God save us all thrum a death the like o' her death!"

"They wur a quare long time findin' her!"

"They wur."

"Wud ye be wantin' five poun's fur yer wee heifer, John McClurg?" said James O'Hara.

"I wud, indeed, an' a bit more on top of it!"

"They foun' her jus' where she went down," continued Mawhinney, in the voice of a man who is reciting an oft-told tale. "Man, it's quare the way the body returns like that!"

"Aye!"

"Who's thon man wi' the tall hat an' the long coat on him, d'ye know?" asked one that stood by of Mawhinney, as a man in a frock-coat knocked at the door.

"I nivir seen him afore," replied Mawhinney. "He's a stranger in this town, I'm thinkin'. D'ye know him, James?"

"I do not," replied O'Hara. "Mebbe he's come be the train. The mail's in now. Thonder's Patrick Magrath with the mail-car comin' roun' the corner!"

"Ye're mebbe right!" Mawhinney resumed the recital of his tale. "Did ye see the piece in the Derry paper about her?" he said. "Thon was the quare bit. An' there was a piece of portry be the young wumman in the post-affice!"

"Aye, I saw that. It was quare an' nice. I didden know thon wumman cud do the like o' that!"

"Ah, sure she's in Government sarvice, issen she? . . ."

"The paper said she was the quare, clivir, wee girl,

an' tuk a lotta prizes at the school in Derry her da sent her to. They must 'a' spent a power o' money on her trainin'!"

"They did that. They nivir grudged her nathin'. It's a quare pity of them!"

"Aye, it only shows ye shudden make a god of yer childher! . . ."

Two young men, one of whom carried a costly wreath in his hands, went up to the door, and presently were admitted to the house.

"Fur dear sake, luk at thon wreath!" exclaimed John Mawhinney. "Man, thon must 'a' cost somethin'!"

"Aye, it's thrum the young men at the Y.M.C.A. She was goin' to be married to one o' them. Did ye nivir hear about it?"

"Naw. What was his name?"

"I think it wus young McCracken!"

"What! Thon lad?"

"Aye. It'll be a cut-up for him, this! . . . John McClurg, will ye take six poun' ten for yer heifer?"

"Mebbe I wud if it was affered to me! . . ."

"There's manny a Cathlik would be willin' to give a wreath, too, I'm thinkin'!" said John Mawhinney.

"Aye, that's true enough. Sure, there's no room for bigitry where death is! . . . Wur ye thinkin' o' makin' me the affer, James?"

O'Hara walked a little way from the group, and then, squirting tobacco juice before him, returned to it. "Ah, I was just wondherin' if ye wud take it if it was affered t' ye. I wudden affer more'n five poun' for it meself! . . ."

"Ah, well, it wudden be no good you afferin' that amount. I wudden part wi' it fur the money!"

"There's a brave crowd here now," said O'Hara, turning towards the crowd. "It'll be a big procession, I'm thinkin'!"

"It will that. But I've seen bigger. There was the time Dr. Cochrane died. D'ye mind that? That was a procession an' a half!"

"Aye, it was indeed. Near a mile long that was! . . ."

The door of the house opened, and a number of persons entered.

"They'll be startin' soon," said Mawhinney.

"Ah, well, God help her, she'll soon be oura all this. It's the long sleep til the Day o' Judgement!"

"Ye're right there. Ye are indeed! . . ."

The door slowly re-opened, and men came forth bearing the yellow coffin on their shoulders. A great quietness descended upon the village street, and each man in it removed his hat and, if he were a Catholic, crossed himself and prayed for the repose of the dead girl's soul. Here and there a woman wrapped her shawl about her face and wept. The bearers carried the coffin across the street to the lane leading to the churchyard, and the people in the street fell in behind, and marched slowly towards the grave. A bell tolled softly, and in the house from which the body had just been borne a woman was heard crying and lamenting.

"I'll give ye six poun's fur yer wee heifer," said James O'Hara, as the body went by.

"Ah, God rest her sowl!" murmured McClurg, marking himself with the sign of the cross on the head and breast. "I cudden take less nor six poun' ten!"

"I cudden give more nor six poun'! . . ."

"Well, ye'll not get it fur the price. It's six poun' ten or nathin'!"

"Ye're the hard man to bargain wi'! . . ."

"I'm not hard at all! . . . Mebbe, they're better dead young nor dead oul'!"

"Will ye not budge yer price?"

"I will not!"

"They're in the graveyard now. . . . Come on down til Maloney's public-house, an' I'll sale the bargain wi' ye."

PADRAIC FALLON

Something

in a Boat

❋

The Whittys lived in the Crook, a southerly niche of sun,
the best farm, and the best dwelling house, in the Island.
It was known as "Mary the Burrows," though Mary's husband, Jack Tom, was the legal owner, to whom Mary
brought nothing as a dowry but a couple of stony fields on
a hill-top where she had ground her strength like a razor
in the three years of her first marriage.

Mary should have been happy. She had Jack Tom, a
slow, strong, humorous man, who could warm a house on
any kind of a night, and a son, John, who might have been
spat out of his father's mouth. Yet, on the night of a station, when the priest was praising the place she had, the
fine weather-slated house with its byres and piggeries and
white dairies, and said that she must be a very happy
woman, she looked at him in amazement, and then at
Jack Tom, who knocked out his pipe on the hob and
laughed at her.

From CELTIC STORY, edited by Aled Vaughan, London, Pendulum.

91

"D'you know, Father," Jack Tom said, "the poor woman was born with a worm in her."

"A worm, Jack?"

"The worm of Care, Father. He gives her no rest. Night, noon and morning she finds something to worry her."

"I wouldn't think that of her, then."

"How would you, and that peaceful face on her? She's sitting there now forninst you, and you'd think her bit of knitting was all she had in her mind, but give her five minutes and she'll be wondering if the geese are hanging long enough to be tender for your dinner tomorrow and she'll be out to the dairy to pinch them, or she'll be up- stairs to see if your bed is all right, or she'll be out in the valley-field to see if the sheep haven't picked a way into the oats . . ."

And Mary smiled while they all laughed at her. But five minutes later she had left her knitting on the chair and disappeared.

That was the way with her. She gave herself to the life around her like a mother does. Her nerves went out delicately into the weather and the fields. She went up and down with the mercury. For husband and son and farm she had a sixth sense. She never intruded on them. She drew them together instead, as if they had to pass through her mind to become real to themselves. She knew what they wanted before they did, and when son and husband were alone with her at night before they went to bed, she watched them out of her dark eyes without seeming to watch, speaking very little herself, just looking up from her knitting now and then as if to make sure that they lived outside of her as well as inside her.

It didn't take her long to feel the new restlessness that came over her son. She didn't speak of it until she saw there was no sign of it leaving him. And even then she waited, denying its existence to herself until Jack Tom opened the subject himself one night at the fire when John came in late.

"I suppose you were over in Murtagh's, Johnny."

"I was not."

"Or in Glynn's?"

"No. Why would I be?"

Jack Tom put a spit neatly into the fire. "Well, isn't it time you put a rope on some good girl? Time you made your mother a grandmother?"

Mary looked up, startled, to find her husband's slow wink waiting for her. Her eyes went to John, but he was filling his pipe and showing no sign of confusion.

"She'll have to wait a while longer, then," he said. "For it's on me mind to see a bit of the world first. I suppose you'll be able to manage without me for a month. I want to have a look at the city. Dear God, it's staring me in the face every day from the other side of the bay since I was a foot high, and would you believe it's not until a month ago that I began to wonder what kind of a world at all was behind the two drowned steeples we see from the Hill."

He lit his pipe from a red turf. Jack Tom smoked on comfortably. But Mary's knitting lay idle in her lap. John went on, warming up. "I counted six steamers yesterday going up the bay, and eight coming out. There must be a great stir in a city like that, and I'm ashamed of me life I haven't put a foot there yet to see what it's like."

"You're no different from another, then," Mary put in quickly, too quickly. "It's few people from the Island ever see the city. And those that do are no better off for it."

He didn't answer her directly. Jack Tom said, "It does nobody any harm to know the world." And Mary glanced at him bleakly.

"What good'll it do him, either?"

John said nothing for a while. He puffed away at his pipe as if he hadn't heard her. She waited for him, her knitting still idly on her lap, but his eyes were on the fire. Outside, the sea was sounding as the ebb turned against the breeze. There would be a faint haze of light over the waters where the city stood.

"I'm thinking you spent your evening on the hill," she prodded. "You could find better things to do than be watching a couple of lamps across the bay. What would you do in the city for a whole month?"

He turned to her. "That's what I was wondering tonight. And I think it best that I go and see. I'll set off on Monday. The hay is up, and the turnips thinned, and I think ye can do without me for a while."

He went off on Monday morning before the sun. She made him his breakfast, still stiff with opposition. But before he went out the door, she blest him three times with holy water, and gave him a hard peck of a kiss. And when he had gone, she went up the hill where she could watch him walk the only road out of the island. She saw the smoke rising from the chimney of her house, and from other chimneys, and the sun stir and strike on the grey morning like a match; she saw the day waken round her in a way that was both sudden and slow, bringing people out of their houses, and cattle out of the fields, and when he had disappeared into the rocks of the cause-way, she came down only half-thinking of all the daily chores she had before her.

Jack Tom was puffing his first pipe at the gate. "You saw him off?" His face was kindly, but untroubled. She stood before him stiffly.

"If you had spoken one word he'd have put his nonsense away from him and stayed at home."

"God be good to you, woman," he said. "It's not to America he's going. Every young thing has its hour of play."

"It's no play to leave him go into a strange city."

"Wisha! Is it a babby in a box you want to make of him? Milk the cows, woman, and don't be always setting fire to yourself!"

He eyed her for a minute, his eyes soft, and a little shy. "He's a good boy," he said, "and we should thank God for him."

II

It was a month before he came back. She was the first
to see him. She was coming in from the yard with two cans
of milk, when the calves, nosing the bar off the gate, made
a rush for her. She had time to step through the outer
gate, and bang it shut, before they caught up on her; but
then she had to go right round the house and in through
the front door. She was turning the gable when she caught
sight of him. She waited just as she was, the cans in her
hands. He whistled, and hurried his stride, his face flush-
ing as he came up to her. She didn't know what to say to
him when he took the cans out of her hands and kissed her.

He was bubbling over with things to tell. He'd had a
great time of it. She sliced bacon for him and fried it with
eggs, and all the time he talked of things he had seen and
people he had met, she watching him and making him eat,
rather than listening. She didn't want to hear, she was
satisfied to look at him.

It was an hour later when she thought of the calves
roaming the yard, and the byre door opening a way for
them into the cows. By that time, three or four neighbouring men had turned up for an evening's conversation, so
she went out herself to turn the calves into the haggard
and lead out the cows. When she returned, the kitchen
was full of neighbours and full of talk. She lit the lamp, and
took her knitting to the hob, her face peaceful again. Now
and again, she would throw a secret eye on her son, smiling mechanically when he laughed or when somebody else
laughed, or she put a friendly question to some of the
neighbours, just to make him feel welcome. No one had
ever seen her so pleasant.

The whole atmosphere of the house, indeed, altered
from that evening. The neighbours began to make a habit
of dropping in for a talk, and she recovered the habit of
listening that she had lost with her first marriage when she
lived back in the hill. She became anxious to put people at

their ease with her, so she rose sufficiently above her own pre-occupations to take some part in the slow saga of the neighbourhood that unwound itself out of the talk around her every night. Names came up out of the past, and she might remember them in her father's mouth, and think back to this event or that, nodding her head, sometimes, even, giving her version of it in her calm slow voice. Men began to like her a little, even to poke a joke at her now and then in Jack Tom's fashion. She would smile at them quietly and go on with her knitting, accepting the fact that it was John and Jack Tom who were at the centre of things and not herself, but very glad that the Island was building itself in talk all around her son. He would find it hard to break a net of that kind, hard to break away from a warm, friendly nest where he had his place. So she welcomed the men who cluttered up her floor; and dredged in her mind for her share of memories. She would light the lamp, and watch her dresser light up with delph and the cover-dishes sparkle on the walls, and take her knitting again to the hob, smiling gently out of her great reserve at the un-shaven faces round her, at the talkers and their talk, and the great rings and clouds of pipe-smoke that made blue haloes over each head. She wanted the Island to get such a grip on her son that he would never dream of leaving it.

The Island, actually, was not an island at all, but a peninsula that sprang out of the land at the entrance to the bay, and after a couple of miles became as narrow as a jetty, and then blew itself out like green glass into a fertile globe of grass and tillage. Visitors were few. They stayed at the little fishing port on the mainland that was also the market-town for the Island; few faced the rough ten-mile road to the scattered village, fewer still the great ugly rip of water to the little jetty. So Mary was surprised one evening when a hatless, young fellow faced her on her threshold, and blessing the house in good Irish, asked for her son. She put him sitting down immediately, and filled him a mug of milk, and then began cautiously to question him. He was talkative and gay, but insisted on speaking to her in the Irish she had all but forgotten. She could make nothing out of him except that he had met John in the city, and had spent many evenings with him, and had now come to see him. He had sailed out from the city. He laughed.

"John told me I wouldn't learn to sail a boat in a twelve-month. Where's the big-mouth at all, Ma'am, until I take him by the scruff of the neck and tug him to the jetty. I'll stuff every word he said to me down his throttle."

His humorous violence drew a polite smile from her. But her face changed when she saw the cockle-shell with the too-tall mast he had moored to the little wall below.

"It's no boat for open water, I'm thinking," she said, "and you all alone in it."

"Ah, sure, that's the sport of it, Ma'am. Danger is the goad in things—"

He stopped abruptly before the look that came over her face. But she said nothing. She had it in mind to fling at him an old Gaelic proverb about the fool and the sea, but she closed her mouth, partly because of island courtesy, partly because the proverb itself touched too closely on memories of her own. She had heard an old man hurl it through his beard the night they brought her father home in an old sail, and she had heard it many times since, when young men, rotten with death and salt water, were laid down in the old graveyard near the Lighthouse.

"A boy can find death easily enough," she said, "without looking that hard for it. I'm thinking you're maybe a bit of a trial to your mother."

His face was masked for a moment. Then, he shrugged. "Maybe I am," he replied. "But a man must live his own life after all, not that of an old woman." He broke into a smile once more. "Only God's apron-strings are long enough for me." His hands went out in a magnificent gesture and his eyes lit. "God in Heaven, woman, what is a man to do but to burst out of himself into the great, wide world. Look at it! It's like a door always open, waiting for you to do something—to—to—I declare to God, I'm on the old hobby-horse again, and you must be thinking I'm mad. Tell me where John is, Ma'am, and I'll take meself after him!"

She was pondering him as she led him into the fields, too courteous to give him a hint of how he had affected her. Only once on the way, as they turned the hill and met the full vista of sea and far mountain together, did she lose her faint, hospitable smile. The boy had stopped suddenly, filled to the eyes with the summer day. "This is the grandest place in the whole world," he muttered. "Look at that sea!"

Then she spoke in spite of herself. "Those that get their living out of it," she said, "have looked their enough at it. Ah, *A Bhuachaill*, let those bargain with it who have to, for when it breaks a bargain there's no court will serve a summons on it."

She was surprised at the way John received the young man. In his surprise, he almost folded him in his arms. His eyes shone. Then, the conventions of the Island took him, and he grew still and courteous after the Island fashion. She could see he was very happy. She left them unobtrusively, and hurried home to get a bed ready.

For the ten days the Stranger lived in her house, he never knew he was to her, still, *THE STRANGER*. He never guessed that she disliked him, or, more accurately, feared him, she was so quietly elaborate in the ways she tended his comfort, so suavely hospitable in obedience to the island code. He impressed her more than she wished. Outside, in the fields, where he lent a helping hand with the oats, he was not nearly the equal of Jack Tom or John, or any other man on the Island, but indoors, by the fire, when the neighbours foregathered after darkfall, his keen mind went leaping about like a swordsman. He danced through the histories of things and ripped them wide open. He gave them book-facts, and annotated their private sagas. He put things back in a schedule of time, and hung events up before them in colored calendars. They became alive to their background. He gave them word-for-word accounts of famous Fenian trials, and quoted long speeches that Irishmen had made before packed Juries. Then he moved into modern days, and told them of the new movement towards liberation that was beginning to stir all over the country. He made them conscious of Ireland in a new way, of a struggle that was not over, but beginning; he roused them into an awareness of things outside their immediate lives. Before he left, nearly every young man on the Island wanted to join the Volunteers. But he wouldn't have it. He told them to think it over for a couple of months, and John could come and see him about it.

He went off in his little boat, after a breath-taking jibe at the end of the jetty that made every island man there wince and roar instructions at him. In reply, he ran up a little flag that they hadn't seen until then. It was a Tricolour, Green, and White, and Gold, and the tiny craft bobbed away with it over the southerly swell with a nice breeze on her port quarter.

III

But when he had gone, Mary found he had left himself, or plenty of himself, behind. The Island seemed to remember it was not really an island at all but a part of the mainland where things were happening or about to happen. The young men started to gather on the hill of an evening, feeling that on a thousand other hills throughout Ireland, young men were gathering, too. They began to learn the rudiments of drill, and John spent hours under the lamp pondering a little book. Sometimes, forty or fifty young lads in fours would swing around her gable. Sometimes, she would see them creeping on their bellies through the fields. Sometimes, she would hear shouted words of command out in the dark, and know John's voice. And she didn't like it. But she never said anything. It was only a new kind of a play, she told herself, that was all. And Jack Tom laughed. "The Island," he said, with a spit, "is only a babby-house nowadays."

"Will it bring the police after them?" she queried.

"Sure, all Ireland is drilling, Woman, and they'll stop it there first if they're going to stop it at all."

That eased her for a while. Then, John started to bring home a weekly paper, and the reading disturbed her afresh. Big battles in Europe, English victories, German victories, the Russian Steamroller. It brought things to her door, and when she heard the drilling still go on in the loud winter evenings, with plover and oyster-catcher piping above the strand, she had moments of blind terror. The newspaper counted the dead in paper figures that meant nothing to her, but when John shouted *HALT!* and *GROUND ARMS!* on the hill, she had wit enough to sense that there was a point where drilling turned into war and death. So, one night, she forced herself to speak to him.

"I don't like that newspaper coming into the house, John."

"And why not, Mother?"

"It's too full of a troubled world. We're safe from the big war here," she went on significantly, "that is, if we stay quiet." And she repeated, to get her hint clear, "If we stay quiet."

He was unlacing his boots, his pipe going. "I suppose you don't like me to be drilling? Is that it?"

"Drilling is only the beginning," she said. "The beginning of war. And what war would we be fighting in the Island here? Aren't we as well off as we want to be?"

His words came slowly. "While the English hold us," he said, "we're not men except we fight to put them out."

"I don't see any English on the Island, John."

"They're in Ireland, Mother, and what are we, only a part of Ireland. We're as good a people as they are. There's no reason why we should let them rule us."

Her knitting lay idle on her lap. Her eyes were unhappy and grave as she searched for the words that would convince him. "England is too strong for you to beat," she said at last. "You'll only be one of those men that die in gaol or at the end of the hangman's rope. Will you give up the drill for my sake? I can ask that, for it's well I earned you in bringing you into the world."

He pondered for a bit, his open face showing that he was giving her more than a courteous consideration. Then he shook his head. "I can't, Mother. I'd be ashamed before myself if I didn't do what was laid on me to do."

They were silent for a while, and the silence embarrassed both of them. A cockerel gave a choked and sleepy crow in the hen-house outside, the room filled with the heavy thunder of the sea. Inside, in the west room, Jack Tom knocked the dottle out of his last pipe and drawled, "If ye've settled the world now between ye, maybe ye'd go to bed and let me settle meself." Mary stood up. "'Tis time we did go to bed," she said. She started to cover the fire with ash, so as to preserve the red seed until the morning, but before she had finished it, she was speaking once more. "I'll have to talk to The Stranger about you," she said. "He led you into this thing, and I'll see that he leads you out again. He'll be out on Sunday, won't he?"

He rose and knocked out his pipe. "He'll be out, indeed," he answered. "But you'll only waste your breath. I'm a full-grown man, and I'm not going back to babby-clothes for anybody."

He turned from her and went into his room.

IV

She got no chance to speak to The Stranger, for on Sunday, instead of breezing in, with half the young men of the Island at his heels, he was making his way by bicycle through the suburbs of Dublin, and on Monday he was in the General Post Office with a rifle on his shoulder, on Friday a bullet shattered the same shoulder, and on the following Monday, he found himself in a prison hospital, and three months later in a prison camp in England. It was, as a matter of fact, exactly two years later when he turned up, and then she said nothing to him beyond the traditional words of welcome and the traditional enquiry after his family. He stayed for three months that time. He had three stiff fingers, but he earned his keep in the fields, working with Jack Tom and John until dewfall. John and himself would disappear then. Sometimes they came home from the sea with a string of codling or bass, John laughing, the other full of humorous complaint.

"Mother in Heaven!" John might say. "A sailor needs no flag to tell him where the wind is. What's the skin on his face for, Man? Can't he feel it there, or if it's aft of him, on the back of his neck?"

And The Stranger would turn a wry and laughing face to Mary. "I jibed her again, Ma'am. We nearly had to swim for it."

Her heart missed a beat. "John can't swim," she said.

"Then we'd have a great time drowning each other."

"Why don't you give it up, Salmon?" John would laugh. "You have a good future as a farm labourer, now that they've taken the school off you, but in a boat, man, you've no future at all, for you're a natural born suicide." And John, now that The Stranger was a stranger no longer, would go off into a fit of laughter at his own wit.

Often, Mary was tempted to ask them where they spent the other evenings, the evenings when they came home late and missed the Rosary that was said in the kitchen every night. She didn't. She daren't force an open break on this new John of hers who went his own way so calmly. He was so complete in himself. He was the same as ever to her, but he had dropped something like a space between them. It was as if he had moved out of her mind into his own. She watched him all the time, and weighed him in her dark, still eyes, their nerves touching in the tension that was between them, and decided to do nothing for a while. After all, the defeat of Easter Week and the years in prison must surely have taught The Stranger some sense. And there was no drilling. She was certain of that.

Then, one day, a week after The Stranger had left for the city in his little boat, two big police constables in bottle-green uniform came into the kitchen on top of her, ostensibly to take particulars of the year's tillage, in reality, as she was to learn in a minute or two, on a more dubious business. One of them sat at the table and took out his bundle of forms, the other carted his bulk to the sugawn chair on the hearth, and pushing the regulation baton askew, ensconced himself comfortably therein. Both took off their caps, and both accepted with dignity the big mugs of buttermilk she proffered them, for the sun was a dead gold over the earth and the land sweated dust.

" 'Tis a grand dwelling you have here, Ma'am," the pompous man on the sugawn said after a bit, when the buttermilk had watered him down.

" 'Tis a modest good holding, sir," she answered, pleased in spite of herself. "But we're good contrivers and we manage, thanks be to God."

"Is there many in the family, Ma'am?"

"I have one son, sir, but he's as good as two. And a husband that's not far behind in spite of the years that are on him."

" 'Tis a great thing to have a good son. A great thing, indeed."

The other constable had his pencil poised. He rubbed a spit on it, and asked her how many acres of potatoes, and how many acres of oats she had, and her full name, and her husband's full name. While he was writing it all down slowly, the pompous one loosened his collar and took his ease.

"It's a great blessing, indeed," he said, "to have a good son about the house, and a credit to any woman in those times if she's able to keep him good. The great thing, I say, is to keep an eye on him, and to direct him. There's an old saying that says, *as the twig is bent, so does the grown tree incline*. There's a power of wisdom in that, mind you, a power of wisdom. What are the boy's predilections, Ma'am?"

"His what, sir?"

"What does he incline for, Ma'am?"

"I don't know, sir, except for hard work and maybe a rabbit hunt of a Sunday."

"Hah! Sound and solid predilections, indeed, Ma'am. I remember meself, before I joined the Force, and the way I took me pleasure of a Sunday in a likewise manner. Keep him to that, Ma'am, and he's safe from trouble, safe from the law. But it's only wisdom to keep your eye on him, for those are bad times. You never know but he might fall in with one of those codgers who're walking the land secretly, fomenting civil war and making fools of decent boys with their claptrap about Irish Freedom. And we never as free as we are this day, masters of our farms for a rent that's only a tithe of what we had to pay one time. Thim boyos should have known the days that are gone, days that you might remember, Ma'am, when there was a rent on your back like a load of stones. Who freed us of that but England? In open Parliament she did it. Isn't that true, Ma'am?"

"It might be," she replied. "Though it's a different story the way I heard it. If ye'd like a cup of tea, now, I'd take pleasure in putting on the kettle for ye. It's no trouble."

"It's no day for tea," the pompous one said. "But I was ever and always a martyr to a good cup of tea."

She made tea for the two Peelers, while they tried to draw her out cunningly. They were unsuccessful, and in the end, the pompous fellow came to the point suddenly.

"I hear you had a queer fellow staying with you lately, Ma'am."

"We had a boy working," she admitted.

"A buck from the city, eh? An organizer of devilment."

"If he's that," she asked, "why isn't he in gaol?"

"There may be reasons, Ma'am, state reasons for that."

"Are ye looking for him?"

"We might be, Ma'am. And we might not. Is he here now?"

"He is not, not since last Sunday."

"Hum. That agrees with our own information. Do you know his new habitation, Ma'am?"

"I do not."

The constables stood up, and the kitchen seemed to fill with them, and overflow out of doors. They put on their caps, and stooped through the door into the sunlight. They had bicycles, she saw.

"Well, well!" the pompous one grunted. "We'll be saying good-day to ye. And maybe I should be leaving you a little bit of advice, for you're a decent woman. Keep that fly-by-night out of your house and away from your son, or it's a nice sting he'll leave in you."

When they took themselves off into the still sunshine, they left a very frightened woman behind them. She forgot their stupidity, and remembered only the gross cunning with which they had filled her kitchen. Behind those big uniforms, like a threat, loomed a history of death and gaol-house, and now it had come suddenly alive before her, actively malignant in the privacy of her own dwelling. She sat down for a long time, savoring shadows; then, she gathered herself and went about her work, a little tighter in the face, a little quicker and more definite in her movements.

When she stirred out for the cows, a black steamer was moving up the sound, riding down its own smoke. Wind south-east, she decided automatically, and enough of it. A beam wind from the city. She was thinking of The Stranger again. The Island had nick-named him the Salmon, because that was the name of his little boat, but he would be The Stranger to her always, the bolt from the blue, the evil chance inside the *pishoge*. And as if he were answering her thought, his little boat came round from under the steamer's quarters, riding her wake perilously, the wind rocked and knocked out of its small sails. Her heart stopped for a moment before the boy's danger and her own native horror of the sea. Then, as a lucky puff took him due aft and he squared away before it with a filled mainsail, she thought to herself that it would have been an easy way out for herself and her son had he taken the sea over the side and gone under. And the thought went with her as she rounded up the cows, and went to seek her son. And even before she met him, it had ceased to shock her.

"He's not to come into the house," she told John. "The Police are looking for him."

He answered her calmly. "They're looking a long time for him. Now that they've had a look here, they won't come again for a while. It'll be safe enough to give him a bed."

She looked at him with terrible eyes, her mouth as grim as granite. "If he puts a foot in my house," she said, "I'll inform the police."

"You'll do as you wish," he answered, his face going grim, too. "There'll be enough houses in the Island to welcome him."

That night, John was late home, without The Stranger. In the morning she asked him where The Stranger was. He wouldn't answer her.

The police came back a week later, this time in force, and with rifles on their backs. They searched her house and the outhouses, and three or four other houses in the neighbourhood, and they took John away with them. In the two days that he was gone she suffered agonies. She was standing at the door when he returned, but instead of meeting him as she wanted to, with her arms wide and her mouth stiff, she sat down by the fire and turned her head away from him. He knew the way it was with her, however, and turned her face round for his kiss. She kept her mask on, though her eyes startled him with their wild brilliance.

That night she said to him, "You'll have to give up all this folly, John. I'm not able for it."

It was the first confession of personal weakness she had ever made. He looked at her sadly, pushing the cap back on his skull till the lamplight caught the peak and made it a halo over him. "I know, Mother," he said awkwardly. "I know. There'll be more of it, too. A lot more, I'm thinking. And there's nothing I can do about it."

He pushed back his chair at that, and went to bed.

v

From that out, she found herself watching the Sound for the little sail-boat. Sometimes, she did see it; more often, she guessed from John's behavior that it had arrived. It sailed no longer from the city, but from one of the many creeks within the bay, so she formed the habit of walking towards the jetty of an evening to look for it before she settled in for the night. She didn't think of The Stranger as a person any more. He was only some odd kind of force that had struck into her life. His face was rubbed out of her consciousness. Sometimes, he had a man's form in her mind, more often he was just a sail, a boat that came and went with evil purpose. She thought of him no longer as someone she had fed and cared for under her roof. She found it difficult to think that she had ever known him at all. And, maybe, that is why she was able, in the end, to do what she did.

For one night, when the little craft was drawn up on the slipway out of the flood, she moved down to it with a couple of obscure tools, some tarred paper, and a handful of corks. She wasn't more than a half-hour doing whatever she did do, but when that was done, the boat was just sufficiently seaworthy to be a deathtrap.

She said the Rosary as usual with Jack Tom, but she didn't go to bed. She sat on the hob with her knitting, listening to the breeze come stronger from the south-west, feeling with her nerves how the tide was dropping back against the wind and the way the sea was turning outside the shelter of the land. It might be happening, all of it, inside her, for she spread out over the night until the sea was breaking in her and birds wading on her strands. Three swans flew low over the house, and their wings plucked music out of her as they passed through her breast. And then she fell asleep.

She awoke, shocked. Something had happened within her that she couldn't bring to consciousness. She had to ponder for a minute before she could remember where she was or why she was there. The old chains of the clock on the wall were the first to catch her eye. And then, the clockface. And then, the hour.

She knew then. Knew everything.

Yet, she didn't scream, or make a sound that would waken Jack Tom out of his sleep in the room within. She stood up slowly, as if she were balancing a basket on her head, looked into John's empty room, then made for the door, and out. There she began to run. Little splutters of rain soused her face, a wet star was burning low-down in the south-east. The glimmering outlines of things rose before her. She ran and ran.

And all the time she knew what she would find. And still she hurried, turning into one great prayer that soared from the earth towards heaven; she flowed up, dissolving like a fountain, gasping. And she came to the jetty.

The boat was gone.

In the first house, they told her what she knew already. Yes, John had gone with the Salmon, seeing the sea was a bit too much for a bad sailor like him. They couldn't understand why she took on, why she went rambling out towards the shore, keening like a tramp-woman, till the dogs were out for miles around the village. Still, being Island people, the women stirred up their fires, and the men got out of bed and put their clothes on and laced their boots. It wouldn't be the first time a mother had dreamed of her son's death on the sea, and more often than not the dream had proved a reality.

So, they were waiting on the hill when the dawn came up on the horizon like the grey back of a whale. But, they saw nothing. And they found nothing. Not even Mary the Burrows found anything, though she stood on the hill and walked the strands for three years afterwards, until she died.

And, maybe, 'twas as well.

Miss Gillespie and the Micks

✳

We called her old Miss Gillespie, although I do not suppose she was more than forty-five or fifty. She was a big stout woman with rosy cheeks and red hair and an enormous bosom. She always seemed to wear far too many clothes and always appeared to be very warm and out of breath. She had practised midwifery until her fondness for drink caused people to lose faith in her. They pitied her, but would not have her attend them in childbirth. Still the brass plate remained on the doorframe of her house: Miss Gillespie, Certified Midwife.

She lived with her brother, a retired sea-captain, in a little house on the outskirts of the village. Her brother was a short, stocky man with a red face and a sailor's roll. He was very quiet and spent most of his time working about the garden, but occasionally he would come down to Johnston's pub and sit in a corner drinking beer and telling yarns about his seafaring days. He had served his apprenticeship under sail, and always spoke with contempt of the

From *The Bell*.

steamship, maintaining that any landlubber could be a sailor nowadays. "It was a sad day," he used to say, "the day they traded a clean spread of canvas for a splutterin', stinkin' donkey-engine."

Our favorite prank used to be letting down the back tire of her bicycle. She always cycled down to Johnston's on Saturday night and left the bicycle outside while she got drunk in the bar parlour. It was a strange thing, but she always seemed to ride much better when she came out of Johnston's. At other times her method of riding was slow and wobbly and uncertain, as if she were on a bicycle for the first time. But on leaving the pub on Saturday nights she would heave her huge body on to the saddle and go pedalling furiously up the narrow street, weaving in and out among carts and dogs and herds of cattle, narrowly missing other cyclists and shouting at anyone who got in the way.

If, however, we had previously removed the valve from the back tire, she would pull up before she had gone more than a few yards, hop clumsily off the saddle and begin to shout at the top of her voice, standing in the middle of the street with one foot on the ground and the other supported on the pedal. The anger and the shouting made her very red in the face, and we who crouched giggling in some nearby doorway could almost have sworn that her hair became redder, too.

Some of the men who always stood about Johnston's would come over to her and ask her what was the trouble. "Och, it's them children again," she would shout. "Sure they'd break a body's heart. They haven't left me what air in me back tire would blow out a candle. Bad cess to them! Of all the meddlin', interferin' wee brats that ever were let into this world, them in this place takes the cake! I'll put the polis on them. Declare to God I will; I'll put the polis on them and have them banished from the country. A pack of common thieves and rogues and liars, that's what they are. A decent, respectable body doesn't get a chance with the likes of them around, so they don't."

Then she would begin to cry and would have to be taken back into Johnston's for consolation while someone repaired her flattened tire.

Half an hour later they would bring her out, bleareyed and breathing heavily through her nose, help her on her bicycle and send up a ragged cheer as she shot off up the street, stiff and solid as a rock, her mouth grim with determination.

Never slackening her pace for a moment, she would push up the hill, past the post-office and the Orange Hall, round the corner and along the straight, wide road to the church. Turning to the right, where the houses of the village began to thin out and to be separated by little plots and patches of meadow, she would come to the home of the O'Hagans, sitting back from the roadway, with dirty children playing around the door, the washing on the hedge and peat-smoke filtering from the slanting chimney.

Invariably, she would ride past the house, looking neither right nor left; then, as though some thought had suddenly occurred to her, she would pull up, leaning to one side and gripping savagely at the inefficient brake, and slowly circle round in the roadway.

The O'Hagans were the largest, and perhaps the poorest, family in the district. The father was a tall, quiet man, who seemed to spend all his time working with a few chickens and a meagre plot behind the house. He was very shy, and was rarely seen in the village. The mother was a little harassed, anxious woman, who only appeared outside the house to draw water from the nearby pump or hang huge quantities of washing on the hedge. They had seven children, the eldest of whom could not have been more than ten years old at that time. They were a very devout couple, and I think now it may have been this very quality of devoutness and passive acceptance of life's hardships that inflamed Miss Gillespie against them.

Pedalling back to the O'Hagans' place, she would hop to the ground and stand astride her bicycle, one foot on the road, the other on the pedal. "Hi, there!" she would call to the children. "Away in and tell yer da I want a word with him. A lot of words! Tell him to come on out here till I give him his character. Go on, ye wee Fenian brats!"

At this the children would run into the house and close the door, and Miss Gillespie's fury would increase. "Are ye never away yet, O'Hagan? Take you and your snivellin' wife and your brood of whelps and brats and away you go—over the Border where ye belong. Away with the lot of ye—you've contaminated the landscape long enough, God knows. Away back to yer chapels and yer Popery and leave honest Christian folk to live in peace. This is a civilized, Protestant country—we want none of your kind here."

She would keep this up for perhaps ten minutes, until hoarseness and shortage of breath forced her to cease. There was never any attempt made to stop her. Passers-by only laughed and teased her into stronger invective. The house presented a blank face to her abuse. We youngsters, crouching behind the hedge, whistled and jeered and threw pieces of clay and dried cowdung at her, but so intense was her absorption in the O'Hagans that she seemed not to notice anything else. When it was over she would remount her bicycle and, still muttering threats and imprecations, ride off up the road toward her own house. Shortly afterwards, the O'Hagans' front door would open and the children would come out to resume their playing, as if nothing had happened.

Some of the older people tried from time to time to break her of this habit (as they also tried to stop her from drinking). Their intentions were good, but their efforts were in vain. Miss Gillespie would not listen to reason. Her personal pride and integrity were as strong as her powers of hatred. She refused to accept instructions from anyone on how to conduct her life. Even the frequent appeals of the local Methodist minister were without effect. "What business is it of yours, how I behave myself?" she said to him once. "You go on preachin' your wee sermons on Sundays and leave us stipend-payers to look after our own lives. What do you care, as long as the money keeps comin' in? Away and convert them heathen O'Hagans and let us good Christian folks alone!"

One week early in Spring there was very heavy snow, and two or three other boys and I went to the door and asked Captain Gillespie if we could clean his path, hoping to earn a few coppers. We didn't get the money, but when we had done he invited us into the house for tea. It was a tidy little house, full of bits of ship's gear and bottled schooners. This was Captain Gillespie's hobby, and he explained the delicate process by which the apparently impossible feat of getting a four-masted ship through the narrow neck of a bottle is accomplished.

Miss Gillespie, who presided at the tea-table, appeared to be in a very irritable mood. Evidently she was annoyed with her brother for having invited us in. She had been baking in the afternoon, and we had big warm farls of soda-bread, oozing with melted butter, and tea which could have supported the original of any of the captain's models. She herself ate and drank little, and, when she had finished, sat glaring and grunting at us while Captain Gillespie recounted one of his interminable tales of adventure in a clipper off Cape Horn.

While we were sitting there, a timid knock was heard at the front door. The captain rose to answer it. We could hear a young, eager voice, and the captain's deep rumbling replies.

Suddenly she looked at the door and shouted, making us jump.

"Who is it, Albert?"

The door opened and her brother came in, closing it after him. He looked rather uncomfortable.

"Er—it's one of the O'Hagan children. He says his father sent him to ask if you'd come down there right away." He coughed nervously. "Mrs. O'Hagan's going to have a baby. They—can't get the doctor. The road's snowed up."

114

He stood there waiting, watching her from under his frowning, bushy eyebrows.

At first Miss Gillespie was unable to speak. Only her reddening face registered her rising anger. Then she said:

"Well, of all the impertinence! Of all the unbelievable impertinence! The likes of *them*, daring to send for me."

"I think you'd better go, Bertha," said her brother. "The woman must be pretty ill."

"Go? Here, go out and tell that brat to go home and tell his da I wouldn't lift a finger to help them, not if they were havin' triplets! The idea of it!" She was shaking like a jelly. Big tears began to roll down her cheeks. "The very idea—them sendin' to *me* for help. Well, don't stand there with yer mouth open. Go and tell him what I said. Chase him out of here before I go out and beat the lugs off him!"

He shrugged his shoulders and went back to the waiting boy. Miss Gillespie seemed to have forgotten our existence. She sat with her hands in her lap and sobs shook her big body. The tears trickled over her fat cheeks and ran down the sides of her nose. "The idea of it," she kept saying, staring at the tablecloth in front of her. "Just fancy, them sendin' for me!" Her voice was thick with tears.

We sat in a cloud of embarrassment,—then, as if we had all had the idea at the same moment, rose and hurried outside. The captain stood at the door, gazing after young O'Hagan as he walked slowly down the road. We thanked him for the tea and, once we were out in the roadway, shed our discomfort and began to laugh at the big woman sitting there crying over the tablecloth. We followed the O'Hagan boy and hung about outside the house, full of curiosity. We could hear the woman groaning and wailing inside. There were none of the children playing round the door.

We began to build a snowman by the roadside, and I climbed into a field and got an old bowler hat off a scarecrow to set on his head. The eldest boy came out and told us his father said not to make so much noise, because his mother was sick. We pelted him with snowballs, and he had to run into the house again.

We got tired waiting, and were about to go back into the village when we saw Miss Gillespie cycling down the road. She was wobbling along the narrow lane between the banks of snow, and we expected at any moment to see her hit the side and tumble off. We waited on the verge of laughter. She did not fall, however, and when she reached us she hopped off and asked angrily what we were doing there. Her black straw hat sat on top of her head, secured by a long pin at each side. Her eyelids were red and swollen. You could hardly see her eyes.

"Away off with ye!" she cried. "Away out of this, before I beat the ears off you with my own two hands."

She pushed the bicycle at us, and we scampered off down the road, jeering and whistling.

Miss Gillespie made as if to mount her bicycle again, hesitated, and then, with a sudden impatient movement, placed it against the low wall at the front of the O'Hagans' house and marched up to the door. We waited no longer, but ran down to the village to tell what we had heard and seen. It was perhaps an hour later when Miss Gillespie came riding down the street, drew up outside Johnston's pub and went into the bar parlour. A few moments later Joe, Mr. Johnston's assistant, came out and wheeled her bicycle inside. It was not long before the word went round that shortly after her arrival Mrs. O'Hagan had given birth to another son.

She stayed later than usual in the pub that night, and then she came pedalling furiously up the hill past the house, puffing and panting, and did not as much as turn her head. Then, twenty yards farther up the road, she suddenly pulled up, made a precarious turn between the snowbanks, and came cycling back. She stopped outside the quiet house, where a dim yellow light shone from the kitchen window. She stood with one foot on the road and the other on the pedal, holding the bicycle up under her.

"Hello there, O'Hagan," she called. "Come out, O'Hagan. Come out here till I tell you what I think of ye. Are ye never away yet, you dirty Fenian dog? Why don't you clear out an' take your yelpin' pups along with ye? We don't want you here, among decent Christian people. Clear out, an' take your woman and her brood with ye!"

She began to cry and to shake the handlebars of her bicycle in impotent rage.

"D'you hear me, you dirty Mick?" she howled. "Away back where you belong, the lot of ye." She paused, as though waiting for some reply, then began to sob and moan in great distress. "Ah, God forgive me!" she wailed. "God forgive me this night, that ever lent a hand to bring a Papish brat into the world!"

DAVID HOGAN

The Leaping Trout

❄

Michael Davin was sitting at the end of a narrow, roughly-made pier of stones which stretched into the brown waters of Lough Dan. He had come that day post-haste from Dublin and this peace was sweet to him. After the toil of cycling over the tortuous mountain roads, so little used that whenever he turned a corner a score of rabbits hurled themselves in a flash of white into their burrows, after the jolting the rugged ground gave him in that long ride, after the strain of riding past half-a-dozen police barracks with three rifles tied along the cross-bar of his bicycle—from such a day the silence, the infinite placidity of the lake was exquisite retreat.

It was evening time in early June. The surface of the lake was broken now and then by a sudden breeze which put its hand upon the water and stretched long fingers out. Whenever these fingers were lifted the lake was a mirror marvellously filled with the reflection of hills and trees and

From THE CHALLENGE OF THE SENTRY, Dublin, The Talbot Press.

the whiteness of the evening sky. From his throne of stones Michael could see the lake bottom through the brown waters. A little farther out the dancing of the flies fascinated him. He watched them land upon the water, sail a little, and then leap into the air to dance again. Dreamily watching that dance, he heard a trout jump close to him. He thought it was close until he saw the widening circle in the water half way across the broad lake. Everything was so still.

Again came the "hullop" of a jumping fish, and Michael saw that a number of rings had begun to appear on that mirror surface. The trout were feeding. Every time the sound came it was the call of a lover to him, and, half-dreaming still, he undid the boat which lay by the simple pier and soon was moving slowly over the quiet lake. Though a fisherman born, he did not want to fish now—just to drift upon the waters, lying back in the boat, seeing only the sky, hearing the faint sounds from the lake-shore, listening to the music of the feeding trout.

At an extra big splash he said to himself: "That was a whopper, surely." And he raised himself slightly in the boat to watch for the next leap. He saw the first circle, well-marked, widening rapidly. As he watched it grow another spout of water leaped into the air, and Michael Davin knew then that it was a stone. In a second the whole furtiveness of a rebel's life repossessed him. He became again nervous, supersensitive, eager, anxious. He crouched back into the boat wondering whence the stone had come, who had thrown it, what was its meaning. Why did not the thrower shout?

Inside the boat he got the oars into position for swift use and began to scan the shore near which the drifting of his boat had carried him. He could see nothing, nobody. The fear that he was being watched by enemy eyes filled him: he could feel them on him. Yet there was nothing to be seen along that shadowy bank except the groups of wind-formed trees that stood along the water's edge. His eyes were drawn towards one of those groups—four twisted trunks standing on a tiny peninsula mirrored in the surrounding waters faintly now for night was coming on. But save four twisted trees he could see nothing. In the breathless hush of the whole world he could hear the trout jumping in the centre of the lake and then from the group of trees which hypnotized him he heard a faint metallic click.

Quicker than thought the oars were out and Michael Davin was pulling wildly away from the shore. His whole being waited for another sound, a sound that would shout its way across from hill to hill, from shore to shore, up the valleys, into the wooded heights, bringing many a waiting column what word? As he waited for that sound Michael Davin had a strange sensation. He felt that he was standing before a great church whose pillars slowly bent forward and began to break into little fragments of dust and stones, the heralds of mighty fall. He had the illusion that he was watching the great copper dome with its towering golden cross slipping slowly towards him and that in a moment the world would be shaken with the fall of it. It seemed to him that unless he rowed ever more swiftly the tottering church would overwhelm him.

That was his illusion as he pulled like a madman across the darkening lake, pulling away from the sound he knew so well, the sound he had heard behind that group of twisted trees—the click of a magazine being replaced in a rifle. That was what he had heard. He knew it was nothing else. For two years he had drilled and marched and fought with the East Wicklow column of the I.R.A. and knew every sound that a rifle gives. Whoever had thrown that stone had wanted him to sit up, that he might be seen—and shot. The click behind the trees meant that whoever held the rifle was determined to take no chances. He was not going to rely on one shot, he had filled his magazine to make sure. But he had not fired. That, Michael could not understand. He had loaded his magazine because he had meant to fire. As Michael sent his light craft skimming over the lake he forgot his expectant fear in meditating on the mystery of the rifle that did not speak.

The night was coming rapidly. Looking again for the clump of trees Michael found that they had melted into the black heights that now encircled the lake. A thought came to him then and he purposely steered the boat across the light that still hovered in the centre of the lake. As he passed from the shadows of one side, across the brightness, steering towards the shadows of the other, he waited again for a shot. It did not come, and soon Michael's boat must have been lost to the silent watcher on the further shore. To make doubly sure, Michael drew his boat up to the pier, rattled the iron ring as if he were making her fast, walked loudly upon the stones, knowing that all those sounds would travel over the waters to the unseen rifleman who stood among the trees. Then with the noiselessness of a cat he crept down to his boat, slid it out into the lake again, and lying in the prow drove it forward silently with his hands as oars. As a mother duck, bringing her brood for their first long swim and sensing always the eye of the hovering hawk, hugs the tree-rimmed shore, so Michael stole from shadow to shadow, round the edge of the lake, across to that side whence the ominous sound had come, and then moved slowly downward towards the treed peninsula. When two hundred yards from it, he silently beached his boat and went forward on foot.

In the oval opening of the hills was the last faint glow of daylight, but the stars had broken through it and the new moon rose above Mullaghcleevaun mountain like the diadem of a fairy queen walking upon its summit. But the light of the stars and the sickle moon could not pierce the shadows of the lake-shore. Michael knew how to walk noiselessly. More than once even in daylight he had gone forward undiscovered to the very elbows of some bivouacking column of the R.I.C. to count their numbers and note their positions. And nobody sitting by that still lake would have heard any sound from that moving thing which stole from tree to tree. At last Michael could see before him the four twisted trunks. His heart leaping within him, he stared at them. After a while he thought he could see gleaming very faintly in the darkness a round of silver. He was not sure, but what he saw seemed like the badge of a constabulary cap. He waited, but the little round of silver did not move. And Michael began to go forward again.

II

What sixth sense is it that enables us to perceive the unseen, to feel the intangible? What mysterious power dominates those moments when we can tell the secret thoughts of our friends, hear the coming of death, feel the world about us full of a presence which the eye sees not nor the ear hears?

Whatever it be, that strange other-world knowledge overwhelmed Michael Davin as he was about to step from the cover of the bushes and go towards the silver circle that glowed in the heart of the twisted trunks. It was so powerful a message that it checked his step, brought him sharply to a halt, and sent him crouching back into the shadows. The four twisted trunks stood before him, and in their midst was the mystery he must solve. Yet it was not towards them he was looking now. Some distance back from the lake-shore, immediately under the ebony cliff that ringed the lake, was a patch of furze. The furze was not visible except as a shadow against the deeper shadow of the hills behind; but towards it Michael found himself gazing expectantly, fearfully.

No sound had come from there or anywhere. The silence of the great lake was supreme. The waters shone faintly in the tremulous light, the black hills stood in a stooping circle about them. Waters and hills were silent as death is silent. Yet Michael knew that the clump of furze had a meaning for him greater even than the silver circle which shone in the midst of the twisted trunks. There was somebody in that clump of furze—somebody who lived. He waited, wondering and afraid.

A twig snapped, and the sound sent the blood drumming in Michael's ears. A moment later he was not sure if he had really seen something move against the black hills. It had no form, no color. It was not so dark as the hills behind it, he thought . . . Yes, it was moving. It was coming nearer, very slowly, ready to fly, full of hesitation. Michael drew back further into the shadow, his eyes always on the wraith which as yet was like the reflection of a cloud passing over the sea at night. He heard last autumn's leaves rustle under a step. The moving form began to take shape, take color. He could see the white shadow of a face, the fainter grey of a dress . . . it was a girl! With cautious, dreading steps she was going towards the four twisted trunks, towards the cap-badge that caught the starlight.

From the security of his cover Michael watched this drama of an unlit stage. He was thrilled, awed. He stared again at the place to which the girl was going. Was his imagination on fire, or could he now really see a man leaning against one of the trunks, a tall burly man, whose head silhouetted against some momentary brightness on the surface of the lake appeared to hang forward, as if he were asleep, or drunk—or dead? A stir brought his gaze back to the other character in the play. She was still only a shadow, but he could see that she was standing quietly, looking in amongst those four trees. She was only a few yards from them, and Michael knew that she must have pierced the secret that they held. Yet she did not show it in her stand. She took another step forward like a wild thing creeping upon its prey. Then, suddenly, she started back, stiffened, stood still. He heard her draw in her breath sharply. He saw that she remained in the crouching position in which she had been creeping forward—as if she had been turned to stone by what she saw.

It seemed hours before she moved again. She fell on her knees and buried her face in her hands. Michael could hear her sobbing. He tried to think of a way to make his presence known without adding to her terror. He must have made some movement, for her hands fell from her face, the sobs ended in a little cry, and she leaped to her feet. Before Michael could think of what to do she had fled back towards the clump of furze, falling once or twice in the blind terror that was on her. She did not hear him call "Mary, Mary," as she ran.

When the last echo of those running steps had been swallowed up in the great silence, Michael himself crept forward to the four twisted trunks . . . Sergeant Edward Hayden of the Laragh barracks was lying dead against the trees. Michael knew him well and knew that for months the sergeant had wanted to capture or kill him, for there was a reward and promotion to be had from the Government for either.

And lying on the ground by his feet Michael found the sergeant's carbine. It seemed to have fallen suddenly from his hands. The magazine was full. The muzzle of the rifle was pointing towards where he had looked up when the splash of the stone woke him from his day dreams. It must have been pointing in that way, too, when death—a death whose wings nobody had heard—swooped down silently upon him. Michael was on his knees by the rifle when he thought of the constabulary cap whose silver badge had spoken to him from the darkness. He found it caught on a branch, and as he stretched out his hand to take it he saw between the sergeant's shoulders the shaft, as it were, of a great arrow.

Overcoming his nausea Michael drew the arrow out. Even in the faint light of the stars he could see the crimson upon its bronze head. He stood gazing at it for a long time, and then, having washed it in the brown water of the lake, he carefully broke its long shaft into many pieces. Going some distance from the body he bent over the water and scooped a hole in the lake bottom. Having placed the pieces there, he covered them with a stone, and without turning back to where the dead sergeant looked upon the sleeping lake, he walked quietly towards the clump of furze.

He could piece the story in his own mind now. He knew where the arrow had come from. Only one house in the Glen had a weapon like that. Tim O'Dowd's house. Tim in his young days was a miner out in Africa, and it was often he told Michael of the Zulu chief who had given him a great bow and a quiver of bronze-headed arrows. Old Tim learnt that the English meant to kill this Zulu chief and warned him; the gift was the chieftain's thanks. Since the trouble started in Ireland Tim had kept the bow and arrow out of sight, and Michael was sure the R.I.C. knew nothing of them. They would never learn now how Sergeant Hayden died, unless the pieces he had buried in the lake were found.

All this Michael was thinking to himself as he strode the path that led over the mountain to Tim O'Dowd's little house. All this and more. For he was thinking of the girl whom he had last seen running and falling, like a wounded fawn. She must have learned by some way that he was upon the lake and was coming to him with some message, or with no message at all. Perhaps she had taken the bow and arrow for them both to fool with. Perhaps she had seen Sergeant Hayden and by intuition knew his mission. She would have followed him then to the lake side, for long ago Michael had taught her to scout and shadow and track a foe. Perhaps as she lay hidden by the clump of furze watching the Sergeant throwing stones near his boat she saw him get the rifle ready for the shot that would make him a Head Constable. And then as the magazine clicked into position and the head leant forward to get the sights into line there came the twang of a bow-string, a little faint noise like one note of a harp, and the tragedy had been given another ending . . .

Old Tim O'Dowd was brought to the door of his cottage by the sound of steps coming down the stony path. When he saw it was Michael Davin he called in to his daughter that "himself" was coming.

JAMES JOYCE

Araby

✳

North Richmond Street, being blind, was a quiet street except at the hour when the Christian Brothers' School set the boys free. An uninhabited house of two storeys stood at the blind end, detached from its neighbours in a square ground. The other houses of the street, conscious of decent lives within them, gazed at one another with brown imperturbable faces.

The former tenant of our house, a priest, had died in the back drawing-room. Air, musty from having been long enclosed, hung in all the rooms, and the waste room behind the kitchen was littered with old useless papers. Among these I found a few paper-covered books, the pages of which were curled and damp: *The Abbot*, by Walter Scott, *The Devout Communicant* and *The Memoirs of Vidocq*. I liked the last best because its leaves were yellow. The wild garden behind the house contained a central

From DUBLINERS, New York, The Viking Press.

apple-tree and a few straggling bushes under one of which
I found the late tenant's rusty bicycle-pump. He had been
a very charitable priest; in his will he had left all his
money to institutions and the furniture of his house to his
sister.

When the short days of winter came, dusk fell before
we had well eaten our dinners. When we met in the street
the houses had grown somber. The space of sky above us
was the color of everchanging violet and towards it the
lamps of the street lifted their feeble lanterns. The cold
air stung us and we played till our bodies glowed. Our
shouts echoed in the silent street. The career of our play
brought us through the dark muddy lanes behind the
houses where we ran the gauntlet of the rough tribes from
the cottages, to the back doors of the dark dripping gardens where odors arose from the ashpits, to the dark odor-
ous stables where a coachman smoothed and combed the
horse or shook music from the buckled harness. When we
returned to the street, light from the kitchen windows had
filled the areas. If my uncle was seen turning the corner we
hid in the shadow until we had seen him safely housed. Or
if Mangan's sister came out on the doorstep to call her
brother in to his tea we watched her from our shadow peer
up and down the street. We waited to see whether she
would remain or go in and, if she remained, we left our
shadow and walked up to Mangan's steps resignedly. She
was waiting for us, her figure defined by the light from the
half-opened door. Her brother always teased her before he
obeyed and I stood by the railings looking at her. Her
dress swung as she moved her body and the soft rope of
her hair tossed from side to side.

Every morning I lay on the floor in the front parlor
watching her door. The blind was pulled down to within
an inch of the sash so that I could not be seen. When she
came out on the doorstep my heart leaped. I ran to the
hall, seized my books and followed her. I kept her brown
figure always in my eye and, when we came near the point
at which our ways diverged, I quickened my pace and

passed her. This happened morning after morning. I had never spoken to her, except for a few casual words, and yet her name was like a summons to all my foolish blood.

Her image accompanied me even in places the most hostile to romance. On Saturday evenings when my aunt went marketing I had to go to carry some of the parcels. We walked through the flaring streets, jostled by drunken men and bargaining women, amid the curses of laborers, the shrill litanies of shop-boys who stood on guard by the barrels of pigs' cheeks, the nasal chanting of street-singers, who sang a *come-all-you* about O'Donovan Rossa, or a ballad about the troubles in our native land. These noises converged in a single sensation of life for me: I imagined that I bore my chalice safely through a throng of foes. Her name sprang to my lips at moments in strange prayers and praises which I myself did not understand. My eyes were often full of tears (I could not tell why) and at times a flood from my heart seemed to pour itself out into my bosom. I thought little of the future. I did not know whether I would ever speak to her or not or, if I spoke to her, how I could tell her of my confused adoration. But my body was like a harp and her words and gestures were like fingers running upon the wires.

One evening I went into the back drawing-room in which the priest had died. It was a dark rainy evening and there was no sound in the house. Through one of the broken panes I heard the rain impinge upon the earth, the fine incessant needles of water playing in the sodden beds. Some distant lamp or lighted window gleamed below me. I was thankful that I could see so little. All my senses seemed to desire to veil themselves and, feeling that I was about to slip from them, I pressed the palms of my hands together until they trembled, murmuring: *"O love! O love!"* many times.

At last she spoke to me. When she addressed the first words to me I was so confused that I did not know what to answer. She asked me was I going to *Araby*. I forgot whether I answered yes or no. It would be a splendid bazaar, she said she would love to go.

"And why can't you?" I asked.

While she spoke she turned a silver bracelet round and round her wrist. She could not go, she said, because there would be a retreat that week in her convent. Her brother and two other boys were fighting for their caps and I was alone at the railings. She held one of the spikes, bowing her head towards me. The light from the lamp opposite our door caught the white curve of her neck, lit up her hair that rested there and, falling, lit up the hand upon the railing. It fell over one side of her dress and caught the white border of a petticoat, just visible as she stood at ease.

"It's well for you," she said.

"If I go," I said, "I will bring you something."

What innumerable follies laid waste my waking and sleeping thoughts after that evening! I wished to annihilate the tedious intervening days. I chafed against the work of school. At night in my bedroom and by day in the classroom her image came between me and the page I strove to read. The syllables of the word *Araby* were called to me through the silence in which my soul luxuriated and cast an Eastern enchantment over me. I asked for leave to go to the bazaar on Saturday night. My aunt was surprised and hoped it was not some Freemason affair. I answered few questions in class. I watched my master's face pass from amiability to sternness; he hoped I was not beginning to idle. I could not call my wandering thoughts together. I had hardly any patience with the serious work of life which, now that it stood between me and my desire, seemed to me child's play, ugly monotonous child's play.

On Saturday morning I reminded my uncle that I wished to go to the bazaar in the evening. He was fussing at the hallstand, looking for the hat-brush, and answered me curtly:

"Yes, boy, I know."

As he was in the hall I could not go into the front parlor and lie at the window. I left the house in bad humor and walked slowly towards the school. The air was pitilessly raw and already my heart misgave me.

When I came home to dinner my uncle had not yet been home. Still it was early. I sat staring at the clock for some time and, when its ticking began to irritate me, I left the room. I mounted the staircase and gained the upper part of the house. The high, cold, empty gloomy rooms liberated me and I went from room to room singing. From the front window I saw my companions playing below in the street. Their cries reached me weakened and indistinct and, leaning my forehead against the cool glass, I looked over at the dark house where she lived. I may have stood there for an hour, seeing nothing but the brown-clad figure cast by my imagination, touched discreetly by the lamplight at the curved neck, at the hand upon the railings and at the border below the dress.

When I came downstairs again I found Mrs. Mercer sitting at the fire. She was an old garrulous woman, a pawnbroker's widow, who collected used stamps for some pious purpose. I had to endure the gossip of the tea-table. The meal was prolonged beyond an hour and still my uncle did not come. Mrs. Mercer stood up to go: she was sorry she couldn't wait any longer, but it was after eight o'clock and she did not like to be out late, as the night air was bad for her. When she had gone I began to walk up and down the room, clenching my fists. My aunt said:

"I'm afraid you may put off your bazaar for this night of Our Lord."

At nine o'clock I heard my uncle's latchkey in the halldoor. I heard him talking to himself and heard the hallstand rocking when it had received the weight of his overcoat. I could interpret these signs. When he was midway through his dinner I asked him to give me the money to go to the bazaar. He had forgotten.

"The people are in bed and after their first sleep now," he said.

I did not smile. My aunt said to him energetically:

"Can't you give him the money and let him go? You've kept him late enough as it is."

My uncle said he was very sorry he had forgotten. He said he believed in the old saying: "All work and no play makes Jack a dull boy." He asked me where I was going and, when I had told him a second time he asked me did I know *The Arab's Farewell to his Steed*. When I left the kitchen he was about to recite the opening lines of the piece to my aunt.

I held a florin tightly in my hand as I strode down Buckingham Street towards the station. The sight of the streets thronged with buyers and glaring with gas recalled to me the purpose of my journey. I took my seat in a third-class carriage of a deserted train. After an intolerable delay the train moved out of the station slowly. It crept onward among ruinous houses and over the twinkling river. At Westland Row Station a crowd of people pressed to the carriage doors; but the porters moved them back, saying that it was a special train for the bazaar. I remained alone in the bare carriage. In a few minutes the train drew up beside an improvised wooden platform. I passed out on to the road and saw by the lighted dial of a clock that it was ten minutes to ten. In front of me was a large building which displayed the magical name.

I could not find any sixpenny entrance and, fearing that the bazaar would be closed, I passed in quickly through a turnstile, handing a shilling to a weary-looking man. I found myself in a big hall girdled at half its height by a gallery. Nearly all the stalls were closed and the greater part of the hall was in darkness. I recognised a silence like that which pervades a church after a service. I walked into the center of the bazaar timidly. A few people were gathered about the stalls which were still open. Before a curtain, over which the words *Café Chantant* were written in colored lamps, two men were counting money on a salver. I listened to the fall of the coins.

Remembering with difficulty why I had come I went

over to one of the stalls and examined porcelain vases and
flowered tea-sets. At the door of the stall a young lady was
talking and laughing with two young gentlemen. I remarked their English accents and listened vaguely to their
conversation.

"O, I never said such a thing!"

"O, but you did!"

"O, but I didn't!"

"Didn't she say that?"

"Yes. I heard her."

"O, there's a . . . fib!"

Observing me the young lady came over and asked me
did I wish to buy anything. The tone of her voice was not
encouraging; she seemed to have spoken to me out of a
sense of duty. I looked humbly at the great jars that stood
like eastern guards at either side of the dark entrance to
the stall and murmured:

"No, thank you."

The young lady changed the position of one of the
vases and went back to the two young men. They began to
talk of the same subject. Once or twice the young lady
glanced at me over her shoulder.

I lingered before her stall, though I knew my stay was
useless, to make my interest in her wares seem the more
real. Then I turned away slowly and walked down the
middle of the bazaar. I allowed the two pennies to fall
against the sixpence in my pocket. I heard a voice call
from one end of the gallery that the light was out. The
upper part of the hall was now completely dark.

Gazing up into the darkness I saw myself as a creature
driven and derided by vanity; and my eyes burned with
anguish and anger.

Counterparts

✳

The bell rang furiously and, when Miss Parker went to the tube, a furious voice called out in a piercing North of Ireland accent:

"Send Farrington here!"

Miss Parker returned to her machine, saying to a man who was writing at a desk:

"Mr. Alleyne wants you upstairs."

The man muttered "*Blast* him!" under his breath and pushed back his chair to stand up. When he stood up he was tall and of great bulk. He had a hanging face, dark wine-coloured, with fair eyebrows and moustache: his eyes bulged forward slightly and the whites of them were dirty. He lifted up the counter and, passing by the clients, went out of the office with a heavy step.

He went heavily upstairs until he came to the second landing, where a door bore a brass plate with the inscription *Mr. Alleyne*. Here he halted, puffing with labor and vexation, and knocked. The shrill voice cried:

From DUBLINERS, New York, The Viking Press.

"Come in!"

The man entered Mr. Alleyne's room. Simultaneously Mr. Alleyne, a little man wearing gold-rimmed glasses on a clean-shaven face, shot his head up over a pile of documents. The head itself was so pink and hairless it seemed like a large egg reposing on the papers. Mr. Alleyne did not lose a moment:

"Farrington? What is the meaning of this? Why have I always to complain of you? May I ask you why you haven't made a copy of that contract between Bodley and Kirwan? I told you it must be ready by four o'clock."

"But Mr. Shelley said, sir——"

"*Mr. Shelley said, sir.* . . . Kindly attend to what I say and not to what *Mr. Shelley says, sir.* You have always some excuse or another for shirking work. Let me tell you that if the contract is not copied before this evening I'll lay the matter before Mr. Crosbie. . . . Do you hear me now?"

"Yes, sir."

"Do you hear me now? . . . Ay and another little matter! I might as well be talking to the wall as talking to you. Understand once for all that you get a half an hour for your lunch and not an hour and a half. How many courses do you want, I'd like to know. . . . Do you mind me now?"

"Yes, sir."

Mr. Alleyne bent his head again upon his pile of papers. The man stared fixedly at the polished skull which directed the affairs of Crosbie & Alleyne, gauging its fragility. A spasm of rage gripped his throat for a few moments and then passed, leaving after it a sharp sensation of thirst. The man recognized the sensation and felt that he must have a good night's drinking. The middle of the month was passed and, if he could get the copy done in time, Mr. Alleyne might give him an order on the cashier. He stood still, gazing fixedly at the head upon the pile of papers. Suddenly Mr. Alleyne began to upset all the papers, searching for something. Then, as if he had been unaware of the man's presence till that moment, he shot up his head again, saying:

"Eh? Are you going to stand there all day? Upon my word, Farrington, you take things easy!"

"I was waiting to see . . ."

"Very good, you needn't wait to see. Go downstairs and do your work."

The man walked heavily towards the door and, as he went out of the room, he heard Mr. Alleyne cry after him that if the contract was not copied by evening Mr. Crosbie would hear of the matter.

He returned to his desk in the lower office and counted the sheets which remained to be copied. He took up his pen and dipped it in the ink but he continued to stare stupidly at the last words he had written: *In no case shall the said Bernard Bodley be* . . . The evening was falling and in a few minutes they would be lighting the gas: then he could write. He felt that he must slake the thirst in his throat. He stood up from his desk and, lifting the counter as before, passed out of the office. As he was passing out the chief clerk looked at him inquiringly.

"It's all right, Mr. Shelley," said the man, pointing with his finger to indicate the objective of his journey.

The chief clerk glanced at the hat-rack, but, seeing the row complete, offered no remark. As soon as he was on the landing the man pulled a shepherd's plaid cap out of his pocket, put it on his head and ran quickly down the rickety stairs. From the street door he walked on furtively on the inner side of the path towards the corner and all at once dived into a doorway. He was now safe in the dark snug of O'Neill's shop, and, filling up the little window that looked into the bar with his inflamed face, the color of dark wine or dark meat, he called out:

"Here, Pat, give us a g.p., like a good fellow."

The curate brought him a glass of plain porter. The man drank it at a gulp and asked for a caraway seed. He put his penny on the counter and, leaving the curate to grope for it in the gloom, retreated out of the snug as furtively as he had entered it.

Darkness, accompanied by a thick fog, was gaining upon the dusk of February and the lamps in Eustace Street had been lit. The man went up by the houses until he reached the door of the office, wondering whether he could finish his copy in time. On the stairs a moist pungent odor of perfumes saluted his nose: evidently Miss Delacour had come while he was out in O'Neill's. He crammed his cap back again into his pocket and re-entered the office, assuming an air of absent mindedness.

"Mr. Alleyne has been calling for you," said the chief clerk severely. "Where were you?"

The man glanced at the two clients who were standing at the counter as if to intimate that their presence prevented him from answering. As the clients were both male the chief clerk allowed himself a laugh.

"I know that game," he said. "Five times in one day is a little bit. . . . Well, you better look sharp and get a copy of our correspondence in the Delacour case for Mr. Alleyne."

This address in the presence of the public, his run upstairs and the porter he had gulped down so hastily confused the man and, as he sat down at his desk to get what was required, he realised how hopeless was the task of finishing his copy of the contract before half past five. The dark damp night was coming and he longed to spend it in the bars, drinking with his friends amid the glare of gas and the clatter of glasses. He got out the Delacour correspondence and passed out of the office. He hoped Mr. Alleyne would not discover that the last two letters were missing.

The moist pungent perfume lay all the way up to Mr. Alleyne's room. Miss Delacour was a middle-aged woman of Jewish appearance. Mr. Alleyne was said to be sweet on her or on her money. She came to the office often and stayed a long time when she came. She was sitting beside his desk now in an aroma of perfumes, smoothing the handle of her umbrella and nodding the great black feather in her hat. Mr. Alleyne had swivelled his chair round to face her and thrown his right foot jauntily upon his left knee. The man put the correspondence on the desk and bowed respectfully but neither Mr. Alleyne nor Miss Delacour took any notice of his bow. Mr. Alleyne tapped a finger on the correspondence and then flicked it towards him as if to say: "*That's all right: you can go.*"

The man returned to the lower office and sat down again at his desk. He stared intently at the incomplete phrase: *In no case shall the said Bernard Bodley be . . .* and thought how strange it was that the last three words began with the same letter. The chief clerk began to hurry Miss Parker, saying she would never have the letters typed in time for post. The man listened to the clicking of the machine for a few minutes and then set to work to finish his copy. But his head was not clear and his mind wandered away to the glare and rattle of the public-house. It was a night for hot punches. He struggled on with his copy, but when the clock struck five he had still fourteen pages to write. Blast it! He couldn't finish it in time. He longed to execrate aloud, to bring his fist down on something violently. He was so enraged that he wrote *Bernard Bernard* instead of *Bernard Bodley* and had to begin again on a clean sheet.

He felt strong enough to clear out the whole office single-handed. His body ached to do something, to rush out and revel in violence. All the indignities of his life enraged him. . . . Could he ask the cashier privately for an advance? No, the cashier was no good, no damn good: he wouldn't give an advance. . . . He knew where he would meet the boys: Leonard and O'Halloran and Nosey Flynn. The barometer of his emotional nature was set for a spell of riot.

His imagination had so abstracted him that his name was called twice before he answered. Mr. Alleyne and Miss Delacour were standing outside the counter and all the clerks had turned round in anticipation of something. The man got up from his desk. Mr. Alleyne began a tirade of abuse, saying that two letters were missing. The man answered that he knew nothing about them, that he had made a faithful copy. The tirade continued: it was so bitter and violent that the man could hardly restrain his fist from descending upon the head of the manikin before him:

"I know nothing about any other two letters," he said stupidly.

"*You—know—nothing.* Of course you know nothing," said Mr. Alleyne. "Tell me," he added, glancing first for approval to the lady beside him, "do you take me for a fool? Do you think me an utter fool?"

The man glanced from the lady's face to the little egg-shaped head and back again; and, almost before he was aware of it, his tongue had found a felicitous moment:

"I don't think, sir," he said, "that that's a fair question to put to me."

There was a pause in the very breathing of the clerks. Everyone was astounded (the author of the witticism no less than his neighbours) and Miss Delacour, who was a stout amiable person, began to smile broadly. Mr. Alleyne flushed to the hue of a wild rose and his mouth twitched with a dwarf's passion. He shook his fist in the man's face till it seemed to vibrate like the knob of some electric machine:

"You impertinent ruffian! You impertinent ruffian! I'll make short work of you! Wait till you see! You'll apologize to me for your impertinence or you'll quit the office instanter! You'll quit this, I'm telling you, or you'll apologize to me!"

He stood in a doorway opposite the office watching to see if the cashier would come out alone. All the clerks passed out and finally the cashier came out with the chief clerk. It was no use trying to say a word to him when he was with the chief clerk. The man felt that his position was bad enough. He had been obliged to offer an abject apology to Mr. Alleyne for his impertinence but he knew what a hornet's nest the office would be for him. He could remember the way in which Mr. Alleyne had hounded little Peake out of the office in order to make room for his own nephew. He felt savage and thirsty and revengeful, annoyed with himself and with everyone else. Mr. Alleyne would never give him an hour's rest; his life would be a hell to him. He had made a proper fool of himself this time. Could he not keep his tongue in his cheek? But they had never pulled together from the first, he and Mr. Alleyne, ever since the day Mr. Alleyne had overheard him mimicking his North of Ireland accent to amuse Higgins and Miss Parker: that had been the beginning of it. He might have tried Higgins for the money, but sure Higgins never had anything for himself. A man with two establishments to keep up, of course he couldn't. . . .

He felt his great body again aching for the comfort of the public-house. The fog had begun to chill him and he wondered could he touch Pat in O'Neill's. He could not touch him for more than a bob—and a bob was no use. Yet he must get money somewhere or other: he had spent his last penny for the g.p. and soon it would be too late for getting money anywhere. Suddenly, as he was fingering his watch-chain, he thought of Terry Kelly's pawn-office in Fleet Street. That was the dart! Why didn't he think of it sooner?

He went through the narrow alley of Temple Bar quickly, muttering to himself that they could all go to hell because he was going to have a good night of it. The clerk in Terry Kelly's said A *crown!* but the consignor held out for six shillings; and in the end the six shillings was allowed him literally. He came out of the pawn-office joyfully, making a little cylinder of the coins between his thumb and fingers. In Westmoreland Street the footpaths were crowded with young men and women returning from business and ragged urchins ran here and there yelling

out the names of the evening editions. The man passed
through the crowd, looking on the spectacle generally
with proud satisfaction and staring masterfully at the office-
girls. His head was full of the noises of tram-gongs and
swishing trolleys and his nose already sniffed the curling
fumes of punch. As he walked on he preconsidered the
terms in which he would narrate the incident to the boys:

"So, I just looked at him—coolly, you know, and
looked at her. Then I looked back at him again—taking
my time, you know. 'I don't think that that's a fair question to put to me,' says I."

Nosey Flynn was sitting up in his usual corner of Davy
Byrne's and, when he heard the story, he stood Farrington
a half-one, saying it was as smart a thing as ever he heard.
Farrington stood a drink in his turn. After a while O'Halloran and Paddy Leonard came in and the story was repeated to them. O'Halloran stood tailors of malt, hot, all
round and told the story of the retort he had made to the
chief clerk when he was in Callan's of Fownes's Street;
but, as the retort was after the manner of the liberal shep-
herds in the eclogues, he had to admit that it was not as
clever as Farrington's retort. At this Farrington told the
boys to polish off that and have another.

Just as they were naming their poisons who should
come in but Higgins! Of course he had to join in with the
others. The men asked him to give his version of it, and he
did so with great vivacity for the sight of five small hot
whiskies was very exhilarating. Everyone roared, laughing
when he showed the way in which Mr. Alleyne shook his
fist in Farrington's face. Then he imitated Farrington,
saying, *"And here was my nabs, as cool as you please,"*
while Farrington looked at the company out of his heavy
dirty eyes, smiling and at times drawing forth stray drops
of liquor from his moustache with the aid of his lower lip.

When that round was over there was a pause. O'Halloran had money but neither of the other two seemed to
have any; so the whole party left the shop somewhat
regretfully. At the corner of Duke Street, Higgins and

Nosey Flynn bevelled off to the left while the other three turned back towards the city. Rain was drizzling down on the cold streets and, when they reached the Ballast Office, Farrington suggested the Scotch House. The bar was full of men and loud with the noise of tongues and glasses. The three men pushed past the whining match-sellers at the door and formed a little party at the corner of the counter. They began to exchange stories. Leonard introduced them to a young fellow named Weathers who was performing at the Tivoli as an acrobat and knockabout *artiste*. Farrington stood a drink all round. Weathers said he would take a small Irish and Apollinaris. Farrington, who had definite notions of what was what, asked the boys would they have an Apollinaris too; but the boys told Tim to make theirs hot. The talk became theatrical. O'Halloran stood a round and then Farrington stood another round, Weathers protesting that the hospitality was too Irish. He promised to get them in behind the scenes and introduce them to some nice girls. O'Halloran said that he and Leonard would go, but that Farrington wouldn't go because he was a married man; and Farrington's heavy dirty eyes leered at the company in token that he understood he was being chaffed. Weathers made them all have just one little tincture at his expense and promised to meet them later on at Mulligan's in Poolbeg Street.

When the Scotch House closed they went round to Mulligan's. They went into the parlour at the back and O'Halloran ordered small hot specials all round. They were all beginning to feel mellow. Farrington was just standing another round when Weathers came back. Much to Farrington's relief he drank a glass of bitter this time. Funds were getting low but they had enough to keep them going. Presently two young women with big hats and a young man in a check suit came in and sat at a table close by. Weathers saluted them and told the company that they were out of the Tivoli. Farrington's eyes wandered at every moment in the direction of one of the young women. There was something striking in her appearance. An immense scarf of peacock-blue muslin was wound round her hat and knotted in a great bow under her chin; and she wore bright yellow gloves, reaching to the elbow. Farrington gazed admiringly at the plump arm which she moved very often and with much grace; and when, after a little time, she answered his gaze he admired still more her large dark brown eyes. The oblique staring expression in them fascinated him. She glanced at him once or twice and, when the party was leaving the room, she brushed against his chair and said "*O, pardon!*" in a London accent. He watched her leave the room in the hope that she would look back at him, but he was disappointed. He cursed his want of money and cursed all the rounds he had stood, particularly all the whiskies and Apollinaris which he had stood to Weathers. If there was one thing that he hated it was a sponge. He was so angry that he lost count of the conversation of his friends.

When Paddy Leonard called him he found that they were talking about feats of strength. Weathers was showing his biceps muscle to the company and boasting so much that the other two had called on Farrington to uphold the national honor. Farrington pulled up his sleeve accordingly and showed his biceps muscle to the company. The two arms were examined and compared and finally it was agreed to have a trial of strength. The table was cleared and the two men rested their elbows on it, clasping hands. When Paddy Leonard said "*Go!*" each was to try to bring down the other's hand on to the table. Farrington looked very serious and determined.

The trial began. After about thirty seconds Weathers brought his opponent's hand slowly down on to the table. Farrington's dark wine-colored face flushed darker still with anger and humiliation at having been defeated by such a stripling.

"You're not to put the weight of your body behind it. Play fair," he said.

"Who's not playing fair?" said the other.

"Come on again. The two best out of three."

The trial began again. The veins stood out on Farrington's forehead, and the pallor of Weathers' complexion changed to peony. Their hands and arms trembled under the stress. After a long struggle Weathers again brought his opponent's hand slowly on to the table. There was a murmur of applause from the spectators. The curate, who was standing beside the table, nodded his red head towards the victor and said with stupid familiarity:

"Ah! that's the knack!"

"What the hell do you know about it?" said Farrington fiercely, turning on the man. "What do you put in your gab for?"

"Sh, sh!" said O'Halloran, observing the violent expression of Farrington's face. "Pony up, boys. We'll have just one little smahan more and then we'll be off."

A very sullen-faced man stood at the corner of O'Connell Bridge waiting for the little Sandymount tram to take him home. He was full of smouldering anger and revengefulness. He felt humiliated and discontented; he did not even feel drunk; and he had only twopence in his pocket. He cursed everything. He had done for himself in the office, pawned his watch, spent all his money; and he had not even got drunk. He began to feel thirsty again and he longed to be back again in the hot reeking public-house. He had lost his reputation as a strong man, having been defeated twice by a mere boy. His heart swelled with fury and, when he thought of the woman in the big hat who had brushed against him and said *"O, Pardon!"* his fury nearly choked him.

His tram let him down at Shelbourne Road and he steered his great body along in the shadow of the wall of the barracks. He loathed returning to his home. When he went in by the side-door he found the kitchen empty and the kitchen fire nearly out. He bawled upstairs:

"Ada! Ada!"

His wife was a little sharp-faced woman who bullied

her husband when he was sober and was bullied by him when he was drunk. They had five children. A little boy came running down the stairs.

"Who is that?" said the man, peering through the darkness.

"Me, pa."

"Who are you? Charlie?"

"No, pa. Tom."

"Where's your mother?"

"She's out at the chapel."

"That's right. . . . Did she think of leaving any dinner for me?"

"Yes, pa. I——"

"Light the lamp. What do you mean by having the place in darkness? Are the other children in bed?"

The man sat down heavily on one of the chairs while the little boy lit the lamp. He began to mimic his son's flat accent, saying half to himself: "*At the chapel. At the chapel, if you please!*" When the lamp was lit he banged his fist on the table and shouted:

"What's for my dinner?"

"I'm going . . . to cook it, pa," said the little boy.

The man jumped up furiously and pointed to the fire.

"On that fire! You let the fire out! By God, I'll teach you to do that again!"

He took a step to the door and seized the walking-stick which was standing behind it.

"I'll teach you to let the fire out!" he said, rolling up his sleeve in order to give his arm free play.

The little boy cried "*O, pa!*" and ran whimpering round the table, but the man followed him and caught him by the coat. The little boy looked about him wildly but, seeing no way of escape, fell upon his knees.

"Now, you'll let the fire out the next time!" said the man, striking at him vigorously with the stick. "Take that, you little whelp!"

The boy uttered a squeal of pain as the stick cut his

thigh. He clasped his hands together in the air and his voice shook with fright.

"O, pa!" he cried. "Don't beat me, pa! And I'll . . . I'll say a *Hail Mary* for you. . . . I'll say a *Hail Mary* for you, pa, if you don't beat me. . . . I'll say a *Hail Mary*. . . ."

PATRICK KAVANAGH

Football

❄

"Go on our Micky—"
"Gut yer man—"
"Bog him—"
A football match is in progress in my imagination, and I must admit that I am not a spectator but in there, ploughing all around me, making myself famous in the parish as a man that never "cowed" even at the risk of a broken neck.
"Aw, Kavanagh, the dhirty eejut."
"How could he be an eejut and him a poet?" one of our supporters replied, and my traducer had no comeback.
The battle raged up and down the stony field. The team we were playing was a disgusting class of a team who used every form of psychological warfare. For instance, when one of them was knocked down he rolled on the ground and bawled like a bull a-gelding.
Then there was the time when I put the ball over the

From *Envoy*.

goal-line and a most useful non-playing member of the opposing team kicked it back into play. We argued and there was the normal row.

The referee came up and interviewed the non-playing member of the opposition, and that man replied: "I never even saw the ball. Do you think I'd tell a lie and me at Holy Communion this morning?"

What could we say to that?

Of course we had our own methods. We never finished a game if towards the end we were a-batin'. We always found an excuse to rise a row and get the field invaded.

Ah, them was the times.

For one year I was virtual dictator of that team, being captain of the team and secretary and treasurer of the club. There was no means of checking up on my cash which gave rise to a lot of ill-founded suspicion. I remember I kept the money in an attaché-case under my bed. It is possible that every so often I visited it for the price of a packet of cigarettes, but nothing serious.

I once went as the club's representative to the County Board. We had to defend ourselves from a protest against us being awarded a certain game on the grounds that the list of players wasn't on water-marked Irish paper. I pointed out that the list was written on the inside of a large Player packet and that Players packets were made in Ireland. This did not impress. Nothing I said impressed as I hadn't the clichés off. It took a good deal of conspiring to depose me from my dictatorial post. Members of the team met in secret groups to know what could be done, but as soon as I got wind of the conspiracy I fired every man of them.

In the end they got rid of me but it was a job.

The man responsible for my deposition was a huge fellow, a blacksmith, a sort of Hindenburg whose word carried weight. He was a great master of the cliché, but sometimes he broke into originality as when the time we were going for the county final he wouldn't let us touch a ball for a week previous as he wanted us to be "ball hungry."

Ball hungry as we may have been we lost the match, and I was blamed, for I was "in the sticks," and let a ball roll through my legs.

The crowd roared in anguish: "Go home and put an apron on you." And various other unfriendly remarks were made such as "Me oul' mother would make a better goalier."

Somebody has said that no man can adequately describe Irish life who ignores the Gaelic Athletic Association, which is true in a way, for football runs women a hard race as a topic for conversation.

The popular newspaper has driven out the football ballad which at one time gave fairly literal accounts of famous matches—

At half-past two the whistle blew
And the ball it was thrown in,
The haro Murphy sazed it and
He kicked it with the win'

Then there was a ballad singer who used to sing— "*The catching and the kickin' was mar-veel-e-us for to see.*"

After the ballad came the local paper where we were all Trojans in defence and wizards in attack. I once got a lot of kudos from a report which described me as "incisive around goal." No one knew the meaning of the word incisive but it sounded good.

These reminiscences have been inspired by a Dublin barman—a native of my own district—who said to me: "I often wonder you never wrote about the time you were playing football for the Grattans. Do you mind the Sunday we played yous below in Jackie's meada beside the river? and big Hughie on the side-line with an ashplant ready to cut the head of e'er a man that kem 'ithin a mile of him?"

"Vaguely," I said.

"Aw, you must remember. Weren't you playing that day?"

148

Then it came back.

She was a brave mother who willingly allowed her son to play football. Most mothers would "be out of their minds" worried over their sons on the playing fields, never knowing when he'd come back to her a "limither for life."

"Many's the good man the same football put an end to. How I remember the poor Poochy Maguire that got the boot in the bottom of the belly and never overed it. If you'd take a fool's advice that you never took you'd lave the football alone."

"Things have changed since them days."

"That'll do you, now. What about young Kiernan of Cross that was killed in Cavan?"

As soon as the player came home he was scrutinized by his mother. She had sharp eyes as a rule and was able to see the deep cut over his eye which he had been trying to conceal with a lock of hair.

"You got a kick?"

"That's only a little thing."

"Little thing! Aw, God knows but it's me that's the unfortunate woman. I heard the roaring down there in that stony meada of Jackie's, and I didn't know at what minute you'd be brought home to me half dead. Did yous win atself?"

"A draw."

"Yous were never able for Donaghmoyne—with all your bummin. Get the black porringer from under the stairs and put them pair of eggs in it. . . . No, never during soot were yous fit to bate Donaghmoyne."

"Only for the referee——"

"Only for something the sky id fall. Yes, only for something the sky id fall."

For all this my imagination finds difficulty in focusing on this period—and one should always trust the imagination to light up vital things. All sporting subjects are superficial. The emotion is a momentary puff of gas, not an experience, and I know now why I have been unable to write about it at length.

One reads a lot about life in England but one hardly ever comes across a novel in which soccer is interwoven—or even cricket, which has been built into an art on the level of music. At the moment we have a poet, John Arlott—who did write a good poem on cricket—pumping out books about that game. Then there are Nevill Cardus and C. B. Fry, all straining for an artistic allusion in their descriptions of Washbrook's drive through the slips or some one else's æsthetic catch at silly point.

I have noted that in *Ulysses,* that compendium of common-place emotions and goings on, only the punter speculating on the result of the Ascot Gold Cup comes into the theme. So sport can't have been very vital, for Joyce had a mind like a sponge. But all these opinions of mine are barren. It is none of my business, and one should always try to extract the comedy from life and not see it moralisingly.

"Hello."

"Hello."

"How are you after the game last Sunday?"

"A stiff leg."

"I know what that means."

"You're right. Can't sit down without the leg straight out in front. Shocking bleddy nuisance. We were in very bad luck. Sure, Paddy Keegan had an open goal in front of him and he shot forty yards wide. The man that id miss that id miss the parish if he fired at the chapel."

"Bad all right."

"Desperate. Pity Trainer wasn't playing. Mother won't let him."

So the two men on opposite sides of a stone fence talk on.

My brother was telling me how one lovely Sunday morning he was taking a stroll outside San Francisco on the edge of the Pacific when he saw hurrying with little bundles under their oxters men of a rural Irish complex.

Sometime later he came upon a Gaelic football match in progress. Everything was as at home: There were the men running up and down the unpaled side-line slicing at the toes which encroached, with hurleys and crying: "Keep back there now, keep back there now." And all around the pitch the familiar battle cries of the Dalcassians were to be heard:

"Gut yer man . . ."

"Bog into him."

Not a man of them had ever left home and the mysterious Pacific was just a bog-hole, gurgling with eels and frogs. Yet, there was something queer and wonderful about the sight, or the thought.

Then Inniskeen came on the field and they were stuffed with pride,

They fell before the Fontenoys like grass before a scythe.

Yes, says he, they fell before the Fontenoys like grass before a scythe.

MARY LAVIN

The Story of
the Widow's Son

❋

This is the story of a widow's son, but it is a story that has
two endings.

    There was once a widow, living in a small neglected
village at the foot of a steep hill. She had only one son, but
he was the meaning of her life. She lived for his sake. She
wore herself out working for him. Every day she made a
hundred sacrifices in order to keep him at a good school
in the town, four miles away, because there was a better
teacher there than the village dullard that had taught
herself.

    She made great plans for Packy, but she did not tell
him about her plans. Instead she threatened him, day and
night, that if he didn't turn out well, she would put him to
work on the roads, or in the quarry under the hill.

    But as the years went by, everyone in the village, and
even Packy himself, could tell by the way she watched him
out of sight in the morning, and watched to see him come
into sight in the evening, that he was the beat of her heart,

From Irish Harvest, edited by Robert Greacen, Dublin, New Frontiers
Press.

and that her gruff words were only a cover for her pride and her joy in him.

It was for Packy's sake that she walked for hours along the road, letting her cow graze the long acre of the wayside grass, in order to spare the few poor blades that pushed up through the stones in her own field. It was for his sake she walked back and forth to the town to sell a few cabbages as soon as ever they were fit. It was for his sake that she got up in the cold dawning hours to gather mushrooms that would take the place of foods that had to be bought with money. She bent her back daily to make every penny she could, and as often happens, she made more by industry, out of her few bald acres, than many of the farmers around her made out of their great bearded meadows. Out of the money she made by selling eggs alone, she paid for Packy's clothes and for the greater number of his books.

When Packy was fourteen, he was in the last class in the school, and the master had great hopes of his winning a scholarship to a big college in the city. He was getting to be a tall lad, and his features were beginning to take a strong cast. His character was strengthening too, under his mother's sharp tongue. The people of the village were beginning to give him the same respect they gave to the sons of the farmers who came from their fine colleges in the summer, with blue suits and bright ties. And whenever they spoke to the widow they praised him up to the skies.

One day in June, when the air was so heavy the scent that rose up from the grass was imprisoned under the low clouds and hung in the air, the widow was waiting at the gate for Packy. There had been no rain for some days and the hens and chickens were pecking irritably at the dry ground and wandering up and down the road in bewilderment.

A neighbour passed.

"Waiting for Packy?" said the neighbour, pleasantly, and he stood for a minute to take off his hat and wipe the sweat of the day from his face. He was an old man.

"It's a hot day!" he said. "It will be a hard push for

Packy on that battered old bike of his. I wouldn't like to
have to face into four miles on a day like this!"

"Packy would travel three times that distance if there
was a book at the other end of the road!" said the widow,
with the pride of those who cannot read more than a line
or two without wearying.

The minutes went by slowly. The widow kept looking
up at the sun.

"I suppose the heat is better than the rain!" she said,
at last.

"The heat can do a lot of harm, too, though," said the
neighbour, absent-mindedly, as he pulled a long blade of
grass from between the stones of the wall and began to
chew the end of it. "You could get sunstroke on a day like
this!" He looked up at the sun. "The sun is a terror," he
said. "It could cause you to drop down dead like a stone!"

The widow strained out further over the gate. She
looked up the hill in the direction of the town.

"He will have a good cool breeze on his face coming
down the hill, at any rate," she said.

The man looked up the hill. "That's true. On the
hottest day of the year you would get a cool breeze coming
down that hill on a bicycle. You would feel the air streaming past your cheeks like silk. And in the winter it's like
two knives flashing to either side of you, and peeling off
your skin like you'd peel the bark off a sally-rod." He
chewed the grass meditatively. "That must be one of the
steepest hills in Ireland," he said. "That hill is a hill worthy
of the name of a hill." He took the grass out of his mouth.
"It's my belief," he said, earnestly looking at the widow—
"it's my belief that that hill is to be found marked with
a name in the Ordnance Survey map!"

"If that's the case," said the widow, "Packy will be
able to tell you all about it. When it isn't a book he has in
his hand it's a map."

"Is that so?" said the man. "That's interesting. A map
is a great thing. A map is not an ordinary thing. It isn't
everyone can make out a map."

The widow wasn't listening.

"I think I see Packy!" she said, and she opened the wooden gate and stepped out into the roadway.

At the top of the hill there was a glitter of spokes as a bicycle came into sight. Then there was a flash of blue jersey as Packy came flying downward, gripping the handlebars of the bike, with his bright hair blown back from his forehead. The hill was so steep, and he came down so fast, that it seemed to the man and woman at the bottom of the hill that he was not moving at all, but that it was the bright trees and bushes, the bright ditches and wayside grasses that were streaming away to either side of him.

The hens and chickens clucked and squawked and ran along the road looking for a safe place in the ditches. They ran to either side with feminine fuss and chatter. Packy waved to his mother. He came nearer and nearer. They could see the freckles on his face.

"Shoo!" cried Packy, at the squawking hens that had not yet left the roadway. They ran with their long necks straining forward.

"Shoo!" said Packy's mother, lifting her apron and flapping it in the air to frighten them out of his way.

It was only afterwards, when the harm was done, that the widow began to think that it might, perhaps, have been the flapping of her own apron that frightened the old clocking hen, and sent her flying out over the garden wall into the middle of the road.

The old hen appeared suddenly on top of the grassy ditch and looked with a distraught eye at the hens and chickens as they ran to right and left. Her own feathers began to stand out from her. She craned her neck forward and gave a distracted squawk, and fluttered down into the middle of the hot dusty road.

Packy jammed on the brakes. The widow screamed. There was a flurry of white feathers and a spurt of blood. The bicycle swerved and fell. Packy was thrown over the handlebars.

It was such a simple accident that, although the widow screamed, and although the old man looked around to see if there was help near, neither of them thought that Packy was very badly hurt, but when they ran over and lifted his head, and saw that he could not speak, they wiped the blood from his face and looked around, desperately, to measure the distance they would have to carry him.

It was only a few yards to the door of the cottages, but Packy was dead before they got him across the threshold.

"He's only in a weakness!" screamed the widow, and she urged the crowd that had gathered outside the door to do something for him. "Get a doctor!" she cried, pushing a young labourer towards the door. "Hurry! Hurry! The doctor will bring him around."

But the neighbours that kept coming in the door, quickly, from all sides, were crossing themselves, one after another, and falling on their knees, as soon as they laid eyes on the boy, stretched out flat on the bed, with the dust and dirt and the sweat marks of life on his dead face.

When at last the widow was convinced that her son was dead, the other women had to hold her down. She waved her arms and cried out aloud, and wrestled to get free. She wanted to wring the neck of every hen in the yard.

"I'll kill every one of them. What good are they to me, now? All the hens in the world aren't worth one drop of human blood. That old clocking hen wasn't worth more than six shillings, at the very most. What is six shillings? Is it worth poor Packy's life?"

But after a time she stopped raving, and looked from one face to another.

"Why didn't he ride over the old hen?" she asked. "Why did he try to save an old hen that wasn't worth more than six shillings? Didn't he know he was worth more to his mother than an old hen that would be going into the pot one of these days? Why did he do it? Why did he put on the brakes going down one of the worst hills in the country? Why? Why?"

The neighbours patted her arm.

"There now!" they said. "There now!" and that was all they could think of saying, and they said it over and over again. "There now! There now!"

And years afterwards, whenever the widow spoke of her son Packy to the neighbours who dropped in to keep her company for an hour or two, she always had the same question to ask; the same tireless question.

"Why did he put the price of an old clocking hen above the price of his own life?"

And the people always gave the same answer.

"There now!" they said, "There now!" And they sat as silently as the widow herself, looking into the fire.

But surely some of those neighbours must have been stirred to wonder what would have happened had Packy not yielded to his impulse of fear, and had, instead, ridden boldly over the old clucking hen? And surely some of them must have stared into the flames and pictured the scene of the accident again, altering a detail here and there as they did so, and giving the story a different end. For these people knew the widow, and they knew Packy, and when you know people well it is as easy to guess what they would say and do in certain circumstances as it is to remember what they actually did say and do in other circumstances. In fact it is sometimes easier to invent than to remember accurately, and were this not so two great branches of creative art would wither in an hour: the art of the story-teller and the art of the gossip. So, perhaps, if I try to tell you what I myself think might have happened had Packy killed that cackling old hen, you will not accuse me of abusing my privileges as a writer. After all, what I am about to tell you is no more of a fiction than what I have already told, and I lean no heavier now upon your credulity than, with your full consent, I did in the first instance.

And moreover, in many respects the new story is the same as the old.

It begins in the same way too. There is the widow

grazing her cow by the wayside, and walking the long roads to the town, weighted down with sacks of cabbages that will pay for Packy's schooling. There she is, fussing over Packy in the mornings in case he would be late for school. There she is in the evening watching the battered clock on the dresser for the hour when he will appear on the top of the hill at his return. And there too, on a hot day in June, is the old labouring man coming up the road, and pausing to talk to her, as she stood at the door. There he is dragging a blade of grass from between the stones of the wall, and putting it between his teeth to chew, before he opens his mouth.

And when he opens his mouth at last it is to utter the same remark.

"Waiting for Packy?" said the old man, and then he took off his hat and wiped the sweat from his forehead. It will be remembered that he was an old man. "It's a hot day," he said.

"It's very hot," said the widow, looking anxiously up the hill. "It's a hot day to push a bicycle four miles along a bad road with the dust rising to choke you, and sun striking spikes off the handlebars!"

"The heat is better than the rain, all the same," said the old man.

"I suppose it is," said the widow. "All the same, there were days when Packy came home with the rain dried into his clothes so bad they stood up stiff like boards when he took them off. They stood up stiff like boards against the wall, for all the world as if he was still standing in them!" "Is that so?" said the old man. "You may be sure he got a good petting on those days. There is no son like a widow's son. A ewe lamb!"

"Is it Packy?" said the widow, in disgust. "Packy never got a day's petting since the day he was born. I made up my mind from the first that I'd never make a soft one out of him."

The widow looked up the hill again, and set herself to raking the gravel outside the gate as if she were in the road for no other purpose. Then she gave another look up the hill.

"Here he is now!" she said, and she rose such a cloud of dust with the rake that they could hardly see the glitter of the bicycle spokes, and the flash of blue jersey as Packy came down the hill at a breakneck speed.

Nearer and nearer he came, faster and faster, waving his hand to the widow, shouting at the hens to leave the way!

The hens ran for the ditches, stretching their necks in gawky terror. And then, as the last hen squawked into the ditch, the way was clear for a moment before the whirling silver spokes.

Then, unexpectedly, up from nowhere it seemed, came an old clocking hen and, clucking despairingly, it stood for a moment on the top of the wall and then rose into the air with the clumsy flight of a ground fowl.

Packy stopped whistling. The widow screamed. Packy yelled and the widow flapped her apron. Then Packy swerved the bicycle, and a cloud of dust rose from the braked wheel.

For a minute it could not be seen what exactly had happened, but Packy put his foot down and dragged it along the ground in the dust till he brought the bicycle to a sharp stop. He threw the bicycle down with a clatter on the hard road and ran back. The widow could not bear to look. She threw her apron over her head.

"He's killed the clocking hen!" she said. "He's killed her! He's killed her!" and then she let the apron fall back into place, and began to run up the hill herself. The old man spat out the blade of grass that he had been chewing and ran after the woman.

"Did you kill it?" screamed the widow, and as she got near enough to see the blood and feathers she raised her arm over her head, and her fist was clenched till the knuckles shone white. Packy cowered down over the carcass of the fowl and hunched up his shoulders as if to shield himself from a blow. His legs were spattered with blood, and the brown and white feathers of the dead hen were stuck to his hands, and stuck to his clothes, and they were strewn all over the road. Some of the short white inner feathers were still swirling with the dust in the air.

"I couldn't help it, Mother. I couldn't help it. I didn't see her till it was too late!"

The widow caught up the hen and examined it all over, holding it by the bone of the breast, and letting the long neck dangle. Then, catching it by the leg, she raised it suddenly above her head, and brought down the bleeding body on the boy's back, in blow after blow, spattering the blood all over his face and his hands, over his clothes and over the white dust of the road around him.

"How dare you lie to me!" she screamed, gaspingly, between the blows. "You saw the hen. I know you saw it. You stopped whistling! You called out! We were watching you. We saw." She turned upon the old man. "Isn't that right?" she demanded. "He saw the hen, didn't he? He saw it?"

"It looked that way," said the old man, uncertainly, his eye on the dangling fowl in the widow's hand.

"There you are!" said the widow. She threw the hen down on the road. "You saw the hen in front of you on the road, as plain as you see it now," she accused, "but you wouldn't stop to save it because you were in too big a hurry home to fill your belly! Isn't that so?"

"No, Mother. No! I saw her all right but it was too late to do anything."

"He admits now that he saw it," said the widow, turning and nodding triumphantly at the onlookers who had gathered at the sound of the shouting.

"I never denied seeing it!" said the boy, appealing to the onlookers as to his judges.

"He doesn't deny it!" screamed the widow. "He stands there as brazen as you like, and admits for all the world to hear that he saw the hen as plain as the nose on his face, and he rode over it without a thought!"

"But what else could I do?" said the boy, throwing out

his hand; appealing to the crowd now, and now appealing to the widow. "If I'd put on the brakes going down the hill at such a speed I would have been put over the handle-bars!"

"And what harm would that have done you?" screamed the widow. "I often saw you taking a toss when you were wrestling with Jimmy Mack and I heard no complaints afterwards, although your elbows and knees would be running blood, and your face scraped like a gridiron!" She turned to the crowd. "That's as true as God. I often saw him come in with his nose spouting blood like a pump, and one eye closed as tight as the eye of a corpse. My hand was often stiff for a week from sopping out wet cloths to put poultices on him and try to bring his face back to rights again." She swung back to Packy again. "You're not afraid of a fall when you go climbing trees, are you? You're not afraid to go up on the roof after a cat, are you? Oh, there's more in this than you want me to know. I can see that. You killed that hen on purpose—that's what I believe! You're tired of going to school. You want to get out of going away to college. That's it! You think if you kill the few poor hens we have there will be no money in the box when the time comes to pay for books and classes. That's it!" Packy began to redden.

"It's late in the day for me to be thinking of things like that," he said. "It's long ago I should have started those tricks if that was the way I felt. But it's not true. I want to go to college. The reason I was coming down the hill so fast was to tell you that I got the scholarship. The teacher told me as I was leaving the schoolhouse. That's why I was pedalling so hard. That's why I was whistling. That's why I was waving my hand. Didn't you see me waving my hand from once I came in sight at the top of the hill?"

The widow's hands fell to her sides. The wind of words died down within her and left her flat and limp. She didn't know what to say. She could feel the neighbours staring at her. She wished that they were gone away about their business. She wanted to throw out her arms to the boy, to drag him against her heart and hug him like a small child. But she thought of how the crowd would look at each other and nod and snigger. A ewe lamb! She didn't want to satisfy them. If she gave in to her feelings now they would know how much she had been counting on his getting the scholarship. She wouldn't please them! She wouldn't satisfy them!

She looked at Packy, and when she saw him standing there before her, spattered with the furious feathers and crude blood of the dead hen, she felt a fierce disappointment for the boy's own disappointment, and a fierce resentment against him for killing the hen on this day of all days, and spoiling the great news of his success.

Her mind was in confusion. She started at the blood on his face, and all at once it seemed as if the blood was a bad omen of the future that was for him. Disappointment, fear, resentment, and above all defiance, raised themselves within her like screeching animals. She looked from Packy to the onlookers.

"Scholarship! Scholarship!" she sneered, putting as much derision as she could into her voice and expression.

"I suppose you think you are a great fellow now? I suppose you think you are independent now? I suppose you think you can go off with yourself now, and look down on your poor slave of a mother who scraped and sweated for you with her cabbages and her hens? I suppose you think to yourself that it doesn't matter now whether the hens are alive or dead? Is that the way? Well, let me tell you this! You're not as independent as you think. The scholarship may pay for your books and your teacher's fees but who will pay for your clothes? Ah-ha, you forgot that, didn't you?" She put her hands on her hips. Packy hung his head. He no longer appealed to the gawking neighbours. They might have been able to save him from blows but he knew enough about life to know that no one could save him from shame.

The widow's heart burned at sight of his shamed face, as her heart burned with grief, but her temper too burned fiercer and fiercer, and she came to a point at which nothing could quell the blaze till it had burned itself out. "Who'll buy your suits?" she yelled. "Who'll buy your boots?" She paused to think of more humiliating accusations. "Who'll buy your breeches?" She paused again and her teeth bit against each other. What would wound deepest? What shame could she drag upon him? "Who'll buy your nightshirts or will you sleep in your skin?"

The neighbours laughed at that, and the tension was broken. The widow herself laughed. She held her sides and laughed, and as she laughed everything seemed to take on a newer and simpler significance. Things were not as bad as they seemed a moment before. She wanted Packy to laugh too. She looked at him. But as she looked at Packy her heart turned cold with a strange new fear.

"Get into the house!" she said, giving him a push ahead of her. She wanted him safe under her own roof. She wanted to get him away from the gaping neighbours. She hated them, man, woman and child. She felt that if they had not been there things would have been different. And she wanted to get away from the sight of the blood on the road. She wanted to mash a few potatoes and make a bit of potato cake for Packy. That would comfort him. He loved that.

Packy hardly touched the food. And even after he had washed and scrubbed himself there were stains of blood turning up in the most unexpected places: behind his ears, under his finger-nails, inside the cuff of his sleeve.

"Put on your good clothes," said the widow, making a great effort to be gentle, but her manners had become as twisted and as hard as the branches of the trees across the road from her, and even the kindly offers she made sounded harsh. The boy sat on the chair in a slumped position that kept her nerves on edge, and set up a further conflict of irritation and love in her heart. She hated to see him slumping there in the chair, not asking to go outside the door, but still she was uneasy whenever he as much as looked in the direction of the door. She felt safe while he was under the roof; inside the lintel; under her eyes.

Next day she went in to wake him for school, but his room was empty; his bed had not been slept in, and when she ran out into the yard and called him everywhere there was no answer. She ran up and down. She called at the houses of the neighbours but he was not in any house. And she thought she could hear sniggering behind her in each house that she left, as she ran to another one. He wasn't in the village. He wasn't in the town. The master of the school said that she should let the police have a description of him. He said he never met a boy as sensitive as Packy. A boy like that took strange notions into his head from time to time.

The police did their best but there was no news of Packy that night. A few days later there was a letter saying that he was well. He asked his mother to notify the master that he would not be coming back, so that some other boy could claim the scholarship. He said that he would send the price of the hen as soon as he made some money.

Another letter in a few weeks said that he had got a job on a trawler, and that he would not be able to write very often but that he would put aside some of his pay every week and send it to his mother whenever he got into port. He said that he wanted to pay her back for all she had done for him. He gave no address. He kept his promise about the money but he never gave any address when he wrote.

. . . . And so the people may have let their thoughts run on, as they sat by the fire with the widow, many a night, listening to her complaining voice saying the same thing over and over. "Why did he put the price of an old hen above the price of his own life?" And it is possible that their version of the story has a certain element of truth about it too. Perhaps all our actions have this double quality about them; this possibility of alternative, and that it is only by careful watching and absolute sincerity, that we follow the path that is destined for us, and, no matter how tragic that may be, it is better than the tragedy we bring upon ourselves.

DONAGH MAC DONAGH

"All the Sweet

Buttermilk . . ."

✳

The most lonesome place I was ever posted to was a little
town twenty miles from the nearest railway, in the County
Mayo, where there was neither cinema, theater nor anything else; the only entertainment was a chat and a smoke,
a drink and an occasional dance. I was always a great one
to fish and take life easy, so it suited me fine, but the Sergeant didn't fancy it at all.

Sergeant Finnegan was a dour looking man and very
close. I never rightly discovered what it was had him
shifted to that place, but it can't have been want of zeal.
He was the most energetic man and the most enthusiastic
man in his search for crime that ever I met. Of course he
was wasting his time looking for crime in Coolnamara,
but what he couldn't find he invented.

Hanlon and Flaherty and myself used to have a grand
easy life of it in old Sergeant Moloney's time; there wasn't
a bicycle lamp in the district, the pubs closed when the
last customer went home, and that was earlier than you'd

From CELTIC STORY, edited by Aled Vaughan, London, Pendulum.

think, and if there was any poteen made nobody came worrying us about it. But Sergeant Finnegan soon changed all that. He wasn't a month in the place till every lad in the county had a lamp on his bike, I even bought one myself; and there was such a row kicked up about the pubs staying open that nobody went home till midnight. They suddenly realized that there must be a great charm in after-hours drinking.

The Sergeant used to have me cross-eyed chasing round the country in search of illicit stills, and as soon as ever I'd get settled down for the evening with my pipe going nicely and the wireless behind my head, he'd be in with some new list of outrages, cattle straying on the road, a camp of tinkers that whipped a couple of chickens, or some nonsense like that.

"Take your feet down off that mantelpiece," he'd say, "and get out on patrol. Who knows what malicious damage or burglary or larceny is going on under the cover of night!" And up I'd have to get, put on my coat and go in next door to listen to the news.

He was a great man for objecting to dance-hall licences, and if he'd had his way there wouldn't have been a foot put on a floor within the four walls of Ireland. On the night of a dance he'd be snooping around to see was there any infringement of the regulations, and his finger itching on the pencil to make notes for a prosecution.

One night there was an all-night dance over in Ballyduv and he sent me over to keep an eye on it.

"I think I better go in mufti, Sergeant," says I. "There's no use in drawing their attention to the Civic Guards being present."

"True. True. Quite true!" says he. So up I went and changed, chuckling to myself. I could have worn a beard and a major-general's outfit and every hog, dog and devil in the place would have known me. But I always enjoyed a dance and I didn't want to be encumbered with a uniform for the stretch of the evening.

When I got to the dance-hall it was about half-ten but

hardly anyone had arrived yet. At an all-night dance they're never in much of a hurry to get started, and besides the lads have to get washed and changed after the day's work. I stood chatting to Callaghan, that owned the hall, for a bit, and then we went over to Hennessy's for a couple of pints. Of course it was well after hours by this time, but with the Sergeant safe in Coolnamara nobody was worrying too much about that. Around about half-eleven we heard the band getting into its stride, so we came back to see how the fun was going.

As soon as I stepped in through the door I saw the grandest looking girl you'd want to see, bronze colored hair, green eyes, and an American dress that was made for her figure.

"Who's that?" says I to Callaghan. "She must be down from Dublin."

"Dublin nothing!" says he, "She's from the mountain beyond. There's a whole family of them, and they're as wild as a lot of mountain goats. Lynch's they are."

"Give us a knock-down," says I, "I'll surely die if I don't meet that one!"

"I will," says he, "but I better say nothing about you being in the Guards."

"And why not?"

"Now never mind. It's what I'm telling you." So he brought me over and introduced me to her.

Well, we got on grand. There was a waltz just starting and I asked her out, and we danced from that out without a break, and when we were tired dancing we went out for a bit of a walk, and I can tell you I wasn't wasting my time.

She told me all about the sister in America, and how anxious she was to get to Dublin, and I could see she was dying down dead to find out what I was, but after Jack Callaghan's warning I made her no wiser.

On about one o'clock we were whirling around when what should I see sloping in through the door but the Sergeant, and he in mufti, too. He gave me a very cold nod and I didn't pretend to take the least bit of notice of him.

"Who's your friend?" says she. "I never saw him before."

"Any more than you saw me!" says I, giving her a squeeze and avoiding the question.

"Who is he, though?" she said again, so I saw there was no way out of it.

"That's Sergeant Finnegan from Coolnamara," says I, "and a greater trouble maker there isn't in the country."

"And what else would he be only a trouble maker, if he's a Guard. If there's one thing I hate in this world it's a Guard, and if there's a thing I hate more it's a Sergeant." I could see I was on very delicate ground and took all the trouble I could not to be any way awkward with my big feet.

"And why is that?" says I, but she only tossed her head and shot the Sergeant dead with both her green eyes.

After a bit some great gawk of a countryman managed to prise her away from me, and off she went, though I felt she'd rather stay. No sooner had she gone than I could feel the Sergeant breathing down the back of my neck.

"Come outside here till I talk to you," says he, and I could see she had her eyes buried in us as we went out the door.

"Do you know who that is?" says he.

"That's a girl called Maeve Lynch," says I. "Isn't she a grand looking thing."

"Her father's the greatest poteen maker in the County of Mayo, and I thought you were long enough in the county to know that."

"Well, that's news to me. He was never prosecuted in my time. How do you know?"

"From information received. Now you keep away from that girl, or it might be worse for you. And keep your mind on your business. Don't you know you have no right to be dancing?"

"I was just seeing could I pick up any information. But things are very quiet."

"Things are never as quiet as they appear. I hope you investigated Hennessy's after closing time."

"You can be bound I did!" says I without a smile.

We went back into the hall, and as soon as I got the Sergeant's back turned I gave Maeve the beck to come on out. As she passed the Sergeant she gave him a glare that must have rocked him back on his heels.

"Are you not going to dance?" says she to me, but instead of answering I drew her out into the dark and slipped an arm around her. We walked along for a while without saying a word. Then she gave my hand a squeeze.

"What did the Sergeant want with you?"

"Ah, he was just chatting."

"You seem to be terrible great with him."

"I wouldn't say that. I just know him."

"Did he say anything about me?"

"What would he say? He doesn't know you, does he?"

"Oh, the dear knows. They're a very nosey crowd, the Guards. Come on back and dance."

"No," I said, "I'm tired. Let's sit down." So we sat down.

When we got back to the dance it was near breaking up and the Sergeant was gone. I was all for taking her home, but there were some cousins of hers there who said they'd take her in a trap, so I arranged to meet her the next Sunday at a dance a few miles away, and away I went singing "The Red Haired Girl" and whistling back at the birds.

I had an early breakfast and was off to the lake with my rod and line long before the Sergeant or Hanlon or Flaherty were stirring. I spent half the day fishing and half the day dreaming, and when I got back in the afternoon the Sergeant was fit to be tied.

"Where were you all day?" says he, "I'll report you to the Superintendent for being absent without leave."

"Oh, indeed I wasn't, Sergeant," says I, "I was on duty all day. I was down at the lake keeping an eye open for poachers." It was fortunate that I had left the half-dozen trout down the town on my way home.

"Poachers!" says he. "And who ever heard of poachers on Cool Lake?"

"You'd never know when they might start. I took the precaution of bringing along a rod as a camouflage!" I could see he was only half convinced, but he let it go.

"Get up on your bike there," says he. "We have work to do." But I told him I'd have to get something to eat first. I had such an appetite that minute that I'd have nearly eaten the sour face off himself. I downed a good meal in record time and the two of us started off.

For a couple of miles the Sergeant never said a word, and I said no more. After a bit I realised we were heading up towards the mountains, a part of the world I wasn't very well acquainted with.

"Where are we off to, Sergeant?" says I.

"We're off on a job that may get you your Sergeant's stripes if you play your cards right. It's that old Maurice Lynch. I have information that he's after running enough poteen to set the whole countryside drunk. He thinks he's as safe as Gibraltar, stuck up here on his mountainside, but it isn't old Sergeant Moloney he has to deal with now. Callaghan told me last night the daughter didn't know about you being in the Guards."

"That's true enough."

"Well, maybe it's just as well you were so busy chasing after her. You'll be able to keep them in chat while I have a look around. You can pretend you came on a social call."

I cursed my day's fishing when I realized that it was too late now to get any word to Maeve. If I'd been in the station when the Sergeant first decided on this expedition I could have sent a message through Callaghan, but here I was now on an empty bog road with the Sergeant glued to my side and every stroke on the pedals bringing us nearer. There was a big push being made against poteen all through the country, and I knew it would go hard with old Lynch if he was caught.

At last we got into the mountains, and after a while we had to get down and walk, and heavy climbing it was.

"There it is now," says the Sergeant. "We'll have to dump the bikes and take to the fields. But you go ahead and I'll follow after at a safe distance."

Here's my chance, said I to myself, and I started hot-foot for the farmhouse. Just as I got up to the gate, a fine handsome girl with red hair came out the door and leaned against the jamb, showing off her figure. I was just going to wave to her when I realized that it wasn't Maeve.

"What can we do for you?" says she, looking very bold at me.

"Listen!" says I, "this is urgent. If you have any poteen about the place, for God's sake tell me where it is till I get rid of it. There's a Sergeant of the Guards on his way across the fields now."

"Poteen?" says she. "Poteen? I seem to have heard of the stuff."

"Look!" I said, "this is no time for fooling. Show me where it is quick till I destroy it. God knows I'm taking enough risk." She stretched her arms over her head and yawned.

"Is your father here?" I said.

"He is not."

"Is Maeve?"

"She is not."

"Well then, show me where it is quick. The Sergeant will be in on top of us in a minute."

"He'll find nothing here."

"Very well then, I give up. But you'll be a sorry girl if your father gets six months or a year in jail.'

"Be off with you now, you have the look of a spy about you. By the big boots I'd take you for a peeler. Go on now before I let out Shep."

I gave a sigh and turned out the gate again. The Ser-

geant was just coming up the field, his uniform standing
out against the country like a scarecrow in the corn.

"Why aren't you inside keeping them out of the way?"
says he.

"There's no one there."

"Better and better. Come on and help me now." And
he was off like a retriever for the barn. I pretended to help
him in his search, but he found no more than I did.

"I'll tell you a little trick I know," says he, and he
caught up a dung-fork that was lying against the wall.
"Come out here now and I'll show you." So I followed him
out again. He went across to the heap of manure that was
lying in the back yard and started to probe around in it
with the fork. I was just standing, admiring the fine sight
of a Sergeant at work when there was the noise of the fork
striking something, and the next moment the Sergeant was
standing up holding a two-gallon jar. He pulled out the
cork and gave the first real smile I ever saw on his face.

"Poteen!" says he, and the way he said it you'd think
it was a poem. Then he whipped it behind his back quick
and I looked round and saw Maeve's sister just coming
round the corner of the house. When she saw the
Sergeant's uniform she shook her fist at the two of us.

"I knew what you were," she said, "I knew! Let you
get out of this now before my father gets back or it'll be
the worse for the pair of you."

"Be careful, young woman!" says the Sergeant. "It is
a very dangerous thing to obstruct a Guard officer in the
discharge of his duty. We are here in search of illicit spirits, and if there is any on the premises it is wiser to tell us
now."

I was leaning against the door of the barn, looking out
over the Mayo mountains, and wondering how long would
poor old Lynch get at the District Court, when what
should I see peeping up over the hedge but another red
head. And this time it was Maeve sure enough. She had
been there all the time watching every move. She gave me
a wicked glare. I winked back. The Sergeant was standing

with his back turned to her, rocking from his heels to his toes playing cat-and-mouse with the sister, and waggling the jar gently behind his back. There wasn't a prouder Sergeant on the soil of Ireland that minute.

I could see that Maeve wasn't quite sure whether I was just a pal of the Sergeant's that came out to keep him company, or a Guard on duty, and she kept glancing from me to the jar that the Sergeant was so busy hiding. She seemed to be asking me a question with her eyes. As there wasn't anything I could do to help her I gave her another wink and a big grin. She looked hard at me, then ducked out of sight behind the hedge. I was just beginning to wonder what had happened to her when she stood up straight, and my heart nearly stopped when I saw the big lump of a rock she had in her fist. I'm not a very narrow-minded man, and I had no particular regard for the Sergeant, but I wasn't going to have him murdered in cold blood before my eyes. If a thing like that came out at the inquest it would look very bad on my record. I was in two minds whether to shout out or not, weighing the trouble Maeve and her family would get into if I did against the trouble I'd get into if I didn't, when she drew back her arm, took wicked and deliberate aim, and let fly. I closed my eyes tight and turned away. When I heard a scream of agony from the Sergeant I closed them even tighter, but I opened them again when I heard what he was shouting.

"Blast it! Blast it! Blast it to hell!" he was roaring, and then I saw the heap of broken crockery at his feet. The sister was in kinks of laughter and there wasn't a sign of Maeve. There was a most delightful smell of the very best poteen on the air, and when the Sergeant threw the handle of the jar on the ground in a rage I realized that it was the jar and not the Sergeant's head that had received the blow. I burst out laughing.

"Who did that?" he shouted at me. "Who did that, you grinning imbecile?" But I shook my head.

"I was just day-dreaming," I said, "I didn't see a thing."

"You'll pay for this!" he said. "You'll pay dearly for this, you inefficient lout! Dereliction of duty! Gross imbecility! Crass stupidity! I'll have the coat off your back for this day's work!" Of course the poor man didn't know what he was saying, but in a way I was nearly sorry for him. He was so sure that he had the case all sewn up. But now, without the contents of the jar any chance of a prosecution was ballooned from the beginning. The Law requires very strict proof in these matters.

The Sergeant and myself searched all through the farm that day. And every day for a week afterwards Flaherty and Hanlon and myself searched it again. But it was labor in vain. It was great weather, though, and I used to spend most of the day lying out in the hay, and after the first day I managed to get Maeve to join me. I had a terrible job persuading her that all Guards aren't as bad as she thought, and that the Sergeant was quite exceptional. Fortunately, Flaherty and Hanlon were in no great hurry to get the searching finished, so I had plenty of time to devote to persuading her. For some reason old Lynch didn't seem to care if we searched till doomsday, and himself and myself struck up a great friendship when I told him about my conversation with Maeve's sister, Mary. So that when Maeve agreed to marry me he put up no objection.

The Sergeant did his level best to have me drummed out of the Guards for marrying a poteen-maker's daughter, but, as I pointed out to the Superintendent, there was no proof that Maurice Lynch ever ran a drop of poteen, and even if he did, wouldn't a Guard in the family be the greatest deterrent against illicit distilling. The Superintendent saw my point, but I'm not so sure that I was right. I've often said that my father-in-law makes the smoothest run of mountain dew it has ever been my good luck to taste.

It was just as well the Sergeant was moved soon after. He was very bitter about the broken jar and would have stopped at nothing to get a conviction. Things have been very quiet and peaceful since he left and crime has practically disappeared from the district.

175

DONAGH MAC DONAGH

Duet for

Organ and Strings

❋

One of the most popular men that ever set foot in the hospital was little Brother MacCormack. He was a grand little man with white hair and a rosy complexion, always very neat in himself and very precise and I often wondered he never became a priest. But maybe the height was against him or the health. Up at St. Bonaventure's he was, the Recordist College, and he had charge of all the vestments and the plate and the ordering, but as soon as his work was done in the evening he'd be down here like a shot, the little coat buttoned up on him and a grand smile for everyone.

He'd wandered around the wards chatting and stopping, and sometimes if he was in the mood, or if one of the patients asked him he'd sit down on the end of a bed and take out a mouth-organ he always carried in his pocket, and he'd start off and play away there till everybody in the

From Irish Harvest, edited by Robert Greacen, Dublin, New Frontiers Press.

ward would forget there was any such thing in the world as worry. Of course some of the old ones used to say that it wasn't right for a Brother to be playing a mouth-organ in a public ward, but the like of them is never satisfied. A grand order they are, the Recordists, and an educated order, and do you think they'd let Brother MacCormack play his mouth-organ if it wasn't perfectly all right with Rome? And a lovely player he was. If I've heard him once I've heard him a hundred times and he could play anything from the "Rose of Tralee" to Tosti's "Farewell" to bring tears to your eyes. I think that was his happiness in a way, playing and giving pleasure, and when all the patients in the beds would sit up and clap at the end he'd smile and nod and brush his eyes as if he was going to cry.

Of course the patients all had a great regard for him and indeed everybody in the hospital had; but the Almoner, Mrs. Teevan, thought there wasn't the like of him in the town. Oh, a villain she was, the same Mrs. Teevan, with a slouthering smile for his reverence you could butter your bread with, and a tongue like a raging devil the minute his back was turned. She was always a great one for the clergy, bringing up flowers for the altar and working for the missions. She used to have the patients here heart-scalded collecting for black babies and most of them with more white ones than they could manage.

But poor Brother MacCormack was too simple to see through her. He thought it was all for the love and honor of God and the glory of old Erin, and he'd stand chatting with her in the ward telling her about the great work the Fathers were doing away among the heathen blacks, and she smiling and bobbing around and saying, "Oh, Brother, isn't it wonderful they see the light! We must all do our little best to help!" I'm telling you, a bit of converting would have done that one no harm!

Well, one day she came rushing up the ward to Brother MacCormack full of excitement, her two big pop eyes lying out on her cheeks with the great news she had. "Do you know who's here, Brother MacCormack," says she, "who's in the hospital this very minute?" and before the unfortunate man had time to get a word in edgeways she bent down and whispered in his ear, "Mr. Wilson!"

Brother MacCormack never batted an eyelid. "Mr. Wilson?" says he. "What Mr. Wilson?"

"Mr. Wilson the Protestant!" says she. "The one that has the vegetable shop down the town."

"Poor man," says Brother MacCormack, "I hope it's nothing serious. I am not personally acquainted with him but from what I hear, he's a most respectable man."

"Yes," hissed Mrs. Teevan, "and a Protestant. Wouldn't this be a grand opportunity to have a little talk with him! You'd never know what problems he might have on his mind. And you being a Recordist and all."

"Yes, Mrs. Teevan, but I'm only a lay Brother," says Brother MacCormack, and I suppose the poor little man had never talked to anyone about their soul in his life. Being in the Recordists he'd leave all that to the high-up men. That's the way they work, you know. They have men for the Mission, and men for teaching, and men for preaching, but Brother MacCormack's job was to look after the surplices and the chalices and leave the saving of souls to those that were trained to it. But Mrs. Teevan could never be made to see that.

"Sure it's no harm to have a chat with him," says she. "Come on down now and I'll introduce you to him. He's a very nice gentlemanly man."

The Brother and Mr. Wilson took a great fancy to one another right away. Mr. Wilson was a great one for music too and had an assload of records at home of John Mac-Cormack and Galli-Curci and all the great singers, and he asked Brother MacCormack right away was he any relation of John's.

"Not that I'm aware of," says he, "but he is a man for whom I have a great admiration. He is certainly a very great singer and a credit to his country. His 'Ave Maria' is a work of art." Mr. Wilson agreed. "We often have him in the evenings," said the Brother. "The Fathers have a great

178

selection of records, you know. Very nice concerts they have."

Well, Mr. Wilson was astounded at Brother Mac-Cormack. He'd never met a Recordist before and he had always had a vision of them as some kind of fellows in purple robes dropping poison in the soup and listening at key-holes. Himself and the Brother had a great old chat about this and that and in the end the Brother took out the mouth-organ and began to play for Mr. Wilson. When he'd finish one tune Mr. Wilson would ask for another, and in the end the little Brother had to run most of the way back to the College to be in time for Benediction.

Mr. Wilson had his appendix out and he was very bad after it and very weak, but Brother MacCormack used to come to see him every day and he'd sit beside the bed and play away to him, delighted when he'd see a smile on Mr. Wilson's face. In the beginning I suppose Brother Mac-Cormack had some idea of converting Mr. Wilson all right, but once the two of them started chatting it was more as a friend he used to come, and besides the doctor warned him that Mr. Wilson had a very bad heart and any kind of excitement was liable to send him off. But Mrs. Teevan was as busy as a nailer going round telling everybody the great work Brother MacCormack was doing, saving the soul of the black Protestant!

Somehow or other this news got to the ears of Brother Augustine of the Aloysians. If Brother MacCormack was small, Brother Augustine was big, with a fine hearty laugh and an easy way with everyone, not like poor little Brother Mac who took a long time to get used to people. Brother Augustine didn't see any reason in the world why the Re-cordists should be assisting all the souls into glory, so one morning when he was sure Brother MacCormack wouldn't be here he stepped up to the hospital to have a look around. He stopped and chatted in all the wards and got everybody in a good humor joking and laughing and telling them funny stories. Then he asked Nurse Casey about Mr. Wilson and how he was getting along.

"Oh, the poor man's very low in himself," says Nurse Casey, "I don't think he's over the operation."

"And I suppose he must be lonely too, especially at this time of the day. I think I'll go in and see him."

Poor Mr. Wilson nearly rose out of the bed with the fright when he saw Brother Augustine coming in, in his habit. Brother MacCormack was so small and neat and the black clothes were so quiet that Mr. Wilson hardly noticed them, but when he saw Brother Augustine coming in as big as a house with the rosary flapping at his side he thought his last hour had come and this was the devil for his soul.

"Good morning, Mr. Wilson," says the Brother, "I'm Brother Augustine and as I was in the hospital I thought I'd just drop in and see you as well as the other patients."

"That was very nice of you," says Mr. Wilson, shivering, "won't you sit down." So Brother Augustine sat down and fumbled under his habit for his cigarettes. This was a great relief to Mr. Wilson and he lay back in his bed with a sigh looking at the big Brother puffing away.

"They tell me Mr. Wilson that you're a great man for the music. That's a very nice taste to have, a very nice taste," says Brother Augustine.

"It is perhaps inherited," says Mr. Wilson, "my father was the organist in the church of St. Bartholomew."

"Oh, an organist was he. Yes. A very nice instrument the organ. There's nothing in the world I like better than music, Mr. Wilson. Nothing at all. Plain Chant of course is my favourite, but a piece out of an opera now, or even a bit by Mozart or Mendelssohn I find soothing. Yes. Very soothing. Ah, there is no pleasure in the world like good music. None at all. And tell me, Mr. Wilson, do you play at all yourself?"

"Only the gramophone, I fear," says Mr. Wilson smiling.

"Ah, yes, the gramophone. Very nice too. Very nice. The community has none unfortunately. Not for many years. But we play you know. We play. Yes, I think I can safely say we are musical. I play the violin myself. Oh, a delightful instrument the violin. A pleasure to play, Mr. Wilson."

"It is certainly a pleasure to hear one well played," says Mr. Wilson.

"I wouldn't claim to be what you might call an expert you know. Just an amateur. But it gives pleasure to the community, Mr. Wilson, and I always think that is a near approach to virtue. I'll tell you what, Mr. Wilson, I'll bring along my violin the next time I'm coming to the hospital and maybe I could play you a few little tunes. Just a few simple melodies you know, but sweet, very sweet."

"You are indeed very kind," says Mr. Wilson.

"No kindness at all only for your kindness in saying so, Mr. Wilson. Well, I must be off now, Mr. Wilson. Yes indeed. But I'll be soon back again, and I'll have my fiddle with me, never fear."

Mr. Wilson never said a word to Brother MacCormack about Brother Augustine, not knowing what kind of professional jealousy might be involved, but from that day out he had his fill and more than his fill of music. In the morning my brave Brother Augustine would be down with his fiddle under his arm and there he'd be for an hour and more playing away like Nero at the burning of Rome. He tried once or twice to start a discussion about religion but Mr. Wilson always managed to turn his mind back to music. Then in the evening Brother MacCormack would step in through the door with the mouth-organ bulging through his breast pocket and a shy little smile on his face, ready to entertain Mr. Wilson. All the music the rest of the hospital got was what leaked out through the door.

This went on grand for a week or so till one day Brother MacCormack happened to get away earlier than usual from the College and stepped right into the middle of one of Brother Augustine's concerts. The big man was just sawing away at "Believe Me if All" when the door opened. Brother MacCormack stood there blushing and fumbling with his hat.

"Come in, Brother MacCormack," says Mr. Wilson.

"This is Brother Augustine. I suppose you know him?"

"Come in, Brother," says Brother Augustine, "you're as welcome as the flowers in May. Oh, indeed, I've often heard of you. Often. Mr. Wilson and myself were just having a little bit of music for ourselves you know. Nothing like the music for keeping the heart up I often say. Nothing. I believe you're a great player yourself, Brother Mac-Cormack. Yes indeed, I've often heard that." Brother Mac-Cormack was still standing at the door.

"Oh, don't be shy, Brother. Come in and make yourself at home why don't you? Sure there isn't a soul here only Mr. Wilson and myself. Come in man. Come in."

"You're very early to-day," said Mr. Wilson as Brother MacCormack came in and shut the door. Brother Mac-Cormack just smiled.

"Well," says Brother Augustine, "maybe I'd best be getting along." And he began to pack his fiddle into its case.

"Don't let me disturb you," says Brother Mac. "I merely happened to be in the building and I dropped in. I'll call back again, Mr. Wilson."

"I think the two of you should stop, unless you're in a hurry, Brother Augustine," says Mr. Wilson, so after a bit of persuading they both stayed and the next thing was they started off to play for one another and for Mr. Wilson. Soon they found they both knew a lot of the same tunes and they played together from that out.

Every day after that they used to arrange to be there together and in the late afternoon you'd think it was a band that was practising in the room. Many's the time we used to go down to listen outside the door and upon my word it was delightful. But not a word about religion was ever said by any of them and often in the morning Mr. Richards the Protestant clergyman used to come down to see Mr. Wilson. When she'd see him coming, Mrs. Teevan's face used to be fit to turn a pint of milk.

There the two Brothers were, playing away one lovely evening in May, when without any warning Mr. Wilson

passed away on them. There he was sitting up in bed chatting and listening one minute, and the next he was as cold
and stiff as King Billy. Brother MacCormack was the first
to notice the change in him, and he gave Brother Augustine a nudge, but the big man was in such great form he
never even noticed. Then Brother MacCormack caught
him by the wrist and pointed to Mr. Wilson. Brother Augustine let the bow fall on the floor and made a run for the
doctor and Brother Mac knelt down and said a prayer.
After a while the Matron came along and Nurse Casey and
the Priest and the doctor; and the two Brothers went out
very quietly, Brother MacCormack with his mouth-organ
in his breast pocket and Brother Augustine with the fiddle
in under his arm.

They were just coming down the corridor here together, not a word out of either of them, when Mrs.
Teevan caught sight of them and caught them up at a run.
She planted herself in front of them, her eyes popping with
rage.

"Look at you!" says she. "Look at the two of you; with
your jigs and your reels, and your fiddles and your mouth-
organs, and your operas and your symphonies, playing
music and making chat instead of instructing the man in
the way he should go, and letting his soul slip down to Hell
between the two of you!"

Brother Augustine was moved very soon after that,
but poor little Brother MacCormack is still to the fore
here, though he never put his foot in this place since. I believe the Order took a very serious view.

MICHAEL MAC GRIAN

Myself
and a Rabbit

✳

The blackberry picker filled her small basket and departed. I hardly noticed her going. The strong sun-heat of
afternoon had taken full possession and made all things
still. All sound and movement had gone into the shadows
to sleep.

I dozed in company with the trees until one sudden
movement nearby broke the calm. I saw a rabbit and it
was acting in a queer way. It ran around in circles and
the erratic orbits grew smaller and smaller until it just
ran up and down a few yards either way.

Then I saw another movement in the grass, an oiled
keen movement showing flashes of rustbrown fur and I
understood why the rabbit was acting so oddly.

The stoat was trailing by scent although only ten
yards away, following the aimless circle of fear. The rabbit
could not escape because the stoat scent was spun around
it, etched indelibly on the still air by its own guideless

From *The Bell*.

movement. It might as well have been shut in a cage for it was powerless to break away to safety through the invisible web of dread.

I stood up. The stoat was very near and the rabbit was jerking about as if in a fit, small whimpering noises rasping in its throat. I knew the sequence. The squeals would increase to screams and then die away to snoring whimpers and the stoat would feed on the warm arterial blood, receiving the fearsoaked heartgush in its own throat.

Maybe it was because my heart went out to the little beast in its grievous terror; maybe I felt its fear akin to something similar in myself: whatever bond had quickly tied us the rabbit hopped stiffly towards me, almost spent. I watched its coming, surprised and forgetting the trailing killer. It came right up to my feet and snuggled against my shoes.

The stoat was on the last hot scent. It saw the huddled form and leaped towards it with awkward little springs, undulating death movement swift as swift water. I snatched for the rabbit's ears and the stoat blundered against my hand.

I have felt the weight of water in a spating stream bearing against my body with a force irresistible; I have watched great breakers gouting through a narrow V of rock, churning and fuming; and I have experienced passion's culmination: I have dreamt dreams wherein I toppled from unknown heights down-rushing to some eternal abyss with the speed of light; and I can imagine the blind pressure of two dead ashed planets chafing lightly together in the gloom of space: but the shock of feeling that small stoat's bite on my forefinger, the blind a-human pressure behind the small white fangs driving their ivory points deep into flesh, gave more realization of force than any of these elemental things.

Instinctively I snatched up the rabbit with the stoat hanging momentarily from my finger. It dropped off, chattering with disappointment, tail bristling and eyes glowing. I made a kick at it, afraid of it, afraid even to touch it with my shoe.

"Go away!" I shouted. "Go away, you crazy wicked bastard!"

It ran around me twice, full of the hot scent and puzzled that it had not led to a kill, then it slipped away into the grass. The rabbit lay in my arms, the long ears close to its neck. It might die, I thought, die from terror, unscathed as it is.

I held it in my arms, sucking my finger and thinking. Soon I forgot about it altogether; all but its terror. I was just conscious of its heart under my fingers, conscious of the swift heart.

Lifting up my head I looked around. The silver lake below me was serene with dappled cloud shadows. About me the lush undergrowth clung to the shade. The wild flowers I should have named drooped in the heat. The tall beeches planted two hundred years before stood in straight immobile lines waiting with terrible patience for their seasonal call. The winding carriage track trebled its length in curves around the edge of an inlet without thought for economy of the cheap labor of a hundred semi-slaves now under the earth they shovelled but did not own.

Myself and a rabbit looking down on that majestic landscape, on all the thick heavy beauty of a year's closing. Myself and a rabbit, fearstricken by every mock shadow of the day's designing, jumping nervously and apologetically at the bark of every mongrel that lived by a law of instinctive distrust.

To stand alone, I thought; to stand alone and unarmed, unarmed but watchful; that was my wish—unarmed, fearful, watchful; haunted perhaps by untold fears lodged in every imagined shadow; mute as the rabbit was mute, and stalked as it was stalked by one vast foolish braggart threat. . . .

The rabbit moved and brought me back. It was more peaceful. I walked down to the cottage, across the lawn, and deep into the hazel thickets until I found a quiet place speckled with green sunlight. There I released the animal.

It crouched close to the earth. Going softly downwind I watched but it did not move. It may die, I thought, just like that, and become a cold tight ball of fur.

When I clapped my hands it paid no heed and I could not watch it any more. As I went back to the cottage I thought about it and became irritated with it. It was a silly animal. It was safe now, and free. To-morrow it might meet the same or another stoat but to-day it was safe and free.

Going into the cottage I sat down, not thinking about anything save of the rabbit in a confused way. My finger was almost painless, less painful than the deep prick of a thorn. It was marked by two punctures alongside the nail.

These were the only stigmata I could show to prove that I had experienced a pressure as omnipotent as the hammer of Thor. So I was led to wonder about the dark strength lying in the jaws of a lion, for instance, and what a fly must feel when nipped by a spider. And I wondered about all these dark a-human forces in nature, of the great and pitiless strength of a gale pressing against a flagging tree: by virtue of his humanity, apparently, man has been spared much in this confused and mighty scheme of existence.

Perhaps oddly enough I thought of the Lord's Prayer, listening again to my mother's voice when my hearing was far more developed than my speech. . . . Forgive us our debts, as we forgive our debtors. And lead us not into temptation, but deliver us from evil. . . .

I wanted to go back to the rabbit, hoping to find it gone. But I could not return for fear it was still crouching there quietly dying from completed terror, quietly dying in the green sunlight under the twisted hazels.

I grew angry at myself and rabbits, cursing them aloud for their silliness. Almost, I wanted to go back and kill the silly beast. I would take it up by the hind legs and bring down the edge of my right hand on its neck with a clean quick blow. It would leap wildly, twitch for a moment, and then lie still forever. Better that than thinking about it patiently dying.

I started to the door, hesitated, turned back. Going over to the camp bed I pulled out a suitcase and started packing.

Outside, the skiffs of wind crinkled patches of the lake's surface, leaving islands of calm dark water between. The tall bulrushes and reeds swayed over gracefully, the varnished green of the rushes catching the slanting sun on their plump rounded stems.

Ten high curlews scythed their way through the cooling air, heading westwards for the rich ripe ooze of the marshes into which they would plunge their curved bills with relish, casting abroad their liquid cry which was the sound of their shape and flight.

The breeze followed them, growing stronger and erasing all the calm dark patches, leapt among the bulrushes, raced over the hazels, and the trees whispered to the lake below.

MICHAEL MC LAVERTY

The Wild
Duck's Nest

✼

The sun was setting, spilling gold light on the low western
hills of Rathlin Island. A small boy walked jauntily along
a hoof-printed path that wriggled between the folds of
these hills and opened out into a crater-like valley on the
cliff-top. Presently he stopped as if remembering something, then suddenly he left the path, and began running
up one of the hills. When he reached the top he was out of
breath and stood watching streaks of light radiating from
golden-edged clouds, the scene reminding him of a picture he had seen of the Transfiguration. A short distance
below him was the cow standing at the edge of a reedy
lake. Colm ran down to meet her waving his stick in the
air, and the wind rumbling in his ears made him give an
exultant whoop which splashed upon the hills in a shower
of echoed sound. A flock of gulls lying on the short grass
near the lake rose up languidly, drifting like blown snow-
flakes over the rim of the cliff.

From The Game Cock, New York, The Devin-Adair Co.

The lake faced west and was fed by a stream, the drainings of the semi-circling hills. One side was open to the winds from the sea and in winter a little outlet trickled over the cliffs making a black vein in their gray sides. The boy lifted stones and began throwing them into the lake, weaving web after web on its calm surface. Then he skimmed the water with flat stones, some of them jumping the surface and coming to rest on the other side. He was delighted with himself and after listening to his echoing shouts of delight he ran to fetch his cow. Gently he tapped her on the side and reluctantly she went towards the brown-mudded path that led out of the valley. The boy was about to throw a final stone into the lake when a bird flew low over his head, its neck a-strain, and its orange-colored legs clear in the soft light. It was a wild duck. It circled the lake twice, thrice, coming lower each time and then with a nervous flapping of wings it skidded along the surface, its legs breaking the water into a series of silvery arcs. Its wings closed, it lit silently, gave a slight shiver, and began pecking indifferently at the water.

Colm, with dilated eyes, eagerly watched it making for the farther end of the lake. It meandered between tall bulrushes, its body, black and solid as stone against the graying water. Then as if it had sunk it was gone. The boy ran stealthily along the bank looking away from the lake, pretending indifference. When he came opposite to where he had last seen the bird he stopped and peered through the sighing reeds whose shadows streaked the water in a maze of black strokes. In front of him was a soddy islet guarded by the spears of sedge and separated from the bank by a narrow channel of water. The water wasn't too deep—he could wade across with care.

Rolling up his short trousers he began to wade, his arms outstretched, and his legs brown and stunted in the mountain water. As he drew near the islet, his feet sank in the cold mud and bubbles winked up at him. He went more carefully and nervously. Then one trouser fell and dipped into the water; the boy dropped his hands to roll it up, he unbalanced, made a splashing sound, and the bird arose with a squawk and whirred away over the cliffs. For a moment the boy stood frightened. Then he clambered on to the wet-soaked sod of land, which was spattered with sea gulls' feathers and bits of wind-blown rushes.

Into each hummock he looked, pulling back the long grass. At last he came on the nest, facing seawards. Two flat rocks dimpled the face of the water and between them was a neck of land matted with coarse grass containing the nest. It was untidily built of dried rushes, straw and feathers, and in it lay one solitary egg. Colm was delighted. He looked around and saw no one. The nest was his. He lifted the egg, smooth and green as the sky, with a faint tinge of yellow like the reflected light from a buttercup; and then he felt he had done wrong. He put it back. He knew he shouldn't have touched it and he wondered would the bird forsake the nest. A vague sadness stole over him and he felt in his heart he had sinned. Carefully smoothing out his footprints he hurriedly left the islet and ran after his cow. The sun had now set and the cold shiver of evening enveloped him, chilling his body and saddening his mind.

In the morning he was up and away to school. He took the grass rut that edged the road for it was softer on the bare feet. His house was the last on the western headland and after a mile or so he was joined by Paddy McFall; both boys, dressed in similar hand-knitted blue jerseys and gray trousers, carried home-made school bags. Colm was full of the nest and as soon as he joined his companion he said eagerly: "Paddy, I've a nest—a wild duck's with one egg."

"And how do you know it's a wild duck's?" asked Paddy slightly jealous.

"Sure I saw her with my own two eyes, her brown speckled back with a crow's patch on it, and her yellow legs——"

"Where is it?" interrupted Paddy in a challenging tone.

"I'm not going to tell you, for you'd rob it!"

"Aach! I suppose it's a tame duck's you have or maybe an old gull's."

Colm put out his tongue at him. "A lot you know!" he said, "for a gull's egg has spots and this one is greenish-white, for I had it in my hand."

And then the words he didn't want to hear rushed from Paddy in a mocking chant, "You had it in your hand! . . . She'll forsake it! She'll forsake it! She'll forsake it!" he said, skipping along the road before him.

Colm felt as if he would choke or cry with vexation.

His mind told him that Paddy was right, but somehow he couldn't give in to it and he replied: "She'll not forsake it! She'll not! I know she'll not!"

But in school his faith wavered. Through the windows he could see moving sheets of rain—rain that dribbled down the panes filling his mind with thoughts of the lake creased and chilled by wind; the nest sodden and black with wetness; and the egg cold as a cave stone. He shivered from the thoughts and fidgeted with the inkwell cover, sliding it backwards and forwards mechanically. The mischievous look had gone from his eyes and the school day dragged on interminably. But at last they were out in the rain, Colm rushing home as fast as he could.

He was no time at all at his dinner of potatoes and salted fish until he was out in the valley now smoky with drifts of slanting rain. Opposite the islet he entered the water. The wind was blowing into his face, rustling noisily the rushes heavy with the dust of rain. A moss-cheeper, swaying on a reed like a mouse, filled the air with light cries of loneliness.

The boy reached the islet, his heart thumping with excitement, wondering did the bird forsake. He went slowly, quietly, on to the strip of land that led to the nest. He rose on his toes, looking over the ledge to see if he could see her. And then every muscle tautened. She was on, her shoulders hunched up, and her bill lying on her breast as if she were asleep. Colm's heart hammered wildly in his ears. She hadn't forsaken. He was about to turn stealthily away. Something happened. The bird moved, her neck straightened, twitching nervously from side to side. The boy's head swam with lightness. He stood transfixed. The wild duck with a panicky flapping, rose heavily, and flew off towards the sea. . . . A guilty silence enveloped the boy. . . . He turned to go away, hesitated, and glanced back at the bare nest; it'd be no harm to have a look. Timidly he approached it, standing straight, and gazing over the edge. There in the nest lay two eggs. He drew in his breath with delight, splashed quickly from the island, and ran off whistling in the rain.

MICHAEL MC LAVERTY

Father Christmas

❄

"Will you do what I ask you?" his wife said again, wiping
the crumbs off the newspaper which served as a tablecloth.
"Wear your hard hat and you'll get the job."

He didn't answer her or raise his head. He was seated
on the dilapidated sofa lacing his boots, and behind him
tumbled two of his children, each chewing a crust of
bread. His wife paused, a hand on her hip. She glanced at
the sleety rain falling into the backyard, turned round,
and threw the crumbs into the fire.

"You'll wear it, John—won't you?"

Again he didn't answer though his mind was already
made up. He strode into the scullery and while he washed
himself she took an overcoat from a nail behind the
kitchen door, brushed it vigorously, gouging out the specks
of dirt with the nose of the brush. She put it over the back
of a chair and went upstairs for his hard hat.

"I'm a holy show in that article," he said, when she

From THE GAME COCK, New York, The Devin-Adair Co.

was handing him the hat and helping him into the over-coat. "I'll be a nice ornament among the other applicants! I wish you'd leave me alone!"

"You look respectable anyhow. I could take a fancy for you all over again," and she kissed him playfully on the side of the cheek.

"If I don't get the job you needn't blame me. I've done all you asked—every mortal thing."

"You'll get it all right—never you fear. I know what I'm talking about."

He hurried out of the street in case some of the neigh-bors would ask him if he were going to a funeral, and when he had taken his place in the line of young men who were all applying for the job of Father Christmas in the Big Store he was still conscious of the bowler hat perched on top of his head. He was a timid little man and he tried to crouch closer to the wall and make himself inconspicu-ous amongst that group of gray-capped men. The rain con-tinued to fall as they waited for the door to open and he watched the drops clinging to the peaks of their caps, swelling and falling to the ground.

"If he had a beard we could all go home," he heard someone say, and he felt his ears reddening, aware that the remark was cast at him. But later when he was following the Manager up the brass-lipped stairs, after he had got the job, he dwelt on the wisdom of his wife and knew that the hat had endowed him with an air of shabby respectability.

"Are you married?" the Manager had asked him, looking at the nervous way he turned the hat in his hand. "And have you any children?" He had answered every-thing with a meek smile and the Manager told him to stand aside until he had interviewed, as a matter of form, the rest of the applicants.

And then the interviews were quickly over, and when the Manager and John were mounting the stairs he saw a piece of caramel paper sticking to the Manager's heel. Down a long aisle they passed with rows of counters at each side and shoppers gathered round them. And though it was daylight outside, the electric lights were lit, and through the glare there arose a buzz of talk, the rattle of money, and the warm smell of new clothes and perfume and confectionery —all of it entering John's mind in a confused and dreamy fashion, for his eye was fastened on the caramel paper as he followed respectfully after the Manager. Presently they emerged on a short flight of stairs where a notice—PRIVATE —on trestles straddled across it. The Manager lifted it ostentatiously to the side, ushered John forward with a sweep of his arm, and replaced the notice with mechanical importance.

"Just a minute," said John, and he plucked the caramel paper from the Manager's heel, crumpled it between his fingers, and put it in his pocket.

They entered the quiet seclusion of a small room that had a choking smell of dust and cardboard boxes. The Manager mounted a step-ladder, and taking a large box from the top shelf looked at something written on the side, slapped the dust off it against his knee, and broke the string.

"Here," he said, throwing down the box. "You'll get a red cloak in that and a white beard." He sat on the top rung of the ladder and held a false face on the tip of his finger: "Somehow I don't think you'll need this. You'll do as you are. Just put on the beard and whiskers."

"Whatever you say," smiled John, for he always tried to please people.

Another box fell at his feet: "You'll get a pair of top boots in that!" The Manager folded the step-ladder, and daintily picking pieces of fluff from his sleeves he outlined John's duties for the day and emphasized that after closing-time he'd have to make up parcels for the following day's sale.

Left alone John breathed freely, took off his overcoat and hung it at the back of the door, and for some reason whenever he crossed the floor he did so on his tiptoes. He lifted the red cloak that was trimmed with fur, held it in his outstretched arms to admire it, and squeezed the life

196

out of a moth that was struggling in one of the folds. Chips of tinsel glinted on the shoulders of the cloak and he was ready to flick them off when he decided it was more Christmassy-looking to let them remain on. He pulled on the cloak, crossed on tiptoes to a looking-glass on the wall and winked and grimaced at himself, sometimes putting up the collar of the cloak to enjoy the warm touch of the fur on the back of his neck. He attached the beard and the whiskers, spitting out one or two hairs that had strayed into his mouth.

"The very I-T," he said, and caught the beard in his fist and waggled it at his reflection in the mirror. "Hello, Santa!" he smiled, and thought of his children and how they would laugh to see him togged up in this regalia. "I must tell her to bring them down some day," and he gave a twirl on his toes, making a heap of paper rustle in the corner.

He took off his boots, looked reflectively at the broken sole of each and pressed his thumb into the wet leather: "Pasteboard—nothing else!" he said in disgust, and threw them on the heap of brown paper. He reached for the top boots that were trimmed with fur. They looked a bit on the small side. With some difficulty he squeezed his feet into them. He walked across the floor, examining the boots at each step; they were very tight for him, but he wasn't one to complain, and, after all, the job was only for the Christmas season and they'd be sure to stretch with the wearing.

When he was fully dressed he made his way down the stairs, lifted his leg over the trestle with the name PRIVATE and presented himself on one of the busy floors. A shop-girl, hesitating before striking the cash-register, smiled over at him. His face burned. Then a little girl plucked her mother's skirt and called, "Oh, Mammy, there's Daddy Christmas!" With his hands in his wide sleeves he stood in a state of nervous perplexity till the shop-girl, scratching her head with the tip of her pencil, shouted jauntily: "First Floor, Santa Claus, right on down the stairs!" He stumbled on the stairs because of the tight boots and when he halted to regain his composure he felt the blood hammering in his temples and he wished now that he hadn't listened to his wife and worn his hard hat. She was always nagging at him, night, noon and morning, and he doing his damned best!

On the first floor the Manager beckoned him to a miniature house—a house painted in imitation brick, snow on the eaves, a door which he could enter by stooping low, and a chimney large enough to contain his head and shoulders, and inside the house stacks of boxes neatly piled, some in blue paper and others in pink.

The Manager produced a hand-bell. "You stand here," said the Manager, placing himself at the door of the house. "Ring your bell a few times—like this. Then shout in a loud, commanding voice: 'Roll up now! Blue for the Boys, and Pink for the Girls.'" And he explained that when business was slack, he was to mount the ladder, descend the chimney, and bring up the parcels in that manner, but if there was a crowd he was just to open the door and shake hands with each child before presenting the boxes. They were all the same price—a shilling each.

For the first ten minutes or so John's voice was weak and self-conscious and the Manager, standing a short distance away, ordered him to raise his voice a little louder: "You must attract attention—that's what you're paid for. Try it once again."

"Blue for the Boys, and Pink for the Girls!" shouted John, and he imagined all the buyers at the neighbouring counters had paused to listen to him. "Blue for the Boys, and Pink for the Girls!" he repeated, his eye on the Manager who was judging him from a distance. The Manager smiled his approval and then shook an imaginary bell in the air. John suddenly remembered about the bell in his hand and he shook it vigorously, but a shop-girl tightened up her face at him and he folded his fingers over the skirt of the bell in order to muffle the sound. He gained more confidence, but as his nervousness decreased he became aware of the tight boots imprisoning his feet, and occasionally he would disappear into his little house and catching the sole of each in turn he would stretch them across his knee.

But the children gave him no peace, and with his head held genially to the side, if the Manager were watching him, he would smile broadly and listen with affected interest to each child's demand.

"Please, Santa Claus, bring me a tricycle at Christmas and a doll's pram for Angela."

"I'll do that! Everything you want," said Father Christmas expansively, and he patted the little boy on the head with gentle dignity before handing him a blue parcel. But when he raised his eyes to the boy's mother she froze him with a look.

"I didn't think you would have any tricycles this year," she said. "I thought you were only making wooden trains."

"Oh, yes! No, yes. Not at all! Yes, of course, I'll get you a nice wooden train," Father Christmas turned to the boy in his confusion. "If you keep good I'll have a lovely train for you."

"I don't want an oul train. I want a tricycle," the boy whimpered, clutching his blue-papered parcel.

"I couldn't make any tricycles this year," consoled Father Christmas. "My reindeers was sick and three of them died on me."

The boy's mother smiled and took him by the hand. "Now, pet, didn't I tell you Santa had no tricycles? You better shout up the chimney for something else—a nice game or a wooden train."

"I don't want an oul game—I want a tricycle," he cried, and jigged his feet.

"You'll get a warm ear if you're not careful. Come on now and none of your nonsense. And Daddy Christmas after giving you a nice box, all for yourself."

Forcibly she led the boy away and John, standing with his hands in his sleeves, felt the prickles of sweat on his forehead and resolved to promise nothing to the children until he had got the cue from the parents.

As the day progressed he climbed up the ladder and down the chimney, emerging again with his arms laden with parcels. His feet tortured him and when he glanced at the boots every wrinkle in the leather was smoothed away. He couldn't continue like this all day; it would drive him mad.

"Roll up!" he bawled. "Roll up! Blue for the Pinks and Boys for the Girls! Roll up, I say. Blue for the Pinks and Boys for the Girls." Then he stopped and repeated the same mistake before catching himself up. And once more he clanged the bell with subdued ferocity till its sound drowned the jingle of the cash-registers and the shop-girls had to shout to be heard.

At one o'clock he wearily climbed the stairs to the quiet room, where dinner was brought to him on a tray. He took off his boots and gazed sympathetically at his crushed toes. He massaged them tenderly, and when he had finished his dinner he pared his corns with a razor blade he had bought at one of the counters. He now squeezed his bare feet into the boots, walked across the room, and sat down again, his face twisted with despair. "Why do I always give in to that woman," he said aloud to himself. "I've no strength—no power to stand up and shout in her face: 'No, no, no! I'll go my own way in my own time!' " He'd let her know to-night the agony he suffered, and his poor feet gathered up all day like a rheumatic fist.

Calmed after this outburst, and reassuring himself that the job was only for three weeks, he gave a whistle of forced satisfaction, brushed the corn-parings off the chair, and went off to stand outside the little house with its imitation snow on the chimney.

The afternoon was the busiest time, and he was glad to be able to stand at the door like a human being and hand out the parcels, instead of ascending and descending the ladder like a trained monkey. When the children crowded too close to him he kept them at arm's length in case they'd trample on his feet. But he always managed to smile as he watched them shaking their boxes or tearing holes in the paper in an effort to guess what was inside. And the parents smiled too when they looked at him wagging his finger at the little girls and promising them dolls at Christmas if they would go to bed early, eat their porridge and stop biting their nails. But before closing time a woman was back holding an untidy parcel. "That's supposed to be for a boy," she said peevishly. "There's a rubber doll in it and my wee boy has cried his eyes out ever since."

"I'm just new to the job," Father Christmas apologized. "It'll never occur again." And he tossed the parcel into the house and handed the woman a new one.

At the end of his day he had gathered from the floor a glove with a hole in one finger, three handkerchiefs, a necklace of blue beads, and a child's handbag containing a half-penny and three tram-tickets. When he was handing them to the Manager he wondered if he should complain about the boots, but the tired look on the Manager's face and his reminder about staying behind to make up parcels discouraged him.

For the last time he climbed the stairs, took off his boots and flung them from him, and as he prepared the boxes he padded about the cool floor in his bare feet, and to ensure that he wouldn't make a mistake he arranged, at one side of the room, the contents for the girls' boxes: dolls, shops, pages of transfers, story books, and crayons; and at the opposite side of the room the toys for the boys: ludo, snakes and ladders, blow football, soldiers, cowboy outfits, and wooden whistles. And as he parcelled them neatly and made loops in the twine for the children's fingers he decided once again to tell his wife to bring his own kids along and he'd have special parcels prepared for them.

On his way out of the store the floors were silent and deserted, the counters humped with canvas covers, and the little house looking strangely real now under a solitary light. A mouse nibbling at something on the floor scurried off between an alleyway in the counters, and on the ground floor two women were sweeping up the dust and gossiping loudly.

The caretaker let him out by a side door, and as he walked off in the rain through the lamp-lighted streets he put up the collar of his coat and avoided the puddles as best he could. A sullen resentment seized his heart and he began to drag from the corners of his mind the things that irritated him. He thought they should have given him his tea before he left, or even a bun and a glass of milk, and he thought of his home and maybe the fine tea his wife would have for him, and a good fire in the grate and the kids in bed. He walked more quickly. He passed boys eating chip potatoes out of a newspaper, and he stole a glance at Joe Raffo's chip-shop and the cloud of steam rolling through the open door into the cold air. The smell maddened him. He plunged his hands into his pockets and fiddled with a button, bits of hard crumbs, and a sticky bit of caramel paper. He took out the caramel paper and threw it on the wet street.

He felt cheated and discontented with everything; and the more he thought of the job the more he blamed his wife for all the agony he had suffered throughout the day. She couldn't leave him alone—not for one solitary minute could she let him have a thought of his own or come to a decision of his own. She must be for ever interfering, barging in, and poking into his business. He was a damned fool to listen to her and to don a ridiculous hard hat for such a miserable job. Father Christmas and his everlasting smile! He'd smile less if he had to wear a pair of boots three sizes too small for him. It was a young fella they wanted for the job—somebody accustomed to standing for hours at a street corner and measuring the length of his spits on the kerb. And then the ladder! That was the bloody limit! Up and down, down and up, like a squirrel in a cage, instead of giving you a stick and a chair where you could sit and really look like an old man. When he'd get home he'd let his wife know what she let him in for. It would lead to a row between them, and when that happened she'd go about for days flinging his meals on the table and belting the kids for sweet damn-all. He'd have to tell her—it was no use suffering devil's torture and saying nothing about it. But then, it's more likely than not she'd put on her hat and coat and go down to the Manager in the morning and complain about the boots, and then he might lose the job, bad and all as it was. Och, he'd say nothing—sure, bad temper never got you anywhere!

He stepped into a puddle to avoid a man's umbrella and when he felt the cold splash of water up the leg of his trousers his anger surged back again. He'd tell her all. He'd soon take the wind out of her sails and her self-praise about the hat! He'd tell her everything.

He hurried up the street and at the door of his house he let down the collar of his coat and shook the rain off his hat. He listened for a minute and heard the children shouting. He knocked, and the three of them pounded to the door to open it.

"It's Daddy," they shouted, but he brushed past them without speaking.

His wife was washing the floor in the kitchen and as she wrung the cloth into the bucket and brushed back her hair with the back of her hand she looked at him with a bright smile.

"You got it all right?"

"Why aren't the children in bed?"

"I didn't expect you home so soon."

"Did you think I was a bus conductor!"

She noticed the hard ring in his voice. She rubbed the soap on the scrubber and hurried to finish her work, making great whorls and sweeps with the cloth. She took off her dirty apron, and as she washed and dried her hands in the scullery she glanced in at him seated on the sofa, his head resting on his hands, the three children waiting for him to speak to them. "It was the hat," she said to herself. "It was the hat did the trick."

"Come on now and up to bed quickly," and she clapped her hands at the children.

"But you have to wash our legs in the bucket."

"You'll do all right for to-night. Your poor father's hungry after his hard day's work." And as she pulled off a jersey she held it in her hand and gave the fire a poke under the kettle. John stared into the fire and when he raised his foot there was a damp imprint left on the tiles. She handed him a pair of warm socks from the line and a pair of old slippers that she had made for him out of pasteboard and a piece of velours.

"I've a nice bit of steak for your tea," she said. "I'll put on the pan when I get these ones into their beds."

He rubbed his feet and pulled on the warm socks. It was good that she hadn't the steak fried and lying as dry as a stick in the oven. When all was said and done, she had some sense in her head.

The children began to shout up the chimney telling Santa Claus what they wanted for Christmas, and when they knelt to say their prayers they had to thank God for sending their Daddy a good job. John smiled for the first time since he came into the house and he took the youngest on his knee. "You'll get a doll and a pram for Christmas," he said, "and Johnny will get a wooden train with real wheels and Pat—what will we get him?" And he remembered putting a cowboy's outfit into one of the boxes. "A cowboy's outfit—hat and gun."

His wife had put the pan on the fire and already the steak was frizzling. 'Don't let that pan burn till I come down again. I'll not be a minute."

He heard her put the kids to bed, and in a few minutes she was down again, a fresh blouse on her and a clean apron.

She poured out his tea and after he had taken a few mouthfuls he began to tell her about the crowd of applicants and about the fellow who shouted: "We'd better all go home," when he had seen him in the hat.

"He was jealous—that's what was wrong with him!" she said. "A good clout on the ear he needed."

He told her about the Manager, the handbell, the blue and pink parcels, the little house, and the red cloak he had to wear. Then he paused, took a drink of tea, cut a piece of bread into three bits, and went on eating slowly.

"It's well you took my advice and wore the hat," she said brightly. "I knew what I was talking about. And you look so—so manly in it." She remembered about the damp stain on the floor, and she lifted his boots off the fender and looked at the broken soles. "They're done," she said, "that's the first call in your wages at the end of the week."

He got up from the table and sat near the fire. She handed him his pipe filled with tobacco, and as she washed the dishes in the scullery she would listen to the little pouts he made while he smoked. Now and again she glanced in at him, at the contented look on his face and the steam rising from his boots on the fender.

She took off her apron, tidied her hair at the looking-glass, and powdered her face. She stole across the floor to him as he sat staring into the fire. Quietly she took the pipe from his lips and put it on the mantelpiece. She smiled at him and he smiled back, and as she stooped to kiss him he knew that he would say nothing to her now about the tight boots.

BRYAN MAC MAHON

The Plain People

of England

(A RECORDING)

❋

I am one of the couple of hundred thousand Irishmen at
present working in factories in Britain. I am home on holi-
days at the moment, having spent the greater part of a year
working in a factory in the North Midlands of England.

Perhaps you have a friend who has spent some years
in the English Midlands. If you have, please ask him—for
my reputation's sake alone if not for your enjoyment—to
read aloud this little string of anecdotes for you. Then
perhaps without leaving your chair you may meet the
Plain People of England, even as I met them. They may
even raise themselves erect and prance around the bed-
spread for your delectation: Sister's Bybee and Alfie Robinson and Meg and Ernest and George and Gertie.

When I came back people said, "What do you think
of England?" Do you suppose I start to tell them? I can
only think of Freddie 'Unter. Freddie 'Unter is a co-
worker of mine in the factory. All the others brag of his

From *The Bell*.

virtuosity at the keyboard. They say, "Little Freddie 'Unter (final r cold dead) very good at pianner" (the definite article abandoned as an archaism). If anybody asks me what I think of England, all I can say is, "Little Freddie 'Unter, very good at pianner."

The first characteristic of the Plain People of England that made a disconcerting impression on me is their surpassing honesty. Other people call this attribute by different names; they call it childishness, literalness, guilelessness, and at the very least and at its most engaging it is called naïveté. I prefer to call it honesty. As far as cuteness goes, the ordinary Irish countryman could put a score of English workmen in a bag and sell them at the nearest fair. As for myself now, I may as well play a spread misère —I'm a born liar. To me, life without whitewashed lies is plain plum-duff. And I abhor plum-duff! Sometimes when I am in less candid moods than at the moment I prefer to call my lying romanticizing or weaving or just downright fiction. But at my best I'm not a dishonest grocer: I'm just a fellow who likes embroidery on life's nightgown.

Picture my reaction when I'm confronted with incidents such as these. I say to the girl working at the machine with me: "When Archie comes in now, say the Boss was through the shop before he came in." She gazes at me, this tough-looking chaw in blue denim trousers and says "Naw, Paddy, it'd be a loi!" Or one day when I was called out for a quarter of an hour to see a friend in another workshop I was asked on my return, "Eh-eh, Pat, where you bin?" "Ah," I said, "I was helping Foster with the accounts." (Foster is the boss of the whole factory, a remote eagle.) The news goes through the shop like a furze-fire. "Eh-eh, would you believe it, Old Foster, 'ee sent for Pat to 'elp 'im with the accounts. Would you believe it?"

Here is another aspect of English life that dumbfounds me. There's a big brawny chap I call Sister's Bybee, who is a wizard with machinery. I don't call him Sister's Bybee to his face, of course: the name is as yet confined to the more intimate passages of my own skull. Tuesday morning this big chap says to me:

"Must get 'ome early Satiday aft'noon." (Everything happens Satiday aft'noon.)

"What for?" I say.

"Must moind sister's bybee."

"Mind your sister's baby!"

"Oh-aw! Oy. Sister's got some shopping to do all Satiday aft'noon."

A pause. I endeavor to digest this. My mental stomach turns queasy at such unwonted fare. I look at the fellow again. After all he *is* a grown man. Cautiously I pursue: "What'll you do if your sister's baby cries?"

Comes wryness indicated by the first deprecatory grin. "Aw, gee, cawn't 'elp it if it croys, Pat, can Oi? I'll do summat."

Short as that conversation was, it stunned me. Monday morning I am impatiently awaiting the arrival of S.B. I ask, "Well, how did you get on with the baby?"

"Very good up to about ten minutes before Sister returned. Then bybee started chewing. Chewing loike 'ell. Gave bybee chocolate and biscuits. Kept bybee gaoing till sister returned. Sister gyve bybee 'is bottle. Bybee all roight then."

The deprecatory grin was the only point contiguous to a smile in all this. Oh, Ireland, isn't it grand you look!

Are the English simple? Jock 'Opkins comes up to me. " 'Eh, Pat, you know Cork? 'Ats it, Cork. Chum o' moine, Reggie Walker, 'ee got job as factory operative in taown in Cork. 'Ee wrotes me letter from taown in County Cork. Would you believe it Pat? Reggie's gaoin' to live in this little plyce. For the rest of 'is loife. 'Ee says 'ee loikes it. Would you believe it, Pat? Oi'll tell you summat else, Pat. Reggie's got naow number on 'is 'ouse. Naow, 'ee asn't got it. So, Oi write letter to Reggie and Oi sye "Reggie, you got naow number on your 'ouse. If you should feel ill your Mom and Pop wouldna be able to find you. Reggie, you got naow number on your 'ouse!" Reggie wrotes to me and he syes 'There ain't naow number on any 'ouse.' Would you believe it, Pat? I wrote to Reggie just the street, just the street. Naow number, Pat, naow number. Naow, wot if Reggie should get very ill. . . . ?"

And now what do you make of my "landlord" friend? I spend a fair amount of my time in the pub or, as we call it, the boozer. The pub fills a more comfortable place in the social life of the English than does its Irish counterpart. Compared with what we consume on this side of the Irish Sea the drink is weak and it would take a bucketful of mild or bitter to make me unsure of myself. The nearest pub to my lodgings is "The White Woman" and I generally go there. But if I'm feeling extra-adventurous I wander far afield to "The Davvo," "The Old Eagle," "The Black Castle," "Anchorage" or "The Deer in the Field." A man who owns his own pub is called a landlord, a man who is managing a place is called a willy. Now and again I go to the outskirts of the town to a pub called "The Dickey Bird." The landlord is an angler of sorts. From what I can gather he goes up to an old black pool in the hills once or twice a year and skull-drags a few roach or perch out from under rusty motor-wheels. When I enter this pub the landlord greets me as a long-lost brother. He has a fascinating face. I am always drawing lines from the vertex of his skull to his lugs and I always get the same result, a triangle of bloody beef.

" 'Ow do, Pat, 'Appy at your work?"

I mimic the vernacular. "All roight, landlord, all roight!"

After the preliminaries he comes to me, greedy all over. Greedy for my tales of the sun and the green air and the silver water.

"You was a-tellin' me of the fishin', Pat. You was a-tellin' me of the fishin'!"

"Oh, the fishing." Then, without preamble I let him have it. "Over in my place I get up at six of a grand summer's morning. I wet a cup of tea and put it to draw on the coals. Then I go out. God, the air! The air and the red sycamores glistenin' in the mornin' sun. The river flows underneath my house. I live in the trees on a sort of a cliff over the river. I go off and try fishin' for a while. I try an inch Silver Devon or a tiny Golden Sprat. Maybe I kill a dozen sea-trout fair. Then I get fed-up of fair fishin'. So I get out me old stroke-haul and land another dozen the short cut."

By this time the landlord is fairly slavering. I have my man timed to a T. I know that he'd almost sell his pub for two dozen sea-trout. His agitated heart pumps an additional pint of blood into his already suffused face. I think perhaps his whitening eyes will never take the pressure. Any moment now they will go Pop! They will; they won't! By hell but they're holding! Slowly the face drains.

"Two dozen sea-trout. Eh, Pat, sea-trout?"

"Aye."

"Sea-trout, Pat. Eh! sea-trout?"

"Aye, that's what I said. Two dozen sea-trout."

In the agony of frustration the man clumps up and down inside the counter. He clutches both sides of his bursting head.

"Aow, Pat, wy in 'ell don't you go to some other boozer? 'Onest, Pat, I canna wear it! I canna wear it! I tell you I canna wear it w'en you talk about the sea-trout."

But I am relentless. "I come home and I throw the trout on the table to the missus. Then I grab a sweet-gallon off the ledge of the dresser and off with me out into our own backfields. I gather a gallonful of lovely cup-mushrooms. Every one of them with a snow-white cap on his head and soft pale-red gills underneath."

"Mushrooms, eh, Pat, Mushrooms? I tell you I canna wear it. I wish you wouldna come 'ere for your jar of beer. I tell you, Pat . . ."

"Trout and mushrooms for breakfast. God, the smell of 'em! I tell you, landlord, it's a feed fit for a King."

"Fit for a King, eh, Pat! I tell you, Pat, I wouldna waste 'em on a bleedin' King! Naow, I tell you w'at, Pat." . . . The landlord blunders out into the unprintable.

Footnote to the foregoing: The landlord's wife accosted me in the bar one evening. She looked me over quizzically. "You the Paddy wot's telling my Albert about the trout and mushrooms?" The woman looked fierce.

I confessed that I was, a little squeamishly.

Then she said, half-pleadingly: "I wish you wouldna do it. Mykin' 'im restless, that's wot you are . . . mykin' 'im restless . . ."

Speaking of squeamishness, the following incident tickled me to death. When I say that I'm a first-class poacher, I'm telling the truth for a change. I was drinking with Bill one night and the talk turned on fishing. Bill said: "Little Alfie Robinson and Oi went fishin' one day. Got into car, see, went away, aoh away up on the 'ills. Aow! car stopped at lyke. We got aout. Little Alfie put maggot on 'ook" (Ask the fellow who can imitate the English accent to repeat that last sentence for you.) " 'Ee threw 'ook out on to water. 'Ook sank. Filled our poipes, began to smoak. Rod started to shyke, up, down, up, down, see! Little Alfie pulled it aout. Aow! Poor little beggar on 'ook. 'Ee was just soa long. Little beggar turned 'is poor little eyes on me. I couldna wear it. I said: 'Alfie, canna you get 'ook out?' Alfie said: 'Naow, 'ees got it swallowed roight down.' I said: 'Canna you save its loife?' 'Ee said: 'Naow, Oi canna. 'Ees got the 'ook roight in 'is stommick.' Little Alfie couldna do note. 'Ee troid, did little Alfie, 'ee troid an' troid, but 'ee couldna save it. Poor little beggar, 'ee had 'is pitiful eyes on me. Oi couldna wear watching it. Oi said: 'Alfie, kill it!' So Alfie killed it. 'Ee bashed its poor little 'ead off. On a rock, see. Oi couldna wear watchin' while 'ee killed it. Oi never went fishin' again. Naow, I couldna wear it. . . ."

(Old Bill and Little Alfie should have seen me at the back of the West Falls one wild morning in April. I had a mad salmon in my armpit with the gaff driven deep into his belly. The fish was pumping blood on to my shirt.)

By the way, as far as I can judge, the women of England are depending on a choice of three Christian names

—Gladys, Doris and Irene. I go into a pub and address the barmaid:

"Aow do, Doris?"

" 'Ow do. Oi ain't Doris."

"Oh, you're Gladys!"

"Naow, oi ain't Gladys."

"Oh, you're Irene!"

"Eh-eh, I'm Irene, Pat. 'Ow did you know?"

Of kindness and cruelty—I am standing outside the door of "The Davvo" at closing-time. What they call in Dublin the "ould wans" are coming out. They are amicable to the point of exhaustion. The term of endearment is "duck." This is the chorus:

"Goo' noi', duck."

"All roight, duck."

"See you tomorrow noight, duck."

This chorus rings in my head all day long. That night I am in "The Old Eagle," and ten minutes before closing-time I think of the old women's chorus of "Goo' noight, duck." The urge to hear them gets the upper hand of me. I make my apologies to the company just at the critical approach of the final drink. They seek the reasons for my departure, and when I confess them, they are indignant thereat. I tell them the truth, which is that I am fascinated by the talk of the old ladies. The business sounds alarmingly threadbare in words. Stony faces confront me. One of the company says, indignantly: "You is only mykin' gyme of them, Pat." Suddenly the chasm between the Englishry and the Irishry yawns at my feet.

The Clonakilty man meets me on his first night in England. I make the sounds of an old hand, so we adjourn for a refresher. I sick the Clonakilty man at the barmaid; she's a bumptious piece o' goods anyhow. The Clonakilty man thrusts his face over the bar as if his face were a weapon. "Have 'oo sht-ow-it?" he threatens.

The barmaid goes back a pace. Her face goes a trifle fish-bellyish.

"Wot's 'ee sying?" Now she is appealing to me.

I sing dumb and give my compatriot a nudge.

He brandishes his features at her. "Have 'oo shtow-it?"

The lady has recovered somewhat. "Wot's 'ee sying? Wot's the blighter sying?"

I whisper in the Corkman's ear: "She's a bit deaf; you'll have to talk out louder."

The man drew a gigantic breath. Expelled in the form of articulation, it could have landed us both in the body of the jail. My final nudge struck him dumb.

"Guinness he wants," I hastened.

"Well, wye the 'ell if the blighter wanted Guinness, didn't he awsk for it? 'Ee was trying to sye summat, but 'ee said note. Wye the 'ell . . ."

To mortify me further, the Clonakilty man did *not* want Guinness: he wanted Beamish, and was loth to part company with his truculence. When my friend was paying for the drinks, he turned his back on the barmaid and dived into his "buzzom" for his old-fashioned purse. The mystified barmaid stood on tiptoe to decipher this antic. She looked belligerently at a meek me as the instigator of this assault.

English humour and Irish humour are seas apart. I am with Ernest in the pub. Charlie is the taciturn person on the other side of Ernest. Charlie makes agreeable noises when Ernest sings his praises. Ernest has his dog with him —a type of lurcher I think it is. Ernest lowers his pint of mild and the dog samples it with a fastidious tongue. Then Ernest gives the dog a loving cuff and says paternally: "Eh, Bully, you greedy beggar, you've 'ad enough." The man finishes his drink. Then, turning to me, without a tinge of malice—just as if it was only a matter of academic interest —he says: "Is it true, Pat, you've got pigs sleeping in kitchen?"

I say: "Well, not in the kitchen exactly. You see, in the winter nights the kitchen is cold, especially coming on for dawn of day, when the fire goes out and the pig is likely to catch a chill. My missus now she generally keeps them in the bed. We've a fine old-fashioned feather tick and it keeps them warm as wool. You'd get used to them after a while. Just like dogs and very affectionate."

Ernest and Charlie weightily ponder this myth.

Ernest says: "I'd rawther dogs. For one thing, they're cleaner."

"All very fine," I say, "but how much a pound are dogs?"

"You got me there, chum, you got me there."

The trait of character in the English that I find most difficult to stomach is their exaggerated affection for animals, especially cats and dogs.

Ernest goes on: "See old Bully here," he says indicating the dog. "'Ee's the third Bully Oi've 'ad. The first Bully 'ee was a prince. Aow, 'ee was a prince. When 'ee got aold my missus says: 'Eh, Ernest, we've got to put old Bully to sleep.' Satiday aft'noon Oi had a few jars o' beer to steady moi nerves and Oi led old Bully to Hospital. Going in the door, Oi found Oi couldna wear the thought of it and I came 'ome. 'Missus,' Oi said, 'Oi canna wear it.' So we 'ad old Bully abaht. 'Ee got bloind and 'ee went abaht knocking at the furniture. My missus said: 'Eh, Ernest, you got to put old Bully to sleep.' Satiday aft'noon Oi was suppin' ale till Oi was feeling rum. Oi led old Bully to 'ospital and Oi put him to sleep. Oi took a wooden box along. When 'ee was asleep Oi took him 'ome. In the box, see? Did the missus croi? Did Oi croi? Did little 'uns croi? We buried 'im in garden; put 'eadstone at 'is 'ead, see? Two years afterwards we 'ad to leave 'ouse—Oi got a job in Notting'am, see? Would you believe it, Pat, we dug up old Bully and put 'im in a new box and took 'im along? Took 'eadstone along, too. Would you believe it, Pat? 'Ouse in Notting'am hadna a garden! Naow. 'Ee was loi-ing abaht ever soa long. Moi missus said . . ."

My landlord's name is George and my landlady's

Gertie. They're a quaint old couple. They keep only three of us lodgers—my brother and his son-in-law with myself. I am sitting in the parlour one evening twiddling my thumbs. George is opposite me reading the paper and smoking. The wireless is on—a gentle musical background to our mood of quiet. At 9 P.M. I twiddle the knobs and poke for Athlone. The news in Irish is on. I tune it in, press my ear close to the speaker, corrugate my forehead and purse my lips. This is my personal declaration of independence. Truth to tell, I understand very little of the news except "gunnaí spéire." I approve at the periods by opening my lips and uttering "Ah!" with intense relish. At a wholly illusory climax I smack my right fist home into my left palm and say "Good!" This draws that old badger, George. I am aware that he has already given me two or three furtive glances over the rims of his spectacles. Conscious that his gaze is fastened on me, I increase the volume and press my ear closer so as not to miss one "tuint" of all this preciousness.

"'At your station, Pat, eh?"

"That's my station." Then, with sham-truculence, "An' he's tellin' every word of the truth."

The news ends. I switch off with every exterior evidence of repletion.

George speaks again. "You know wot it is, cock? You know wot Oi sye to old Gertie abaht you. 'Gertie,' Oi sye, 'Pat never seems loike an alien till Oi 'ear 'is station coming on. Then Pat starts listening to 'is station and Oi just feels aout of it all.' Then Oi sye: 'Eh-eh, Pat's an alien all roight. 'Ee is, but Oi wouldn't ha' known it wi'aout the station.' See what Oi mean, cock?"

In the midst of my shamming I grow ashamed of my inability to speak Irish. Why, man, you should hear the Taffs prattling away to one another, and they do it without the slightest tinge of shame, too. A last word on this subject and I have done. Do the orators declaring Feiseanna open realize that the most important impetus

the revival has had in the last twenty years is given by
seventeen words in that much-harried ditty—"Galway
Bay"—

> "*And the people in the uplands, digging praties,*
> "*Speak a language that the English do not know.*"

Lastly, I have a problem, and, to be candid, I am worried about it. This is it: I can't find the England that I
hate. And, deep in my heart, I do hate that mythical England. But I can't find it in my bones to hate the people that
I have met. I must say that I can't believe that it was Sister's Bybee, or George or Gert or Jack 'Opkins or the landlord of "The Dickey Bird" who sicked the Tans at our
throats. It couldn't be. Why, Old Bill couldn't bear to see a
trout die, much less burn down Cork or Balbriggan. And,
another thing, these people have nothing on their con-
sciences—you should hear Taff sing "The Boys from the
County Cork"—he has that tongue for it that you'd swear
he came from the Coal Quay. So I asked the local Schoolmaster at home about it, and he told me to read "White
Light and Flame," "The Irish Republic," and "Peace by
Ordeal." Maybe, when I've read these, I'll be a bit clearer
about fundamentals—maybe not. But I do wish I could
find the nigger in the woodpile.

And, for my part, I have learned two important
things. I have learned to appreciate honesty in speech, and
I have also learned the precision of keeping one's plighted
word. I add that these tributes of mine are the more valuable to the P. P. E. since they are squeezed out of a most reluctant heart.

I confess that I find an impudent enjoyment in the recording of all this. Was it G.K.C. who flung this type of
witticism at the evolutionists: "We go back a long time
and find a man with a crude drawing of a monkey in his
cave, but we'll have to go back a good deal further before
we'll find a monkey with a crude drawing of a man in his
cave?" It is much the same with me. The English have

been centuries probing us Gaelic insects and rolling us over on our bellies with the points of their ferules. You may prefer to call me an embryonic mass-observationist; I feel more akin to the Neanderthal man or to a monkey with the picture of a man in his cave. I prove something big, but what it is I prove I can't articulate in words. All the while I'm feeling more and more memorable.

In the meantime I solace myself with a score of grand mimicries: " 'Appy at your work?" "Little Alfie put maggot on 'ook." " 'Ee canna doive it, 'ee canna swim it," "Eh-eh, Meg, 'ow's cawt?" "Bybee started chewin' like 'ell," "Little Freddie 'Unter very good at pianner." . . .

BRYAN MAC MAHON

The Cat

and the Cornfield

❇

In Ireland, all you need to make a story is two men with completed characters—say, a parish priest and his sexton. There at once you have conflict. When, as a foil for the sexton, you throw in a mature tinker girl, wild and lissom, love interest is added to conflict. And when, finally, you supply a snow-white cat, a cornfield, and a shrewish woman who asks three questions, the parts if properly put together should at least provide a moderate tale.

    The scene is laid in a village asleep on a summer hill: the hour of the day is mid-morning. The village is made up of a church that lacks a steeple, a pair of pubs—one thatched and the other slated—with maybe a dozen higgledy-piggledy houses divided equally as between thatch and slate. The gaps between the houses yield glimpses of well-foliaged trees beyond which the countryside falls away into loamy fields.

    On the morning of our story, the sexton, a small grumpy fellow of middle age with irregular red features,

From THE RED PETTICOAT, New York, E. P. Dutton.

by name Denny Furey, had just finished sweeping out the brown flagstones of the church porch. He then took up the wire mat at the door and tried irritably but vainly to shake three pebbles out of it.

At the sound of the rattling pebbles, the sexton's white cat which was sitting on the sunny wall of the church beside his master's cabin, looked up and mewed soundlessly.

Denny glanced sourly at the cat. "Pangur Bán," he said, "if you didn't sleep in my breeches and so have 'em warm before my shanks on frosty mornings, I'd have you drowned long 'go!" The cat—he had pale green eyes and a blotch on his nose—silently mewed his misunderstanding.

Suddenly there came a sound of harness bells. A tinker's spring-cart, painted bright green and blue, with a shaggy piebald cob between the shafts, drew slowly past the church gate. Sitting on the near wing of the cart was a tinker girl wearing a tartan dress and a bright shoulder-shawl. Eighteen, perhaps; more likely, nineteen. She had wild fair hair and a nut-brown complexion. Spying the sexton struggling with the mat, her eyes gleamed with puckish pleasure.

Meeting her gaze, Denny grimaced ill-temperedly and then half-turned his back on her. As on a thought he swung around to scowl her a reminder of her duty. Slowly the girl cut the sign of the Cross on herself.

Just beyond the church gateway, the cob's lazy motion came to a halt. The girl continued to stare at the sexton. Angrily Denny dropped the mat. Swiftly he raised his right hand as if he had been taken with a desire to shout: "Shoo! Be off with yourself at once!" The words refused to come.

Pangur Bán raised himself on shuddering legs, arched his back and sent a gracious but soundless mew of welcome in the girl's direction.

"That you may be lucky, master!" the tinker girl said. Then: "Your wife—have she e'er an old pair of shoes?"

"Wife! Wife! I've no wife!" Denny turned sharply away and snatched up his brush.

The girl watched as the sexton's movements of sweeping became indefinably jaunty. Then her smiling eyes roved and rested for a moment on the thatched cabin at the left of the church gate.

Without turning round, Denny shouted: "Nothing for you today!"

The girl was slow in replying. Her eyes still fast on the cabin, she said: "I know you've nothin' for me, master!" She did not draw upon the reins.

Denny stopped brushing. His stance indicated that again he was struggling to say: "Be off!" Instead of speaking, he set his brush against the church wall, turned his head without moving his shoulders and looked fully at the girl. She answered his eyes with frankness. They kept looking at one another for a long time. At last, his altering gaze still locked in hers, Denny turned his body around.

As if caught in drowse Denny set aside his brush. He donned his hat, then walked slowly toward the church gate. Lost rosaries clinked as the white-painted iron yielded to his fingers. Denny looked to left and to right. Up to this their eyes had been bound fast to one another.

The sunlit village was asleep. Pangur Bán lay curled and still on the warm wall.

A strange tenderness glossed Denny's voice. "Where are you headin' for?" he asked. The gate latched shut behind him.

"Wherever the cob carries me!"

Again the girl's gaze swivelled to the cabin. "Is that your house?" she asked, and then, as she glanced again at the wall: "Is that your cat?"

"Ay! . . . Ay!"

For a long while the girl kept looking at the little house with its small deeply recessed windows. She noted well the dark-green half-door above which shone a latch of polished brass.

"Do you never tire of the road?" Denny asked.

"Do you never tire of being fettered?" the girl flashed. She had turned to look at him directly.

Both sighed fully and deeply. Under the black hat Denny's eyes had begun to smoulder.

Secretly the girl dragged on the rein. As the cob shifted from one leg to another, she uttered a small exclamation of annoyance. Her red and green skirt made a wheel as she leaped from the vehicle and advanced to make an obscure adjustment to the harness. This done she prepared to lead her animal away.

Denny glanced desperately around. Uproad stood a hissing gander with his flock of geese serried behind him. "I'll convey you apass the gander!" he blurted.

The tinker girl glanced at the gander; her mouth-corners twitched in a smile. She made a great to-do about gathering up the reins and adjusting her shawl. As she led the animal away, Denny moved to the far side of the road and kept pace with her as she went. Walking thus, apart yet together, they left the village and stepped downhill. Once the sexton glanced fearfully over his shoulder; the village was not so much asleep as stone-dead.

As the white road twisted, the village on the hillock was unseen. The cob—a hairy, bony animal—moved swiftly on the declivity so that Denny had to hurry to keep up with the girl and her animal.

The splendor of the summer accompanied them. The gauds of the harness were winking in the bright light. The countryside was a silver shield inclining to gold. Their footfalls were muted in the limestone road dust. Muted also were the noise of the horse's unshod hooves and the ringing of the harness bells. At last they came to the foot of the hillock. Here the road ran between level fields. Denny looked over his shoulder and saw Pangur Bán fifty yards behind him walking stealthily on the road margin.

"Be off!" the sexton shouted.

Pangur Bán paused to utter his soundless mew.

The girl smiled. They walked on for a space. Again Denny turned. "Be off, you Judas!" he shouted. He snatched up a stone and flung it at the cat.

The instant the stone left the sexton's hand, Pangur

judged that it was going to miss him. He remained utterly
without movement. When the stone had gone singing
away into stillness, the cat went over and smelled at a
piece of road metal the bounding stone had disturbed.
Pangur mewed his mystification into the sky; then spurted
faithfully on.

The road again twisted. Now it was commanded by
the entrance to the village on the hillock.

Here in a cornfield at the left-hand side of the road,
the ripening corn was on the swing from green to gold.
The field was a house of brightness open to the southern
sky. Directly beside their boots a gap offered descent to the
sown ground. The cob stopped dead and began to crop the
roadside grass.

"Let us sit in the sun," the sexton ventured. He indicated the remote corner of the cornfield.

The girl smiled in dreamy agreement. With slow
movements she tied her cob to the butt of a whitethorn
bush. The pair walked along by the edge of the corn and
sat down on the grassy edge of the farthest headland. Here
the corn screened them from the view of a person passing
on the road. The fierceness and lushness of growth in this
sun-trap had made the hedge behind them impenetrable.
Denny set his hat back on his poll. Then he took the girl's
hand in his and began to fondle it. Points of sweat appeared on his agitated face.

Twice already, from the top of the grassy fence,
Pangur Bán had stretched out a paw in an attempt to descend into the cornfield. On each occasion thistles and
thorns tipping his pads had dissuaded him from leaping.
Through slim upended ovals of dark pupil the cat ruefully
eyed the cropping horse, then turned to mew his upbraid-
ings in the direction of his master. Tiring of this, he settled himself patiently to wait.

Pangur Bán sat with his tail curled around his front
paws. His eyes were reluctant to open in the sunlight. His
ears began to sift the natural sounds of the day.

Reading his Office, the huge old priest walked the village. Glancing up from his breviary, he noticed the brush idle against the church wall: he also spied the wire mat that lay almost concealed on the lawn grass. The impudence of the gander the priest punished with a wave of his blackthorn stick. Standing on the road in front of the sexton's cabin, he sang out: "Denny! Denny Furey!" There was no reply.

The priest shuffled to the church door and in a lowered voice again called for his sexton. At last, with an angry shrug of his shoulders, he again turned his attention to his breviary. Still reading, he sauntered downhill and out into the open country.

After a while he raised his eyes. First he saw the brown and white pony, then he spied the flame that was the cat burning white beside the olive cornfield.

The old man's face crinkled. He grunted. Imprisoning his stick in his left armpit, he began to slouch in the direction of Pangur Bán. From time to time his eyes strayed over the gilt edging and the colored markers of his book.

Denny glanced up from his sober love-making.

"Divine God!" he exclaimed.

The girl was leaning back on the grass: her posture tautened a swath of green hay to silver. She was smiling up at the sky as she spaced her clean teeth along a grass stem.

Reaching the cat, the priest halted. "Pangur Bán," he wheedled in a low voice. His eyes were roving over the cornfield. The cat tilted his back against the lower may leaves, set his four paws together and drooped as if for a bout of languid gaiety.

For a moment or two the priest tricked with the cat. Then he threw back his shoulders. "To think that I don't see you, Denny Furey!" he clarioned.

Denny and the girl were silent and without movement. About them the minute living world asserted itself in the snip of grasshoppers.

Again the priest thundered: "Nice example for a sexton!"

The sweat beaded above Denny's eyebrows. His

thighs began to shiver in the breeches his cat slept in. The girl peered at the priest through the altering lattice of the corn-heads. Her expression was quizzical as she glanced at Denny.

From the roadway came again the dreaded voice: "If it's the last thing I do, Denny Furey, I'll strip you of your black coat!"

At this moment a shrewish woman, wearing a black and green shawl, thrust around the bend of the road. She was resolutely headed for the village.

Seeing the woman approach, the priest quickly turned his face away from the cornfield and resumed his pacing along the road. His lips grew busy with the Latin psalms.

Peeping out and recognizing the newcomer, Denny Furey at first swore softly, then he began to moan. "The parish will be ringin' with the news before dark!" he sniffled.

The woman blessed the priest so as to break him from his Office: then in a tone of voice that expressed thin concern: "Did I hear your voice raised, Father?"

The priest lowered his shaggy eyebrows. "Sermons don't sprout on bushes, my good woman!"

"Ah! Practisin' you were!"

Her crafty eyes alighted on the white cat. "Would it be bird-chasin' the sexton's cat is?"

"It could be, now that you mention it!"

There was a pause. The conversation of the wheat spars was only one step above silence. Flicking the corn-field and the cart with a single glance, the woman said, in a half whisper: "People say that tinker girls 'd pick the eye out of your head!"

"Did you never hear tell of the virtue of charity, woman?" the priest growled.

The woman made her crumbled excuses. It suited the priest not to accept them. Hurriedly she walked away. Resentment was implicit in the puffs of road-dust that spouted from beneath her toe-caps. Before the village swallowed her up, she looked over her shoulder. The priest was standing in mid-road waiting to parry this backward glance.

Again the priest turned his attention to the cornfield. With a sound half-grunt, half-chuckle, he untied the cob, and leading it by the head, turned away in the direction of the village.

The instant the harness bells began to ring, the tinker girl sprang to her feet and raced wildly but surefootedly along the edge of the cornfield. "Father!" she cried out. "Father!"

The priest came to a halt. Well out of the range of his stick, the girl stopped. "So I've drawn you, my vixen!" the priest said.

Breathlessly, the girl bobbed a half-curtsy.

"What're you goin' to do with my animal, Father?"

"Impounding him I am—unless you get that sexton o' mine out of the cornfield at once."

The girl leaped on to the low fence: "Come out o' the cornfield," she shouted, "I want to recover my cob!"

There was a pause. Then Denny shuffled to his feet. The cat stood up and mewed loyal greetings to his lord.

The priest stood at the horse's head. The angry girl was on the fence; her arms akimbo. Shambling dismally, Denny drew nearer. When he had reached the roadway, the tinker girl cried out: "I was goin' my road, Father, when he coaxed me into the cornfield!"

Denny opened his mouth, but no words came. He began to blink his moist eyes. His mouth closed fast. He kept his distance from the priest's stick. As Pangur Bán began rubbing himself against the end of the beloved breeches, the sexton gave the cat the side of his long boot and sent him careening into the bushes.

"*A chait*, ou'r that!" he said.

"Aha, you scoundrel!" the priest reproved, "Can you do no better than abuse a dumb animal?"

Turning to the girl: "Take your cob! And if I catch

you in this village again, by the Holy Man, I'll give you the length and breadth of my blackhorn!"

"He said he'd convey me apass the gander, Father!"

Three times she lunged forward. Three times her buttocks winced away. At last she mustered courage enough to grasp the winkers. Clutching the ring of the mouthpiece, she swung the pony downroad. When she had gained a few yards she leaped lightly on to the broad board on the side of the cart and slashed at the cob's rump with the free dangle of the reins. The animal leaped forward.

The priest, the sexton, the cat. The sunlit, rustling cornfield.

"Come on, me bucko!" the priest said grimly.

He began to lead the way home. The sexton trailed a miserable yard or two behind. Glory was gone out of his life. The wonderful day seemed to mock him. The future was a known road stretching before his leaden legs. What he had thought would prove a pleasant bauble had turned to a crown of thorns. In the past, whenever he had chafed against the drab nature of his existence, he had consoled himself thus: "One day, perhaps today, I'll run and buy me a hoop of bright colors."

Denny began to compare his soul to a pebble trapped in a wire mat of despair.

Gradually the priest became infected with Denny's moroseness. Side by side, the priest and his sexton continued to move homewards. In the faraway, the sound of the harness bells was a recessional song of adventure.

Behind the pair and at a discreet distance, Pangur Bán traveled quietly. Now and again he paused to mew his loyalty into the sunny world.

GEORGE MOORE

Julia Cahill's Curse

❊

"And what has become of Margaret?"

"Ah, didn't her mother send her to America as soon as
the baby was born? Once a woman is wake here she has
to go. Hadn't Julia to go in the end, and she the only one
that ever said she didn't mind the priest?"

"Julia who?" said I.

"Julia Cahill."

The name struck my fancy, and I asked the driver to
tell me her story.

"Wasn't it Father Madden who had her put out of the
parish? But she put her curse on it, and it's on it to this
day."

"Do you believe in curses?"

"Bedad I do, sir. It's a terrible thing to put a curse on
a man, and the curse that Julia put on Father Madden's
parish was a bad one, the divil a worse. The sun was up at
the time, and she on the hilltop raising both her hands.

From The Untilled Field, Philadelphia, Lippincott.

And the curse she put on the parish was that every year a roof must fall in and a family go to America. That was the curse, your honor, and every word of it has come true. You'll see for yourself as soon as we cross the mearing."

"And what became of Julia's baby?"

"I never heard she had one, sir."

He flicked his horse pensively with his whip, and it seemed to me that the disbelief I had expressed in the power of the curse disinclined him for further conversation.

"But," I said, "who is Julia Cahill, and how did she get the power to put a curse upon the village?"

"Didn't she go into the mountains every night to meet the fairies, and who else could've given her the power to put a curse on the village?"

"But she couldn't walk so far in one evening."

"Them that's in league with the fairies can walk that far and as much farther in an evening, your honor. A shepherd saw her; and you'll see the ruins of the cabins for yourself as soon as we cross the mearing, and I'll show you the cabin of the blind woman that Julia lived with before she went away."

"And how long is it since she went?"

"About twenty year, and there hasn't been a girl the like of her in these parts since. I was only a gossoon at the time, but I've heard tell she was as tall as I'm myself, and as straight as a poplar. She walked with a little swing in her walk, so that all the boys used to be looking after her, and she had fine black eyes, sir, and she was nearly always laughing. Father Madden had just come to the parish; and there was courting in these parts then, for aren't we the same as other people—we'd like to go out with a girl well enough if it was the custom of the country. Father Madden put down the ball alley because he said the boys stayed there instead of going into Mass, and he put down the crossroad dances because he said dancing was the cause of many a bastard, and he wanted none in his parish. Now there was no dancer like Julia; the boys used to gather

about to see her dance, and who ever walked with her under the hedges in the summer could never think about another woman. The village was cracked about her. There
was fighting, so I suppose the priest was right: he had to
get rid of her. But I think he mightn't have been as hard
on her as he was.

"One evening he went down to the house. Julia's people were well-to-do people, they kept a grocery store in the
village; and when he came into the shop who should be
there but the richest farmer in the country, Michael
Moran by name, trying to get Julia for his wife. He didn't
go straight to Julia, and that's what swept him. There are
two counters in that shop, and Julia was at the one on the
left hand as you go in. And many's the pound she had
made for her parents at that counter. Michael Moran says
to the father, 'Now, what fortune are you going to give
with Julia?' And the father says there was many a man who
would take her without any; and that's how they spoke,
and Julia listening quietly all the while at the opposite
counter. For Michael didn't know what a spirited girl she
was, but went on arguing till he got the father to say fifty
pounds, and thinking he had got him so far he said, 'I'll
never drop a flap to her unless you give the two heifers.'
Julia never said a word, she just sat listening. It was then
that the priest came in. And over he goes to Julia; 'And
now,' says he, 'aren't you proud to hear that you'll have
such a fine fortune, and it's I that'll be glad to see you
married, for I can't have any more of your goings-on in my
parish. You're the encouragement of the dancing and
courting here; but I'm going to put an end to it.' Julia
didn't answer a word, and he went over to them that were
arguing about the sixty pounds. 'Now why not make it
fifty-five?' says he. So the father agreed to that since the
priest had said it. And all three of them thought the marriage was settled. 'Now what will you be taking, Father
Tom?' says Cahill, 'and you, Michael?' Sorra one of them
thought of asking her if she was pleased with Michael; but
little did they know what was passing in her mind, and

when they came over to the counter to tell her what they had settled, she said, 'Well, I've just been listening to you, and 'tis well for you to be wasting your time talking about me,' and she tossed her head, saying she would just pick the boy out of the parish that pleased her best. And what angered the priest most of all was her way of saying it— that the boy that would marry her would be marrying herself and not the money that would be paid when the book was signed or when the first baby was born. Now it was agin girls marrying according to their fancy that Father Madden had set himself. He had said in his sermon the Sunday before that young people shouldn't be allowed out by themselves at all, but that the parents should make up the marriages for them. And he went fairly wild when Julia told him the example she was going to set. He tried to keep his temper, sir, but it was getting the better of him all the while, and Julia said, 'My boy isn't in the parish now, but maybe he is on his way here, and he may be here to-morrow or the next day.' And when Julia's father heard her speak like that he knew that no-one would turn her from what she was saying, and he said, 'Michael Moran, my good man, you may go your way: you'll never get her.' Then he went back to hear what Julia was saying to the priest, but it was the priest that was talking. 'Do you think,' says he, 'I am going to let you go on turning the head of every boy in the parish? Do you think,' says he, 'I'm going to see you gallavanting with one and then with the other? Do you think I'm going to see fighting and quarrelling for your like? Do you think I'm going to hear stories like I heard last week about poor Patsy Carey, who has gone out of his mind, they say, on account of your treatment? No,' says he, 'I'll have no more of that. I'll have you out of my parish, or I'll have you married.' Julia didn't answer the priest; she tossed her head, and went on making up parcels of tea and sugar and getting the steps and taking down candles, though she didn't want them, just to show the priest that she didn't mind what he was saying. And all the while her father trembling, not knowing what would happen, for the priest had a big stick, and there was no saying that he wouldn't strike her. Cahill tried to quiet the priest, he promising him that Julia shouldn't go out any more in the evenings, and bedad, sir, she was out the same evening with a young man and the priest saw them, and the next evening she was out with another and the priest saw them, nor was she minded at the end of the month to marry any of them. Then the priest went down to the shop to speak to her a second time, and he went down again a third time, though what he said the third time no-one knows, no-one being there at the time. And next Sunday he spoke out, saying that a disobedient daughter would have the worst devil in hell to attend on her. I've heard tell that he called her the evil spirit that set men mad. But most of the people that were there are dead or gone to America, and no-one rightly knows what he did say, only that the words came pouring out of his mouth, and the people when they saw Julia crossed themselves, and even the boys who were most mad after Julia were afraid to speak to her. Cahill had to put her out."

"Do you mean to say that the father put his daughter out?"

"Sure, didn't the priest threaten to turn him into a rabbit if he didn't, and no-one in the parish would speak to Julia, they were so afraid of Father Madden, and if it hadn't been for the blind woman that I was speaking about a while ago, sir, it is to the Poor House she'd have to go. The blind woman has a little cabin at the edge of the bog—I'll point it out to you, sir; we do be passing it by— and she was with the blind woman for nearly two years disowned by her own father. Her clothes wore out, but she was as beautiful without them as with them. The boys were told not to look back, but sure they couldn't help it.

"Ah, it was a long while before Father Madden could get shut of her. The blind woman said she wouldn't see Julia thrown out on the road-side, and she was as good as her word for wellnigh two years, till Julia went to America, so some do be saying, sir, whilst others do be saying she joined the fairies. But 'tis for sure, sir, that the day she left the parish Pat Quinn heard a knocking at his window and somebody asking if he would lend his cart to go to the railway station. Pat was a heavy sleeper and he didn't get up, and it is thought that it was Julia who wanted Pat's cart to take her to the station; it's a good ten mile; but she got there all the same!"

"You said something about a curse?"

"Yes, sir. You'll see the hill presently. A man who was taking some sheep to the fair saw her there. The sun was just getting up and he saw her cursing the village, raising both her hands, sir, up to the sun, and since that curse was spoken every year a roof has fallen in, sometimes two or three."

I could see he believed the story, and for the moment I, too, believed in an outcast Venus becoming the evil spirit of a village that would not accept her as divine.

"Look, sir, the woman coming down the road is Bridget Coyne. And that's her house," he said, and we passed a house built of loose stones without mortar, but a little better than the mud cabins I had seen in Father Mac-Turnan's parish.

"And now, sir, you will see the loneliest parish in Ireland."

And I noticed that though the land was good, there seemed to be few people on it, and what was more significant than the untilled fields were the ruins for they were not the cold ruins of twenty, or thirty, or forty years ago when the people were evicted and their tillage turned into pasture—the ruins I saw were the ruins of cabins that had been lately abandoned, and I said:

"It wasn't the landlord who evicted these people."

"Ah, it's the landlord who would be glad to have them back, but there's no getting them back. Everyone here will have to go, and 'tis said that the priest will say Mass in an empty chapel, sorra a one will be there but Bridget, and she'll be the last he'll give communion to. It's said, your honor, that Julia has been seen in America, and

I'm going there this autumn. You may be sure I'll keep a lookout for her."

"But all this is twenty years ago. You won't know her. A woman changes a good deal in twenty years."

"There will be no change in her, your honor. Sure hasn't she been with the fairies?"

VAL MULKERNS

The World
Outside

✳

Most of the children were early that morning, creeping in
subdued and stiff in the unaccustomed shoes, their faces
and limbs shining from prolonged scrubbing. Some of the
boys looked unusually ugly because of having had their
hair savagely attacked with scissors and bowl the previous
night by over-zealous mothers, but the girls were glossy and
braided and comely, and looked much more confident
than the boys, as if handling inspectors would not be much
trouble to them. The school master scanned all the faces
sharply, planning the traditional reshuffle. Something
nervous and trusting in the general atmosphere prompted
him to put them at ease, though he was jumpy enough himself.

"Tell me, is it the same crowd at all I have before me,
or is it some swanky gang down from Dublin for the day?"
he grinned at them in Irish, and a relieved pleased ripple
of laughter went over the desks. "Let me see now, we'll

From *Irish Writing*.

234

have to have yourself in the front, Mary Mannion, to show off that brave red ribbon, and let you take yourself to the back desk, Tomás Peig where with God's help you'll get a chance to show the Inspector how to do fractions." The point was that Mary was easy on the eyes and utterly brainless, and Tomás Peig was a bright lad and back benchers were inevitably questioned. "We'll have you over by the window, Muiris, and our friend with the red head in the second row. Will you get those boots back on you this minute, Tadg, and I'll fly the hide off you if I see them anywhere except where they're meant to be. Do you think now that it was to decorate the floor for me your mother went to Clifden last week and handed out a mint of money. No, Sir, well you may be sure the answer is No Sir, and take heed of what I said to you, if you value that hide of yours." But as the reshuffling went on, they understood the unusual bantering humor for what it was, an effort to put them at ease, and their faces beamed gratefully back at him. They were being examined, and God knew what horrible things would happen to them if they failed to please the inspector, and here was Boozy, the decent man, and he with nothing to fear being a Master, soft as butter with them to drive away their nervousness.

"Now listen to me the lot of you. If he speaks to you in Irish don't answer him back in a blast of English just to show that you know it. Answer him in Irish. Now if he speaks to you in English, what are you to do, Mary Mannion?"

"Answer him in Irish, sir," said Mary with a bright confident smile. There was a gale of laughter, and Mary was prodded incredulously by her neighbours.

" 'Tis a professor of Logic we'll make out of you. If he speaks to you in English, what will *you* do, tell her, Martin Flaherty?"

"Answer him in English, sir."

"Right. Now keep that in your heads. The next thing to remember is if he asks the class in general a question and you think you know the answer, put up your hands.

Don't be afraid. He won't eat you if you happen to be
wrong. He's probably a fine, well-fed man. The only people whose hands I don't want to see up for anything are
Mary Mannion and Micilín Seán Mullen, because they
have a job keeping up with the best of us, and we'll give
them a rest to-day. Next year with the help of God they'll
be ready for anything. Do you hear that now, the pair of
you?"

"Yes, sir." Micilín Seán was beaming with relief and
Mary Mannion was sulking.

"Right. Now the next thing to remember is—" his
eyes suddenly caught sight of a figure at the gate—"that
he's coming up the path this minute, and let you keep as
still as mice while I call the register." There were sighs
and gasps and rapid intakes of breath all around, and then
utter petrified silence, and everybody answering "Annso, a
Mhaighistear" in an unrecognizable whisper.

Mr. Mulvey was gray and hunched and small, with
heavy-lidded gloomy eyes and a mouth turning down
hopelessly at the corners. A first glance, before he opened
his mouth, suggested that his voice would be a sick wind
among the reeds, but in fact it was big and jolly and when
he laughed, which was frequently, you had the fantastic
impression that some enchantment had been worked before your eyes and that this was certainly not the man who
had walked into the room. It was difficult to say whether
his life had taken the form of a victorious battle against his
natural temperament, or whether it was only his appearance which belied him. His clothes were silver gray and
faultlessly pressed, and he carried a neatly rolled black
umbrella and a black brief-case.

As he stepped into the room out of the thickening
rain, the children scraped to their feet and stood looking
at him with dismay. They were more used to fat tweedy
red-faced inspectors with patches of leather down their
jackets. He shook hands with and spoke a few pleasant
words to Mr. McGlynn, and then turned to the pupils with

his incredible smile, which showed square healthy white teeth, slightly prominent, and produced numbers of answering smiles. He was delighted to see them all, absolutely delighted, and hoped to learn more this morning than he had ever done at school. Would they sit down now, and attend to Mr. McGlynn's lesson, and later on he'd have a chat with them. He sat down on the chair which had been placed for him near the window, opened his brief-case, and became again, in a moment, the gloomy little gray man who had entered the room. The schoolmaster finished calling the register, closed the book, and sent Mary Mannion across with it to the inspector. Then the lesson began, Geography. The large map of Europe behind the master's desk was covered by a map of Mexico, and as was his usual custom, he began by giving them a general impression of the country itself, the color, the atmosphere, then something of its history. His words were alive and interesting, because omnivorous reading of everything from strictly technical works or anthropological works to things like Graham Greene's "The Lawless Roads" had produced complete familiarity. It happened to be Mexico to-day because that was the stage of the syllabus they had reached, but it was the same with everywhere, when he was sober, that is. The three maps which he drew with quick strokes, one of the physical regions, one of the climatic regions, and the third showing produce, were accurate and even beautiful with their lively blending colors. Then the class was set to work, an intricate business because of the different ages. Little working groups were put together, and a résumé of what in particular each had to tackle was given, and the older pupils were set some questions on the lesson.

All this time, the bent little depressed figure by the window appeared to be taking no notice. The register had been scrutinized and laid aside, and also some sample exercise books, and then he seemed to give all his attention to some private papers. The Arithmetic lesson went by, and the Irish grammar lesson, and then towards midday, when a rising wind was lashing the rain against the windows, he stood up and the transfiguring smile shone out.

"Well now, I suppose you're all fit for bed, after the work you've done this morning, what?" He drew the required laugh from them, and rubbed his small gray hands happily together. "But before we let you off home there are one or two things which have been puzzling me for some time." He changed rapidly to English. "Tell me, is Mexico in the Northern Hemisphere or in the Southern Hemisphere?" The hands shot up, and so did Mary Mannion's, but it was rapidly lowered. "I see my little friend here with the red ribbon knows and doesn't know. Which hemisphere is Mexico in, will you tell me now, like the sound woman you are?"

"The Southern Hemisphere, sir," said Mary Mannion with superb confidence and a shake of the head. There were the inevitable gasps from the class, and Mr. Mulvey smiled still more brilliantly.

"I don't think we all agree with you there, do we?," and there was an enthusiastic chorus of "No sir!" "The last time I was in Mexico," he went on, directly addressing Mary Mannion, who was smiling engagingly at him, "it was in the Northern Hemisphere. Will you remember that, because I don't think it's moved since then?"

"Yes, sir. No, sir," said Mary Mannion with another engaging smile.

"Well now there's another thing that's been puzzling me. A few weeks ago I went into the dining room of my house in Galway and two of the children had apples, nice big red ones. Seán said, 'Daddy, I'll give you half mine,' and Máire said, 'I'll give you three-eighths of mine, Daddy.' Now I thought a while before I decided which I'd take, and I want you to think now. Which was the more decent offer of the two, Seán's or Máire's?" The hands went up slowly, three, four, six, then ten. "Difficult question to put to a poor simple father, wasn't it? How did I know which to take?" Again he was speaking Irish.

"I'd have taken the both of them, sir," said Mary Mannion in lamentable English, beside herself with the notice she had achieved.

"Ní thuigim," said Mr. Mulvey, with another brilliant smile, and then ignored her. "Well, will you tell me, the boy at the back, there?"

Tomás Peig, to the schoolmaster's joy, got smartly to his feet, held back his fair head and spoke up very clearly. "Seán's offer was the one you should have taken, sir, because he was giving you four-eighths (or a half) and Máire was only giving you three-eighths."

"Splendid. If I had been as bright as you now, I wouldn't have done myself out of the eighth of a fine apple."

Before they had quite finished laughing, the inspector turned to the schoolmaster and said, "I think the best thing we can do now is to send them off home for the rest of the day because they're too clever for us."

When they had all filed out into the cloakroom in clattering happiness, Mr. Mulvey's gloomy gray eyes roamed for a while about the schoolmaster's face before the smile broke again and he held out his hand. "That was the only Geography lesson in Ireland that's ever interested me," he said. He glanced quickly again at the schoolmaster's qualifications listed on the sheet before him, and asked sharply: "What are you doing here? We could do with plenty more of your kind in the national schools throughout the country but—?" He shrugged, half-smiling the question.

"It suits me here," Peter McGlynn said briefly, "I like it."

The inspector shrugged again. "If you ever wanted a change, my friend Dr. Linnane in Galway would jump at a man like you—preparing boys for University scholarships, that sort of thing."

"Thanks," the schoolmaster said without interest, "I'll remember if I ever decide to change. It's very kind of you."

"Nonsense," Mulvey replied, with an old-fashioned air, gathering his things together and fastening the brief-case. "You lived for some time in Mexico, I take it?"

"No. My Grand Tour took the form of a day trip to Liverpool. I never slept a night outside this country in my life."

"Remarkable. I taught, myself, for seven years in Mexico City and you brought it back into this classroom today, the heat, the filth, the color, the indolence, the preposterous fascination of the place. It's remarkable."

"No," Peter McGlynn smiled, "it's Baedeker, and a studious youth, and Graham Greene and a trick of the tongue. You'll not refuse a bite of lunch with me in our one and only hostelry, Pats Flaherty's?"

"I will now," said the inspector warmly, "I spend my life having lunch with clerical managers and a man can do with a bit of civilization now and again."

Pats' wife had clearly taken some trouble to see that the catering arrangements of Ballyconnolly would stand up to inspection quite as well as the school. As soon as she had received the schoolmaster's order two days previously, she had set to work, scouring and polishing the little square room off the bar, hunting out her best lace table-cloth, unused since the previous inspector's visit, and fixing a formidable array of family photographs along the mantelpiece. Despite these, the warm, low-ceilinged little room with its scarlet geraniums and looped lace curtains was welcoming to the two men as they stepped in out of the bitter wild morning. The place was permeated by the fragrance of roasting fowl, stewed apples and strong spirits, blending deliciously with the bitterness of turf-smoke. Kate Pats Flaherty bustled busily in and out, talking all the time.

" 'Tis frozen and demented the pair of you must be with the hunger, now. Ah, sure I often heard it said a man that works with his brain needs twice the feeding of a man that works with his body, and why wouldn't he, indeed? There was a cousin of my own, Mr. Mulvey, sir, and there

he is before ye on the mantelpiece with the white face
there in the middle, and hadn't they got him starved in
the college above in Dublin and he going in for a priest.
Night and day he was at the books, God pity him, and he
no more than a lad, and there wasn't he only out a priest
a few months, and his brother not even married, when he
took a delicacy and died on his poor mother, God between
us and all harm. 'Twas a fright to the world the way she
took it, bawling and crying every time she'd look at a
priest for years after. There she is for you now, Mr. Mc-
Glynn, on the bend of the mantelpiece with the feathery
hat down near her nose, but sure God is good and didn't
the second lad, a fine big puck of a boy, go in for a priest
after, and he's a curate below in Kerry now. Another sup
of that soup, Mr. Mulvey, sir? Or the Master? Well now,
I'll have that bird on the table before you'll be finished
licking your lips. There he is to your north now, Mr.
Mulvey, sir, with the fine soft plucks on him and the holy
book in his hands. We had him here now, and you could
have seen him only a few weeks ago, and there was never a
lad like him for feeding, and wouldn't he need it, I ask
you, and him not to be dying on us like his poor brother,
God rest his soul." Half of this oration was in English and
half in Irish, and during journeys to the kitchen and to
the bar the rich strong voice came clearly back to her
guests, of whom she expected and desired no response. It
was only when the last course had been cleared away and
the bottle of whiskey ordered by the schoolmaster was between them on the table, and the smoke from their cigarettes was rising to the low ceiling, that Kate Pats Flaherty
drew the door behind her, put her head around it again
and said: "I'll leave ye now to yourselves to talk to your
heart's content and if there's any other thing in the world
ye want, leave a screech out of ye and I'll hear it."

She went, and the door closed at last. In the brief satisfied silence the rain beat in gusty blasts against the window, and the wind swept down the chimney to set the turf
leaping and blazing. The hunched gray man in the gray

clothes was the first to speak, lifting the gloomy eyes that were flecked now with a faint humor.

"There's Ireland for you now, McGlynn, all of it. Unending rain rattling the windows, and inside a kindly woman boasting about her clerical relations, and two men drinking whiskey, and outside the rest of the world. If Michelangelo painted the Resurrection on her smoky ceiling she wouldn't give it a look or him a thank-you if her portly cousin His Reverence were within miles of the place. Once upon a time we exported scholars and culture to the Continent. Now we export nothing but beasts and priests, God help us." And there began one of those inevitable discussions on what's wrong with the country, that never end and are more common in Ireland than discussions on religion or sex. But before the well-worn tracks had been followed to within reach of their muddy end, the talk under the direction of Mr. Mulvey took a turn to Mexico, and from there to Spain where he had found his wife, the daughter of a Spaniard who had a ballet company in Mexico but who had left his daughter in Spain to be educated. In the warm half-forgotten enchantment of good whiskey on which the brain floated away like a dead flower and only the senses and the imagination were taut and alive, the schoolmaster felt the sun like the caressing tongue of some fantastic animal, at once savage and tender, and smelled the fruit piled high in the narrow streets, and the bitterness of cheap wine, shivered at the sudden white chill inside the vaulted Cathedrals where black-eyed women chattered and laughed before Mass began and felt no urge to leave their personalities like gifts outside the church door, at which filthy mewling beggars held out diseased limbs; he watched the cypresses shooting eager and dark into warm, star-filled air tingling with the music of De Falla to which a girl was dancing like a flame, twisting and writhing in the dark agony of exorcism; narrow martyred faces of El Greco floated in a golden mist beside the warm sensual beauties of Velasquez and in a timeless jumble of history real and imagined the sweet sane voice of a woman saint blended with the fat bass of a wandering peasant demanding an island of his master; and over it all, rising and falling like a sea of sound was the music of Albeniz, the 'Iberia,' of which every note was as familiar as the sound of rain beating on gray stone.

He had no clear memory of when exactly the little gray inspector left him, but only a vague impression of a warm handgrip and a voice urging him to visit the house in Galway to meet Maria, and look at some Spanish etchings and some Mexican carvings, and he vaguely remembered too standing at the door of Pats Flaherty's and watching the huddled gray figure disappearing through driving rain in the direction of his car, and then he remembered turning back into the fire-broken shadows of the bar, the tang of spirits and turf-smoke in his nostrils, and his head bemused with sunlight.

The Devil
and O'Flaherty

✳

"The devil and O'Flaherty couldn't do it; no, they couldn't," said the old carman to me when I told him that I had to be in Galway before ten o'clock. "Why, man, if we had a racehorse, we couldn't do it. You won't catch that train to-night, take my word for it."

The rain was coming down in torrents and the west wind blew a full gale from the sea. Where there were trees by the roadside the wind made the weirdest music in their bare branches. The full moon was somewhere up in the sky if the astronomers were to be believed, but it was completely hidden from us. I was wet to the skin, tired, weary and hungry. The driver was in no better condition. The horse was just dragging his legs after him and his head bobbed up and down like a child's toy horse. The wind shrieked, making a sound like devils' music. The horse started. The driver jumped down and, slowly as the horse went before, he now went very much slower, as

From THE WOMAN AT THE WINDOW AND OTHER STORIES, translated from the Irish by Eamonn O'Neill, Dublin, The Talbot Press.

the driver held him by the bridle and tried to coax him forward. I said a lot of things about that horse, about Galway carmen, about the weather, the place and other things, but I fear the printer would be ashamed to read them. The driver, however, paid no attention to what I said. Probably he had heard similar language pretty often before. In any case he went on in his own way, as he did not mount the car again until we had gone a couple of miles of the wet road, muddy and full of ruts.

He was between me and the wind, and from time to time I heard him mutter something. "The Devil" was what I heard oftenest, but sometimes I caught the words "The Devil and O'Flaherty." Though I was swearing under my breath myself, I was becoming interested in the driver's mutterings. "O'Flaherty!" "Who was O'Flaherty? What had he to do with the Devil? I thought of every story I had ever heard about devils assuming the form of men. Was O'Flaherty a devil in human form? Where did he live? When? What was his appearance? Did he leave any family? Did they take after the father who begot them, or the mother who bore them?

The sky cleared somewhat. The astronomers were right. The moon came out. The driver had been silent for some time.

"Over there on the top of the cliff he lived," he said suddenly.

I started.

"Who?" I said. "The Devil, was it?"

"No, but his heir. O'Flaherty Dubh."

I put him a few questions and soon he let himself go.

"Over there he lived," he said, "till the devil came for him in the end. He was a landlord but, even so, many a hundred pounds did he owe all over the country. God help you, man! If he had a couple of thousand a year itself, he was well able to get through it. Racehorses, gambling, dogs, eating and drinking, music and dancing by day and by night. Women—oh! shut up, man! He scandalized the whole countryside. He did, indeed!"

245

The driver lit his pipe, and I lit mine, but not without difficulty. The driver seemed willing to continue his story.

"Was he married, did you say?" he said, answering me. "Didn't I tell you he was? He wasn't much more than twenty when he married an earl's daughter from Munster —a kind, charitable, charming woman—but where's the wife who could live in the same house with a man who had a wife in every village from here to Dublin? After the birth of her fifth son she had to return to Munster. The child had not even been baptized when seven carriages drove up to her to the door one night. O'Flaherty himself was in the first carriage. All the occupants—men and women—were under the influence of drink and were singing ribald songs. She tried to keep them out, but they forced the door. They locked her up in one of the top rooms and then pandemonium reigned downstairs. They say that her heart was broken that night. She had left her husband, but the blessing of the people went with her. It did, indeed.

"I tell you that she brought her sons with her too, but he took them from her again after instituting legal proceedings. And didn't he rear them well, piously, and properly! They never went to school and the teaching they got from their father—well, much good it did them. If their father killed a man without rhyme or reason they applauded the deed and said that never was such a fine deed done in Ireland. It was amazing to see these five young men going mad through the country scaring man and beast. I saw one of them myself—Redmond he was called —being hanged in Galway. He had killed his own brother all over a woman.

"He had nine others at home between sons and daughters. Mind, I don't say that his wife returned. Oh, no! not likely! But he got another wife—what's this her name was? No matter. He had three more sons and two daughters by her. What's the use of talking? People wouldn't have said much, perhaps, were it not that he was a bad man in other respects. He never gave anything in charity, and after a night's feasting it was not to the poor that he gave the leavings next day but to his dogs. My father told me that, one morning he went there with a car, he saw the dogs and the poor scrambling for the remnants of the preceding night's banquet. O'Flaherty himself was present enjoying the fun. My father struck him. Were it not that the other man was drunk my father would not have got a month's imprisonment."

By this time we were approaching the town.

"What was the end of him?" I asked.

"Well, indeed, it's hard to say truly," he answered, "for there are many versions of the story, but mine is the true one if it was the truth that Big Jack, the bailiff, told me. As I have already said, he owed thousands throughout the country and there was a law then in force that if a man died in debt his body might be seized. He fell ill. He was not at home when the stroke seized him, but hunting with his sons in the hills. He was taken to a little cottage from which he had evicted the tenants years before. He died very shortly. His sons made a coffin to take him home in and they "keened" him bitterly. While they were "keening" a man walked in—apparently a huntsman. He was really a bailiff and his assistants were not far off. He expressed sympathy with the young men. He gave them a drink out of a bottle he had in his pocket. They fell asleep.

"It was night—a terrible night like this. Five young men were asleep on the floor. An old man lay cold and stiff in his coffin. Four others getting ready to carry away the body. Two candles stuck in bottles gave them light. They took hold of the coffin, lifted it and put it on their shoulders. A peal of thunder burst over the mountain cabin and the wind rose. The door was shattered and the lights went out. The body-snatchers trembled. One of the young men stirred and yawned.

" 'Oh! oh! he's alive. He's alive,' said one of the bailiffs.

"They put down the coffin on the floor. They were

247

terror-stricken. They re-lit the candles and took a swig out of the bottle.

" 'Better wait and see will the night clear up,' said one of them.

"They agreed, and all four sat down on the floor around the body. They had another swig out of the bottle. A pack of cards was produced and they began to play.

"The night calmed down. There wasn't the least sound to be heard anywhere save the snoring of the young men in their heavy sleep and the falling of the cards on the coffin-lid. The bailiffs themselves got drowsy and fell asleep one by one. The two candles which were stuck in bottles at the head of the coffin were still lighting. One of the bailiffs moved his hand. The cards were all scattered on the floor except one—the one we call the 'devil's own' —and that one lay, menacing and bright as it seemed— right over the heart of the corpse. Again the bailiff moved his hand. This time it touched the card and the card touched one of the bottles and the bottle and candle were knocked over. An odd, shapeless shadow crossed the white wall. The floor about the coffin was littered with dry grass and chips of wood. In a twinkling the place was ablaze. The bailiffs escaped. O'Flaherty's sons also got away, except one who tried to carry off the body. He was burned alive. The body was burned—the cabin was burned. But the people never believed that this was the way O'Flaherty died. The old charred walls of the cabin are still there to prove that it was the devil himself that came to take home his heir with him."

We were now in the City of Galway.

"Where will you sleep to-night?" asked the driver.

"I shan't sleep at all, I fear," said I, and I didn't.

FRANK O'CONNOR

The Drunkard

❋

It was a terrible blow to Father when Mr. Dooley on the terrace died. Mr. Dooley was a commercial traveller with two sons in the Dominicans and a car of his own, so socially he was miles ahead of us, but he had no false pride. Mr. Dooley was an intellectual, and, like all intellectuals the thing he loved best was conversation, and in his own limited way Father was a well-read man and could appreciate an intelligent talker. Mr. Dooley was remarkably intelligent. Between business acquaintances and clerical contacts, there was very little he didn't know about what went on in town, and evening after evening he crossed the road to our gate to explain to Father the news behind the news. He had a low, palavering voice and a knowing smile, and Father would listen in astonishment, giving him a conversational lead now and again, and then stump triumphantly in to Mother with his face aglow and ask: "Do you know what Mr. Dooley is after telling me?" Ever

From THE STORIES OF FRANK O'CONNOR, New York, Alfred Knopf.

since, when somebody has given me some bit of information off the record I have found myself on the point of asking: "Was it Mr. Dooley told you that?"

Till I actually saw him laid out in his brown shroud with the rosary beads entwined between his waxy fingers I did not take the report of his death seriously. Even then I felt there must be a catch and that some summer evening Mr. Dooley must reappear at our gate to give us the low-down on the next world. But Father was very upset, partly because Mr. Dooley was about one age with himself, a thing that always gives a distinctly personal turn to another man's demise; partly because now he would have no one to tell him what dirty work was behind the latest scene at the Corporation. You could count on your fingers the number of men in Blarney Lane who read the papers as Mr. Dooley did, and none of these would have overlooked the fact that Father was only a laboring man. Even Sullivan, the carpenter, a mere nobody, thought he was a cut above Father. It was certainly a solemn event.

"Half past two to the Curragh," Father said meditatively, putting down the paper.

"But you're not thinking of going to the funeral?" Mother asked in alarm.

" 'Twould be expected," Father said, scenting opposition. "I wouldn't give it to say to them."

"I think," said Mother with suppressed emotion, "it will be as much as anyone will expect if you go to the chapel with him."

("Going to the chapel," of course, was one thing, because the body was removed after work, but going to a funeral meant the loss of a half-day's pay.)

"The people hardly know us," she added.

"God between us and all harm," Father replied with dignity, "we'd be glad if it was our own turn."

To give Father his due, he was always ready to lose a half day for the sake of an old neighbour. It wasn't so much that he liked funerals as that he was a conscientious man who did as he would be done by; and nothing could have consoled him so much for the prospect of his own death as the assurance of a worthy funeral. And, to give Mother her due, it wasn't the half-day's pay she begrudged, badly as we could afford it.

Drink, you see, was Father's great weakness. He could keep steady for months, even for years, at a stretch, and while he did he was as good as gold. He was first up in the morning and brought the mother a cup of tea in bed, stayed at home in the evenings and read the paper; saved money and bought himself a new blue serge suit and bowler hat. He laughed at the folly of men who, week in week out, left their hard-earned money with the publicans; and sometimes, to pass an idle hour, he took pencil and paper and calculated precisely how much he saved each week through being a teetotaller. Being a natural optimist he sometimes continued this calculation through the whole span of his prospective existence and the total was breathtaking. He would die worth hundreds.

If I had only known it, this was a bad sign; a sign he was becoming stuffed up with spiritual pride and imagining himself better than his neighbours. Sooner or later, the spiritual pride grew till it called for some form of celebration. Then he took a drink—not whisky, of course; nothing like that—just a glass of some harmless drink like lager beer. That was the end of Father. By the time he had taken the first he already realized that he had made a fool of himself, took a second to forget it and a third to forget that he couldn't forget, and at last came home reeling drunk. From this on it was "The Drunkard's Progress," as in the moral prints. Next day he stayed in from work with a sick head while Mother went off to make his excuses at the works, and inside a fortnight he was poor and savage and despondent again. Once he began he drank steadily through everything down to the kitchen clock. Mother and I knew all the phases and dreaded all the dangers. Funerals were one.

"I have to go to Dunphy's to do a half-day's work," said Mother in distress. "Who's to look after Larry?"

"I'll look after Larry," Father said graciously. "The little walk will do him good."

There was no more to be said, though we all knew I didn't need anyone to look after me, and that I could quite well have stayed at home and looked after Sonny, but I was being attached to the party to act as a brake on Father. As a brake I had never achieved anything, but Mother still had great faith in me.

Next day, when I got home from school, Father was there before me and made a cup of tea for both of us. He was very good at tea, but too heavy in the hand for anything else; the way he cut bread was shocking. Afterwards, we went down the hill to the church, Father wearing his best blue serge and a bowler cocked to one side of his head with the least suggestion of the masher. To his great joy he discovered Peter Crowley among the mourners. Peter was another danger signal, as I knew well from certain experiences after Mass on Sunday morning: a mean man, as Mother said, who only went to funerals for the free drinks he could get at them. It turned out that he hadn't even known Mr. Dooley! But Father had a sort of contemptuous regard for him as one of the foolish people who wasted their good money in public-houses when they could be saving it. Very little of his own money Peter Crowley wasted!

It was an excellent funeral from Father's point of view. He had it all well studied before we set off after the hearse in the afternoon sunlight.

"Five carriages!" he exclaimed. "Five carriages and sixteen covered cars!" There's one alderman, two councillors and 'tis unknown how many priests. I didn't see a funeral like this from the road since Willie Mack, the publican, died.

"Ah, he was well liked," said Crowley in his husky voice.

"My goodness, don't I know that?" snapped Father. "Wasn't the man my best friend? Two nights before he died—only two nights—he was over telling me the goings-on about the housing contract. Them fellows in the Corporation are night and day robbers. But even I never imagined he was as well connected as that."

Father was stepping out like a boy, pleased with everything: the other mourners, and the fine houses along Sunday's Well. I knew the danger signals were there in full force: a sunny day, a fine funeral, and a distinguished company of clerics and public men were bringing out all the natural vanity and flightiness of Father's character. It was with something like genuine pleasure that he saw his old friend lowered into the grave; with the sense of having performed a duty and the pleasant awareness that however much he would miss poor Mr. Dooley in the long summer evenings, it was he and not poor Mr. Dooley who would do the missing.

"We'll be making tracks before they break up," he whispered to Crowley as the gravediggers tossed in the first shovelfuls of clay, and away he went, hopping like a goat from grassy hump to hump. The drivers, who were probably in the same state as himself, though without months of abstinence to put an edge on it, looked up hopefully.

"Are they nearly finished, Mick?" bawled one.

"All over now bar the last prayers," trumpeted Father in the tone of one who brings news of great rejoicing.

The carriages passed us in a lather of dust several hundred yards from the public-house, and Father, whose feet gave him trouble in hot weather, quickened his pace, looking nervously over his shoulder for any sign of the main body of mourners crossing the hill. In a crowd like that a man might be kept waiting.

When we did reach the pub the carriages were drawn up outside, and solemn men in black ties were cautiously bringing out consolation to mysterious females whose hands reached out modestly from behind the drawn blinds of the coaches. Inside the pub there were only the drivers

and a couple of shawly women. I felt if I was to act as a
brake at all, this was the time, so I pulled Father by the
coattails.

"Dadda, can't we go home now?" I asked.

"Two minutes now," he said, beaming affectionately.
"Just a bottle of lemonade and we'll go home."

This was a bribe, and I knew it, but I was always a
child of weak character. Father ordered lemonade and two
pints. I was thirsty and swallowed my drink at once. But
that wasn't Father's way. He had long months of abstinence behind him and an eternity of pleasure before. He
took out his pipe, blew through it, filled it, and then lit it
with loud pops, his eyes bulging above it. After that he
deliberately turned his back on the pint, leaned one elbow
on the counter in the attitude of a man who did not know
there was a pint behind him, and deliberately brushed the
tobacco from his palms. He had settled down for the evening. He was steadily working through all the important
funerals he had ever attended. The carriages departed and
the minor mourners drifted in till the pub was half full.

"Dadda," I said, pulling his coat again, "can't we go
home now?"

"Ah, your mother won't be in for a long time yet," he
said benevolently enough. "Run out in the road and play,
can't you?"

It struck me as very cool, the way grown-ups assumed
that you could play all by yourself on a strange road. I
began to get bored as I had so often been bored before. I
knew Father was quite capable of lingering there till
nightfall. I knew I might have to bring him home, blind
drunk, down Blarney Lane, with all the old women at
their doors, saying: "Mick Delaney is on it again." I knew
that my mother would be half crazy with anxiety; that
next day Father wouldn't go out to work; and before the
end of the week she would be running down to the pawn
with the clock under her shawl. I could never get over the
lonesomeness of the kitchen without a clock.

I was still thirsty. I found if I stood on tiptoe I could

just reach Father's glass, and the idea occurred to me that it would be interesting to know what the contents were like. He had his back to it and wouldn't notice. I took down the glass and sipped cautiously. It was a terrible disappointment. I was astonished that he could even drink such stuff. It looked as if he had never tried lemonade.

I should have advised him about lemonade but he was holding forth himself in great style. I heard him say that bands were a great addition to a funeral. He put his arms in the position of someone holding a rifle in reverse and hummed a few bars of Chopin's Funeral March. Crowley nodded reverently. I took a longer drink and began to see that porter might have its advantages. I felt pleasantly elevated and philosophic. Father hummed a few bars of the Dead March in *Saul*. It was a nice pub and a very fine funeral, and I felt sure that poor Mr. Dooley in Heaven must be highly gratified. At the same time I thought they might have given him a band. As Father said, bands were a great addition.

But the wonderful thing about porter was the way it made you stand aside, or rather float aloft like a cherub rolling on a cloud, and watch yourself with your legs crossed, leaning against a bar counter, not worrying about trifles but thinking deep, serious, grown-up thoughts about life and death. Looking at yourself like that, you couldn't help thinking after a while how funny you looked, and suddenly you got embarrassed and wanted to giggle. But by the time I had finished the pint, that phase too had passed; I found it hard to put back the glass, the counter seemed to have grown so high. Melancholia was supervening again.

"Well," Father said reverently, reaching behind him for his drink, "God rest the poor man's soul, wherever he is!" He stopped, looked first at the glass, and then at the people round him. "Hello," he said in a fairly good-humored tone, as if he were just prepared to consider it a joke, even if it was in bad taste, "who was at this?"

There was silence for a moment while the publican

and the old women looked first at Father and then at his glass.

"There was no one at it, my good man," one of the women said with an offended air. "Is it robbers you think we are?"

"Ah, there's no one here would do a thing like that, Mick," said the publican in a shocked tone.

"Well, someone did it," said Father, his smile beginning to wear off.

"If they did, they were them that were nearer it," said the woman darkly, giving me a dirty look; and at the same moment the truth began to dawn on Father. I suppose I must have looked a bit starry-eyed. He bent and shook me.

"Are you all right, Larry?" he asked in alarm.

Peter Crowley looked down at me and grinned.

"Could you beat that?" he exclaimed in a husky voice.

I could, and without difficulty. I started to get sick. Father jumped back in holy terror that I might spoil his good suit, and hastily opened the back door.

"Run! run! run!" he shouted.

I saw the sunlit wall outside with the ivy overhanging it, and ran. The intention was good but the performance was exaggerated, because I lurched right into the wall, hurting it badly, as it seemed to me. Being always very polite, I said "Pardon" before the second bout came on me. Father, still concerned for his suit, came up behind and cautiously held me while I got sick.

"That's a good boy!" he said encouragingly. "You'll be grand when you get that up."

Before, I was not grand! Grand was the last thing I was. I gave one unmerciful wail out of me as he steered me back to the pub and put me sitting on the bench near the shawlies. They drew themselves up with an offended air, still sore at the suggestion that they had drunk his pint.

"God help us!" moaned one, looking pityingly at me, "isn't it the likes of them would be fathers?"

"Mick," said the publican in alarm, spraying sawdust

on my tracks, "that child isn't supposed to be in here at all. You'd better take him home quick in case a bobby would see him."

"Merciful God!" whimpered Father, raising his eyes to heaven and clapping his hands silently as he only did when distraught, "what misfortune was on me? Or what will his mother say? . . . If women might stop at home and look after their children themselves!" he added in a snarl for the benefit of the shawlies. "Are them carriages all gone, Bill?"

"The carriages are finished long ago, Mick," replied the publican.

"I'll take him home," Father said despairingly. . . . "I'll never bring you out again," he threatened me. "Here," he added, giving me the clean handkerchief from his breast pocket, "put that over your eye."

The blood on the handkerchief was the first indication I got that I was cut, and instantly my temple began to throb and I set up another howl.

"Whisht, whisht, whisht!" Father said testily, steering me out the door. "One'd think you were killed. That's nothing. We'll wash it when we get home."

"Steady now, old scout!" Crowley said, taking the other side of me. "You'll be all right in a minute."

I never met two men who knew less about the effects of drink. The first breath of fresh air and the warmth of the sun made me groggier than ever and I pitched and rolled between wind and tide till Father started to whimper again.

"God Almighty, and the whole road out! What misfortune was on me didn't stop at my work! Can't you walk straight?"

I couldn't. I saw plain enough that, coaxed by the sunlight, every woman old and young in Blarney Lane was leaning over her half-door or sitting on her doorstep. They all stopped gabbling to gape at the strange spectacle of two sober, middle-aged men bringing home a drunken small boy with a cut over his eye. Father, torn between the shamefast desire to get me home as quick as he could, and the neighbourly need to explain that it wasn't his fault, finally halted outside Mrs. Roche's. There was a gang of old women outside a door at the opposite side of the road. I didn't like the look of them from the first. They seemed altogether too interested in me. I leaned against the wall of Mrs. Roche's cottage with my hands in my trousers pockets, thinking mournfully of poor Mr. Dooley in his cold grave on the Curragh, who would never walk down the road again, and, with great feeling, I began to sing a favorite song of Father's.

> *Though lost to Mononia and cold in the grave*
> *He returns to Kincora no more.*

"Wisha, the poor child!" Mrs. Roche said. "Haven't he a lovely voice, God bless him!"

That was what I thought myself, so I was the more surprised when Father said "Whisht!" and raised a threatening finger at me. He didn't seem to realize the appropriateness of the song, so I sang louder than ever.

"Whisht, I tell you!" he snapped, and then tried to work up a smile for Mrs. Roche's benefit. "We're nearly home now. I'll carry you the rest of the way."

But, drunk and all as I was, I knew better than to be carried home ignominiously like that.

"Now," I said severely, "can't you leave me alone? I can walk all right. 'Tis only my head. All I want is a rest."

"But you can rest at home in bed," he said viciously, trying to pick me up, and I knew by the flush on his face that he was very vexed.

"Ah, Jasus," I said crossly, "what do I want to go home for? Why the hell can't you leave me alone?"

For some reason the gang of old women at the other side of the road thought this very funny. They nearly split their sides over it. A gassy fury began to expand in me at the thought that a fellow couldn't have a drop taken without the whole neighbourhood coming out to make game of him.

"Who are ye laughing at?" I shouted, clenching my fists at them. "I'll make ye laugh at the other side of yeer faces if ye don't let me pass."

They seemed to think this funnier still; I had never seen such ill-mannered people.

"Go away, ye bloody bitches!" I said.

"Whisht, whisht, whisht, I tell you!" snarled Father, abandoning all pretence of amusement and dragging me along behind him by the hand. I was maddened by the women's shrieks of laughter. I was maddened by Father's bullying. I tried to dig in my heels but he was too powerful for me, and I could only see the women by looking back over my shoulder.

"Take care or I'll come back and show ye!" I shouted. "I'll teach ye to let decent people pass. Fitter for ye to stop at home and wash yeer dirty faces."

" 'Twill be all over the road," whimpered Father. "Never again, never again, not if I lived to be a thousand!"

To this day I don't know whether he was forswearing me or the drink. By way of a song suitable to my heroic mood I bawled "The Boys of Wexford," as he dragged me in home. Crowley, knowing he was not safe, made off and Father undressed me and put me to bed. I couldn't sleep because of the whirling in my head. It was very unpleasant, and I got sick again. Father came in with a wet cloth and mopped up after me. I lay in a fever, listening to him chopping sticks to start a fire. After that I heard him lay the table.

Suddenly the front door banged open and Mother stormed in with Sonny in her arms, not her usual gentle, timid self, but a wild, raging woman. It was clear that she had heard it all from the neighbours.

"Mick Delaney," she cried hysterically, "what did you do to my son?"

"Whisht, woman, whisht, whisht!" he hissed, dancing from one foot to the other. "Do you want the whole road to hear?"

"Ah," she said with a horrifying laugh, "the road knows all about it by this time. The road knows the way you filled your unfortunate innocent child with drink to make sport for you and that other rotten, filthy brute."

"But I gave him no drink," he shouted, aghast at the horrifying interpretation the neighbours had chosen to give his misfortune. "He took it while my back was turned. What the hell do you think I am?"

"Ah," she replied bitterly, "everyone knows what you are now. God forgive you, wasting our hard-earned few ha'pence on drink, and bringing up your child to be a drunken corner-boy like yourself."

Then she swept into the bedroom and threw herself on her knees by the bed. She moaned when she saw the gash over my eye. In the kitchen Sonny set up a loud bawl on his own, and a moment later Father appeared in the bedroom door with his cap over his eyes, wearing an expression of the most intense self-pity.

"That's a nice way to talk to me after all I went through," he whined. "That's a nice accusation, that I was drinking. Not one drop of drink crossed my lips the whole day. How could it when he drank it all? I'm the one that ought to be pitied, with my day ruined on me, and I after being made a show for the whole road."

But next morning, when he got up and went out quietly to work with his dinner-basket, Mother threw herself on me in the bed and kissed me. It seemed it was all my doing, and I was being given a holiday till my eye got better.

"My brave little man!" she said with her eyes shining. "It was God did it you were there. You were his guardian angel."

FRANK O'CONNOR

The Majesty

of the Law

❉

Old Dan Bride was breaking brosna for the fire when he heard a step on the path. He paused, a bundle of saplings on his knee.

Dan had looked after his mother while the life was in her, and after her death no other woman had crossed his threshold. Signs on it, his house had that look. Almost everything in it he had made with his own hands in his own way. The seats of the chairs were only slices of log, rough and round and thick as the saw had left them, and with the rings still plainly visible through the grime and polish that coarse trouser-bottoms had in the course of long years imparted. Into these Dan had rammed stout knotted ash-boughs that served alike for legs and back. The deal table, bought in a shop, was an inheritance from his mother and a great pride and joy to him though it rocked whenever he touched it. On the wall, unglazed and fly-spotted, hung in mysterious isolation a Marcus Stone print, and beside the door was a calendar with a picture of

From THE STORIES OF FRANK O'CONNOR, New York, Alfred Knopf.

a racehorse. Over the door hung a gun, old but good, and
in excellent condition, and before the fire was stretched
an old setter who raised his head expectantly whenever
Dan rose or even stirred.

He raised it now as the steps came nearer and when
Dan, laying down the bundle of saplings, cleaned his
hands thoughtfully in the seat of his trousers, he gave a
loud bark, but this expressed no more than a desire to
show off his own watchfulness. He was half human and
knew people thought he was old and past his prime.

A man's shadow fell across the oblong of dusty light
thrown over the half-door before Dan looked round.

"Are you alone, Dan?" asked an apologetic voice.

"Oh, come in, come in, sergeant, come in and welcome," exclaimed the old man, hurrying on rather uncertain feet to the door which the tall policeman opened and
pushed in. He stood there, half in sunlight, half in shadow,
and seeing him so, you would have realized how dark the
interior of the house really was. One side of his red face
was turned so as to catch the light, and behind it an ash
tree raised its boughs of airy green against the sky. Green
fields, broken here and there by clumps of red-brown rock,
flowed downhill, and beyond them, stretched all across the
horizon, was the sea, flooded and almost transparent with
light. The sergeant's face was fat and fresh, the old man's
face, emerging from the twilight of the kitchen, had the
color of wind and sun, while the features had been so
shaped by the struggle with time and the elements that
they might as easily have been found impressed upon the
surface of a rock.

"Begor, Dan," said the sergeant, " 'tis younger you're
getting."

"Middling I am, sergeant, middling," agreed the old
man in a voice which seemed to accept the remark as a
compliment of which politeness would not allow him to
take too much advantage. "No complaints."

"Begor, 'tis as well because no one would believe
them. And the old dog doesn't look a day older."

The dog gave a low growl as though to show the sergeant that he would remember this unmannerly reference to his age, but indeed he growled every time he was mentioned, under the impression that people had nothing but ill to say of him.

"And how's yourself, sergeant?"

"Well, now, like the most of us, Dan, neither too good nor too bad. We have our own little worries, but, thanks be to God, we have our compensations."

"And the wife and family?"

"Good, praise be to God, good. They were away from me for a month, the lot of them, at the mother-in-law's place in Clare."

"In Clare, do you tell me?"

"In Clare. I had a fine quiet time."

The old man looked about him and then retired to the bedroom, from which he returned a moment later with an old shirt. With this he solemnly wiped the seat and back of the log-chair nearest the fire.

"Sit down now, sergeant. You must be tired after the journey. 'Tis a long old road. How did you come?"

"Teigue Leary gave me the lift. Wisha now, Dan, don't be putting yourself out. I won't be stopping. I promised them I'd be back inside an hour."

"What hurry is on you?" asked Dan. "Look, your foot was only on the path when I made up the fire."

"Arrah, Dan, you're not making tea for me?"

"I am not making it for you, indeed; I'm making it for myself, and I'll take it very bad of you if you won't have a cup."

"Dan, Dan, that I mightn't stir, but 'tisn't an hour since I had it at the barracks!"

"Ah, whisht, now, whisht! Whisht, will you! I have something here to give you an appetite."

The old man swung the heavy kettle onto the chain over the open fire, and the dog sat up, shaking his ears with an expression of the deepest interest. The policeman unbuttoned his tunic, opened his belt, took a pipe and a plug of tobacco from his breast pocket, and crossing his legs in an easy posture, began to cut the tobacco slowly and carefully with his pocket knife. The old man went to the dresser and took down two handsomely decorated cups, the only cups he had, which, though chipped and handleless, were used at all only on very rare occasions; for himself he preferred his tea from a basin. Happening to glance into them, he noticed that they bore signs of disuse and had collected a lot of the fine white turf-dust that always circulated in the little smoky cottage. Again he thought of the shirt, and, rolling up his sleeves with a stately gesture, he wiped them inside and out till they shone. Then he bent and opened the cupboard. Inside was a quart bottle of pale liquid, obviously untouched. He removed the cork and smelt the contents, pausing for a moment in the act as though to recollect where exactly he had noticed that particular smoky smell before. Then, reassured, he stood up and poured out with a liberal hand.

"Try that now, sergeant," he said with quiet pride.

The sergeant, concealing whatever qualms he might have felt at the idea of drinking illegal whisky, looked carefully into the cup, sniffed, and glanced up at old Dan.

"It looks good," he commented.

"It should be good," replied Dan with no mock modesty.

"It tastes good too," said the sergeant.

"Ah, sha," said Dan, not wishing to praise his own hospitality in his own house, " 'tis of no great excellence."

"You'd be a good judge, I'd say," said the sergeant without irony.

"Ever since things became what they are," said Dan, carefully guarding himself against a too-direct reference to the peculiarities of the law administered by his guest, "liquor isn't what it used to be."

"I've heard that remark made before now, Dan," said the sergeant thoughtfully. "I've heard it said by men of wide experience that it used to be better in the old days."

264

"Liquor," said the old man, "is a thing that takes time. There was never a good job done in a hurry."

" 'Tis an art in itself."

"Just so."

"And an art takes time."

"And knowledge," added Dan with emphasis. "Every art has its secrets, and the secrets of distilling are being lost the way the old songs were lost. When I was a boy there wasn't a man in the barony but had a hundred songs in his head, but with people running here, there and everywhere, the songs were lost. . . . Ever since things became what they are," he repeated on the same guarded note, "there's so much running about the secrets are lost."

"There must have been a power of them."

"There was. Ask any man today that makes whisky do he know how to make it out of heather."

"And was it made of heather?" asked the policeman.

"It was."

"You never drank it yourself?"

"I didn't, but I knew old men that did, and they told me that no whisky that's made nowadays could compare with it."

"Musha, Dan, I think sometimes 'twas a great mistake of the law to set its hand against it."

Dan shook his head. His eyes answered for him, but it was not in nature for a man to criticize the occupation of a guest in his own home.

"Maybe so, maybe not," he said noncommittally.

"But sure, what else have the poor people?"

"Them that makes the laws have their own good reasons."

"All the same, Dan, all the same, 'tis a hard law."

The sergeant would not be outdone in generosity. Politeness required him not to yield to the old man's defence of his superiors and their mysterious ways.

"It is the secrets I'd be sorry for," said Dan, summing up. "Men die and men are born, and where one man

drained another will plough, but a secret lost is lost forever."

"True," said the sergeant mournfully. "Lost forever."

Dan took his cup, rinsed it in a bucket of clear water
by the door and cleaned it again with the shirt. Then he
placed it carefully at the sergeant's elbow. From the dresser
he took a jug of milk and a blue bag containing sugar;
this he followed up with a slab of country butter and—a
sure sign that he had been expecting a visitor—a round
cake of homemade bread, fresh and uncut. The kettle sang
and spat and the dog, shaking his ears, barked at it angrily.

"Go away, you brute!" growled Dan, kicking him
out of his way.

He made the tea and filled the two cups. The sergeant cut himself a large slice of bread and buttered it
thickly.

"It is just like medicines," said the old man, resuming
his theme with the imperturbability of age. "Every secret
there was is lost. And leave no one tell me that a doctor is
as good a man as one that had the secrets of old times."

"How could he be?" asked the sergeant with his
mouth full.

"The proof of that was seen when there were doctors
and wise people there together."

"It wasn't to the doctors the people went, I'll engage?"

"It was not. And why?" With a sweeping gesture the
old man took in the whole world outside his cabin. "Out
there on the hillsides is the sure cure for every disease.
Because it is written"—he tapped the table with his thumb
—"it is written by the poets 'wherever you find the disease
you will find the cure.' But people walk up the hills and
down the hills and all they see is flowers. Flowers! As if
God Almighty—honor and praise to Him!—had nothing
better to do with His time than be making old flowers!"

"Things no doctor could cure the wise people cured,"
agreed the sergeant.

"Ah, musha, 'tis I know it," said Dan bitterly. "I

know it, not in my mind but in my own four bones."

"Have you the rheumatics at you still?" the sergeant asked in a shocked tone.

"I have. Ah, if you were alive, Kitty O'Hara, or you, Nora Malley of the Glen, 'tisn't I'd be dreading the mountain wind or the sea wind; 'tisn't I'd be creeping down with my misfortunate red ticket for the blue and pink and yellow dribble-drabble of their ignorant dispensary."

"Why then indeed," said the sergeant, "I'll get you a bottle for that."

"Ah, there's no bottle ever made will cure it."

"That's where you're wrong, Dan. Don't talk now till you try it. It cured my own uncle when he was that bad he was shouting for the carpenter to cut the two legs off him with a handsaw."

"I'd give fifty pounds to get rid of it," said Dan magniloquently. "I would and five hundred."

The sergeant finished his tea in a gulp, blessed himself and struck a match which he then allowed to go out as he answered some question of the old man. He did the same with a second and third, as though titillating his appetite with delay. Finally he succeeded in getting his pipe alight and the two men pulled round their chairs, placed their toes side by side in the ashes, and in deep puffs, lively bursts of conversation, and long, long silences, enjoyed their smoke.

"I hope I'm not keeping you?" said the sergeant, as though struck by the length of his visit.

"Ah, what would you keep me from?"

"Tell me if I am. The last thing I'd like to do is waste another man's time."

"Begor, you wouldn't waste my time if you stopped all night."

"I like a little chat myself," confessed the policeman.

And again they became lost in conversation. The light grew thick and colored and, wheeling about the kitchen before it disappeared, became tinged with gold;

the kitchen itself sank into cool greyness with cold light on the cups and basins and plates of the dresser. From the ash tree a thrush began to sing. The open hearth gathered brightness till its light was a warm, even splash of crimson in the twilight.

Twilight was also descending outside when the sergeant rose to go. He fastened his belt and tunic and carefully brushed his clothes. Then he put on his cap, tilted a little to side and back.

"Well, that was a great talk," he said.

" 'Tis a pleasure," said Dan, "a real pleasure."

"And I won't forget the bottle for you."

"Heavy handling from God to you!"

"Good-bye now, Dan."

"Good-bye, sergeant, and good luck."

Dan didn't offer to accompany the sergeant beyond the door. He sat in his old place by the fire, took out his pipe once more, blew through it thoughtfully, and just as he leaned forward for a twig to kindle it, heard the steps returning. It was the sergeant. He put his head a little way over the half-door.

"Oh, Dan!" he called softly.

"Ay, sergeant?" replied Dan, looking round, but with one hand still reaching for the twig. He couldn't see the sergeant's face, only hear his voice.

"I suppose you're not thinking of paying that little fine, Dan?"

There was a brief silence. Dan pulled out the lighted twig, rose slowly and shambled towards the door, stuffing it down in the almost empty bowl of the pipe. He leaned over the half-door while the sergeant with hands in the pockets of his trousers gazed rather in the direction of the laneway, yet taking in a considerable portion of the sea line.

"The way it is with me, sergeant," replied Dan unemotionally, "I am not."

"I was thinking that, Dan; I was thinking you wouldn't."

There was a long silence during which the voice of the thrush grew shriller and merrier. The sunken sun lit up rafts of purple cloud moored high above the wind.

"In a way," said the sergeant, "that was what brought me."

"I was just thinking so, sergeant, it only struck me and you going out the door."

"If 'twas only the money, Dan, I'm sure there's many would be glad to oblige you."

"I know that, sergeant. No, 'tisn't the money so much as giving that fellow the satisfaction of paying. Because he angered me, sergeant."

The sergeant made no comment on this and another long silence ensued.

"They gave me the warrant," the sergeant said at last, in a tone which dissociated him from all connection with such an unneighbourly document.

"Did they so?" exclaimed Dan, as if he was shocked by the thoughtlessness of the authorities.

"So whenever 'twould be convenient for you—"

"Well, now you mention it," said Dan, by way of throwing out a suggestion for debate, "I could go with you now."

"Ah, sha, what do you want going at this hour for?" protested the sergeant with a wave of his hand, dismissing the notion as the tone required.

"Or I could go tomorrow," added Dan, warming to the issue.

"Would it be suitable for you now?" asked the sergeant, scaling up his voice accordingly.

"But, as a matter of fact," said the old man emphatically, "the day that would be most convenient to me would be Friday after dinner, because I have some messages to do in town, and I wouldn't have the journey for nothing."

"Friday will do grand," said the sergeant with relief that this delicate matter was now practically disposed of. "If it doesn't they can damn well wait. You could walk in there yourself when it suits you and tell them I sent you."

269

"I'd rather have yourself there, sergeant, if it would be no inconvenience. As it is, I'd feel a bit shy."

"Why then, you needn't feel shy at all. There's a man from my own parish there, a warder; one Whelan. Ask for him; I'll tell him you're coming, and I'll guarantee when he knows you're a friend of mine he'll make you as comfortable as if you were at home."

"I'd like that fine," Dan said with profound satisfaction. "I'd like to be with friends, sergeant."

"You will be, never fear. Good-bye again now, Dan. I'll have to hurry."

"Wait now, wait till I see you to the road."

Together the two men strolled down the laneway while Dan explained how it was that he, a respectable old man, had had the grave misfortune to open the head of another old man in such a way as to require his removal to hospital, and why it was that he couldn't give the old man in question the satisfaction of paying in cash for an injury brought about through the victim's own unmannerly method of argument.

"You see, sergeant," Dan said, looking at another little cottage up the hill, "the way it is, he's there now, and he's looking at us as sure as there's a glimmer of sight in his weak, wandering, watery eyes, and nothing would give him more gratification than for me to pay. But I'll punish him. I'll lie on bare boards for him. I'll suffer for him, sergeant, so that neither he nor any of his children after him will be able to raise their heads for the shame of it."

On the following Friday he made ready his donkey and butt and set out. On his way he collected a number of neighbours who wished to bid him farewell. At the top of the hill he stopped to send them back. An old man, sitting in the sunlight, hastily made his way indoors, and a moment later the door of his cottage was quietly closed.

Having shaken all his friends by the hand, Dan lashed the old donkey, shouted: "Hup there!" and set out alone along the road to prison.

SEAN O'FAOLAIN

Teresa

❋

On the platform at Dieppe, at a corner so near the sea and the boat as to be part of the quay, there stood a small nun, flanked by three shapeless bags of that old-fashioned kind known as portmanteaux. Lovely as a black wall-flower, large-eyed by nature, her eyes were now enormous: for she was looking across the quays with delight at the sun-blazing confections of houses on the other side. Now and again an old nun came hobbling up to her from the busier end of the platform, muttering something that drew a shadow across the lovely face, and then hobbling away again, head down, to this official and that official, wavering around like a top as each one hurriedly threw a few words at her and rushed past. At last the old nun came back to the novice, with her two hands out in appeal. The novice, followed by the old nun, at once walked straight down to the first official she saw and said in clear English:

From THE MAN WHO INVENTED SIN, New York, The Devin-Adair Co.

"Where is the train for Rouen?"

The official glanced at her, then smiled, then bowed, and said politely, indeed with deference:

"There it is, mademoiselle," and pointed to it.

"Mais non, non," babbled the old nun. "Pas aller à Rouen! Aller à Leesoo!"

"That's all right, Sister Patrick," said the other. "We change at Rouen." And taking charge of the situation, she led the still-protesting nun up to the waiting train, put in the bags, helped—almost pushed—the old woman before her, and settled herself for the journey. The old woman clambered out again, red with fluster. Once more she ambushed official after official, all of whom said a word so like "Wrong" that she insisted on hauling out her companion.

"Listen, Sister Patrick," begged the novice, with saintly patience. "I know the route backwards. It's Dieppe, Rouen, Elbeuf St. Aubin, Serquigny, and then Lisieux. This is the train."

The guard confirmed this, as far as concerned Rouen, and they clambered in at the last moment; but the old woman was still saying that they would never get to "Leesoo," that they would find themselves landed in Paris in the middle of the night, that she had told Mother Mary Mell not to send her, that thirty-one years is too long out of a country for anyone to remember the language, and so on and so on, while the younger nun gazed wide-eyed out of the window at the passing fields.

"Our pilgrimage has begun," she said in a dreamy voice, almost to herself.

"And what's going to be the end of it at this rate?" snapped the old woman. But then she gave a frightened look at the little face before her. The big eyes had lowered. A tremble was flitting across the red lips. The old woman immediately calmed down, laid a rough hand on the novice's knee, and said, gently, "Sure, don't mind me, Sister Teresa. I'm all of a flusther. We're on the road now. Just as you say. When we get to Leesoo, 'twill be all right, a gilly. Saint Teresa will look after you and . . . Look't, I have no sense. We should be eating our lunch."

"I'd love a cup of tea!" said the girl. "I have a raging headache."

"Tut tut," clucked the old woman, and then she grabbed the girl's flank. "Are ye wearing your double petticoat, Sister Teresa?"

"Yes, Sister," said Teresa, with a blush and a warning look into the corner of the carriage, where an old Frenchman was devouring a roll and slugging red wine.

"Have ye the red-flannel drawers on ye?" demanded the old nun.

"Yes, Sister. Sssh!"

"There's nothing like red flannel next the skin," said the nun, fiddling with the lunch-parcel. " 'Tis a touch of cold you've got."

" 'Twas the heat down under that deck," said Teresa, and big floods of water entered her eyes. Her chaperone did not notice. "I never saw Dieppe from the sea," she whimpered. "And Mother Mary Mell says that it's lovely from the sea."

"Will ye have egg and cress, or tomato?" asked the old woman, too intent on her own appetite to take notice of anything else. "We earned it," she laughed, with a happy look about her and a countrywoman's smile and nod to the old "Clemenceau" in the corner. He just dug a chunk of his roll off with his penknife, wiped the back of his hand right and left across his mustaches, and with an idle glance at her, opened both mouth and eyes simultaneously to devour the chunk.

The nuns began to nibble their food. Two hens could not have pecked more nimbly or neatly. Their traveling-companion finished his lunch almost before they had well begun. He carefully stowed away his bottle, produced a long cheroot, and began to fill the carriage with smoke. Then, to the dismay of the novice, he leaned across and closed the window tightly. By the time she had finished eating, she had already begun to lean her aching head on her palm. In minute imitation of the Frenchman, the old woman rubbed her mustaches and her beard clean of crumbs, leaned back, closed her eyes, began to eat chocolates and to breathe through her nose. She woke with a start to hear Teresa say to the Frenchman:

"C'est assez chaud, monsieur. Veuillez bien ouvrir la fenêtre."

The old tiger-face glared, growled, tapped his chest fiercely, poured out a flood of uncompromising French, and leaned back. His sideward glare thereafter was like a cat ready to pounce.

"What's that?" asked the old nun apprehensively.

"My head," groaned Teresa.

"Offer it up, girl," advised the old woman. "Offer it up to Saint Teresa for the success of your intention."

"I've offered it up on the boat the whole way over," retorted the novice.

" 'Tis a cross," said the old woman easily. " 'Tis put on you by Saint Teresa to try you. Suffer it for her sake."

The girl looked at her coldly. Then she observed that they had a second traveling-companion. He was a cavalry officer, who, with more consideration than their "Clemenceau," was walking up and down in the corridor to smoke his pipe. Each time he passed the door he glanced up at his luggage on the rack. She raised her eyes appealingly the next time he passed. He paused, glanced at her, was about to pass on, paused again to look. A tiny gesture of her hand, a widening of her eyes held him. He came in, sat down, looked around him, and stared at her.

"Monsieur," she begged. "J'ai mal à la tête. La fenêtre. Est-ce que nous pouvons l'ouvrir?"

"With pleasure," he said, in English, stalked over to it and slapped it down.

A raucous argument started up at once between the officer and his fellow-countryman. Sister Patrick sat up, glared at her charge, and drew herself in from the combatants. The argument ended with the abrupt flight of the old man, cursing as he went, a laugh from the officer, and a frightened smile from the novice, accompanied by a glance at her chaperone, who, in the greatest suspicion of the officer, had lowered her head to look crookedly at him, like a duck, out under her coif. He was stroking his little line of mustache and smiling at Teresa. When Patrick slewed full around to survey her charge, Teresa had cast her eyes down demurely on her clasped hands.

Presently the officer got up, and went out to smoke another pipe. Every time he passed, he bowed in to the two nuns. Teresa never looked higher than his knees. When he had passed for about the sixth time, Patrick said:

"Sister, do you realize that officer is bowing to us every two minutes?"

"He is very kind," said the little nun. "Everybody is very kind," she sighed, and began to pray on her beads.

But when he passed again, and bowed, the old nun said crossly:

"I believe you're looking at him, Sister Teresa!"

Teresa shook her head sadly and looked out of her big eyes at her chaperone.

"It is sad," she said. "He will be killed in the wars," and her eyes swam with tears.

"And what's that to you?" whispered the old nun angrily.

"He reminds me of my brother, Jim, in the army," said Teresa. "He will be killed on the battlefield too. Oh, let us pray for the pair of them."

The old nun could not refuse to do this, so they prayed together, and when the officer passed, and bowed, and smiled, the two nuns bowed and smiled back, and went on with their prayers for the repose of his soul when he would be killed in the wars. But he was useful at Rouen. He bought them two lovely cartons of café-au-lait, with buttered rolls, and showed them where the auto-rail would start. Then for the last time he bowed, and smiled, and went away, and they never saw him again.

II

It was the fading hour of day before their little auto-rail came and took the two travellers (and about eight others) trotting out of Rouen. A light haze of rain began to float down through the air. They passed a village deep in trees. There the first lights were beginning to contest the supremacy of the day. Soon the rain shone in rivulets on the lighted windows of the auto. The other travellers leaned closer together in a kind of animal companionship and chattered in loud voices, as if to keep the night at bay.

"I wonder," murmured Teresa, "what are they doing now back in Saint Anthony's?"

"Ah, yes!" sighed the old nun wearily. "It makes England seem very far away to think of Saint Anthony's now."

"And Dublin?" smiled the novice sadly.

"Ha!" said the old nun, with a yawn that dropped the subject into vacancy. Her youth and her friends were too remote for serious reflection.

"I know what my sisters are doing now in Dublin," whispered Teresa. "Having tea and making plans for the night." And she looked out at the evening shower and the thickening night. "I wish I never came," she said suddenly. "I feel terribly lonely."

"Sssh! Tut tut!" chided the old nun; she had begun to eat more chocolates, and did not want to talk.

"It's all right for you," complained the novice. "You're going to meet your aunt. I'll know nobody in Lisieux. And if I find out there that I have no vocation, what'll I do?"

"Now, now, now," grumbled the old woman, "you know you'll get peace and calm in Leesoo. The saint will reveal your heart to you. You'll quieten down. You'll know that all these scruples of yours mean nothing at all. Sure, we all had them!" In spite of herself she became impatient. Her soothing voice gradually took on an edge. "And anyway, goodness knows, you were eager enough to come! And let me tell you it isn't every Reverend Mother would let you. And it's not a holiday you're on, Miss. It's thinking of the holy saint you should be, and not of gillygooseys in Dublin."

The novice withdrew into herself. She was too tired to pray; from sheer repetition the words were becoming meaningless.

Presently the old nun said, as if she were thinking aloud:

"And even if I have an aunt . . . Ha! . . . I suppose she won't know me."

She stopped again and folded her hands deep into her sleeves.

"Thirty-one years," she mused to the window.

The auto-rail rattled along for several miles. Then, Patrick leaned over and said comfortably:

"A terror for the hot milk at night. She'd drink two pints of it. Sure, 'twas enough to kill a plough-horse."

From that on she kept on letting occasional little gasps of laughter escape her. It was as if somebody tickled her every three minutes. Then, after a protracted giggle out of each side of her mouth, she went off into a beatific sleep and the broad smile never left her face until they stopped abruptly in Lisieux.

As they left the station and emerged on the great square, Teresa cried in delight:

"But it's really a big place!"

Through the rain the little town shone into the station like a prismatic waterfall. She saw a green neon light flitting through the wetness over a hotel door. She saw a vis-à-vis crawling shiningly across the Place, and it made the town seem both cosy and intimate, and at the same time enormous and important. But Patrick had flown into a hurry and scurry, fumbling with her umbrella, and clutching her bags, and gazing all around her in a new rush of timidity; the two, in this conflict of absorption, nearly lost one another in the crush. The novice said:

"Oh, Sister Patrick! Couldn't we have one cup of tea in a restaurant before we go to the Hostel?"

"Wh-a-t?" cried Patrick, hunching up her shoulders, and laying her hand on her guimpe like a stage French-woman. "Mon Pethite, que dites vous? Du thé? Vous savez bien . . . Vous savez bien que nous . . . Il faut . . . Il faut . . ." She groaned furiously. "I can't talk French. I told Mother Mary Mell . . . Are you talking about tea? Do you realize, Miss, that you're on a pilgrimage? Gosther-ing in the middle of the street! Hurry! Hurry!"

They did hurry, under their two black umbrellas, like two ants with top-heavy loads. Suddenly Teresa stopped and sneezed resolutely; once . . . twice . . . four times. Patrick towered over her. She started to gibber at her like a baboon.

"You're after getting a cold on me! That's yourself, and your window, and your fine officer!" Teresa sneezed a fifth time. "Are you sure," demanded Patrick, "that you have the double petticoat?"

The novice's big eyes were directed miserably into a confectioner's window. It was bright with the brightest cakes.

"Dear Sister Patrick!" she wheedled. "Don't you think we could have one small, tiny little cup of tea?"

The nun opened her mouth to say "No," looked at the window, looked at Teresa, and after a struggle said:

"Well! Since you have a cold coming on you, I'll let you have just one hot cup of coffee. Just one, mind you!"

It was warm in the café. Patrick had an éclair. Over their heads a radio kept weaving waltzes that made the novice sway gently on her chair. Patrick had two éclairs. The novice made her coffee last as long as possible. Patrick had a third éclair. Then, in spite of a fleck of cream on her jaw, Patrick's face was unusually forbidding as she looked up and said:

"Well, Miss, I hope you're feeling better now?"

"Thank you very much, Sister," said Teresa, and rose with an air of firm resignation. "We must go to the Hostel."

A bell rang eight o'clock as they emerged. They wasted ten minutes searching for the Hostel, a bald faced house rising plumb from the pavement. Its brass tipped, reed-woven half-screens were damply inhospitable. Its closed door and iron grille were shining with the rain. The lay-sister who drew the slide of the grille spoke in unintelligible, provincial French, of which they understood only one word, "Impossible!"

"Quoi?" squawked Patrick, clawing the grille, as the slide shot to in her face. "What did that wan say?"

The bell jangled down the hall again. This time the lay-sister was even more emphatic, and therefore even less intelligible, and she became still less intelligible as Patrick hung to the grille and blustered in Franco-English. Teresa firmly pushed her aside, with a calm sanity:

"Vous ne comprenez pas. Tout est bien arrangé. Notre mère a écrit une lettre à votre mère. . . ."

The lay-sister interrupted. She said, "Trop tard." She said, "Huit heures." She said these words several times. She closed the grille with the slowness of a curiosity that commented on the folly of the two foolish virgins who had come too late. Teresa turned to Patrick, and burst into peals of laughter at the look of horror on her face.

"We're too late!" she cried, joyously. "Now we must go to a hotel!"

Patrick rent her.

"You and your tea! You did it deliberately! Wait until we get back to Mother Mary Mell! I'll tell her you're not fit to be a nun! You're a little flitthermouse! You're a gillygoosey! What a pilgrim we have in you! There's your answer for you! You're not fit to be a nun! You're a slip! You're a miss! What're we going to do? What'll my aunt say to me? What'll Mother Mary Mell say to me? What's going to happen to us?"

Teresa began to cry. Patrick at once hushed her tirade, unfurled her umbrella (it was as big as a bookmaker's), dragged up two of the bags and set off, in a mouth-buttoned fury, to find a hotel. The rain was now a downpour. Their bags weighted them down. She halted. She gave the girl a look that was worse than a blow, shoved her into a doorway, and said, "Don't stir from there till I come back." She left the bags in her care, and butted out into the rain.

Men kept approaching the door, and seeing the nun, they would stop dead, and push away. At first this merely frightened her for she did not realize her predicament: but suddenly a cistern flushed noisily behind her and she recognized that she was standing in the doorway of a *cabinet*. Clutching her bags, she fled down the street, down a side street, another side street, and halted panting under a café awning.

The old proprietor came out and looked at her, cocked his head to one side, bowed, considered her, smiled, said that it was a bad night, and wiped his indifference on to the tabletop. Then he gazed around him, looked at her again, shrugged, and went indoors. More men passed her, on their way in or out, always pausing, after the first glance, to smile and bow. Twice she got up to fly, wondered whether Patrick would ever find her, sat again on the damp iron chair. A drunken old man with a beard finally put her to flight by taking off his hat, leaning on the tabletop, and starting a flowery speech. She ran into a gendarme who was accompanying Sister Patrick down the street. Patrick threw her two hands up to the sky preparatory to a tornado of abuse. She was soaked; her guimpe was a rag; her coif hung around her face like lace. Before she could speak, Teresa hurled herself on the old woman's breast and sobbed out all her awful adventures, so that the gendarme and the nun calmed her with difficulty. They took her bag, then, and led her, whimpering, to the little pension-pub that Patrick had chosen for their night's lodging. There Patrick put her into bed, in a cosy little room all to herself, with red stuff curtains and a dusty-looking carpet—it was nearly thread-bare—and with her own two hands Patrick lit a fire, brought an omelette, rolls, and coffee, and tucked her in for the night; and all the time Patrick kept begging her pardon for that outburst at the Hostel. What with the comfort, the kindness, and the vestigial excitement, the little novice was melted to tears of happiness.

"Our pilgrimage is beginning," she whispered happily to Patrick. "Isn't it, dear Sister Patrick?"

" 'Twill begin in the morning," temporized Patrick. "And then the saint will smoothen everything out."

Right cheek touched right cheek, and left cheek touched left cheek, in the way of all nuns kissing. Old fingers laid out her glossy black hair on the pillow. The light went out. A rough palm smoothed her forehead. The door clicked. The flames flickered on the ceiling.

In Kent, at Saint Anthony's, the only sound around the convent at night had been the crackle of twigs in the damp wood, the hoo-hoo of an owl. Here she heard footsteps in the street below, an occasional motor-car swishing over the cobbles, the soft, whispering downfall of April rain. Looking up at the wavering ceiling, she attended to those sounds, whose tumult, and whose unfamiliarity, and whose suggestiveness made England and her convent, Dublin and her home, utterly remote—less part of another country than part of another life. More than anything else they said, "The pilgrimage has begun!" They said, "O dear Saint Thérèse, I will leave all things in thy hands." They said, "O most omnipotent God, I yield all the world to Thee."

"I want to be a saint!" she cried out, and beat the coverlet with her palm. And at that she fell asleep, curled up in bed as softly as a cat.

III

Only the hens were awake as they walked to first Mass at Saint Pierre. The sun was glittering in the water between the cobblestones. Teresa felt that she alone possessed the town. She felt that all things converged on the forthcoming visit to the shrine. Even the warm prophecy of the steam rising from the streets and the cloudless whiteness of the sky seemed not something general to everybody in the world, but particular to her life alone. She whispered to Patrick, "Thérèse is calling! I hear her!" Patrick nodded, too excited to speak.

After breakfast they began the ritual of Lisieux. Les Buisonnets, the Martin home (Saint Thérèse Martin), was exactly as they had foreseen it, just like all the photos and descriptions in biographies of the saint. They saw the "trim lawn in front of the house," and "the useful kitchen-garden at the back." From the attic windows there was the expected "distant view over the plain." Teresa said to Patrick, with a sigh of happiness:

"It was all made for her. If I had lived here, I, too, would have been a saint!"

Patrick nodded in agreement with the general proposition. For the novice to say that she could have been a saint was merely a way of saying that God had chosen one and could as easily have chosen another.

" 'Tis Heaven!" she murmured, and clasped Teresa's hand.

It was the same in the sacristy of the Carmelite convent, where the saint's hair lies strewn under glass in its reliquary, and the walls are covered by mementoes of those who have paid honor to her memory—decorations, orders, swords, letters from all over the world. Here, where Patrick became almost incoherent at the prospect of meeting her aunt, thirty-one years after, now a Reverend Mother in the Carmelites, Teresa filled with sadness.

"The folly of the world!" she murmured, sighing again and again. "They honor her now. They did not know the sorrow of her heart while she was alive."

The two touched cheek to cheek again.

A Carmelite lay-sister next led them to the grave of the saint. From that they would go on to the convent proper to meet Patrick's aunt. They began to palpitate in mutual sympathy. The grave calmed them by its simplicity.

When they rose, the aunt stood beside them. Patrick toddled to her with cries of joy. The aged woman, her head a mere skull, her hands bony and ridged, gave no sign of recognition other than to say, "God bless you, my child." Old Patrick drew back like a frightened child. Timidly she introduced the novice. She explained falteringly why they had come.

"She's not sure if she wants to be a nun, Mother."

The Carmelite looked at the novice. She, too, at once drew back. But the Carmelite smiled to hear the English name, Teresa, and took her hand gently and led her (Patrick following) across the garden to the convent anteroom. On the way she talked of simple things like the budding shrubs and the blessing of the rain. They sat in the ante-room and the Carmelite rang a bell.

They talked of the price of vegetables, until a faint passage of light in one wall drew their eyes to the grille— the last portal of the inner Carmelite hermitage. Behind the grille was a gauze, and presently Teresa's eyes made out, behind the gauze, a still face from which the gauze had eroded all recognizable character. All she could see was the vaguest outline of a countenance. As if she realized in that second how the discipline of the Order must have likewise eroded from the little girl of Les Buissonets all human emotion, and in a flash of understanding knew what sacrifice really means, she flung herself at the Carmelite's knees and cried out hysterically:

"Ma mère! I have no vocation!"

Patrick intervened hurriedly:

"Pay no heed to her. She's upset and sick in herself. The child doesn't know what she wants."

The aged Carmelite waved her aside and lifted the novice to her feet. Looking into her face with a clear eye, she said, after a frightening silence:

"Could you be a Carmelite?"

"No!" panted the novice, and she drew back, as if she were at that moment about to be imprisoned behind the grille.

"If you cannot be a Carmelite, my child, you can be nothing."

"She'd be happy enough," intervened Patrick comfortably, "in an easier Order."

"She will be happy—we will all be happy—only in Heaven," said the Carmelite coldly. "Could you not even try to be a Carmelite?" asked the aged woman.

"No!" begged the novice. "I couldn't do it!"

"Why not?"

"To be always shut in?" trembled the girl.

"It is an enclosed Order," agreed the Superioress calmly.

"I couldn't stand it!"

"How do you know?" catechized the Superioress.

For answer the girl burst into such a sobbing wail that Patrick drew her to her broad bosom and turned on her aunt.

"Ye have no heart!" she upbraided. "Badgering the poor child! 'Tisn't that we expected from you! Don't heed her," she comforted Teresa. "My poor little girsha! Don't mind her. Sure we can't all be saints. You'll do your best. You can't do more."

"But," sobbed Teresa, "I want to be a saint. 'Tis to . . . to . . . to be a saint I joined the nuns." Her voice came out through her nose, miserably. "If I can't be a saint, I don't *want* to be a nun!"

The old woman comforted her, and finally restored her to a whimpering silence. Looking up, they saw they were alone. The grille was closed. The veil was hidden. The Superioress had gone.

The two pilgrims went back to their pension. That afternoon, without discussion, they went on to Saint Malo. There the novice was expected to find bodily rest, as at Lisieux she had been expected to find calm of soul.

IV

Saint Malo faces across a wide estuary the modern watering-place of Dinard. At night they saw the lights in the hotels, and cafés, and more colored lights beaded all around the roof of the casino; and sometimes they heard music across the still surface of water. Steamers from

Southampton and the Channel Islands floated in the bay at anchor. Patrick was charmed with her room in the convent where they stayed. It looked directly across at Dinard. She wrote to Mother Mary Mell that she had a "grandstand," and that she was thinking of going across in a rowboat some night to gamble in the Casino and make the fortune of the Order. Becoming serious in a postcript, she said that Teresa had not yet made up her mind, but that she was "behaving with the most edifying devotion."

Not only did the novice attend every service in the convent, but she had become pious beyond description, daily spending long hours alone in adoration in the chapel. But when Patrick noticed that she left her lunch untouched on her table on the third day of her arrival, and went up to the novice's cell to ask if this were wise, she made a frightening discovery. She found that the mattress and bedclothes had been rolled up and put away under the bed, and all the girl's flannel underclothing was hanging in her cupboard. At once she went down to the chapel, and hissed at the solitary worshipper to come out, beckoning madly with her bony finger.

"Sister Teresa," she said severely, "you are refusing your food. Is there any reason for this?"

The novice hung her head and said nothing.

"Answer me, Sister."

Still the novice kept her eyes on the parquet.

"I command you, Sister, to answer me."

"There is no reason," whispered the novice.

"Then eat up your food in future," ordered the nun. "Do you want to make a skeleton out of yourself?" And she added more easily, "Don't you know right well I'm supposed to bring you home as plump as a duck?"

The novice raised two large, sad eyes.

"Sister Patrick," she begged, "I will obey if you command me. But I want to do penance for my sins, and for the sins of the world. I feel I have received a higher command."

"What higher command?" blustered the old woman, taken aback. "What on earth are you talking about, Sister?"

Teresa sighed.

"The sins of the world are all about us," she smiled sadly. "I see them every night from my window, across the water, in the dens and gambling-houses. All lit up like the fires of Hell to lure poor souls astray. I dreamed the first night I came here that the Devil lives over there. I saw his red eyes in the air. I saw that this convent was put here specially to atone for the wickedness that surrounds it."

"Holy Mother!" cried the nun. "What are you talking about, girl? Sister Teresa, let me tell you that if you ate a proper supper . . . And by the same token, Miss, no wonder you have dreams if you sleep on the laths of the bed. Do you," she threatened, "sleep on the laths of the bed?"

The novice once more hung her head, and once more she had to be bullied into replying.

"I do, Sister," she confessed unhappily.

"Well, then, let there be an end of it! What right have you to be going on with these andrewmartins off of your own bat? You know right well you must ask permission of your superior before you do the like. And that reminds me," she cried, grabbing the girl's flank, and then standing back from her in horror, with her gummy mouth open. "You haven't a stitch on you! Go upstairs at once, Miss, and dress yourself properly. I'll be after you in two minutes. I'm worn out and tormented with your vagaries! Ten times I told Mother Mary Mell . . ."

She pointed upstairs—a figure of Justice.

The novice went, tearful, head-hanging. In two minutes the old nun followed. She opened the door of the cell. The girl lay on the ground, her arms stretched out like a crucifix, her dilated eyes fixed as on a vision over her head. The old nun entered the room, closed the door, and thundered:

"Get up out o' that!"

The novice did not move.

"Miss!" said the old woman, pale as a sheet, "how dare you disobey me!"

The novice trembled as if a wind had ruffled her spirit. With her heart battering inside in her, Patrick walked over and looked down. The big brown eyes, so strikingly dark in that pale pink-and-white face, stared up past her. Patrick looked up at the electric light bulb. She looked all about her. The thick-moted afternoon sun slanted in across the bed. A hissing suspiration below the window was followed by the little groan of the gravel dragging back under the wave. Then she saw a slimy brown insect, with wavering head, creep to the white ear of the novice, and she screamed:

"An earwig! Climbing into your ear!"

Teresa sat up as if she was stung. The fright passed. The two looked at each other with hate in their eyes. At the door, Patrick said:

"I'll wait in the garden."

In complete silence they walked four miles that afternoon. They did the same the following morning. That was their last full day. On the final afternoon Patrick spoke:

"We will be in Saint Anthony's to-morrow night. Do you know, yet, my dear, if you have a vocation?"

"I have decided to join the Carmelites," said the novice.

They halted. They looked across the sea-wall into the blue of Dinard. A few lights were already springing up over there—the first dots in the long, golden necklet that already they had come to know so well. A lone sea-gull squawked over the glassy water. The sunset behind the blue pinnacles of the resort was russet.

"And what's wrong with our own Order, Sister dear?" asked Patrick of the vacancy before her.

"I feel, dear Sister Patrick," judged the novice, staring ahead of her, "that it is too worldly."

"How is it too worldly?" asked Patrick in a whisper.

"Well, dear Sister Patrick," pronounced the novice, "I see, for example, that you all eat too much."

The little wavelets fell almost inaudibly, drunken with the fullness of the tide, exhausted and soothed by their own completion.

"I shall tell Mother Mary Mell that you think so," whispered the old nun.

"There is no need, dear Sister. It will be my duty to tell her myself. I will pray for you all when I am in the Carmelites. I love you all. You are all kind and generous. But, dear Sister, I feel that very few nuns really have the right vocation to be nuns." Patrick closed her eyes tightly. The novice continued: "I will surrender myself to the divine Love. The death I desire is the death of Love. The death of the Cross."

They heard only the baby tongues of the waves. The evening star blazed in the russet sky. The old nun saw it, and she said, in part a statement, in part a prayer, in part a retort:

"Sweet Star of the Sea!"

Teresa raised her dark eyes to the star and she intoned in her girlish voice the poem of Saint Thérèse:

> "Come, Mother, once again,
> Who camest first to chide.
> Come once again, but then
> To smile—at eventide."

The old nun fiddled with her beads. She drew long breaths through her nose. She tried several times to speak. She gestured that they must go back. They turned and walked slowly back to the convent, side by side; the old nun as restless as if she were in bodily agony, the novice as sedate and calm as a statue. After a while Patrick fumbled in her pocket, and found a chocolate, and popped it into her mouth. Then she stopped chewing, and threw an eye at her companion. At the look of intense sorrow in the face beside her, she hunched up her shoulders and as silently as she could, she gulped the fragments whole.

On the journey homeward they did not speak one

word to each other: all the way to Rouen in the trotting auto-rail; in the clanking train to Dieppe; on the boat; in the English train. In silence they arrived at Saint Anthony's, among the dank beechwoods, now softly dripping, in time to hear the first hoo-hoo of the owl, and to troop in with the rest of the community for evening chapel. Mother Mary Mell barely had time to ask the old nun how she had enjoyed her holiday—that first holiday in thirty-one years. Patrick's eyes fluttered. She recalled the lights of Dinard.

"It was lovely, Mother!"

Mary Mell caught the flicker of hesitation. Just as they crossed the tessellated threshold of the chapel, she whispered quickly, "And Teresa?"

Patrick who had been waiting for that question ever since the final afternoon in Saint Malo, and yet had no answer ready, took refuge behind the chapel's interdiction of silence. She smiled reassuringly, nodded, smiled, nodded again, and then, very solemn and pious, she walked in with her head down. She said her prayers badly. She slept hardly at all that night. She heard every crackling branch and fluttering night-bird. For what, in the name of the Most High, was she to say to Mary Mell? And what was she to say to the community in the morning? As she tossed and tumbled, she thought of Teresa sleeping peacefully in her cell, and the old woman burst into tears of rage.

In the morning there was no Teresa. She had left the convent, through a ground-floor window, before anybody was awake, and gone on the milk-train to London. She had walked across the city at that hour when the sun emphasizes the position of the East End, and the sleepers in the Parks that she traversed are unwrapping their newspaper-blankets. A sister-in-law coming out to collect the morning post found a nun sitting on the doorstep. She had breakfast, in a tennis-frock, along with the family.

She saw the convent only once again—about two years later when she brought her husband to see it. As they got out of the train she looked up into the familiar beeches at the steam of the engine caught in the branches, and she remembered how every train used to make the woods seem infinitely lonely and the convent darker and more melancholy, because that white steam suggested people travelling, and the luxury of the world she had renounced. Her George, who was a Protestant, and who was much excited by this expedition, nodded solemnly, and began to get an uncomfortable feeling that he was married to a nun. They were entertained politely. Old Sister Patrick did not appear. As they left, the starting train again sent its gushes of steam into the branches, and now those branches again seemed to Teresa to clutch not only at the white smoke but at her own heart. She felt that the woods enclosed a refuge from the world of which she had, irrevocably, become a part. As she snuggled down into her fur collar she gazed out of her big eyes at her husband, and said, with a shake of her little head:

"Ah George! George! You will never know what I gave up to marry you!"

He smiled adoringly at her as, in obedience to a gesture, he leaned over to put a cigarette between her rouged lips.

"My precious Teresa," he murmured softly, and patted her knee.

She shook her head at him again, with a pitying smile.

"Has it upset you, my sweet?" he asked dismally.

Saying never a word, she kept gazing at him fixedly, as if he were a stranger. He huffed, and hawed, and hedged himself behind his newspaper, looking as despondent as he considered proper. For as he explained to his colleagues in the morning, his wife was "a very spiritual woman" and on occasions like this she always made him feel that he had the soul of a hog.

SEAN O'FAOLAIN

Persecution

Mania

✳

There are two types of Irishman I can't stand. The first is always trying to behave the way he thinks the English behave. The second is always trying to behave the way he thinks the Irish behave. That sort is a roaring bore. Ike Dignam is like that. He believes that the Irish are witty, so he is for ever making laborious jokes. He has a notion that the Irish have a gift for fantasy, so he is constantly talking fey. He also has a notion that the Irish have a magnificent gift for malice, mixed up with another idea of the Irish as great realists, so he loves to abuse everybody for not having more common sense. But as he also believes that the Irish are the most kind and charitable people in the world he ends up every tirade with an "Ah, sure, God help us, maybe the poor fellow is good at heart." The result is that you do not know, from one moment to the next, whom you are talking to—Ike the fey, or Ike the realist, Ike the malicious, or Ike the kind.

I am sure he has no clear idea of himself. He is a polit-

From *The Bell*.

ical journalist. I have seen him tear the vitals out of a man, and then, over a pint, say, with a shocked guffaw,

"I'm after doin' a terrible thing. Do you know what I said in my column this morning about Harry Lombard? I said, 'There is no subject under the sun on which the eloquence does not pour from his lips with all the thin fluidity of asses' milk.' Honest to God, we're a terrible race. Of course, the man will never talk to me again."

All as if Right Hand had no responsibility for Left Hand. But the exasperating thing is that his victims do talk to him again, and in the most friendly way, though why they do it I do not know considering some of the things he says and writes about them. He is the man who said of a certain woman who is in the habit of writing letters to the press in defence of the Department of Roads and Railways: "Ah, sure, she wrote that with the Minister's tongue in her cheek." Yet the Minister for Roads and Railways is one of his best friends, and he says, "Ike Dignam? Ah, sure! He's all right. The poor divil is good at heart." And the cursed thing is that Ike *is* good at heart. I have long since given up trying to understand what this means. Something vaguely connected with hope and consolation and the endless mercy of God?

Ike naturally has as many enemies as friends, and this is something that *he* cannot understand. Somebody may say,

"But you're forgetting, Ike, what you said about him last year. You said every time he sings *Galway Bay* he turns it into a street puddle."

Ike will laugh delightedly.

"That was only a bit o' fun. Who'd mind that?"

"How would you like to have things like that said about yourself?"

He will reply, valiantly,

"I wouldn't mind one bit. Not one bit in the world. I'd know 'twas all part of the game. I'd know the poor fellow was really good at heart."

A few weeks ago he got a taste of his own medicine.

He committed the folly of granting to his rivals the ancient wish of all rivals, "That mine enemy would write a book." The subject of his book—it was a pamphlet rather than a book—was *The Irish Horse in Irish History*, and it was savagely disembowelled in an anonymous review in one of the popular weeklies. The sentence that wounded him, as it was intended to do, said: "Mr. Dignam's knowledge of hunters is weak, of hacks most profound."

That very afternoon I met him in Mooney's on the quay. He was staring into the boghole deeps of a pint of porter. Seeing me he turned such a morose eye on me that I could tell he had been badly hit.

"You saw what the *Sun* said about my book?" he asked, and when I nodded: "That's a low paper. A low rag. A vicious-minded rag. That's what it is. Full of venom and hate and lust for power. And," he added, slapping the counter, "destruction!"

"Somebody getting his own back, I suppose?"

"What did I ever do to anybody? Only a bit of give and take. What's done every day of the week in journalism. Surely to Gawd nobody takes me as seriously as all that!"

"Well, that's more or less all your reviewer did with your book."

Again the indignant palm slapped the mahogany.

"That's exactly what I dislike about that review. The mean implication. The dirty innuendo. Why couldn't he come out and say it in the open like a man? It's the anonymity of the thing that's so despicable." Here he fixed me with a cunning eye. "Who do ye think wrote it?"

I spread my hands.

"I think," he said sourly, "that it was Mulvaney wrote it. I made a hare of him one time in my column. But I'm not sure. That's the curse of it. He hasn't enough brains to write it." He gazed at me for a moment through his eyelashes. "You didn't write it yourself, by any chance?"

I laughed and told him I hadn't read his book. I'd bought it, of course (which I had not), and had every intention of reading it (which was also untrue).

"Or could it be that drunk Cassidy," he said. "That fellow has it in for me ever since I said that he spoke in the Dail with the greatest sobriety." He laughed feebly. "Everyone knew what I meant. Do you think it might be Cassidy?"

"Ikey, it might be a dozen people."

"It could be anybody," he snarled. "Anybody! Damn it all if I ever say a thing I say it straight out from the shoulder. Why can't they come into the open?" He leaned nearer and dropped to a whisper. "I was thinking it might be that redheaded bastard from the All Souls Club. That fellow thinks I'm anti-clerical. And," he guffawed, "I'm not! That's the joke of it, I'm not!"

"What in the name of all that's holy," I asked crossly, "has anti-clericalism got to do with horses?"

He scratched his head fiercely and moaned and shook it.

"Ye never know. The people in this country have as much sense when it comes to religion . . . Tell me, did ye ever hear of a thing called Discovery of Documents?"

It was only then I fully realized how badly he had been hit.

"You're not being such an idiot as to be thinking of taking this thing to law?"

"Look't! I don't give one tinker's curse about what anybody says against me, but the one thing I *must* know is who wrote it! If I don't find out who wrote it I'll be suspecting my best friends for the rest of my born days."

"Well," I said, finishing my drink and leaving him, "happy hunting to you."

A couple of days later I saw him cruising towards me along O'Connell Street glowing like a sunrise.

"I'm on the track of that," he shouted at me from fifteen yards off. "I'm off on the right scent," he babbled, and I had time to remember what he was talking about while he explained how he had worked up a friendship with a girl in the office of the *Sun*. " 'Tis none of the people I suspected at all. Do you know who I think wrote it now?"

"God knows, maybe you wrote it yourself."

He shook with laughter.

" 'Twould be great publicity if I could say I did." Then he glowered. "They're entirely capable of saying I did. If they thought anybody would believe 'em. No!" he gripped my arm. " 'Twas a woman did it. I should have guessed it from the word Go."

"Who is she?"

"I don't know," he said, sadly.

"Then why did you say . . . ?"

"I had a dhream about it. Didn't I see the long, lean, bony hand holding the pen, coming out like a snake from behind a red curtain! Didn't I see the gold bangle on the wrist and all?"

"Did you pull the curtain to see who it was?"

"I pulled and I pulled," Ike assured me enthusiastically. "Dear Gawd, I was all the night pullin'!"

"And," I suggested bitterly, "I suppose the curtain was made of iron? You know, Ikey, you'll go crackers if you go on like this."

With his two hands he dragged his hat down on his head as if he wanted to extinguish himself.

"I will," he cried, so loudly that passers-by turned to look at the pair of us. "I'll go stark, staring, roaring mad if I don't find out who wrote that dirty thing about me."

"Look," I pleaded, "what does it all matter? The whole thing is gone completely out of everybody's head but your own. It's all over and done with. And even supposing you did find out who wrote it, what could you do then?"

He folded his arms and gazed down O'Connell Street like Napoleon looking over the Atlantic from Saint Helena.

"I'd write a Limerick on him. I'd *shrivel* him. I wouldn't leave a peck on his bones. As a matter of fact," cocking an eye on me, "I've done it already. I wrote ten Limericks the other night on ten different people who might have written that review. I'm thinking of publishing the whole lot of 'em, and if the cap fits they can share it and wear it."

And before I could stop him he recited to the sky four blistering quatrains on *Irish Bards and Botch Reviewers*. I took his arm:—

"Ikey, that'll be ten enemies you'll make instead of one! Come in here, Ikey, and let me talk to you like a father."

We went across to Mooney's and I talked for half an hour. I told him we had all been through this sort of thing. I told him that no man who cannot grow an epidermis against malice should try to live in small countries like ours. I said that all that matters is a man's work. I assured him, Heaven forgive me, that he had written a masterly record of *The Irish Horse in Irish History* and that that was the main thing. I developed this soundly into the theory that everything is grist to the mill, and that instead of worrying about this silly review he should go home and write a comic piece about it for *Dublin Opinion*, which, indeed, he could do very well. I built him up as Dignam *solus contra mundum*. He agreed to every word of it. We parted cordially. He was in the happiest temper.

Three days later he came striding towards me, beaming. From afar he hailed my passing ship, roaring like a bosun:—

"I found out that bastard! Mulvaney! A friend of mine charged him with it and he didn't deny it."

"Good. You're satisfied now."

"I am. I don't give a damn about it now. Sure that fellow's brains are all in his behind. Who'd mind anything he'd say?"

"The whole thing is of no importance."

"None what-so-ever."

"Splendid. It's all over now."

"Finished. And done with."

"Grand."

"I sent him a hell of a postcard."

"No!"

"I did," he chortled, "I did. All I wrote on it was what I said to yourself:—'Your Second Front is your Behind.' An open postcard. It was a terrible thing to do," he beamed. "Oh, shocking!" His laughter gusted.

"And you put your name to that?"

"I did not. What a fool I'd be! That'll keep him guessing for a while. 'Twill do him no harm in the world. He's not a bad poor gom. Ah! Sure! The poor divil is good at heart."

Off he went, striding along, as happy as a child. I went into Mooney's. There at the counter was Mulvaney, sucking his empty pipe, staring in front of him, his bushy eyebrows as black as night. I wheeled quickly but he caught the movement and called me. His hand strayed to his breast pocket.

"I'm after receiving a very myst-e-e-rious communication," he said sombrely.

I did not hear what else he said. I realized that you could do nothing with these people. I realized that the only sensible thing to do was to write a satire on the whole lot of them. I began to wonder could I get any editor anywhere to publish it anonymously.

LIAM O'FLAHERTY

The Hawk

❋

He breasted the summit of the cliff and then rose in wide circles to the clouds. When their undertendrils passed about his outstretched wings, he surged straight inland. Gliding and dipping his wings at intervals, he roamed across the roof of the firmament, with his golden hawk's eyes turned down, in search of prey, toward the bright earth that lay far away below, beyond the shimmering emptiness of the vast blue sky.

Once the sunlight flashed on his gray back, as he crossed an open space between two clouds. Then again he became a vague, swift shadow, rushing through the formless vapor. Suddenly his fierce heart throbbed, as he saw a lark, whose dewy back was jeweled by the radiance of the morning light, come rising toward him from a green meadow. He shot forward at full speed, until he was directly over his mounting prey. Then he began to circle slowly, with his wings stiff and his round eyes dilated, as if

From The Stories of Liam O'Flaherty, New York, Devin-Adair.

in fright. Slight tremors passed along his skin, beneath the compact armor of his plumage—like a hunting dog that stands poised and quivering before his game.

The lark rose awkwardly at first, uttering disjointed notes as he leaped and circled to gain height. Then he broke into full-throated song and soared straight upward, drawn to heaven by the power of his glorious voice, and fluttering his wings like a butterfly.

The hawk waited until the songbird had almost reached the limit of his climb. Then he took aim and stooped. With his wings half-closed, he raked like a meteor from the clouds. The lark's warbling changed to a shriek of terror as he heard the fierce rush of the charging hawk. Then he swerved aside, just in time to avoid the full force of the blow. Half-stunned, he folded his wings and plunged headlong toward the earth, leaving behind a flutter of feathers that had been torn from his tail by the claws of his enemy.

When he missed his mark, the hawk at once opened wide his wings and canted them to stay his rush. He circled once more above his falling prey, took aim, and stooped again. This time the lark did nothing to avoid the kill. He died the instant he was struck; his inert wings unfolded. With his head dangling from his limp throat, through which his lovely song had just been poured, he came tumbling down, convoyed by the closely circling hawk. He struck earth on a patch of soft brown sand, beside a shining stream.

The hawk stood for a few moments over his kill, with his lewd purple tongue lolling from his open beak and his black-barred breast heaving from the effort of pursuit. Then he secured the carcass in his claws, took wing, and flew off to the cliff where his mate was hatching on a broad ledge, beneath a massive tawny-gold rock that rose, over-arching, to the summit.

It was a lordly place, at the apex of a narrow cove, and so high above the sea that the roar of the breaking waves reached there only as a gentle murmur. There was no other sound within the semicircle of towering limestone walls that rose sheer from the dark water. Two months before, a vast crowd of other birds had lived on the lower edges of the cliffs, making the cove merry with their cries as they flew out to sea and back again with fish. Then one morning the two young hawks came there from the east to mate.

For hours the rockbirds watched them in terror, as the interlopers courted in the air above the cove, stooping past each other from the clouds down to the sea's edge, and then circling up again, wing to wing, winding their garland of love. At noon they saw the female draw the male into a cave, and heard his mating screech as he treaded her. Then they knew the birds of death had come to nest in their cove. So they took flight. That afternoon the mated hawks gamboled in the solitude that was now their domain, and at sundown the triumphant male brought his mate to nest on this lofty ledge, from which a pair of ravens had fled.

Now, as he dropped the dead lark beside her on the ledge, she lay there in a swoon of motherhood. Her beak rested on one of the sticks that formed her rude bed, and she looked down at the distant sea through half-closed eyes. Uttering cries of tenderness, he trailed his wings and marched around the nest on his bandy legs, pushing against her sides, caressing her back with his throat, and gently pecking at her crest. He had circled her four times, before she awoke from her stupor. Then she raised her head suddenly, opened her beak, and screamed. He screamed in answer and leaped upon the carcass of the lark. Quickly he severed its head, plucked its feathers, and offered her the naked, warm meat. She opened her mouth wide, swallowed the huge morsel in one movement, and again rested her beak on the stick. Her limp body spread out once more around the pregnant eggs, as she relapsed into her swoon.

His brute soul was exalted by the consciousness that

he had achieved the fullness of the purpose for which nature had endowed him. Like a hound stretched out in sleep before a blazing fire, dreaming of the day's long chase, he relived the epic of his mating passion, while he strutted back and forth among the disgorged pellets and the bloody remains of eaten prey with which the rock was strewn.

Once he went to the brink of the ledge, flapped his wings against his breast, and screamed in triumph, as he looked out over the majestic domain that he had conquered with his mate. Then again he continued to march, rolling from side to side in ecstasy, as he recalled his moments of tender possession and the beautiful eggs that were warm among the sticks.

His exaltation was suddenly broken by a sound that reached him from the summit of the cliff. He stood motionless, close to the brink, and listened with his head turned to one side. Hearing the sound again from the summit, the same tremor passed through the skin within his plumage, as when he had soared, poised, above the mounting lark. His heart also throbbed as it had done then, but not with the fierce desire to exercise his power. He knew that he had heard the sound of human voices, and he felt afraid.

He dropped from the ledge and flew, close to the face of the cliff, for a long distance toward the west. Then he circled outward, swiftly, and rose to survey the intruders. He saw them from on high. There were three humans near the brink of the cliff, a short way east of the nest. They had secured the end of a stout rope to a block of limestone. The tallest of them had tied the other end to his body, and then attached a small brown sack to his waist belt.

When the hawk saw the tall man being lowered down along the face of the cliff to a protruding ledge that was on a level with the nest, his fear increased. He knew that the men had come to steal his mate's eggs; yet he felt helpless in the presence of the one enemy that he feared by instinct. He spiraled still higher and continued to watch in agony.

The tall man reached the ledge and walked carefully

to its western limit. There he signaled to his comrades, who hauled up the slack of his rope. Then he braced himself, kicked the brink of the ledge, and swung out toward the west, along the blunt face of the cliff, using the taut rope as a lever. He landed on the eastern end of the ledge where the hawk's mate was sitting on her nest, on the far side of a bluff. His comrades again slackened the rope, in answer to his signal, and he began to move westward, inch by inch, crouched against the rock.

The hawk's fear vanished as he saw his enemy relentlessly move closer to the bluff. He folded his wings and dove headlong down to warn his mate. He flattened out when he came level with the ledge and screamed as he flew past her. She took no notice of the warning. He flew back and forth several times, screaming in agony, before she raised her head and answered him. Exalted by her voice, he circled far out to sea and began to climb.

Once more he rose until the undertendrils of the clouds passed about his outstretched wings and the fierce cold of the upper firmament touched his heart. Then he fixed his golden eyes on his enemy and hovered to take aim. At this moment of supreme truth, as he stood poised, it was neither pride in his power nor the intoxication of the lust to kill that stiffened his wings and the muscles of his breast. He was drawn to battle by the wild, sad tenderness aroused in him by his mate's screech.

He folded his wings and stooped. Down he came, relentlessly, straight at the awe-inspiring man that he no longer feared. The two men on the cliff top shouted a warning when they saw him come. The tall man on the ledge raised his eyes. Then he braced himself against the cliff to receive the charge. For a moment, it was the eyes of the man that showed fear, as they looked into the golden eyes of the descending hawk. Then he threw up his arms, to protect his face, just as the hawk struck. The body of the doomed bird glanced off the thick cloth that covered the man's right arm and struck the cliff with a dull thud. It rebounded and went tumbling down.

When the man came creeping round the bluff, the mother hawk stood up in the nest and began to scream. She leaped at him and tried to claw his face. He quickly caught her, pinioned her wings, and put her in his little sack. Then he took the eggs.

Far away below the body of the dead hawk floated, its broken wings outstretched on the foam-embroidered surface of the dark water, and drifted seaward with the ebbing tide.

LIAM O'FLAHERTY

The Tent

❄

A sudden squall struck the tent. White glittering hailstones struck the shabby canvas with a wild noise. The tent shook and swayed slightly forward, dangling its tattered flaps. The pole creaked as it strained. A rent appeared near the top of the pole like a silver seam in the canvas. Water immediately trickled through the seam, making a dark blob.

A tinker and his two wives were sitting on a heap of straw in the tent, looking out through the entrance at the wild moor that stretched in front of it, with a snowcapped mountain peak rising like the tip of a cone over the ridge of the moor about two miles away. The three of them were smoking cigarettes in silence. It was evening, and they had pitched their tent for the night in a gravel pit on the side of the mountain road, crossing from one glen to another. Their donkey was tethered to the cart beside the tent.

When the squall came the tinker sat up with a start and looked at the pole. He stared at the seam in the canvas

From THE STORIES OF LIAM O'FLAHERTY, New York, Devin-Adair.

for several moments and then he nudged the two women and pointed upwards with a jerk of his nose. The women looked but nobody spoke. After a minute or so the tinker sighed and struggled to his feet.

"I'll throw a few sacks over the top," he said.

He picked up two brown sacks from the heap of blankets and clothes that were drying beside the brazier in the entrance and went out. The women never spoke, but kept on smoking.

The tinker kicked the donkey out of his way. The beast had stuck his hind quarters into the entrance of the tent as far as possible, in order to get the heat from the wood burning in the brazier. The donkey shrank away sideways still chewing a wisp of the hay which the tinker had stolen from a haggard the other side of the mountain. The tinker scrambled up the bank against which the tent was pitched. The bank was covered with rank grass into which yesterday's snow had melted in muddy cakes.

The top of the tent was only about eighteen inches above the bank. Beyond the bank there was a narrow rough road, with a thick copse of pine trees on the far side, within the wired fence of a demesne, but the force of the squall was so great that it swept through the trees and struck the top of the tent as violently as if it were standing exposed on the open moor. The tinker had to lean against the wind to prevent himself being carried away. He looked into the wind with wide-open nostrils.

"It can't last," he said, throwing the two sacks over the tent, where there was a rent in the canvas. He then took a big needle from his jacket and put a few stitches in them.

He was about to jump down from the bank when somebody hailed him from the road. He looked up and saw a man approaching, with his head thrust forward against the wind. The tinker scowled and shrugged his shoulders. He waited until the man came up to him.

The stranger was a tall, sturdily built man, with a long face and firm jaws and great sombre dark eyes, a fighter's face. When he reached the tinker he stood erect with his feet together and his hands by his sides like a soldier. He was fairly well dressed, his face was clean and well shaved, and his hands were clean. There was a blue figure of something or other tattooed on the back of his right hand. He looked at the tinker frankly with his sombre dark eyes. Neither spoke for several moments.

"Good evening," the stranger said.

The tinker nodded without speaking. He was looking the stranger up and down, as if he were slightly afraid of this big, sturdy man, who was almost like a policeman or a soldier or somebody in authority. He looked at the man's boots especially. In spite of the muck of the roads, the melted snow and the hailstones, they were still fairly clean, and looked as if they were constantly polished.

"Travellin'?" he said at length.

"Eh," said the stranger, almost aggressively. "Oh! Yes, I'm lookin' for somewhere to shelter for the night."

The stranger glanced at the tent slowly and then looked back to the tinker again.

"Goin' far?" said the tinker.

"Don't know," said the stranger angrily. Then he almost shouted: "I have no bloody place to go to . . . only the bloody roads."

"All right, brother," said the tinker, "come on."

He nodded towards the tent and jumped down into the pit. The stranger followed him, stepping carefully down to avoid soiling his clothes.

When he entered the tent after the tinker and saw the women he immediately took off his cap and said: "Good evening." The two women took their cigarettes from their mouths, smiled and nodded their heads.

The stranger looked about him cautiously and then sat down on a box to the side of the door near the brazier. He put his hands to the blaze and rubbed them. Almost immediately a slight steam rose from his clothes. The tinker handed him a cigarette, murmuring: "Smoke?"

The stranger accepted the cigarette, lit it, and then looked at them. None of them were looking at him, so he "sized them up" carefully, looking at each suspiciously with his sombre dark eyes. The tinker was sitting on a box opposite him, leaning languidly backwards from his hips, a slim, tall, graceful man, with a beautiful head poised gracefully on a brown neck, and great black lashes falling down over his half-closed eyes, just like a woman. A womanish-looking fellow, with that sensuous grace in the languid pose of his body which is found only among aristocrats and people who belong to a very small workless class, cut off from the mass of society, yet living at their expense. A young fellow with proud, contemptuous, closed lips and an arrogant expression in his slightly expanded nostrils. A silent fellow, blowing out cigarette smoke through his nostrils and gazing dreamily into the blaze of the wood fire. The two women were just like him in texture, both of them slatterns, dirty and unkempt, but with the same proud, arrogant contemptuous look in their beautiful brown faces. One was dark-haired and black-eyed. She had rather a hard expression in her face and seemed very alert. The other woman was golden-haired, with a very small head and finely-developed jaw, that stuck out level with her forehead. She was surpassingly beautiful, in spite of her ragged clothes and the foul condition of her hair, which was piled on her tiny skull in knotted heaps, uncombed. The perfect symmetry and delicacy of her limbs, her bust and her long throat that had tiny freckles in the white skin, made the stranger feel afraid of her, of her beauty and her presence in the tent.

"Tinkers," he said to himself. "Awful bloody people."

Then he turned to the tinker.

"Got any grub in the place . . . eh . . . mate?" he said brusquely, his thick lips rapping out every word firmly, like one accustomed to command inferiors. He hesitated before he added the word "mate," obviously disinclined to put himself on a level of human intercourse with the tinker.

The tinker nodded and turned to the dark-haired woman.

"Might as well have supper now, Kitty," he said softly.

The dark-haired woman rose immediately, and taking

a blackened can that was full of water, she put it on the brazier. The stranger watched her. Then he addressed the tinker again.

"This is a hell of a way to be, eh?" he said. "Stuck out on a mountain. Thought I'd make Roundwood to-night. How many miles is it from here?"

"Ten," said the tinker.

"Good God!" said the stranger.

Then he laughed, and putting his hand in his breast pocket, he pulled out a half-pint bottle of whiskey.

"This is all I got left," he said, looking at the bottle.

The tinker immediately opened his eyes wide when he saw the bottle. The golden-haired woman sat up and looked at the stranger eagerly, opening her brown eyes wide and rolling her tongue in her cheek. The dark-haired woman, rummaging in a box, also turned around to look. The stranger winked an eye and smiled.

"Always welcome," he said. "Eh? My curse on it, any-way. Anybody got a corkscrew?"

The tinker took a knife from his pocket, pulled out a corkscrew from its side and handed it to the man. The man opened the bottle.

"Here," he said, handing the bottle to the tinker. "Pass it round. I suppose the women'll have a drop."

The tinker took the bottle and whispered to the dark-haired woman. She began to pass him mugs from the box.

"Funny thing," said the stranger, "when a man is broke and hungry, he can get whiskey but he can't get grub. Met a man this morning in Dublin and he knew bloody well I was broke, but instead of asking me to have a meal, or giving me some money, he gave me that. I had it with me all along the road and I never opened it."

He threw the end of his cigarette out the entrance.

"Been drinkin' for three weeks, curse it," he said.

"Are ye belongin' to these parts?" murmured the tin-ker, pouring out the whiskey into the tin mugs.

"What's that?" said the man, again speaking angrily, as if he resented the question. Then he added: "No. Never been here in me life before. Question of goin' into the work-house or takin' to the roads. Got a job in Dublin yesterday. The men downed tools when they found I wasn't a member of the union. Thanks. Here's luck."

"Good health, sir," the women said.

The tinker nodded his head only, as he put his own mug to his lips and tasted it. The stranger drained his at a gulp.

"Ha," he said. "Drink up, girls. It's good stuff."

He winked at them. They smiled and sipped their whiskey.

"My name is Carney," said the stranger to the tinker. "What do they call you?"

"Byrne," said the tinker. "Joe Byrne."

"Hm! Byrne," said Carney. "Wicklow's full o' Byrnes. Tinker, I suppose?"

"Yes," murmured the tinker, blowing a cloud of cigarette smoke through his puckered lips. Carney shrugged his shoulders.

"Might as well," he said. "One thing is as good as another. Look at me. Sergeant-major in the army two months ago. Now I'm tramping the roads. That's boiling."

The dark-haired woman took the can off the fire. The other woman tossed off the remains of her whiskey and got to her feet to help with the meal. Carney shifted his box back farther out of the way and watched the golden-haired woman eagerly. When she moved about her figure was so tall that she had to stoop low in order to avoid the roof of the tent. She must have been six feet in height, and she wore high-heeled shoes which made her look taller.

"There is a woman for ye," thought Carney. "Must be a gentleman's daughter. Lots o' these shots out of a gun in the county Wicklow. Half the population is illegitimate. Awful bloody people, these tinkers. I suppose the two of them belong to this Joe. More like a woman than a man. Suppose he never did a stroke of work in his life."

There was cold rabbit for supper, with tea and bread and butter. It was excellent tea, and it tasted all the sweeter on account of the storm outside which was still raging. Sitting around the brazier they could see the hailstones driving through a grey mist, sweeping the bleak black moor, and the cone-shaped peak of the mountain in the distance, with a whirling cloud of snow around it. The sky was rent here and there with a blue patch, showing through the blackness.

They ate the meal in silence. Then the women cleared it away. They didn't wash the mugs or plates, but put everything away, probably until morning. They sat down again after drawing out the straw, bed-shape, and putting the clothes on it that had been drying near the brazier. They all seemed to be in a good humour now with the whiskey and the food. Even the tinker's face had grown soft, and he kept puckering up his lips in a smile. He passed around cigarettes.

"Might as well finish that bottle," said Carney. "Bother the mugs. We can drink outa the neck."

"Tastes sweeter that way," said the golden-haired woman, laughing thickly, as if she were slightly drunk. At the same time she looked at Carney with her lips open.

Carney winked at her. The tinker noticed the wink and the girl's smile. His face clouded and he closed his lips very tightly. Carney took a deep draught and passed him the bottle. The tinker nodded his head, took the bottle and put it to his lips.

"I'll have a stretch," said Carney. "I'm done in. Twenty miles since morning. Eh?"

He threw himself down on the clothes beside the yellow-haired woman. She smiled and looked at the tinker. The tinker paused with the bottle to his lips and looked at her through almost closed eyes savagely. He took the bottle from his lips and bared his white teeth. The golden-headed woman shrugged her shoulders and pouted. The dark-haired woman laughed aloud, stretched back with one arm under her head and the other stretched out towards the tinker.

"Sht," she whistled through her teeth. "Pass it along, Joe."

He handed her the bottle slowly, and as he gave it to her she clutched his hand and tried to pull him to her. But he tore his hand away, got up and walked out of the tent rapidly.

Carney had noticed nothing of this. He was lying close to the woman by his side. He could feel the softness of her beautiful body and the slight undulation of her soft side as she breathed. He became overpowered with desire for her and closed his eyes, as if to shut out the consciousness of the world and of the other people in the tent. Reaching down he seized her hand and pressed it. She answered the pressure. At the same time she turned to her companion and whispered:

"Where's he gone?"

"I dunno. Rag out."

"What about?"

"Phst."

"Give us a drop."

"Here ye are."

Carney heard the whispering, but he took no notice of it. He heard the golden-headed one drinking and then drawing a deep breath.

"Finished," she said, throwing the bottle to the floor. Then she laughed softly.

"I'm going out to see where he's gone," whispered the dark-haired one. She rose and passed out of the tent. Carney immediately turned around and tried to embrace the woman by his side. But she bared her teeth in a savage grin and pinioned his arms with a single movement.

"Didn't think I was strong," she said, putting her face close to his and grinning at him.

He looked at her seriously, surprised and still more excited.

"What ye goin' to do in Roundwood?" she said.

"Lookin' for a job," he muttered thickly.

She smiled and rolled her tongue in her cheek.

"Stay here," she said.

He licked his lip and winked his right eye. "With you?"

She nodded.

"What about him?" he said, nodding towards the door.

She laughed silently. "Are ye afraid of Joe?"

He did not reply, but, making a sudden movement, he seized her around the body and pressed her to him. She did not resist, but began to laugh, and bared her teeth as she laughed. He tried to kiss her mouth, but she threw back her head and he kissed her cheek several times.

Then suddenly there was a hissing noise at the door. Carney sat up with a start. The tinker was standing in the entrance, stooping low, with his mouth open and his jaw twisted to the right, his two hands hanging loosely by his sides, with the fingers twitching. The dark-haired woman was standing behind him, peering over his shoulder. She was smiling.

Carney got to his feet, took a pace forward, and squared himself. He did not speak. The golden-headed woman uttered a loud peal of laughter, and, stretching out her arms, she lay flat on the bed, giggling.

"Come out here," hissed the tinker.

He stepped back. Carney shouted and rushed at him jumping the brazier. The tinker stepped aside and struck Carney a terrible blow in the jaw as he passed him. Carney staggered against the bank and fell in a heap. The tinker jumped on him like a cat, striking him with his hands and feet all together. Carney roared: "Let me up, let me up. Fair play." But the tinker kept on beating him until at last he lay motionless at the bottom of the pit.

"Ha," said the tinker.

Then he picked up the prone body, as lightly as if it were an empty sack, and threw it to the top of the bank.

"Be off, you—," he hissed.

Carney struggled to his feet on the top of the bank and looked at the three of them. They were all standing now in front of the tent, the two women grinning, the tinker scowling. Then he staggered on to the road, with his hands to his head.

"Good-bye dearie," cried the golden-headed one.

Then she screamed. Carney looked behind and saw the tinker carrying her into the tent in his arms.

"God Almighty!" cried Carney, crossing himself.

Then he trudged away fearfully through the storm towards Roundwood.

"God Almighty!" he cried at every two yards. "God Almighty!"

SEUMAS O'KELLY

Michael and Mary

❋

Mary had spent many days gathering wool from the whins
on the headland. They were the bits of wool shed by the
sheep before the shearing. When she had got a fleece that
fitted the basket she took it down to the canal and washed
it. When she had done washing it was a soft, white, silky
fleece. She put it back in the brown sally basket, pressing it
down with her long, delicate fingers. She had risen to go
away, holding the basket against her waist, when her eyes
followed the narrow neck of water that wound through the
bog.

      She could not follow the neck of yellow water very
far. The light of day was failing. A haze hung over the great
Bog of Allen that spread out level on all sides of her. The
boat loomed out of the haze on the narrow neck of the canal
water. It looked, at first, a long way off, and it seemed to
come in a cloud. The soft rose light that mounted the sky
caught the boat and burnished it like dull gold. It came
leisurely, drawn by the one horse, looking like a Golden

From THE GOLDEN BARQUE, Dublin, The Talbot Press.

Barque in the twilight. Mary put her brown head a little to one side as she watched the easy motion of the boat. The horse drew himself along deliberately, the patient head going up and down with every heavy step. A crane rose from the bog, flapping two lazy wings across the wake of the boat, and, reaching its long neck before it, got lost in the haze.

The figure that swayed by the big arm of the tiller on *The Golden Barque* was vague and shapeless at first, but Mary felt her eyes following the slow movements of the body. Mary thought it was very beautiful to sway every now and then by the arm of the tiller, steering a Golden Barque through the twilight.

Then she realised suddenly that the boat was much nearer than she had thought. She could see the figures of the men plainly, especially the slim figure by the tiller. She could trace the rope that slackened and stretched taut as it reached from the boat to the horse. Once it splashed the water, and there was a little sprout of silver. She noted the whip looped under the arm of the driver. Presently she could count every heavy step of the horse, and was struck by the great size of the shaggy fetlocks. But always her eyes went back to the figure by the tiller.

She moved back a little way to see *The Golden Barque* pass. It came from a strange, far-off world, and having traversed the bog went away into another unknown world. A red-faced man was sitting drowsily on the prow. Mary smiled and nodded to him, but he made no sign. He did not see her; perhaps he was asleep. The driver who walked beside the horse had his head stooped and his eyes on the ground. He did not look up as he passed. Mary saw his lips moving, and heard him mutter to himself; perhaps he was praying. He was a shrunken, misshaped little figure and kept step with the brute in the journey over the bog. But Mary felt the gaze of the man by the tiller upon her. She raised her eyes.

The light was uncertain and his peaked cap threw a shadow over his face. But the figure was lithe and youthful.

He smiled as she looked up, for she caught a gleam of his teeth. Then the boat had passed. Mary did not smile in return. She had taken a step back and remained there quietly. Once he looked back and awkwardly touched his cap, but she made no sign.

When the boat had gone by some way she sat down on the bank, her basket of wool beside her, looking at *The Golden Barque* until it went into the gloom. She stayed there for some time, thinking long in the great silence of the bog. When at last she rose, the canal was clear and cold beneath her. She looked into it. A pale new moon was shining down in the water.

Mary often stood at the door of the cabin on the headland watching the boats that crawled like black snails over the narrow streak of water through the bog. But they were not all like black snails now. There was a Golden Barque among them. Whenever she saw it she smiled, her eyes on the figure that stood by the shaft of the tiller.

One evening she was walking by the canal when *The Golden Barque* passed. The light was very clear and searching. It showed every plank, battered and tarstained, on the rough hulk, but for all that it lost none of its magic for Mary. The little shrunken driver, head down, the lips moving, walked beside the horse. She heard his low mutters as he passed. The red-faced man was stooping over the side of the boat, swinging out a vessel tied to a rope, to haul up some water. He was singing a ballad in a monotonous voice. A tall, dark, spare man was standing by the funnel, looking vacantly ahead. Then Mary's eyes travelled to the tiller.

Mary stepped back with some embarrassment when she saw the face. She backed into a hawthorn that grew all alone on the canal bank. It was covered with bloom. A shower of the white petals fell about her when she stirred the branches. They clung about her hair like a wreath. He raised his cap and smiled. Mary did not know the face was so eager, so boyish. She smiled a little nervously at last. His face lit up, and he touched his cap again.

The red-faced man stood by the open hatchway going

into the hold, the vessel of water in his hand. He looked at Mary and then at the figure beside the tiller.

"Eh, Michael?" the red-faced man said quizzically. The youth turned back to the boat, and Mary felt the blush spreading over her face.

"Michael!"

Mary repeated the name a little softly to herself. The gods had delivered up one of their great secrets.

She watched *The Golden Barque* until the two square slits in the stern that served as port holes looked like two little Japanese eyes. Then she heard a horn blowing. It was the horn they blew to apprise lock-keepers of the approach of a boat. But the nearest lock was a mile off. Besides, it was a long, low sound the horn made, not the short, sharp, commanding blast they blew for lock-keepers. Mary listened to the low sound of the horn, smiling to herself. Afterwards the horn always blew like that whenever *The Golden Barque* was passing the solitary hawthorn.

Mary thought it was very wonderful that *The Golden Barque* should be in the lock one day that she was travelling with her basket to the market in the distant village. She stood a little hesitantly by the lock. Michael looked at her, a welcome in his eyes.

"Going to Bohermeen?" the red-faced man asked.

"Ay, to Bohermeen," Mary answered.

"We could take you to the next lock," he said, "it will shorten the journey. Step in."

Mary hesitated, as he held out a big hand to help her to the boat. He saw the hesitation and turned to Michael.

"Now, Michael," he said.

Michael came to the side of the boat, and held out his hand. Mary took it and stepped on board. The red-faced man laughed a little. She noticed that the dark man who stood by the crooked funnel never took his eyes from the stretch of water before him. The driver was already urging the horse to his start on the bank. The brute was gathering his strength for the pull, the muscles standing out on his haunches. They glided out of the lock.

It was half a mile from one lock to another. Michael had bidden her stand beside him at the tiller. Once she looked up at him and she thought the face shy but very eager, the most eager face that ever came across the bog from the great world.

Afterwards, whenever Mary had the time, she would make a cross-cut through the bog to the lock. She would step in and make the mile journey with Michael on *The Golden Barque*. Once, when they were journeying together, Michael slipped something into her hand. It was a quaint trinket, and shone like gold.

"From a strange sailor I got it," Michael said.

Another day that they were on the barque, the blinding sheets of rain that often swept over the bog came upon them. The red-faced man and the dark man went into the hold. Mary looked about her, laughing. But Michael held out his great waterproof for her. She slipped into it and he folded it about her. The rain pelted them, but they stood together, Michael holding the big coat folded about her. She laughed a little nervously.

"You will be wet," she said.

Michael did not answer. She saw the eager face coming down close to hers. She leaned against him a little and felt the great strength of his arms about her. They went sailing away together in *The Golden Barque* through all the shining seas of the gods.

"Michael," Mary said once, "is it not lovely?"

"The wide ocean is lovely," Michael said. "I always think of the wide ocean going over the bog."

"The wide ocean!" Mary said with awe. She had never seen the wide ocean. Then the rain passed. When the two men came up out of the hold Mary and Michael were standing together by the tiller.

Mary did not go down to the lock after that for some time. She was working in the reclaimed ground on the headland. Once the horn blew late in the night. It blew for a long time, very softly and lowly. Mary sat up in bed listening to it, her lips parted, the memory of Michael on *The*

Golden Barque before her. She heard the sound dying away in the distance. Then she lay back on her pillow, saying she would go down to him when *The Golden Barque* was on the return journey.

The figure that stood by the tiller on the return was not Michael's. When Mary came to the lock the red-faced man was telling out the rope, and where Michael always stood by the tiller there was the short strange figure of a man with a pinched, pock-marked face.

When the red-faced man wound the rope round the stump at the lock, bringing the boat to a stand-still, he turned to Mary.

"Michael is gone voyaging," he said.

"Gone voyaging?" Mary repeated.

"Ay," the man answered. "He would be always talking to the foreign sailors in the dock where the canal ends. His eyes would be upon the big masts of the ships. I always said he would go."

Mary stood there while *The Golden Barque* was in the lock. It looked like a toy ship packed in a wooden box.

"A three-master he went in," the red-faced man said, as they made ready for the start. "I saw her standing out for the sea last night. Michael is under the spread of big canvas. He had the blood in him for the wide ocean, the wild blood of the rover." And the red-faced man, who was the Boss of the boat, let his eyes wander up the narrow neck of water before him.

Mary watched *The Golden Barque* moving away, the grotesque figure standing by the tiller. She stayed there until a pale moon was shining below her, turning over a little trinket in her fingers. At last she dropped it into the water.

It made a little splash, and the vision of the crescent was broken.

SEUMAS O'KELLY

Nan Hogan's House

❋

When Mrs. Paul Manton lifted the latch and pushed open
the door of Nan Hogan's house she was rooted to the spot
by the sight which presented itself to her view.

Nan Hogan was propped up by the side of the hearth
in a weird collection of old clothes, or, as Mrs. Manton
called them, "old brillauns gathered together in long ages
and generations." But Nan Hogan's uncompromising head
and shoulders rose out of the pillows, and her one fearless
steel-grey eye took Mrs. Paul Manton in with steady and
frank displeasure.

"The Lord save us, what come over you, Nan Hogan?" Mrs. Manton asked.

"The weakness came over me," Nan Hogan made answer in her traditional note of discontent.

"And there isn't a spark of fire in the place," Mrs.
Manton declared, moving down to the hearth.

"What does that signify," Nan Hogan said. "People

From Hillsiders, Dublin, The Talbot Press.

ought to be thankful to have a spark of life in their bodies, and they maybe with neighbors that don't care the toss of a button whether they're dead or living."

Nan gathered some of the clothes up about her as she spoke. Mrs. Manton made no reply. She brought an armful of turf from a box in a corner, and built up a fire on the hearth.

"When were you taken bad?" she asked as she fanned the flames with her apron.

"Last night, ma'am," Nan replied, coldly. "If it might concern you to know the exact hour I'm sorry I can't strengthen your knowledge."

"Is it the rheumatism?" Mrs. Manton went on, ignoring Nan's tone.

"No, ma'am, it isn't no rheumatism, for that's always in the four bones of me."

Mrs. Manton gave some hot milk to the patient.

"I thought it was a nice place," Nan Hogan said, sipping the milk, "where a woman was left to die on the floor with nothing more Christian near her than a drowsy cat." And Nan made a feeble movement with one of her feet in the heap of clothes to throw off a sleepy cat ensconced in the arm of an old jacket. The cat only rolled over softly, and curled himself into the remains of a once glorious mantilla.

"Couldn't you make a noise, or call out or do something?" Mrs. Manton suggested.

"I could indeed, pet," Nan replied, sarcastically, "if I had the strength for it. But what is a body to do when the weakness is upon her? There I was, going over them articles of clothes, contriving to see what sort of a skirt I might be making out of them, when, lo and behold, the power went out of my limbs. I just lay back, ma'am, where I am, and pulled the clothes the best way I could about me, to keep from perishing."

"I'll be making the bed for you," Mrs. Manton said, going into the little room.

"It's case equal where a body is left to rot," Nan went on in the same monotonous voice—a monotonous, metallic voice which had long ago lost all its provoking rasp for Mrs. Paul Manton. "But I was thinking to myself that Kilbeg would cut a handsome figure when it was published to the world that it let an oul' creature die without the comfort of priest or the charity of doctor."

Mrs. Manton in the room inside began to rattle the furniture and make a noise. It was her way for resenting Nan Hogan's tone. Nan perked her head when she heard the racket in the room, and her voice rose higher and shriller. "And more betoken," she cried, "there's them in Kilbeg that wouldn't ask better than hearing of a sudden death. There's one cabin-hunter in Kilbeg that'd go down on her bare marrow-bones to give thanks that I died with the company of a cat by the black hearth."

For some reason a chair got knocked over at this moment in the room, and Nan Hogan lay back a little, a certain expression of ugly satisfaction in her face. Presently Mrs. Manton came out and did some tidying-up about the kitchen. Then she removed the bundle of rags from around Nan Hogan, stowing them away in the big bin that stood over against the wall. But when it came to helping Nan Hogan to bed Mrs. Paul Manton's natural vigour gave way. The woman was so helpless that she could not put a leg under her.

"Didn't I tell you I was crippled?" Nan demanded. "I suppose, ma'am, you take me for a liar and an impostor, and the grave opening up in front of me?"

"The cramps are in your legs, Nan Hogan," Mrs. Manton said, "and no wonder. I'll be going out for Mrs. Denny Hynes."

And while Mrs. Manton was away for help Nan Hogan sat dismantled on her floor, her one eye looking out of the little window with that eternal and unblinking pessimism which gave her such a sinister appearance. Mrs. Paul Manton and Mrs. Denny Hynes helped Nan Hogan into her bed as gently as they could.

"I'm beholden to you," Nan said with dry scepticism. "But it's not long I'll be troubling the people of Kilbeg."

"Tim O'Halloran will be over to-morrow," Mrs. Manton said. "He'll be coming with the relief. And maybe he could send you a doctor."

"It's great good that will be to me, indeed," Nan said with a little hard laugh. "You might as well be telling me that Kilbeg will be giving me the compliment of a big funeral when it gets shut of me."

The women had to listen to a good deal of the same kind of criticism of Kilbeg for the rest of the day.

When the news of Nan Hogan's sudden weakness spread through Kilbeg any of the people who could at all spare a little time "took a chase down to see what way the creature was."

Accordingly, for the rest of the day, there was a continual movement of visitors over the little stile and down the strip of road leading into Nan Hogan's house.

Her house stood right at the bottom of the village, pushed in, so to speak, from the irregular line of cabins and with its back turned upon them all. Kilbeg in its construction had never come under the tyranny of the architect or the conventionality of the engineer. There was no designing, no mapping and planning, no consideration of aspect, and no surveying of the site. The houses were put up by the people according as they were wanted, and under conditions of the most perfect individual liberty. One cabin, so to speak, did not care a snap for the other, and showed it. If you were a sociable person, for instance, you hooked your habitation on to a number of others. If you were of a retiring disposition you planted yourself away in from the road or went down into a dip in the ground. If you were aggressive or overbearing you put your house on a commanding view, and if you were nasty and wanted to be disagreeable you built your cabin in front of your enemy's door, so that he would have to walk about your house to get in or out of his own, and the movements of his family would be under your constant observation. The cabins of Kilbeg were pitched according to the temperaments of the inhabitants, so that you could almost tell by looking at them what manner of mortal sheltered under each roof. Nan Hogan's house gave expression to Nan's opinion of Kilbeg, for no matter what other cabin door you stood at, Nan's house had an angle pointing at you.

Nan Hogan sat propped up on her bed all day receiving her visitors. She measured every fresh arrival with her solitary eye. Her tongue never faltered in its grim humour. Every word of caustic greeting held its sting. The sour expression never faded from the features as the hours passed, nor the tone of discontent from her voice. But I doubt much if Cleopatra in all her glory ever relished a parade of obsequious beauties kowtowing before her throne as much as Nan Hogan relished her levee in Kilbeg that day. There was only one cloud on the brilliancy of her reception—Sara Finnessy never turned up. The very sight of Sara Finnessy stirred up every inch of venom in Nan Hogan. For Sara Finnessy to cross her threshold, while she enjoyed all the advantage of her sudden weakness, would spell a very ecstasy to the patient.

The bitterness between Nan Hogan and Sara Finnessy was very real and of long standing. It went back to the day that Nan found herself utterly alone and deserted in her cabin. The last of her family, the boy upon whom all her affections were lavished, had gone away from her that day. With him had disappeared the eldest boy of Sara Finnessy, "a rascal who left Kilbeg that he might cheat and swindle the wide world," Nan Hogan had said. These two youthful adventurers of Kilbeg had joined a band of wanderers who were taking flight from the hills about Ballinaiske "to sail the waters of all the oceans in their sailoring." Nan Hogan believed, as she believed in her God, that it was young Finnessy who had lured her boy from his home, and all her bitterness was heaped upon the head of Sara Finnessy from that day to this.

The people had pity for Nan Hogan. She had never what they called "the even temper or the mannerly way," but most of them knew her when she was a proud woman with her family about her. God had taken her man from

Nan Hogan, leaving her with a young family of two daughters and two boys. She had striven to bring up her little family. The eldest girl went in the decline just as she was gathering the shape of a woman. The second girl married a boy over from Boherlahan, and they emigrated to America. They were understood to be striving the best way they could in the Republic down to this day. The second boy wasted away after his sister, and the night he was waked Nan Hogan sat by his bed telling the people that poor Thomaseen had never any heart for the rough world.

It was a poor story enough, this story of Nan Hogan. It can be understood how her heart wound itself about the only one left her of her flock, the eldest boy, an active, strong, big-hearted, giddy-headed, impulsive youth. It cannot be so easily understood how Nan Hogan felt when one day that boy left her alone in her house and in the world. It was little wonder she had the pity of Kilbeg. She had seen all her care scattered to the far places of the world, or drawn to the grave, and if she strove on after that, keeping her cabin together, putting in her day's work in the fields and contriving to sustain her independence, it was, as her neighbours said, because she had the courage of her own heart.

It was not unnatural, therefore, if Nan Hogan became soured against the world—that is to say, Kilbeg. The one privilege left her was the right to complain, and she took advantage of it to the full. The neighbours bore with her as well as their humanity allowed them; they tried to remember her sorrow, and left her the comfort of her tongue—all except Sara Finnessy, whose peculiar psychological construction allowed her to give Nan Hogan no great latitude. "A ranting old hare," Sara Finnessy called Nan Hogan, but Sara Finnessy's toleration extended so far that she kept out of Nan's way as far as the geographical disposition of Kilbeg would permit.

However, if Nan Hogan was denied the comfort of an attack on Sara Finnessy, while she had the advantage of her sudden weakness, it was some sort of consolation to her to see Christy Finnessy crossing her threshold in the cool of the evening. Christy came in heavily to the house, and fully conscious that he bore, in the judgment of the patient, the burden of his woman's sins. The eye of Nan Hogan kindled when she heard the step of Christy Finnessy upon her floor.

"I hear 'tis how you were taken bad sudden," Christy said in his stupid way, stooping rather unnecessarily as he entered the doorway of the little room. Nan looked at him with her searching eye, her mouth drawn tight and hard. Christy thought, with a little pang of relief, that maybe Nan's speech was taken from her in the attack. The thought was short-lived.

"I suppose," said Nan, "that you were sent down to take the dimensions of me coffin?"

"Well, no, Nan, I was not," Christy put in mildly.

"You're a great man," Nan said in her level voice; "a great man, Christy Finnessy, and I always said it. I never thought of you yet but that I remembered the saying that God makes the back for the burden."

Christy moved down to the end of the room where Nan held him in her eye. "God is good," Christy said, with a feeble attempt at light-heartedness.

"The courage that always stood to you," Nan said, "the courage and the strength of your back. You may well thank God for giving you both, or it's long long ago Sara Finnessy would be in the company of Mrs. Lowry and myself—two widow-women with mourning in our hearts."

"Mrs. Lowry had wisdom," Christy managed to put in. "She never gave herself over to the grief like you did, Nan Hogan."

Nan Hogan hitched herself on her pillow with an air of roused interest that made Christy Finnessy's heart sink.

"The more I ponder over your case, Christy," Nan said, "the more respect I have for your strength. 'If he was another,' I'd say to myself, 'she'd have him stretched long ago the day.' And sure the harmless poor men of the hills ought never be done giving their praise to you. What one of them knew but that it might be himself would fall into Sara's hands when she was roving the country on the lookout? But like the brave heart you had, my son, you took away the danger the day she led you up to the marriage rails."

"Well," said Christy, bridling, "I never had any regrets over that same day."

"That's it, honey," said Nan, "you bore up, all your life with the courage of ten men. No one ever yet heard the poor word of complaint on your lips, only you to be striving over the road like a mule that'd be put to the pull of a great caravan. You were never without the admiration of the people."

It was with great relief Christy Finnessy saw the Widow Lowry bustling into the little room. The Widow settled the pillows about Nan, and laid critical fingers on her forehead.

"You're fine and natural, thank God," the Widow Lowry said. "It was only just a passing fit."

"What odds does it make?" Nan said. "And indeed you oughtn't to be giving such sad word for Christy Finnessy to be bringing back home with him. It's little welcome there'll be before him if he hasn't the story to tell that Nan Hogan is drawing on to her last gasp."

"Christy Finnessy has no wish to carry the black word," the Widow said, and Christy looked his thanks to the Widow.

"Christy's wish indeed!" Nan exclaimed. "When was Christy's wish of any account in the house of Sara Finnessy? Isn't it only now I was telling him of the respect and admiration he had of the world. No one ought to know that better than yourself, ma'am, you a woman that put a couple of men through your own hands."

The Widow Lowry laughed good-humoredly. "I'll do for a few more of them yet," she said.

"Then if that be your way," said Nan Hogan, "you're the fortunate woman you didn't strike on Christy Finnessy. When Sara didn't as much as sour the man's temper, sure he'd be like a fiery young colt to-day if he fell into your own hands."

Christy Finnessy moved down to the door.

"I must put a coal in the pipe at the fire," he said, going out into the kitchen.

Nan's voice followed him out. "Tell Sara," she said, "that she isn't shut of Nan Hogan yet. That funeral she's expecting won't move up the village for another while. And there's no telling who might not be going before her. God be praised. Christy Finnessy, you're the greatest constitution of a man that ever threw a shadow across the floor."

Nan lay back on her pillows, her eye closing, and her face, the Widow Lowry thought, becoming more pallid.

"You have no right to be over-reaching yourself," the Widow said, testily.

Nan's eye opened and took in the Widow with some concern. "I'd be satisfied," she said, "if that Christy Finnessy was not such a moonsaun. I'm in dread now he won't bring my words up home with him. It's a poor case when a body is stretched with the dint of weakness, maybe to be wasting me words on a man that has no retention for them."

When Christy Finnessy got home he sat down by the fire.

"Well," his woman asked expectantly, "what way is she?"

"She says," Christy said, "that she has a weakness." And he knocked the heel of his pipe of tobacco out on the palm of his hand.

"And has she," Mrs. Finnessy asked.

"Well," Christy said, refilling the pipe, "if she has I'm thinking it must be in her tongue. She's keeping her intellect clear to the last."

Mrs. Sara Finnessy leaned over to her man. "Was she saying anything?" she asked, the battle-light coming into her eyes in anticipation.

"She was. She was saying many a thing."

"Giving out about myself, I'll engage," Sara suggested.

Christy yawned and stretched out his toes to the fire.

"I couldn't rightly say," he said. "She was talking in a sort of back-hand way. And whether or which it's all gone from me memory now. It went from me and I coming up the road." And as Christy could not be got beyond this declaration his woman looked upon him with open contempt.

When the Widow Lowry was coming up home later she saw Sara Finnessy leaning up miserably against the side of the door, her hands folded under her arms.

"She's gone into a kind of a drowse," the Widow told her. "Was Christy telling you anything?"

"No, ma'am, he was not," Mrs. Finnessy replied. "There's no comfort to be had in him. 'Tisn't the first time in my life that I felt the hardship of a man that has no gift of retention."

And the Widow Lowry caught the same note of pained regret in the tone of Sara Finnessy as she had detected in the voice of Nan Hogan.

The Widow Lowry laughed a little to herself as she turned in to her home. "Christy," she said, "has taken the good out of the day for both of them. He's the poorest ambassador that stands in the country."

When Tim O'Halloran, the relieving officer, came to Kilbeg from Boherlahan the next day with the outdoor relief to a few destitute people, he found Nan Hogan in a poor way. She was shrunken up in the bed.

"Leave the few shillings on the dresser, Tim," she said.

"I must send the doctor to you, Nan," Tim said. "You're looking a bit shook."

"I got a weakness," Nan explained, "a great weakness in the legs. It's more through good luck than through any neighbourly grace that you hadn't an ugly case in me this day, Tim O'Halloran. I suppose it wouldn't be any great pleasure to you to find me a corpse upon the floor. But it was nearly coming to that through the charity of Kilbeg."

"You'd be better off in the hospital," Tim said. "You'd get the right care there."

"Is it to send me into the Poorhouse you have a mind?" Nan asked quickly, some of the old fire coming into her eye.

"It would be the best place for you," Tim answered, bluntly.

Nan Hogan looked steadily and suspiciously at him for a minute. "Tim O'Halloran," she demanded, "has any person in Kilbeg put you up to send me to the Poorhouse?"

"I wouldn't like to rob Kilbeg of its store of wisdom," Tim answered. "I'm coming to it long enough, and I never expected any great enlightenment from its people. They never disappointed me."

This reply was much to Nan's heart.

"It would be like a shaft of light shining down from heaven to Sara Finnessy if she saw me heading for the Poorhouse," Nan said.

"Well, now," said Tim, in his most judicial tone, "maybe if she thought that the good treatment would put you on your legs again it would put a cloud over the light."

Nan remained thinking over this view very quietly for some time.

"And, indeed, Nan," Tim urged, "you're no great envy to anyone as long as you're stretched there the way you are. It might be a great satisfaction to Sara Finnessy to say that Nan Hogan was now no more than Denny Hynes, a bed-ridden man."

And Tim left Nan Hogan to ponder over his words while he went out to deliver some instructions to the neighbours. Tim advised the neighbours that it was well to hammer it into the head of Nan Hogan that it was the great wish of Sara Finnessy's heart to see her lying helpless on her bed until the Lord called her.

He had some difficulty in getting the neighbours to play upon the prejudices of the patient. They resented the Poorhouse for any person in Kilbeg. It was only when Tim O'Halloran laid the lie of Nan Hogan at their feet that the Widow Lowry and Mrs. Paul Manton consented to do his bidding.

The news that Nan Hogan was about to be removed in the ambulance to the Poorhouse cast a gloom over Kilbeg. The Workhouse Car, as they called it, was only seen in Kilbeg in years of acute distress. The very thought of it was repugnant to every heart upon the hillsides. Many of the people said they would almost as soon carry out Nan Hogan in her coffin as see her taken away in the Poorhouse Car. It was to them an emblem of death and pestilence and horror, a black vulture that hovered over places where the people lay broken, a thing that had direct descent from the Famine, that carried with it an atmosphere of soup-houses and proselytism, that smelt of a foul traffic in soul-selling and body-snatching, the relic of a tyranny that held the memory of the Penal Laws in the grind of its wheels.

The Widow Lowry and Mrs. Paul Manton went in and out to the sick room that day with an instinctive feeling that public opinion outside was against them in this work. It was only the belief that the end justified the means—that Nan Hogan's recovery depended upon her treatment in the hospital—that kept them to their promise to Tim O'Halloran.

The Widow Lowry was in the kitchen, looking after the preparation of some medicine which had been provided for the patient when Mrs. Manton came out of the room to lend a hand. Mrs. Manton found the Widow Lowry fiddling rather blindly among the delft on the dresser.

"What's delaying you?" Mrs. Manton asked, going up to her. The Widow turned away, groping for the fireplace with a little cry. Mrs. Manton caught a sight of her face.

"Do you think, now, that this is going to do Nan Hogan any good?" Mrs. Manton demanded severely. The Widow sat down on a stool by the fire.

"I couldn't help thinking of the way this home was scattered," the Widow said. "To think of her man, and her children, and the heart she kept up through it all. I had my own troubles, God knows, but what were they to the troubles of Nan Hogan!"

"That's a nice way to be helping the woman," Mrs. Manton said. "It's a shame for you, a great shame for you." Mrs. Manton tried to keep up the severity in her voice, but the last word broke in a little gasp. She, like the Widow

Lowry, had to grope for the fireplace. They sat down to-gether, two dim figures in the smoke on Nan Hogan's hearth, wiping their eyes in their aprons and crying quietly.

"I was here when the weight of her troubles came upon her one by one, but I never thought it would come to this."

"Did he say when the Car was to be here?" in a whis-per that was full of the pending dread.

"I hadn't the courage to ask him."

The Poorhouse Car came rumbling up through the vil-lage when the shadows were deepening. But it would take more than the charity of the gathering night to cloak the ugliness of the Poorhouse Car. The shaggy, ill-kept, slow-looking brute that drew it seemed conscious of the weight behind him. The driver, in his pauper clothes, sat lop-sided on the seat, the whip dangling from his hands in a spirit-less, slipshod fashion. The Car was black and heavy and lurched over the road like a ship that had lost its ballast, a dark, covered-in structure, with a door at the back. The shafts tilted over the shoulders of the horse, as if the harness were a misfit and the horse too small for the vehicle. The people stood silent by the way as it came up, the children running frightened into the houses, for they had heard such evil things of this spectre during the day that it held more terror for them than the Headless Coach.

Mrs. Manton and the Widow Lowry heard the sound of the wheels turning upon the road from a great distance. They bustled about the room, talking a little wildly and making such noise as might kill the sound for Nan Hogan. But Nan, too, had heard the ominous rumble. She spoke no word, but her eye was fixed on the little window of the room waiting for the thing to make a dark shadow across it. It passed at last, a hitched-up patch of black in the dim light. Tim O'Halloran came in with a few of the men, walk-ing softly and speaking in undertones. Mrs. Paul Manton and the Widow Lowry were making Nan ready for the journey, talking to her with forced cheerfulness, when sud-denly Mrs. Paul Manton threw up her arms, and stepping out from the door fled from Nan Hogan's house. The

Widow Lowry, whose voice had become a little breathless, thought to cover the retreat as well as she could, but Nan was wonderfully alert and susceptible to the things going on about her. A wan smile passed over her face when she saw Mrs. Manton throwing up her arms and clearing. She still held her peace, and was carried out in a dead silence by the men to the waiting vehicle which loomed before the door. The feet of the men shuffled over the ground, and Nan saw the figures of neighbours standing about in the shadows. She had been carried quite close to the door of the ambulance when something seemed to strike her.

"Lock the door of the house," she called out in her well-known voice. A few people fumbled at the door, found the key, and turned it in the lock.

The Widow Lowry was saying to one of the women, "Talk of courage and heart! The world never yet saw the like of it!"

"Kilbeg isn't shut of Nan Hogan yet," Nan's voice sang out from the ambulance door.

Tim O'Halloran was busy seeing to the care of the patient, and the Widow Lowry to singing her praises, or they would have made some effort to prevent the blunder that followed. In the confusion at the door a woman got hold of the key just as Nan called out from the Poorhouse Car— "Bring me that key, now. I'm not giving it up yet."

A figure stepped towards the ambulance, and held out the key. The next moment a loud wail broke out upon the air.

It was Sara Finnessy who held out the key to Nan Hogan. Kilbeg never could say whether she did it in malice or in mistaken repentance, for Sara Finnessy herself scorned to make a declaration. But whatever the motive, it had an instantaneous effect on Nan Hogan. She wailed and screamed in the ambulance and the people began to gather excitedly close to the vehicle. Sara Finnessy threw the key, some said in terror, into the ambulance and rushed up the road home. Nan Hogan was seen to be battling with her arms in the ambulance with the woman who had come as sort of companion from the Poorhouse. She was tearing the wraps from about her and could be seen dimly, like a spectre, fighting her way to the door of the vehicle. Presently she reached it, clinging to the door and swaying about like a wraith making loud complaint and calling on the people to take her back into her home. Tim O'Halloran pleaded with her to go quietly, but Nan battled with the courage of despair.

The people were now drawn close about the Poorhouse Car and Tim O'Halloran could hear hoarse murmurs breaking out among them. Tim O'Halloran knew the people of Kilbeg. He knew that the painful battle Nan Hogan was making was rousing anger in their hearts, and that it only required a lead from one man or one woman to stir them to action and violence. He knew that should one blow be struck Nan Hogan would be forcibly carried back to her house, and the Poorhouse Car wrecked—reduced to matchwood—before her door. It was a moment for decisive action. Tim O'Halloran turned to the crowd. "Fardy Lalor," he called out, "stand here by the step."

Fardy Lalor moved up to the door of the ambulance, and stood there quietly, his face to the crowd. Tim O'Halloran caught the screaming patient in his arms and carried her bodily into the van. He stepped back, slammed the door, and shouted to the driver to move on.

Kilbeg never witnessed such a distressing sight before. The Poorhouse Car lurched slowly up the village, the muffled screams and protests of Nan Hogan coming from within, Tim O'Halloran and Fardy Lalor walking close to the doorstep like a bodyguard, and an excited crowd of people behind them. It was not until they were a mile out on the Boherlahan road that the wails of Nan Hogan died away within the hideous conveyance. Then the people began to fall back.

Tim O'Halloran wiped the perspiration from his forehead, and heaved a sigh of relief. "They were within an ace of killing her," he said. "Only for yourself, Fardy Lalor, there would be bad work in Kilbeg this night."

334

"She'll never do any good after this," Fardy Lalor answered.

Tim O'Halloran shook his head. "I know Nan Hogan a great long while," he said. "I saw her putting many a storm over her head. You'll see her back in Kilbeg again."

While Nan Hogan was undergoing treatment in the Boherlahan Union Hospital, she did not surrender her right to give audible expression to her thoughts. Nan's thoughts were not sweetened by her surroundings. But she had no longer a monopoly in gloomy speculation, for her fellow-sufferers in the ward were all more or less inclined to take a morbid view of life. This fact took a great deal of point from Nan's outlook. She had a feeling that she was only throwing ink on a black sky. There was no satisfaction in holding parleys with patients who paid back gloom for gloom. She missed the lively background of Kilbeg, the conflict of outlook that brought out the light and shade of her battling will.

Instinctively, Nan Hogan turned her attention to one Maura Casey, a sprightly little woman, who had been promoted from the able-bodied ward of the Poorhouse to the position of helper in the hospital. Maura Casey was a sort of understrapper to the nurses described, I believe, in official documents as a wardsmaid. The nurses and doctor had, in Nan Hogan's view, become so much a part of the ritual of the hospital that she got little satisfaction in their company. They kept the machinery of the place in smooth motion, were sort of skilled engineers, who oiled the ailments of the day and greased the pains of the night. They kept the life in you up to the last possible moment, and when they could keep it in you no longer, they passed you out for disposal by another department. But Maura Casey, Nan Hogan felt, was nearer to the humanities; the only person who seemed to be out of gear in the place, whose movements and manners were not regulated by invisible machinery. Maura came in the door carrying some breath of the irresponsible world outside about her. To Maura Casey, therefore, Nan turned for fleeting moments of companionship. The fact that Maura Casey could only lend her ear to Nan Hogan whenever the eyes of the authorities were off guard, sweetened the acquaintanceship.

Maura Casey was not for some time very responsive, for she was some five years "looking at cases" in that place. Her interest in earthly woes had in that time and in the peculiar circumstances, got somewhat blunted. It was the talk of Nan Hogan about her house and the constancy of a dream which haunted her sleeping hours, that aroused the interest of Maura Casey. Nan would tell Maura Casey about her house and her dream while Maura scrubbed the floor about her bed.

Nan Hogan's description of her house would sound fantastic to anybody who knew Kilbeg, but when one is reduced to fiddling on the one string the temptation to introduce variations, with, perhaps, some flighty passages, some thrills and shivers, proves too strong for the artistic temperament. Maura Casey got it into her head that Nan Hogan, under stress of a sudden weakness in the legs, had to leave a splendid dwelling in the village of Kilbeg to the mercy of a most unworthy cat. The effect of this picture of the abandoned mansion in Kilbeg was heightened by the dream of Nan Hogan, faithfully recorded to Maura Casey the morning following its persistent recurrence. It was under cover of this remarkable dream that Nan Hogan introduced, with lawful embellishments, the villain of the piece, Sara Finnessy. Sara Finnessy was described with great relish by Nan Hogan, so much relish that Maura Casey would kneel back on her heels on the floor until the lather of disinfecting soap evaporated from her scrubbing brush. Maura Casey felt that the gallows had been cheated of at least one female monster. She could see this woman fiend dancing a strange, triumphant dance about a closed up, silent house, throwing a sort of Highland Fling at the front door, capering round the gables in a crazy reel, and bringing the performance to a close with an ecstatic, standing jump on to the roof. Maura Casey had no imagination, but this picture was put magically before her by Nan Hogan in her descriptions of her nightly vision.

The thing grew so much on Maura Casey that one day, when she had got a few hours' leave of absence from Boherlahan Hospital she was seized with such an overpowering curiosity that she footed it over to Kilbeg to view the deserted mansion of Nan Hogan, and, if possible, and at a safe distance, steal a look at the thrilling Sara Finnessy.

Maura Casey saw both wonders in Kilbeg, and came back with a droop in the corners of her mouth. When Nan Hogan continued her recitals afterwards Maura Casey paid less heed to her words, and more to her scrubbing brushes. "Raving the woman is," Maura Casey told herself, "raving for death."

But the empty cabin in Kilbeg had an unexpected psychological effect on Maura Casey. It was such a cabin as she had often ambitioned. She had been a woman who knocked about from one workhouse to another, tramping over the roads, before she settled down in Boherlahan, and earned her promotion to the hospital. Like many other homeless creatures, Maura Casey lacked the love of wandering that is of the gipsy and tinker blood. She was a wanderer through necessity, and not from choice. Maura Casey had always held an opinion that she was a born housekeeper, and that it was one of the ironies of life, the caprices of Fate, that she should never be able to claim a little house of her own. She liked to hang about small cabins for that reason, fancying to herself what she could be doing had she the ownership of one. For the same reason she liked rather lonely, out-of-the-way, quiet places, her instinct telling her that if she ever could lay claim to a cabin of her own her best chance lay in such places.

Maura Casey, with the home hunger in her heart, had faced the winds and the unending journeys for many years, until a bad winter came with a heavy fall of snow. She had been caught on the hills in the midst of it, and had suffered so much from exposure that she sought the sanctuary of

Boherlahan Union and stayed there ever since. Her ambition to become a housekeeper and a householder was nipped, and lay dormant until she saw Nan Hogan's empty house in Kilbeg, after which she got into the habit of long spells of silent reflection in the intervals of her labor in the hospital.

Soon after Nan Hogan missed Maura Casey from the hospital. She was told that Maura had given up the job— "taken her discharge," as they put it—and had gone out again into the world. Nan Hogan became low-spirited as a result, even though they were, as she said, "coaxing back a little life to her limbs."

In the meantime, Kilbeg had settled down to its normal condition, and the agitation created by the distressing departure from Kilbeg had subsided to various speculations as to whether Nan was ever likely to return to her home.

One fine morning, however, Kilbeg was astonished to see smoke coming out of the chimney of Nan Hogan's house. It went up into the blue air with a sort of flourish, proclaiming to the world that life was once more active under the roof. The wild word went about that Nan Hogan had mysteriously returned in the dead of the night. The people who were earliest astir tumbled over each other across the little stile and down the little pathway to give her welcome. The front door was locked against them, and there was no response to a few impatient thumps upon it. The Widow Lowry was the first to make her way in by the backyard. She found the back door wide open.

A strange woman was sitting by the hearth, enjoying a cup of tea with an air of great contentment. She looked very much at home, and quite unmoved by the astounded appearance of the Widow.

"Who—who are you?" the Widow asked at last, as the rest of the people grouped themselves about her.

"Me? —Oh, I'm Maura Casey."

"Maura Casey?"

"The same, ma'am. Maura Casey, over from Boherlahan."

"What is she doing here?" Paul Manton asked of his neighbours.

"House-keeping," Maura Casey made answer.

There was a little embarrassed silence, during which Maura Casey went on enjoying her early cup of tea.

"And where is Nan Hogan?" Mrs. Manton demanded.

"She's in the hospital, talking by day and raving by night."

"Raving by night?"

"Ay, she's raving for death."

"And how do you know?"

"Why shouldn't I know? Was I in the Boherlahan hospital for nothing?"

"Was it Nan sent you to the house?"

Maura Casey laid down her cup and saucer, and wiped her mouth with her apron with a gesture that proclaimed her satisfaction with the tea. Then she walked over collectedly to the door, standing up close to Mrs. Paul Manton.

"I'm thinking, ma'am," Maura Casey said, "that Kilbeg was never noted for the manners of its people."

The people drew back a little from Maura Casey. She carried about her the air of a woman who knew her business and was sure of her authority.

"It's rather soon to be talking of manners," Mrs. Manton said, with some show of doubt. "Was it Nan Hogan gave you the rights of her house?"

"That, ma'am, makes no matter at all to you. When I ask the rights of your house, if you have one, it'll be time enough for you to show the height of your breeding."

"The law will settle it all," Paul Manton said, walking slowly away, most of the people following him in silence. Mrs. Paul Manton and the Widow Lowry lingered behind.

"Did you say," the Widow asked in a more conciliatory tone, "that poor Nan Hogan is raving for death?"

"That she is. And if you are a friend of Sara Finnessy you'd best be telling her not to go next or near Nan Hogan while she lasts."

This revelation of inside information into the state of Nan Hogan's mind on the part of the newcomer had a very convincing effect on the Kilbeg women. They were ready to back down and continue the interview with Maura Casey, in the hope of gathering more insight into her person and history.

"Is it how she sent you to keep the house aired and warm for her, thinking she'd be coming back soon?" Mrs. Manton asked, with some show of acknowledging Maura Casey's authority.

"It is no wish of Nan Hogan," Maura Casey replied, "that her mind should be made known to any person in this place."

And Maura Casey, with an active movement, tucked up her skirt over her petticoat and dashed into her household activities. The Widow Lowry and Mrs. Paul Manton took the hint and departed.

People hung about the house all day. Every movement of the new arrival was noted and duly commented upon. Maura Casey, it was conceded, was a woman of wonderful energy. Already Nan Hogan's house was beginning to brighten and take on a fresh, cared-for appearance.

"I tell you what," a man said, "Nan Hogan knew what she was doing when she sent the like of that woman into her house."

Sara Finnessy was expected to show some sort of welcome to the newcomer. It struck people that a substitute—any sort of a substitute—for Nan Hogan would be satisfactory to Mrs. Finnessy. Sara Finnessy was moody, however, and reserved her judgment on the unexpected development until the close of the day. Then she broke out.

"She's an impostor," Sara Finnessy declared. "She's a regular impostor, and Kilbeg should rout her out of the place."

But the people somehow did not warm to this view. The very suddenness of the woman's appearance, the mystery of her coming, and the uncertainty of her authority to occupy Nan Hogan's house, gave her an interest that was

not without its magic for Kilbeg. They would not like to see
her routed, and to Sara Finnessy's battle call there was no
response.

But Sara Finnessy felt too strongly on the matter to remain inactive. There was a little thrill of excitement—not
unmixed with delight—when she was seen stepping over the
stile and walking down to Nan Hogan's house with an air
of grim determination.

Maura Casey was seated in from the doorway darning
a stocking, when the shadow of Sara Finnessy fell across
her. Maura Casey's fingers twitched a little when she looked
up.

"Come, you impostor, clear out of this place."

Sara Finnessy's attitude was one of battle right from the
start. She wrapped the little shawl across her shoulders
with a movement that held a threat. She stepped into Nan
Hogan's house.

Maura Casey backed away from her.

"You're Sara Finnessy?" she asked.

"Mrs. Sara Finnessy, by your leave, well known to
Kilbeg, and all belonging to me likewise."

Sara Finnessy cleared her throat in anticipation for a
lengthy warfare, and she had a pleasant feeling that Maura
Casey had not much of a tongue. The tongue was the only
weapon known to the womenfolk of Kilbeg, and Sara Finnessy felt conscious of her strength. But Maura Casey had
travelled much, and had seen many sights. She had had
her mind broadened on the resources of civilisation in times
of grave crisis. Her hand went out for the broom of heather
that stood behind the door.

"Quit your sweeping and give me your rights to this
place," Sara Finnessy demanded imperiously.

Sara Finnessy got the first stroke of the broom on the
side of the head. She staggered over to the little window,
her hands to her head. Like all incompetent people who
rely too much on the power of words she was completely
demoralised by the first touch of well-directed action.

"Uff," said Maura Casey, and this time Sara Finnessy

had it on the poll. She made a dash for the door, and as she reached it the thud caught her between the shoulders. Sara Finnessy staggered across the threshold, and as the people who stood out on the road awaiting developments saw her face a little murmur of amazement broke out amongst them.

Sara Finnessy made a sprint for the stile, but Maura Casey was on her heels. She swung the broom as if she were a juggler with an Indian club.

"Uff!" Maura Casey grunted every time she caught her mark. When Sara Finnessy half tumbled over the stile she began to shout for Christy, but Christy was at home, making a horse of himself on the floor for the children.

Maura Casey stood on the stile with her broom, and watched Sara Finnessy running up the road home, her hair flying behind her. The people standing before Maura Casey on the road broke out into an ill-suppressed shout, not un-mixed with laughter and admiration.

"Bedad," a man said, "that's the quickest bit of work I saw since the Boherlahan Races."

"Who'd think Sara Finnessy could be put down in two minutes?" a woman spoke up. "The devil's cure to her!" she cried.

"Now, me hearties," Maura Casey declared, as she poised on the stile, looking like a parody of Galatea on the Pedestal, "I'll do for Kilbeg what the schoolmaster never did for it. I'll teach it some manners."

And she turned into Nan Hogan's house, feeling victorious but not happy. If the people could see her five minutes after, they would behold her lying face downward on the bed in the little room, sobbing hysterically.

Sara Finnessy was not seen for the rest of the evening. Neither was her man, Christy.

"God help Christy," the Widow Lowry said with a queer look on her face.

When Fardy Lalor went in to Meg he sat down on a chair, and laughed until the baby threatened him with his fat kithogue.

"Praise be to God," Fardy said, "to see that little woman

putting Mrs. Finnessy over the stile. She scattered Sara's hairpins east and west."

For the rest of the week Maura Casey devoted herself to her duties in Nan Hogan's house with unabated vigour. But the question of her occupancy was, as Paul Manton had said, a matter to be settled by the law.

The law came in the shape of Tim O'Halloran. Tim was agent for the landlord of Nan Hogan's house and the other houses in Kilbeg. They were not a valuable property. "They brought in a few shillings," was Tim O'Halloran's way of putting it.

Tim O'Halloran was surprised to hear that Nan Hogan's house was occupied by Maura Casey, but, like the wise man that he was, he did not express any opinion on the point to the people of Kilbeg. He looked thoughtfully down upon the road for some time and then went in to interview Maura Casey.

Kilbeg never knew what transpired at the interview, but when Tim O'Halloran came out he headed for Mrs. McDermott's farmhouse at the Lough.

"You might as well be giving her an odd day when you have it. She says she often worked in the fields and is a good warrant to weed," Tim O'Halloran said.

"I'll give her a trial," Mrs. McDermott said. "But wasn't she a venturesome woman to as good as break into the house?"

"Well, she's in it now, and the house is the better of her. Not a taste she had to live on but a bag of potatoes and a grain of tea. She had a few shillings leaving the Poorhouse."

"But what's going to happen if Nan Hogan comes out of the hospital and finds the strange woman in her house?"

Tim O'Halloran's long face broke into one of those wintry smiles that sometimes passed over it.

"That'll be a matter for another day," he said. "We must take some things in this world by instalments, and at the last leave a lot of reckoning to the Almighty."

That day Maura Casey threw open her front door to the world. Kilbeg took it as a declaration of her independence. The law had given her its sanction, but the news got out that up to this Maura Casey had been, as Mrs. Finnessy surmised, " a regular impostor."

"Well," Paul Manton said to his woman, "Tim O'Halloran knows his own business best, but it's a strange turn in the history of Nan Hogan's house."

"She looks secure enough," Mrs. Paul Manton replied, "but believe you me, she'll have a queer stroke of fortune in front of her when Nan Hogan comes out."

Paul slapped his knee with his hand. "Out she'll come," he declared. "It'll be one of the greatest sights ever seen in Kilbeg when Nan Hogan stands there on one side of the threshold and Maura Casey stands on the other."

"Nan Hogan has the rights of the house," Mrs. Manton declared. "Every stick in the place belongs to her. It's queer law if she's bested out of her place, and I'd say that if Tim O'Halloran had the wisdom of every saint on the calendar."

Maura Casey was given an odd day's work by the neighbouring farmers. She went up and down the village with an independent gait. Sara Finnessy called things after her a few times as she passed, but as Sara Finnessy took care to call out from the battlements of her own citadel, Maura Casey went her way if not in peace, at least in silence.

There was no word of Nan Hogan's homecoming, and Maura Casey was steadily improving her position. Not a week passed that she did not effect some change in the house, for she worked with all the enthusiasm of one new to her art and careless of the conventions. She was whitewashing at a time when no person had ever seen whitewashing in Kilbeg before. Once she brought home the remains of a pot of crimson paint, and Kilbeg opened its eyes when it saw the sashes of Nan Hogan's windows flaring out at them from the white of the walls. So struck was Maura herself with the effect that next day she started to paint the door. But the paint gave out when only half the door had been covered, so that the contrast between the half that was crimson and the half that was of the drab, common to all doors in Kilbeg, proved really startling. No sooner had the sensation of the door died down than Kilbeg learned that Maura Casey had gotten a clocking hen and a setting of eggs. Two geraniums planted in tin cannisters made their appearance on the window sill. Cheap colored prints were going up on the kitchen walls with a rapidity that took away the breath of Kilbeg. When anybody was seen going down to Maura Casey some of the neighbours asked:— "Is it going down to see the picture gallery you are?" Nan Hogan's taste in house decoration had been of the most ascetic description, so that the people began to wonder what she would say, and, still more, what she would do, if she ever turned up in Kilbeg again.

"Be this and be that," said Paul Manton, "unless Nan Hogan gathers her legs under her soon she won't know her own house when she sees it."

Mrs. Paul Manton felt the weight of the wrong to Nan Hogan and to her house pressing so heavily upon her mind that one day she made a journey to Boherlahan and paid a visit to Nan Hogan in the hospital.

Nan Hogan received her with much scepticism, and took the opportunity of giving vent to many fresh complaints of Kilbeg, which she had evolved in her mind in the enforced quiet of the place.

When, however, Mrs. Paul Manton cleared her throat, looked cautiously up and down the ward, leaned in over the bed, and whispered to the patient, Nan Hogan's eye became very fixed and stern, and her mouth drawn and tight.

"And there she is in your house to this hour, Nan, as cocked up with herself as if she owned Kilbeg," Mrs. Manton concluded.

"The treachery of Kilbeg," Nan Hogan murmured sadly at last, "the treachery of Kilbeg."

"Kilbeg isn't to blame," Mrs. Manton ventured.

Nan Hogan's eye came round slowly, and fixed itself searchingly on Mrs. Manton's flushed face.

"To say," said Nan Hogan, "that there was a whole village full of ye there, one bigger and abler than another, and for all that a handful of a woman could defy ye all! To say that the little place of a woman stretched in her sickness was at the mercy of the first wanderer on the roads—leave me alone!"

Nan Hogan turned towards the wall with a sigh.

Mrs. Paul Manton endeavoured to comfort and coax her, but Nan Hogan kept her face to the wall. "I don't want ever to see Kilbeg again," she would say, "or one belonging to it. I'm done with Kilbeg for ever."

When Mrs. Manton got out of the hospital she wiped the perspiration from her face. "I'd be better pleased," she told herself, "if I never set foot in this place. Nan Hogan is done for now."

Nan Hogan lay in bed all night with her face to the wall. But in the morning she sat up suddenly in bed and looked about her with a changed face. There was an eagerness, an agitation, in her expression, a battle-light in her eye. Before half an hour there was witnessed in the Boherlahan Hospital a scene which upset all medical theories and confounded all scientific reasoning. The nurses were horrified to see Nan Hogan struggle out of bed and attempt to walk upon the floor. She swayed about a little in her nightdress, then held on to the head of the bed. They went to her assistance and persuaded her to lie down. But every half hour Nan Hogan was up again "practising for a dance," as one of the other patients put it. Neither the nuns nor the nurses could get any good of Nan Hogan. She wanted the strength of her limbs, she told them, and was going her own way about getting it. For three days Nan Hogan shocked the medical adviser and worried the nurses, but by the third day she was able to walk about.

"I'll be leaving this place now," she announced, "and if there is any justice in heaven I'll never see it again. I'll fight Kilbeg from Mary Hickey's house down to my own cabin before they get me into the Poorhouse Car again."

Pa Cloone was driving from Boherlahan and gave Nan Hogan a lift when she came out into the world once more. Nan sat on a sack of hay, taking the familiar scene in with her unsympathetic eye as she drove to Kilbeg. She spoke no word to Pa Cloone, and Pa's expression was one of extraordinary but well suppressed delight. He left Nan down at the side leading to her cabin. They had driven quietly through the village, but already the people were rushing from their houses and surrounding Nan, shaking her hands and giving her welcome. Nan's voice rose over the turmoil.

"Quit your lies and stand back from my path," she cried. "Kilbeg had always treachery in its heart."

The people hung back a little as Nan struggled over the stile. Her eye was riveted on her cabin.

"Did the world ever see such conduct," she shouted, pointing to the door in all its half-painted glory. "Making a mock of my house, and robbing me of all my belongings."

The door was opened, and Maura Casey stood on the doorstep with a dishcloth in her hand. When she beheld Nan Hogan the dishcloth fell from her unnerved fingers and she stepped back. Nan came down to the door and stood before it. Maura Casey was drawn up inside, a flush of anxiety on her cheeks. The two women stared at each other for a little while, Nan Hogan's head drawn a little to one side, owing to the exigencies of her one eye.

"Can it be," Nan asked at last, "that you have the assurance to stand there in front of me?"

"Come into the house," Maura Casey made answer, nervously.

Nan backed away a step.

"I'll go into my house surely," she said, "but not until the air of it is fit for a Christian. Out you come, Maura Casey, you whipster, and never show your face in Kilbeg again."

Maura Casey stood her ground.

"Come into the house," she repeated.

"Never!" Nan Hogan cried, waving her arms dramatically. "Never, so long as you stand upon my floor. Back with you to the fit place you left behind you."

The people craned their necks over the wall at the stile, breathlessly following the struggle. It went on for a long while. Maura Casey said little, but Nan Hogan said much. She painted an imaginary career for Maura Casey which lacked neither force nor scandal.

"Well," Maura Casey said at last, "if you won't come in, stay where you are." And she closed out the door.

Nan Hogan turned her attention for some time to the people of Kilbeg, and what she had to say to them was not flattering. Mrs. Manton and the Widow Lowry made unavailing efforts to bring about an understanding between the two women. Nan Hogan would not go into the house, and Maura Casey would not come out of it. There was no getting the situation beyond this deadlock.

"As I said before," Paul Manton declared, "it's all a matter of the law."

"The treachery of Kilbeg!" Nan Hogan declared, turning her eye to Heaven in mute appeal.

"Tim O'Halloran has the settling of it all," Paul Manton insisted. "He left the house to Maura Casey, and it belongs to Nan Hogan. Let Tim O'Halloran mend what he made if he has logic enough for it."

Nan Hogan walked over to the closed door, and, putting her back to it, sat down upon the threshold, raising an ologone that went out over the hills.

The people's sympathies were all with Nan Hogan. She was one of themselves, and Maura Casey was a stranger. But the men were loth to carry out an eviction, to, as one of them said, "make dirty bailiffs and black-livered emergency-men of ourselves." If it happened to be a man who held the fort they would have kicked him out on the road long ago, but when it came to laying a hand on a little handful of a woman they sought excuses. If any force were considered necessary there was an impression that it was a case for the women, but the women remembered how Sara Finnessy had fared. There was a suggestion of strength and fight and determination in the closed-out door and the quiet of the house that Maura Casey held. She was sitting tight, holding on to the nine points of the law which she held within her grasp. The people were uncertain and baffled, and at

once agreed with Paul Manton that it was a case for Tim
O'Halloran. Accordingly, a jennet was tackled to a cart
and two young fellows posted hot foot to Boherlahan to ac-
quaint Tim O'Halloran with the extraordinary situation
which he had created in Kilbeg.

"Well," said Tim O'Halloran, when he had been acquainted with the facts, "Boherlahan is a wide union and a
wild union, with mountains and lakes and forests and many
strange people, but there is more torment to be got in a
corner of Kilbeg than in the length and breadth of it."

On the way to Kilbeg Tim O'Halloran did some quiet
thinking, and the gossoons who drove the cart concluded
that he was trying to solve in his mind the problem concerning Nan Hogan's house.

However, when they reached Kilbeg they were astonished that Tim O'Halloran refused to be driven straight to
the scene of action. Instead, he ordered them to let him
down at Paul Manton's door, and he at once held a council
of war in the kitchen. He sat rubbing his chin, while the people came in to give him the full details of the situation. Nan
Hogan continued to sit on the door-step of the house, caoin-
ing and lamenting and going over the troubles of her life,
while Maura Casey lay low within.

"Where is Sara Finnessy?" Tim O'Halloran asked at
last.

"Above in her own house. She's afraid to show her
nose on account of the skelping she got."

"Send her down to me," Tim O'Halloran ordered.

It took a big deputation and a great deal of persuasion
to induce Sara Finnessy to make her appearance, but at last
she came.

Tim O'Halloran ordered the people out of the kitchen,
and was left alone with Sara Finnessy.

"This is a bad business," Tim began.

"It's a business that has no concern for me at all, Tim
O'Halloran," Sara made answer.

"I think you're mistaken in that, Sara."

"Devil a bit, then."

"You and Nan Hogan have been a long time at daggers drawn."

"If we have, that's Nan Hogan's fault."

"I know it is, Sara. But this business of the house is all in your hands now. You're the one person in the world to settle it."

"Me?" Sara Finnessy exclaimed, looking at Tim O'Halloran incredulously.

"No other, Sara."

Sara laughed sarcastically.

"It's your one chance in the world to make it up with Nan Hogan."

"There's no making up with the like of her."

"It's for you to go down and rout Maura Casey out of the house in front of Nan. That'll make up the breach."

"Is it to face Maura Casey? And she like a badger below in the house."

"She'll be too much afeard to fight this time, Sara."

"I wouldn't face her for the weight of Kilbeg in gold— except I had a hatchet or something," Sara added, grimly.

"Look here, Sara Finnessy," Tim O'Halloran said, rousing himself, "there's nothing thought of you by the people since Maura Casey put you out over the stile. You have no respect in Kilbeg since that, and if you be wishful to remove that stain and make it up with Nan Hogan now's your chance. And if you do it well there won't be one thought half as much of as yourself for the rest of your life. It's a great chance entirely for you, Sara Finnessy."

"I tell you it would take a hatchet, Tim O'Halloran," Sara Finnessy insisted, but Tim, with some satisfaction, saw a look of ambition beginning to show in the face of Sara Finnessy.

"Go in by the back door, grab the broom, and drive her out with it over the stile before the eyes of Nan Hogan and of Kilbeg. Where you made the blunder before was not to grab the broom first. It was all a matter of who had it first."

"She might rise the tongs to me," Sara suggested.

"Don't give her time. But she won't. She's too much in

dread of the people now. They'll be around the house. I'll
have a few gossoons ready to go in if she takes the tongs at
you."

Tim pressed home the case, and Sara Finnessy came
round gradually. By the time she stepped out of the house,
her inherent love of conflict was burning in her eyes. She
wanted to pay off Maura Casey for the crushing humiliation she had put upon her. Her fingers were twitching for
the broom as she set forth to the battle.

Tim O'Halloran raised a coal on the tongs to light his
pipe, and then settled himself comfortably in his chair, that
fleeting, wintry smile passing over his long face.

Sara Finnessy acted on Tim O'Halloran's plan of campaign. She got quietly to the back of Nan Hogan's house and
pushed in the door softly, then made a grab at the broom.
She glanced about the kitchen. It was empty. She took a little run for the front door and threw it open.

Nan Hogan was on the top note of one of her lamenta-
tions when she felt the door at her back swing open. She
glanced round, gathered herself to her feet, and panted at
the sight of the apparition before her. Sara Finnessy swung
the broom over her head, her eyes wild-looking and excited.

At the same moment Maura Casey stepped out from
the little room. She took in the situation with a glance, and
stood perfectly still, her back to the wall.

"God leave me my reason," Nan Hogan exclaimed,
"but is it Sara Finnessy I see in my house?"

"Out of the woman's house," Maura Casey exclaimed.

Sara Finnessy made a wild sweep of the broom at
Maura Casey. It swept Maura's face, and the next instant
Maura had one end of it in her hands. Sara thought to jerk
it from her, but Maura Casey was accustomed to hold on to
whatever little things came within her grasp in life.

There was a little scuffle over by the room door. Sara
Finnessy often declared afterwards that she would have
won the day only the sight became scattered in her eyes. As
it was, she felt Maura Casey pressing her against the wall,
and the next thing that she remembered was to feel hard,

long fingers about the scruff of her neck. A quiver went down her spine, for she knew at once that they were the bony fingers of Nan Hogan. She got a few jerks from behind, and felt herself staggering over the threshold of the door. She was conscious of a jeering murmur in a crowd of onlookers outside, and with a last desperate effort turned back to the door, her hands out for the first enemy that came within her reach.

"Close out the door or she'll murder us!" Nan Hogan cried, and the door was slapped out on Sara Finnessy's face. She beat her hands on the door in vain. But as the crowd was becoming greater and more boisterous at the stile, and as the door was secured inside, Sara Finnessy was much relieved to feel Christy's hand on her shoulder.

"Come home out of this," Christy said.

"I will," Sara cried hysterically. "I'll leave them to the judgment of God."

When Tim O'Halloran, from his comfortable chair by Paul Manton's fire, saw Christy Finnessy leading his woman up home, "and she having all the signs and tokens of ignominious defeat written upon her face," he hitched back the chair a bit. "It was quicker than I expected," he said.

A moment later Mrs. Manton came running into the house.

"Was it you sent Sara Finnessy down to rout Maura Casey out of the house?" she asked.

"Ay, it was then," Tim admitted quietly.

"Well, you only made bad worse," Mrs. Manton said.

"And are the other two inside now?" Tim asked.

"They are, and the sorra a word or sign out of them."

"Very well," Tim said. "I'll be on my way home now. This business has nearly cost me the length of a day, and I having many a thing to attend to."

Mrs. Manton looked after Tim O'Halloran as he struck up the Boherlahan road, a puzzled look on her face. Gradually a light broke in upon her, and her face lengthened out. She sat down on a chair, folded her arms, and wagged her head slowly. "Well," she said at last, "the devil is shook on you, Tim O'Halloran."

However, things were not so quiet inside Nan Hogan's house as the people thought. Nan was rather excited, for Sara Finnessy's thumps on the door frightened her while they lasted. Maura Casey, on the other hand, stood drawn to one side of the door, the broom gripped ready in her hand. It was just as well for Sara Finnessy that the door held out. When Christy was heard leading his woman away, Maura Casey left the broom carefully behind the door. Nan Hogan sank into a chair with a sigh.

"Well," said Nan at last. "I came in, after all, Maura Casey. You may thank Sara Finnessy for it, or a step I'd never take on the floor while you were here."

"When did you leave the hospital?" Maura asked, mildly.

"This morning, thank God," Nan replied. "And I was no sooner seen by the stile outside than the cutthroats of Kilbeg came running down to welcome me. When I get my strength back I'll let them know what I have weighing on my mind."

Maura Casey fixed up the fire on the hearth and set the kettle to boil. Nan's eye followed her movements with growing scorn. When Maura Casey reached out for the teapot on the dresser Nan turned on her.

"Don't lay a hand on that teapot," she cried. "Don't think you're going to come round me. I'm not as soft as you fancy, Maura Casey."

Maura laid down the teapot and turned to Nan. Her face was troubled and anxious-looking.

"Won't you let me be in the house with you?" she asked.

"Is it my house to hold the scruff of Boherlahan?" Nan demanded.

"I'm used to the house now. I wouldn't like the thoughts of the roads again."

"It's little concern I have for your thoughts."

"I could be doing many a thing for you. I could be working at the farmers' places an odd day and bringing in a few shillings."

"You can work when and where you wish, but you'll be cutting your stick out of this place."

"You're not too well yet, Nan Hogan. If you get taken with the weakness again they'll be bringing you back into hospital."

"No," Nan cried, with some alarm. "The Poorhouse Car will never stand at my door again."

"Tim O'Halloran will find means of getting you out."

Nan Hogan looked out the window with her one eye, her mouth twitching a little. Maura Casey could see the shadow of a great terror falling across her face.

"Don't be upsetting me with your talk," Nan said at last. "You can make a shake down for yourself in the corner here for to-night. It's too late for the roads now. But to-morrow morning you'll gather together whatever things you have belonging to you in this place and leave my house."

Nan walked into the room and closed out the door. Maura Casey heard her shooting the bolt on the inside. She sat down by the fire miserably. After all, it was a hard thing to face the wandering life again when she had tasted the sweets of a home. Now and then Maura Casey's eyes would travel about the kitchen, lingering on articles which had become dear to her. She stayed by the fire the best part of the night, crying quietly to herself. Then she made a sort of bed by the hearth and slept a little.

In the morning Maura Casey renewed the fire. She scattered some crumbs on the floor for the hen and her young brood, and did other duties about the place. Then she heard Nan Hogan shooting the bolt from the door.

"Maura Casey," Nan called.

Maura Casey pushed in the room door. Nan Hogan was sitting up in bed, having only reached out to draw the bolt.

"What noise is that I heard? Is it a stray hen that came in with a clutch of chickens?"

"She's my own hen. I got her and the eggs from Mrs. O'Hea. Eleven of them she brought out. A body wouldn't feel until the like of them would be laying fine eggs."

"Well," Nan said, "you can be bringing them with you."

"I'll leave them where they are. What way could I contrive to bring them, Nan Hogan?"

"As to that flower pot," Nan said, pointing to the geranium in the cannister on the window, "it's not wholesome. You can be giving it to one of the children."

"Are you getting up now, Nan Hogan?" Maura Casey asked, measuring Nan Hogan's attitude in the bed with a shrewdness that was bringing a ray of hope into her heart.

"Not now," Nan said, a little disconcerted.

"Aren't you feeling well?" Maura insisted, stepping in a little way to the room.

Nan Hogan's eye fell.

"I'm feeling elegant," she said.

"You haven't the weakness in the legs again?"

"I over-reached myself yesterday. I'll be all right bye and bye."

Maura Casey went out into the kitchen and returned after some time with a cup of tea and some toast. Without a word she laid them in Nan Hogan's lap as she sat on the bed, and walked out again.

Presently the rain came down in torrents. Maura Casey stood at the door looking out over the wet country. "It would be a hard day on the roads," she said to herself.

When she went into the room again the tea and the toast had disappeared. Nan Hogan was still sitting up in bed, a great brown beads in her hands, swaying a little from side to side, as she recited the Rosary.

Maura Casey took up the cup and saucer and turned to leave the room. Nan Hogan paused in her devotions and looked at Maura Casey.

"What time will you be quitting this place?" she asked.

"The rain is very heavy," Maura Casey made answer.

"Tell me, Maura Casey," Nan went on, "had you ever

anyone belonging to you sailing the waters of the oceans?"

"Never," Maura answered, "I was always alone."

"I have a son on the seas," Nan said, "and the rest of my care are in heaven. I do be praying to them to send him back to me."

And Nan Hogan went on with her prayers.

Maura Casey went out into the kitchen. She made spasmodic efforts to do a few things about the place. But she spent most of the time listening with alert ears for any sound of stirring in the room, her hands twitching, opening and clasping as she listened. Every now and then she would murmur under her breath, "She might never be able to put them under her again."

The day was drawing to a close when the room door opened, and Nan Hogan came out dressed and walking a little helplessly.

"Did any of the traitors of Kilbeg ask to darken my door to-day?" she asked, coming out.

"An odd one of them was crossing the stile," Maura Casey said, "but I said it was not your wish for any of them to come in. I told them you were in a long sleep after the fatigue of your sickness."

Nan Hogan gave a little grunt of satisfaction. "They might be in no hurry to face me," she said, "when I gather the clearness of my mind together."

Maura Casey moved to the door and looked up at the sky. "The rain is coming heavy yet," she said.

Nan Hogan went down and sat by the fire.

"Well," she said, "I ought to be thankful to the mercy of God that I am by my own fire again. Another month of that rotten place in Boherlahan and the heart would be broke across in me."

"The comfort of a house is a great thing surely," Maura Casey said, standing at the door, looking out over the desolate country, her eyes following the mist that rose and broke upon the hills.

Nan Hogan looked at Maura Casey with her sharp eye. "You look very drooping in yourself," she said. "You're like an old sick hen that'd stay up on the perch the hours of the day, the wings hanging by her."

"I'm thinking of the deep roads and the pair of boots I have," Maura Casey said.

"Ay," Nan Hogan went on, raising the tongs to settle up the fire, "there do be many a turn and twist in the story that stretches behind a person's life. I suppose a day or two ago you were standing out there in the sun, pluming your fine feathers, and thinking all to yourself that Nan Hogan would never gather a leg under her to go between you and the grabbing of her house."

"There was no grabbing about it," Maura Casey answered. "I kept it well with the activity of my two hands, Nan Hogan."

Maura Casey came in from the door, and took down a thin shawl from a nail on the backdoor, which she threw over her shoulders. "The rain is over now," she said.

Nan Hogan stood up and went to the door, halting and limping. She looked up at the sky.

"You could be putting no more trust in that sky," she said, "than you could be depending on the neighbourly grace of Kilbeg."

"I'll be on my road now, Nan Hogan," Maura Casey answered.

Nan did not pretend to hear her as she stood at the door. "Look at the big, loaded cloud up from the West. It'll be washing every blade of grass on the hills."

She closed out the door and limped back to the fire. Then her eyes ranged over the flaring pictures on the walls, the faces of patriots and politicians, saints and writers, staring from a hoarding of caricatures. "Please God," Nan said, ranging her disapproving eye over them, "I'll make a bonfire of them to-morrow."

Maura Casey paused a little, looking intently at Nan Hogan. Nan sat down in her old seat by the fire, then reached out for a stool which she settled the other side of the hearth.

"Maura Casey," Nan said, "I was speaking to you to-day about that son of mine travelling the wide waters of the world. He was taken from under this roof by the greatest rascal that ever left the heart of a woman stripped of its comfort. Sit down here until I be telling you of the grace and beauty of the boy that went sailoring from me."

Maura Casey's fingers trembled a little as she hung the shawl up on the nail. She went over and sat down on the stool by Nan Hogan's hearth.

When the night had fallen on Kilbeg, two carefully shawled figures, with enough space in front of the faces to allow a single eye to see out, stole very noiselessly over the stile leading down to Nan Hogan's house and crept cautiously up to the little window, through which they peered into the kitchen. Outlined against the fire they could see two distinct figures sitting on two stools—the figure of Nan Hogan and the figure of Maura Casey. Nan Hogan was speaking, leaning a hand on Maura Casey's arm as she spoke. Maura Casey was listening very intently, every now and then turning her head away from Nan and wiping something from her eyes surreptitiously.

The Widow Lowry's elbow nudged Mrs. Paul Manton at the window outside. The Widow's shawled head stooped over to Mrs. Manton's shawled head.

"She's telling her the troubles of her life," the Widow whispered. "Little wonder she's drawing tears from her."

Mrs. Manton's head nodded in agreement. "They look like a pair of well-matched cronies," she whispered back. "It'll be the making of Nan Hogan to have someone to discourse to by the fire in the night."

"And if she ever gets taken sick again she'll have one at hand accustomed to handle cases like her."

"It's my opinion," the Widow Lowry said, "that Tim O'Halloran was working for this end all the while."

"He's a caution when it comes to a matter of clever stratagems. He has the understanding of the world. See how he used Sara Finnessy to bring them two creatures together."

"Look! They are going upon their knees by the hearth. Nan is taking out her Rosary Beads."

BRIAN O'NOLAN

The Martyr's Crown

*

Mr. Toole and Mr. O'Hickey walked down the street together in the morning.

Mr. Toole had a peculiarity. He had the habit, when
accompanied by another person, of saluting total strangers; but only if these strangers were of important air and
costly raiment. He meant thus to make it known that he had
friends in high places, and that he himself, though poor, was
a person of quality fallen on evil days through some undis-
closed sacrifice made in the interest of immutable principle
early in life. Most of the strangers, startled out of their private thoughts, stammered a salutation in return. And Mr.
Toole was shrewd. He stopped at that. He said no more to
his companion, but by some little private gesture, a
chuckle, a shake of the head, a smothered imprecation, he
nearly always extracted the one question most melodious
to his ear: "*Who was that?*"

Mr. Toole was shabby, and so was Mr. O'Hickey, but

From *Envoy*.

Mr. O'Hickey had a neat and careful shabbiness. He was an older and a wiser man, and was well up to Mr. Toole's tricks. Mr. Toole at his best, he thought, was better than a play. And he now knew that Mr. Toole was appraising the street with beady eye.

"Gorawars!" Mr. Toole said suddenly.

We are off, Mr. O'Hickey thought.

"Do you see this hop-off-my-thumb with the stick and the hat?" Mr. Toole said.

Mr. O'Hickey did. A young man of surpassing elegance was approaching; tall, fair, darkly dressed; even at fifty yards his hauteur seemed to chill Mr. O'Hickey's part of the street.

"Ten to one he cuts me dead," Mr. Toole said. "This is one of the most extraordinary pieces of work in the whole world."

Mr. O'Hickey braced himself for a more than ordinary impact. The adversaries neared each other.

"*How are we at all, Sean a chara?*" Mr. Toole called out.

The young man's control was superb. There was no glare, no glance of scorn, no sign at all. He was gone, but had left in his wake so complete an impression of his contempt that even Mr. Toole paled momentarily. The experience frightened Mr. O'Hickey.

"Who . . . who was *that?*" he asked at last.

"I knew the mother well," Mr. Toole said musingly. "The woman was a saint." Then he was silent.

Mr. O'Hickey thought: there is nothing for it but bribery—again. He led the way into a public house and ordered two bottles of stout.

"As you know," Mr. Toole began, "I was Bart Conlon's right-hand man. We were through 'twenty and 'twenty-one together. Bart, of course, went the other way in 'twenty-two."

Mr. O'Hickey nodded and said nothing. He knew that Mr. Toole had never rendered military service to his country.

"In any case," Mr. Toole continued, "there was a certain day early in 'twenty-one and orders come through that there was to be a raid on the Sinn Fein office above in Harcourt Street. There happened to be a certain gawskogue of a cattle-jobber from the County Meath had an office on the other side of the street. And he was well in with a certain character by the name of Mick Collins. I think you get me drift?"

"I do," Mr. O'Hickey said.

"There was six of us," Mr. Toole said, "with meself and Bart Conlon in charge. Me man the cattle-jobber gets an urgent call to be out of his office accidentally on purpose at four o'clock, and at half-four the six of us is parked inside there with two machine-guns, the rifles and a class of a homemade bomb that Bart used to make in his own kitchen. The military arrived in two lurries on the other side of the street at five o'clock. That was the hour in the orders that come. I believe that man Mick Collins had lads working for him over in the War Office across in London. He was a great stickler for the British being punctual on the dot."

"He was a wonderful organizer," Mr. O'Hickey said.

"Well, we stood with our backs to the far wall and let them have it through the open window and them getting down offa the lurries. Sacred godfathers! I never seen such murder in me life. Your men didn't know where it was coming from, and a lot of them wasn't worried very much when it was all over, because there was no heads left on some of them. Bart then gives the order for retreat down the back stairs; in no time we're in the lane, and five minutes more the six of us upstairs in Martin Fulham's pub in Camden Street. Poor Martin is dead since."

"I knew that man well," Mr. O'Hickey remarked.

"Certainly you knew him well," Mr. Toole said, warmly. "The six of us was marked men, of course. In any case, fresh orders come at six o'clock. All hands was to proceed in military formation, singly, by different routes to the house of a great skin in the Cumann na mBan, a widow be the name of Clougherty that lived on the south side. We were all to lie low, do you understand, till there was fresh orders to come out and fight again. Sacred wars, they were very rough days them days; will I ever forget Mrs. Clougherty! She was certainly a marvellous figure of a woman. I never seen a woman like her to bake bread."

Mr. O'Hickey looked up.

"Was she," he said, "was she . . . all right?"

"She was certainly nothing of the sort," Mr. Toole said loudly and sharply. "By God, we were all thinking of other things in them days. Here was this unfortunate woman in a three-story house on her own, with some quare fellow in the middle flat, herself on the ground floor, and six blood-thirsty pultogues hiding above on the top floor, every man-jack ready to shoot his way out if there was trouble. We got feeds there I never seen before or since, and the *Independent* every morning. Outrage in Harcourt Street. The armed men then decamped and made good their escape. I'm damn bloody sure we made good our escape. There was one snag. We couldn't budge out. No exercise at all—and that means only one thing . . ."

"Constipation?" Mr. O'Hickey suggested.

"The very man," said Mr. Toole.

Mr. O'Hickey shook his head.

"We were there a week. Smoking and playing cards, but when nine o'clock struck, Mrs. Clougherty come up, and, Protestant, Catholic or Jewman, all hands had to go down on the knees. A very good . . . strict . . . woman, if you understand me, a true daughter of Ireland. And now I'll tell you a damn good one. About five o'clock one evening I heard a noise below and peeped out of the window. Sanctified and holy godfathers!"

"What was it—the noise?" Mr. O'Hickey asked.

"What do you think, only two lurries packed with military, with my nabs of an officer hopping out and running up the steps to hammer at the door, and all the Tommies sitting back with their guns at the ready. Trapped! That's a nice word—*trapped!* If there was ever rats in a cage, it was me unfortunate brave men from the battle of Harcourt Street. God!"

"They had you at what we call a disadvantage," Mr. O'Hickey conceded.

"She was in the room herself with the teapot. She had a big silver satteen blouse on her; I can see it yet. She turned on us and gave us all one look that said: *Shut up, ye nervous lousers.* Then she foostered about a bit at the glass and walks out of the room with bang-bang-bang to shake the house going on downstairs. And I seen a thing . . ."

"What?" asked Mr. O'Hickey.

"She was a fine—now you'll understand me, Mr. O'Hickey," Mr. Toole said carefully; "I seen her fingers on the buttons of the satteen, if you follow me, and she leaving the room."

Mr. O'Hickey, discreet, nodded thoughtfully.

"I listened at the stairs. Jakers I never got such a drop in me life. She clatters down and flings open the halldoor. This young pup is outside, and asks—awsks—in the law-de-daw voice, 'Is there any men in this house?' The answer took me to the fair altogether. She puts on the guttiest voice I ever heard outside Moore Street and says, 'Sairtintly not at this hour of the night; I wish to God there was. Sure, how could the poor unfortunate women get on without them, officer?' Well lookat. I nearly fell down the stairs on top of the two of them. The next thing I hear is, 'Madam this and madam that,' and 'Sorry to disturb and I beg your pardon,' 'I trust this and I trust that,' and then the whispering starts, and at the wind-up the halldoor is closed and into the room off the hall with the pair of them. This young bucko out of the Borderers in a room off the hall with a headquarters captain of the Cumann na mBan! *Give us two more stouts there, Mick!*"

"That is a very queer one, as the man said," Mr. O'Hickey said.

"I went back to the room and sat down. Bart had his gun out, and we were all looking at one another. After ten minutes we heard another noise."

Mr. Toole poured out his stout with unnecessary care.

"It was the noise of the lurries driving away," he said at last. "She'd saved our lives, and when she come up a while later she said 'We'll go to bed a bit earlier to-night, boys; kneel down all.' That was Mrs. Clougherty the saint."

Mr. O'Hickey, also careful, was working at his own bottle, his wise head bent at the task.

"What I meant to ask you was this," Mr. O'Hickey said, "that's an extraordinary affair altogether, but what has that to do with that stuck-up young man we met in the street, the lad with all the airs?"

"Do you not see it, man?" Mr. Toole said, in surprise. "For seven hundred years, thousands—no, I'll make it millions—of Irish men and women have died for Ireland. We never rared jibbers; they were glad to do it, and will again. But that young man was *born* for Ireland. There was never anybody else like him. Why wouldn't he be proud?"

"The Lord save us!" Mr. O'Hickey cried.

"A saint I called her," Mr. Toole said, hotly. "What am I talking about—she's a martyr and wears the martyr's crown to-day!"

JIM PHELAN

Bell Wethers

❄

"I declare to God, Packy—I mane Mr. Dollan—there isn't a pound in money on Mullaravogue Mountain. Not wan pound, among sixty of us." The big round-shouldered peasantman shuffled awkwardly, glanced at the crowd of others like himself, then looked back, furtive as a frightened child, at the man before him.

Packy Dollan sat on a barrel of flour, one leg swinging loosely. He propped an elbow on a box of bacon, and set his chin in his hand, to watch with a good-humored smile while the peasant hurried to speak again in growing embarrassment.

"I'm telling ye, Packy, there isn't as much as half-a-crown between us," the big man emphasised. "Not until after the June fair. An' that's the truth." Again he glanced at the crowd for support.

Timid, sheepish, turning from side to side, they still kept silent. Only huddling a little closer to one another and

From Bog Blossom Stories, London, Sidgwick & Jackson.

to the speaker, they peeped for brief instants, in hope or fear or incomprehension, at the smiling red-faced man on the barrel.

Dollan stood up slowly, brushed a smudge of flour from his trousers, and wiped his hands on his white apron. Still smiling, he hummed a few bars of a song, ignoring the peasantmen, and glanced out from the window of the store-room at the wide sweep of heathery mountain outside. Then, with a short laugh, he whipped an account book from a shelf and faced the first speaker.

"Wisha God help ye, John Joe Mooley me poor fella," he grinned. "Sure it's the deservin' case that ye are! Not even half-a-crown. Nor none of these others," he went on, with a humorous shake of his head as he surveyed the group of men who filled the store. "Yerra, John Joe," he finished with a succession of admiring grins, "sure it's yer-self has the gift o' the gab—but is it a millionaire ye're takin' me for?" He opened the account book, on the top of the bacon-box.

Slowly the men grouped themselves a little nearer, seemingly fascinated by the book. Packy Dollan swept the crowd with a wide intimate grin, nodded with twinkling eyes whenever a man met his gaze for a moment, and toyed with the account book, as if they were all participants in some huge joke.

Gradually his insistent grin forced answering half-smiles from the men around. Dollan paused, with his fore-finger between the pages of the book, and sat erect for a second.

"Sixty of ye," he continued, in the same jocular tone. "Sixty-two I make it, be the book—owin' me forty pound each on an average. But sure," he went on quizzically to John Joe Mooley, "sure a hundher' pound, or a couple of hundher' pound, isn't big enough to matter. No, indeed!" He laughed loudly, and again the crowd of peasants, after a few seconds, pretended to share his merriment.

For a minute or more Packy continued to smile at the crowd. Then he opened the book and commenced to read:

—"John Joe Mooley, forty-seven pound, twelve shillin's an' thruppence. Am I right or wrong, John Joe?"

The only immediate answer was a long, snorting, animal breath from the group of men. Then, gradually, they drew still closer around the account book, as the reading continued:—"Mickeen MacHugh O'Byrne, thirty-nine pound, eight an' ten. Am I right or wrong, Mickeen?"

Awkwardly and with childish heavings, the men shook their rounded shoulders into a pretence of laughing agreement with Packy, as if an unpleasant and difficult lesson were being read by a popular schoolmaster. Only from time to time they looked out of the window, in sudden pain and fear, at the big heathery tops they called home.

Mullaravogue was three rocky mountain crests and the whole of a smaller hill. Behind, westward, the black unbroken mass of the main mountain range cut off the world, carried no village, not even a hamlet. Westward was no road.

Down in the lower levels, on the east front of Mullaravogue, where the last small byway from civilization petered out, the little town of Barnasleeve clung to the side of the foot-hills. With its main street a mountain pass but thinly disguised, its very name meaning in Irish "the mountain gap," Barnasleeve was the first or last stop on the way out of or into the mountain lands.

A single large pub overlooked the middle of the street, the name "P. Dollan" over the door. Beside it, a smaller shop bore the same name, with the added information, "Transport contractor. Funerals attended with promptness and civility. Cars for hire."

On the other side of the pub four converted cottages made a roomy general shop, with a big grocery store at one end, where the flat, impassive voice of Packy Dollan read slowly:—"Martin Mike Dockery, forty-two pound, four an' eight. Am I right or wrong, Martin Mike?"

Backing the little town, the sprawling stony mountain laid its greenish-brown arms around score after score of tiny peasant holdings. Circling each home was the scrap of tillage, eternally defended against the inroads of gorse and heather and rolling rock. Between and above were the untilled tops of Mullaravogue, peaceful and lovely, cut into chequered patterns by the myriad low stone walls, white fleeces showing here and there in the squares of gold and green.

Inland, the dark, rocky bulk of the chief range separated Mullaravogue from the vaguely-suggested Ireland beyond. There was no peasant home on the heights, not a pass worthy of the name, not a road across the range. Everything went up, or came down, through Barnasleeve. The droning voice from the grocery store seemed to be emphasising the fact.

"Danny Jem Ryan, thirty-eight pound four an' six. Am I right, Danny Jem? Paddy Gaffney, forty-wan pound nine an'—"

On the mountains around Barnasleeve there was a stock joke about Packy Dollan. Packy, the hillmen would say, was willing to sell you a cradle or hire you a hearse—he got you coming and going. Everything in Barnasleeve was Packy's.

Starting from nothing, Dollan had worked hard all his life. First adding penny to penny, in a tiny shop, then putting pound beside pound as he prospered, later piling the hundreds into Barnasleeve's only bank, Packy had grown.

The story is common enough in Ireland or in any peasant country. Some one man discovers that he can collect the wealth of a region by supplying necessities. Later and inevitably he becomes the dominant commercial force of his district.

The Irish have a word for it. The small-town merchant who gradually achieves a stranglehold on his neighbours is called a gombeen-man. Gomba, in Gaelic, means vaguely a bit or scrap. Gombeen is the diminutive. A textbook of economics might well be condensed into the single word.

Long before he was thirty, Packy Dollan had grasped the importance of Barnasleeve's geographical position. The

368

little town at the foot of the mountains was the only bridge between the hillmen and civilization. There was no way out, from the lofty backlands, into the world of commerce, except through Barnasleeve. While Packy owned the only five shops in the town, the only pub, the only two motor lorries. Packy was the gombeen.

Half wild, sheepish and timid, mostly unlettered, the men from the hillsides had to come out from their heathery tops, sooner or later, to buy and sell. They bought from, and sold to, Packy. The voice inside the store-room was summarising the results.

"An' Dickeen Cullahan, last," Packy was saying, "Forty-wan pound, eleven an' three. Right, Dickeen?" Cullahan nodded and laughed awkwardly. Packy looked around at the crowd, folding his arms with the account book against his chest, a wide grin of comical discomfiture on his face.

The men scraped their feet on the ground, fumbled in their pockets, peered sideways at one another, fidgeted still more, but kept silent. Dollan waited a few minutes, then suddenly opened a back page of the book.

"Two thousand four hundher' an' ninety-five pound eighteen an' eightpence," he said flatly, "of *my* money, is gone up there on top of Mullaravogue, in flour an' bacon an' tobacco an' the rest. Near twenty-five hundher' pound. Twenty—five—hundher'—pound."

A long, loud, combined exhalation came from the men as Dollan named the total. They peeped at one another, and immediately huddled even closer, exactly like a flock of sheep. Packy laughed.

" 'Tis the great jokers ye are," he commented, nodding approval. "The great jokers. Them that has nothin' can pay nothin'. No. So now ye're all that happy—aye, happy—because ye have nothin'. So me twenty-five hundher' pound is gone, up there."

He turned to the window and looked up at the Mullaravogue tops. The peasants followed his gaze, and Dollan turned back on them suddenly. "All happy," he repeated, and his hearty laugh rang out into the little street. "Because ye have nothin' an' can pay nothin'. Aye."

"After the June fair, Packy—" commenced John Joe Mooley. The other grinned and nodded, silencing him. He opened the book at an early page and glanced at it carelessly, then left it down on a box.

"Them debts," he remarked jocularly, "has been pilin' up from the bits an' pieces left over after the June fair or the December fair for the last twenty year. Now they make two thousand five hundher' pound. Yerra, John Joe, will ye stop jokin' about June fairs before ye make me die laughin'."

Acute discomfort showed among the peasantmen, while the shopkeeper still smiled. Gradually, in the silence, a guilty, hang-dog expression appeared on each face, as if Packy had caught them out in some mean and sordid conspiracy to cheat him. Then, the silence continuing, the men stared at the gombeen in blank and hopeless calm. They had nothing, could pay nothing, could do nothing.

"There must be seven or eight hundher' sheep up there on the tops of Mullaravogue, John Joe," said Dollan, quietly and in a casual voice, scarcely above his breath. The crowd of peasants drew back in haste, as if the gombeen had suddenly produced a bomb.

On the Mullaravogue tops, where the many small flocks of mountain sheep grazed in common, gross wasteful patches of gorse alternated with vast ragged rocks, with here and there a small patch of grass or a square of temporarily-good grazing where the gorse had been burnt away.

Up here, all the sheep of Mullaravogue herded together, indiscriminately, each with its owner's brand on fleece or ear, until the time came to separate them, for slaughter or sale or shearing. That meant, until they or their fleece went down into Barnasleeve, to Packy Dollan.

To the hillmen, the sheep were eternal and unchanging, as much part of their lives as the thatch in the cottage roofs or the water in the mountain streams. A man might sell two sheep, or five lambs, or ten fleeces—he always had

370

the same number of sheep, nearly enough, never thought of them as property.

All the little farms produced corn, potatoes, turnips and the like, for sale. These were the hillmen's main preoccupation and source of income, such as it was. The sheep were almost a by-product, a means of extracting each year a few pounds from the otherwise-sterile tops of Mullaravogue.

Hardly one of the little peasant homes was without thirty or forty sheep, somewhere on the mountain. Fifteen or twenty pounds a year, no more, came in profit from each small flock. But it was money for practically nothing, money from the patches between the rocks and gorse, and in a district where every shilling counted it was important.

It had never struck any of the peasants that their ragged flocks were capital. The sheep were there. Now and then they yielded a few pounds. But they were still there, like the turf in the bog or the roof on the house. No one had ever thought of them as property. Except Packy Dollan.

On the afternoon that Packy dropped his bombshell about the number of sheep on the mountain, the hillmen's first reaction had been to stare as if the gombeen had uttered some insane, sacrilegious obscenity. Swiftly they had realized that instead he was pronouncing something like a sentence of death. Packy had known his twenty-five hundred pounds were safe. The hillmen had not.

With infuriating stupidity, each peasant had evaded Dollan's questions as to how many sheep he had. Sure a man couldn't say, they explained. Them sheep was up there all together, and indeed 'twould be hard to tell which was whose, until say the June fair.

Sure now Mr. Dollan must understand, they explained, with fear in their voices and eyes. Them sheep was all mixed up, on the mountain, everyone's together, one here and there like. Sure a man never bothered, on Mullaravogue, barring when he went to shear or to sell a few lambs or the like. One here and there.

Packy had snarled for a second, and then the good-humored grin had reappeared. The peasantmen seemed to shrink in height as he spoke.

"Aye faith," Dollan had summed up. "So not one of ye knows where his sheep are, nor how many he has. No. Just one here and there. Ye've all got just one here and there. But when they're all together there's so many that a man can't count his own either! Wisha ye'll kill me with laughin'. Now—what about me twenty-five hundher' pound?"

In the end, the hillmen had shambled out into the street of Barnasleeve, not even looking at one another. Packy had made it all sound so simple, so businesslike. He was coming up Mullaravogue himself, on the following Saturday. Sure they could laugh at him if they liked, jokers that they were. But there must be near seven hundred sheep up there *somewhere*.

"At three pound apiece—that'd be fair; am I right or wrong, John Joe?—at three pound apiece—"

"Sheep is near five pound apiece in Dublin market," Mooley interjected, apologetically and without much hope in his voice.

"Thrue, begob," the gombeen agreed. "Thrue enough. But the tops of Mullaravogue isn't Dublin market, no. At three pound apiece I'll be losin' near five hundher' pound. But sure that's betther than losin' the lot. Saturday, John Joe. Saturday." The hillmen sidled out.

On the Saturday morning most of the men grouped in the mountain track near John Joe Mooley's farm. They made no attempt to discuss the gombeen's coming visit, merely stared in sheepish and stupid abasement at one another, as if some tragedy or blight had descended but had left them speechless.

Dollan was brisk and friendly, when he left his car outside Mooley's where the steep narrow lane ended, and approached the crowd of hillmen on foot. He refused point-blank to go up the mountain until he had had a drink, wherefore the car yielded up four bottles of whiskey. Four other bottles followed, and some at least of the peasantmen's gloom was gone, before Packy would agree to start up the steep rocky track to the tops.

"Begor I'll be a farmer meself wan of these days," he laughed, as he handed John Joe Mooley a tool like a pair of pliers. "Take that, John Joe—sure I'd maybe punch holes in me own ears with it." He added a slightly-exaggerated hiccup, and the crowd started slowly up the track.

Mooley carried the "punch," an instrument for marking the ears of sheep to indicate ownership. He seemed not to notice that the punch-mark was "P.D.", and gradually Dollan became more confidential while they worked their way up the hill. He held the peasant's arm for a moment, as they struggled across a narrow stretch of the path between sheer rocks, then stepped out a little more briskly behind the single straggling file of men ahead.

"I want to be fair, John Joe," he reiterated. "Fair." Soberly and competently he conveyed an impression that the whiskey had been too strong or too plentiful, that he was in an expansive and generous mood. "Sure I don't care if I do lose a few hundher' pound—we're all neighbours together. Y'see, John Joe?"

Mooley made vague noises of assent, with only a single glance at the man who proclaimed his generosity. Dollan caught his arm again.

"Get me enough sheep to cover some of me money, John Joe," the gombeen said loudly. "Some of it. An' don't take too much from anyone. No. Just one here an' there." He laughed whiskily as he repeated the peasantmen's own phrase. "Just one here an' there, John Joe."

The crowd of men strung out up the mountain in a long broken line, each with a sheepdog or two near his heels. Continually they called short phrases to one another, up or down the track, but all their talk was mere practical gossip about rocks or gorse, about tracks and grazing, with no word of the gombeen or his obvious intention to clear the mountain of sheep for the first time in centuries.

Now and then one or two halted, to look back towards

Mooley and Dollan at the rear, glancing at John Joe as if he were a leader, although he came nearly last and hardly spoke. Then they shuffled upward again.

The track became steeper, then swiftly steeper still, and Dollan's laughing protests came more often. Up near one of the rocky crests, where the path climbed through a tiny narrow gorge into an open space, the crowd of men and dogs halted, waiting for Dollan and Mooley to come through.

The pass was barely a yard wide, blue ragged rocks closing in sharply on either side, before they fell away at a small flat pasture. Loose boulders here and there had been rolled aside, so that the sheep could pass, and occasionally some steeper "step" had had a few stones hauled into place, by some peasant of the distant past, assisting nature.

Near the top of the narrowest part, a thick flat slab of rock had been tilted out of the way, years ago, that the track might be passable. Propping it, untouched for decades, a small rock-buttress lay almost buried in heather and gorse trodden short by the tiny hooves of generation after generation of sheep.

In the rock-propping, the improvised buttress, the hoof-treading, was the whole story of Mullaravogue, down the centuries. John Joe Mooley drew a long breath, seeming to realize something of the kind, as his eyes took in the familiar details. For a moment he stumbled awkwardly, and the small rock-buttress moved, for perhaps the first time in a century. John Joe stumbled again.

Packy was stating, in jocular pretence at anger, that he would go no farther, when the short slab of rock fell inward. Not big enough to injure Dollan, the slab merely fetched a curse and a grin from him as it held his leg fast, leaving him to stand awkwardly in the middle of the little pass.

"Hey, John Joe," yelled the gombeen man, with a laughing grimace. "Come an' get this bloody rock off me leg. Devil another foot I'll go anyway. Hey, John Joe."

Embarrassed and contrite, sweating in perturbation and shame, the hillman made an immediate attempt to move the rock with his hands. The rock did not rise, and Dollan cursed.

"I'll just find me a log of a tree, Mr. Dollan," John Joe explained apologetically. "Then I can get a couple of the boys to heave that rock back. Besides, ye have no farther to go. The boys'll be getting the flocks down off the tops in the manetime, for ye to mark yer own. Just a minute, Mr. Dollan." He hurried up the track.

The hillmen moved upward and outward. Still their talk was in short practical phrases, about where a log was to be got, where the sheep were likely to be, where was the best place to get them together, which dogs were to accompany which men. Small, short, practical hillside phrases. In a few seconds Packy was alone.

He heard the men calling to one another across the clumps of gorse and rock, as they moved away uphill, spreading and scattering in search of the sheep, shouting to the dogs, venturing guesses as to where a log or stake might be found, up there where there was little but rock and heather. Then there was silence.

Dollan eased himself into position, to wait. Several minutes passed before he heard anything, and he was beginning to realize that logs would be as scarce as diamonds on the tops of Mullaravogue. Then he heard a sound up the path, and looked forward impatiently for John Joe Mooley.

There was a dull clonking, an occasional lonely note from a bell that sounded cracked. From the other side of the clearing a single sheep descended, crossed the open space, and stopped.

Around his neck he carried a rusty bell, and his horns were long although curved and useless as weapons. After a short glance he went back across the open space and stood there, the bell silent. Packy watched him in amusement and pleasure, trying to guess the owner's identity from the faded red brand on the fleece.

Far up the mountain, and away to the right, there sounded a distant halloing and barking of dogs. The bell wether moved a few yards, looking up towards the noise. The bell clonked, flatly, and a few sheep came into the open, to stand huddling near the first. When the noise came again, from the other side of the hill, the big wether crossed to look and listen, clonking his way past the others and returning to stand passively among them.

Scrambling and hurried, a little group of sheep appeared from between two clumps of gorse. Down the rocks in front half a dozen others showed. The flock in the open space was growing, and Dollan noted its size with grim pleasure. He sent an angry shout up the mountain for Mooley, then bent forward in an attempt to free his leg.

There was no answer to his call, but the peasants seemed to be coming nearer, slowly, calling to the dogs, halloing to one another across the mountain. For a moment the gombeen gave way to anger and irritation, then relaxed in something approaching delight as he realized that the flock of sheep had grown to an enormous size.

Two thousand, Packy computed roughly. Two thousand! He would have been satisfied, would have been doing good business, if Mullaravogue had only yielded up a few hundred sheep. The flock before him was worth ten thousand pounds, or more, at the lowest figure.

Ten thousand pounds. While Mooley and the rest were making pretence of being ruined, here was ten thousand pounds on the bare hillside. The gombeen grinned.

He looked up at the clonking of the bell. The big wether came slowly across and looked at him, then clonked his way back to the others. Up and round the mountain the shouting and the noise of the dogs increased. The bell wether moved across the open again, and hurried back, with a rhythmic clonking, while more sheep came in from the heather.

From the rear of the flock there came a sudden movement, as another score of sheep dashed into the clearing, while the barking of dogs came nearer. The bell wether walked slowly towards Dollan again. For a moment the man and the sheep measured glances. The bell clonked once.

Packy was chuckling, at the thought that the bell wether had the same big, quiet stupid face as John Joe Mooley, when the sheep made a sudden frightened spring into the narrow gap. The bell clonked.

Dollan swore laughingly as the wether squeezed past him, straining the trapped leg into a painful position. Then another sheep, and another, sprang to follow the bell wether, and Packy laughed no longer. For the next five minutes he fought desperately, against the thrust of soft fleeces and the drive of strong little bodies trembling with fear, and against the jabbing of small hard hooves.

"Oh, God Almighty preserve us," called John Joe Mooley, half an hour later. "Oh God protect us—who'd have thought sheep could do *that?*"

Peering and blowing, glancing sideways, huddling together, the crowd of hillmen collected in the open space above the gap. One by one, solemnly and with every mark of sorrow, they crossed themselves as they looked down at the place where the gombeen man had waited.

Spread over the gap, mud-like and spongy, with scraps of clothes here and there and with the lower part of a leg still gripped between the rocks, a flattened red-brown mush of blood and dirt bore the marks of many thousand small feet.

JAMES PLUNKETT

Weep for Our Pride

✳

The door of the classroom was opened by Mr. O'Rourke just as Brother Quinlan was about to open it to leave. They were both surprised and said "Good morning" to one another as they met in the doorway, and Mr. O'Rourke, although he met Brother Quinlan every morning of his life, gave an expansive but somehow unreal smile and shouted his "good morning" with bloodcurdling cordiality. They then withdrew to the passage outside to hold a conversation.

In the interval English Poetry books were opened and the class began to repeat lines. They had been given the whole of a poem called "Lament for the Death of Eoghan Ruadh" to learn. It was very patriotic and dealt with the poisoning of Eoghan Ruadh by the accursed English, and the lines were very long, which made it difficult. The class hated the English for poisoning Eoghan Ruadh because the lines about it were so long. What made it worse was that it was the sort of poem Mr. O'Rourke loved. If it was "Hail to

From THE TRUSTING AND THE MAIMED, New York, Devin-Adair.

thee, blythe spirit" he wouldn't mind so much. But he could declaim this one for them in a rich, fruity, provincial baritone and would knock hell out of anybody who had not learned it.

Peter had not learned it. Realizing how inadequate were the few minutes left to him he ran his eyes over stanza after stanza and began to murmur fragments from each in hopeless desperation. Swaine, who sat beside him, said

"Do you know this?"

"No," Peter said. "I haven't even looked at it."

"My God," Swaine breathed in horror, "you'll be mangled."

"You could give us a prompt."

"And be torn limb from limb?" said Swaine with conviction. "Not likely."

Peter closed his eyes. It was all his mother's fault. He had meant to come to school early to learn it but the row delayed him. It had been about his father's boots. After breakfast she had found that there were holes in both his shoes. She held them up to the light which was on because the November morning was wet and dark.

"Merciful God, child," she exclaimed, "there's not a sole in your shoes. You can't go out in those."

He was anxious to put them on and get out quickly, but everybody was in bad humour. He didn't dare to say anything. His sister was clearing part of the table and his brother Joseph, who worked, was rooting in drawers and corners and saying to everybody, "Where the hell is the bicycle pump? You can't leave a thing out of your hand in this house."

"I can wear my sandals," Peter suggested.

"And it spilling out of the heavens—don't be daft, child." Then she said, "What am I to do at all?"

For a moment he hoped he might be kept at home. But his mother told his sister to root among the old boots in the press. Millie went out into the passage. On her way she trod on the cat, which meowed in intense agony.

"Blazes," said his sister, "that bloody cat."

She came in with an old pair of his father's boots, and he was made try them on. They were too big.

"I'm not going out in those," he said. "I couldn't walk in them."

But his mother and sister said they looked lovely. They went into unconvincing ecstasies. They looked perfect they said, each backing up the other. No one would notice.

"They look foolish," he insisted. "I won't wear them."

"You'll do what you're told," his sister said. They were all older than he and each in turn bullied him. But the idea of being made look ridiculous nerved him.

"I won't wear them," he persisted. At that moment his brother Tom came in and Millie said quickly:

"Tom, speak to Peter—he's giving cheek to mammy." Tom was very fond of animals. "I heard the cat," he began, looking threateningly at Peter who sometimes teased it. "What were you doing to it?"

"Nothing," Peter answered. "Millie walked on it." He tried to say something about the boots but the three of them told him to shut up and get out to school. He could stand up to the others but he was afraid of Tom. So he had flopped along in the rain feeling miserable and hating it because people would know he was poor when he had to wear his father's boots.

The door opened and Mr. O'Rourke came in. He was a huge man in tweeds. He was a fluent speaker of Irish and wore the gold Fainne in the lapel of his jacket. Both his wrists were covered with matted black hair.

"Filidheact," he roared and drew a leather from his hip pocket.

Then he shouted "Dun do leabhar" and hit the front desk a ferocious crack with the leather. Mr. O'Rourke was an ardent Gael who gave all his orders in Irish. Someone passed him up a poetry book and the rest closed theirs or turned them face downwards on their desks.

Mr. O'Rourke, his eyes glaring terribly at the ceiling, from which plaster would fall in fine dust when the 3rd year students tramped in or out, began to declaim

*"Did they dare, Did They Dare, to slay Eoghan Ruadh
  O'Neill?
  Yes, they slew with poison him they feared to meet with
  steel."*

He clenched his powerful fists and held them up rigidly before his chest.

*"May God wither up their hearts, may their blood cease to
  flow,
May they walk in living death who poisoned Eoghan
  Ruadh."*

Then quite suddenly, in a businesslike tone, he said, "You
—Daly."

"Me sir?" said Daly, playing for time.

"Yes, you fool," thundered Mr. O'Rourke. "You."

The rest could have drowned Daly for saying "Me
sir?" It put Mr. O'Rourke in bad humor.

Daly rose and repeated the first four lines. When he
was halfway through the second stanza Mr. O'Rourke
bawled "Clancy." Clancy rose and began to recite. They
stood up and sat down as Mr. O'Rourke commanded while
he paced up and down the aisles between the seats. Twice
he passed close to Peter. He stood for some time by Peter's
desk bawling out names. The end of his tweed jacket lay
hypnotically along the edge of Peter's desk. Cummins stumbled over the fourth verse and dried up completely.

"Line," Mr. O'Rourke bawled. Cummins, calmly pale,
left his desk and stepped out to the side of the class. Two
more were sent out. Mr. O'Rourke walked up and down
once more and stood with his back to Peter. Looking at the
desk at the very back he suddenly bawled "Farrell."

Peter's heart jerked. He rose to his feet. The back was
still towards him. He looked at it, a great mountain of tweed
with a frayed collar over which the thick neck bulged in
folds. He could see the antennae of hair which sprouted
from Mr. O'Rourke's ears and could smell the chalk-and-ink
schoolmaster's smell of him. It was a trick of Mr. O'Rourke's

to stand with his back to you and then call your name. It made the shock more acute. Peter gulped and was silent.

"Wail . . ." prompted Mr. O'Rourke.

Peter said "Wail . . ."

Mr. O'Rourke paced up to the head of the class once more.

"Wail—wail him through the island," he said as he walked. Then he turned around suddenly and said "Well, go on."

"Wail, wail him through the island," Peter said once more and stopped.

"Weep," hinted Mr. O'Rourke.

He regarded Peter closely, his eyes narrowing.

"Weep," said Peter, ransacking the darkness of his mind but finding only emptiness.

"Weep, weep, weep," Mr. O'Rourke said, his voice rising.

Peter chanced his arm. He said, "Wail, wail him through the island, weep, weep, weep."

Mr. O'Rourke stood up straight. His face conveyed at once shock, surprise, pain.

"Get out to the line," he roared, "you thick, lazy, good-for-nothing, bloody imbecile. Tell him what it is Clancy." Clancy dithered for a moment, closed his eyes and said,

"Sir—Wail, wail him through the island, weep, weep for our pride
Would that on the battle field our gallant chief had died."

Mr. O'Rourke nodded with dangerous benevolence. As Peter shuffled to the line the boots caught the iron upright of the desk and made a great clamor. Mr. O'Rourke gave him a cut with the leather across the behind. "Did you look at this, Farrell?" he asked.

Peter hesitated and said uncertainly, "No sir."

"It wasn't worth your while, I suppose."

"No sir. I hadn't time, sir."

Just then the clock struck the hour. The class rose. Mr. O'Rourke put the leather under his left armpit and crossed himself. "In ainm an athair," he began. While they recited the Hail Mary, Peter, unable to pray, stared at the leafless rain-soaked trees in the square and the serried rows of pale, prayerful faces. They sat down.

Mr. O'Rourke turned to the class.

"Farrell hadn't time," he announced pleasantly. Then he looked thunderously again at Peter. "If it was an English penny dreadful about Public Schools or London crime you'd find time to read it quick enough, but when it's about the poor hunted martyrs and felons of your own unfortunate country by a patriot like Davis you've no time for it. You're the makings of a fine little Britisher." With genuine pathos Mr. O'Rourke then recited,

> *"The weapon of the Sassenach met him on his way*
> *And he died at Cloch Uachter upon St. Leonard's day."*

"That was the dear dying in any case, but if he died for the likes of you Farrell it was the dear bitter dying, no mistake about it."

Peter said, "I meant to learn it."

"If I can't preach respect for the patriot dead into you, then honest to my stockings I'll beat respect into you. Hand."

Peter held it out. He pulled his coat sleeve down over his wrist. The leather came down six times with a resounding impact. He tried to keep his thumb out of the way because if it hit you on the thumb it stung unbearably. But after four heavy slaps the hand began to curl of its own accord, curl and cripple like a little piece of tinfoil in a fire, until the thumb lay powerless across the palm, and the pain burned in his chest and stiffened in his toes. But worse than the pain was the fear that he would cry. He was turning away when Mr. O'Rourke said, "Just a moment, Farrell, I haven't finished."

Mr. O'Rourke gently took the fingers of Peter's hand,

smoothing them out as he drew them once more into position. "To teach you I'll take no defiance," he said, in a friendly tone, and raised the leather. Peter tried to hold his crippled hand steady.

He could not see properly going back to his desk and again the boots deceived him and he tripped and fell. As he picked himself up, Mr. O'Rourke, about to help him with another, though gentler, tap of the leather, stopped and exclaimed, "Merciful God, child, where did you pick up the boots?"

The rest looked with curiosity. Clancy, who had twice excelled himself, tittered. Mr. O'Rourke said, "And what's the funny joke Clancy?"

"Nothing, sir."

"Soft as a woman's was your voice, O'Neill, bright was your eye," recited Mr. O'Rourke in a voice as soft as a woman's, brightness in his eyes. "Continue, Clancy." But Clancy, the wind taken out of his sails, missed and went out to join the other three. Peter put his head on the desk, his raw hands tightly under his armpits, and nursed his wounds while the leather thudded patriotism and literature into the other, unmurmuring, four.

Swaine said nothing for a time. Now and then he glanced at Peter's face. He was staring straight at the book. His hands were tender, but the pain had ebbed away. Each still hid its rawness under a comfortably warm armpit.

"You got a heck of a hiding," Swaine whispered at last. Peter said nothing.

"Ten is too much. He's not allowed to give you ten. If he gave me ten I'd bring my father up to him."

Swaine was small, but his face was large and bony and when he took off his glasses sometimes to wipe them there was a small red weal on the bridge of his nose. Peter grunted and Swaine changed the subject.

"Tell us who owns the boots. They're not your own."

"Yes they are," Peter lied.

"Go on," Swaine said. "Who owns them? Are they your brother's?"

"Shut up."

"Tell us," Swaine persisted. "I won't tell a soul. Honest." He regarded Peter with sly curiosity. He whispered avidly. "I know they're not your own, but I wouldn't tell it. We sit beside one another. We're pals. You can tell me."

"Curiosity killed the cat . . ." Peter said.

Swaine had the answer to that. With a sly grin he rejoined, "Information made him fat."

"If you must know," Peter said, growing tired, "they're my father's. And if you tell anyone I'll break you up in little pieces. You just try breathing a word."

Swaine sat back, satisfied. If a fellow was expelled or anything mysterious happened, Swaine always knew the ins and outs of it.

Mr. O'Rourke was saying that the English used treachery when they poisoned Eoghan Ruadh. But what could be expected of the English except treachery.

"Hoof of the horse," he quoted, "horn of a bull, smile of a Saxon." Three perils. Oliver Cromwell read his Bible while he quartered infants at their mothers' breasts. People said let's forget all that. But we couldn't begin to forget it until we had our full freedom. Our own tongue, the sweet Gaelic teanga, must be restored once more as the spoken language of our race. It was the duty of all to study and work towards that end.

"And those of us who haven't time must be shown how to find the time. Isn't that a fact, Farrell?" he said. The class laughed. But the clock struck and Mr. O'Rourke put the lament regretfully aside.

"Mathematics," he announced. "Ceimseata."

He had hoped it would continue to rain during lunch time so that they could stay in the classroom. But when the automatic bell clanged loudly and Mr. O'Rourke opened the frosted window to look out, it had stopped. They trooped down the stairs. They pushed and jostled one another. Peter kept his hand for safety on the bannisters. Going down the stairs made the boots seem larger. He made straight for the urinal and stayed there until the old brother whose duty it was for obscure moral reasons to patrol the place had passed through twice. The second time he said to him, "My goodness boy, go out into the fresh air with your playmates. Shoo—boy,—shoo," and stared at Peter's retreating back with perplexity and suspicion.

Dillon came over as he was unwrapping his lunch and said, "Did they dare, did they dare to slap Eoghan Ruadh O'Neill."

"Oh shut up," Peter said.

Dillon linked his arm and said, "You took an awful packet." Then with genuine admiration he added, "You took it super. He aimed for your wrist too. Not a peek. You were wizard. Cripes. When I saw him getting ready for the last four I was praying you wouldn't cry." They were all praying he wouldn't cry.

"I never cried yet," Peter asserted.

"I know, but he lammed his hardest. You shouldn't have said you hadn't time."

"He wouldn't make me cry," Peter said grimly, "not if he got up at four o'clock in the morning to try it."

O'Rourke had lammed him all right, but there was no use trying to do anything about it. If he told his father and mother they would say he richly deserved it. It was his mother should have been lammed and not he.

"The Irish," Dillon added sagaciously, "are an unfortunate bloody race. The father often says so."

"Don't tell me," Peter said with feeling.

"I mean look at us. First Cromwell knocks hell out of us for being too Irish and then Rorky slaughters us for not being Irish enough."

It was true. It was a pity they couldn't make up their minds.

Peter felt the comfort of Dillon's friendly arm. "The boots are my father's," he confided suddenly, "my own had holes." That made him feel better.

"What are you worrying about?" Dillon said, reassuringly. "They look all right to me."

When they were passing the row of water taps with

386

the chained drinking vessels a voice cried, "There's Farrell now." A piece of crust hit Peter on the nose.

"Caesar sends his legate," Dillon murmured. They gathered round.

Clancy said, "Hey boys, Farrell is wearing someone else's boots."

"Who lifted you into them?"

"Wait now," said Clancy, "let's see him walk. Go on—walk Farrell."

Peter backed slowly towards the wall. He backed slowly until he felt the ridge of a downpipe hard against his back. Dillon came with him. "Lay off, Clancy," Dillon said. Swaine was there too. He was smiling, a small cat fat with information.

"Where did you get them Farrell?"

"Pinched them."

"Found them in an ashbin."

"Make him walk," Clancy insisted. "Let's see you walk, Farrell."

"They're my own," Peter said. "They're a bit big—that's all. They'll shrink after a while."

"Come on Farrell—tell us whose they are."

The grins grew wider.

Clancy said, "They're his father's."

"No they're not." Peter denied quickly.

"Yes they are. He told Swaine. Didn't he Swaine? He told you they were his father's."

Swaine's grin froze. Peter fixed him with terrible eyes.

"Well didn't he, Swaine? Go on, tell the chaps what he told you. Didn't he say they were his father's?"

Swaine edged backwards. "That's right," he said, "he did."

"Hey, you chaps," Clancy said, impatiently, "let's make him walk. I vote . . ."

At that moment Peter, with a cry, sprang on Swaine. His fist smashed the glasses on Swaine's face. As they rolled over on the muddy ground, Swaine's nails tore his cheek. Peter saw the white terrified face under him. He beat at it in frenzy until it became covered with mud and blood.

"Cripes," Clancy said in terror, "look at Swaine's glasses. Haul him off lads." They pulled him away and he lashed out awkwardly with the big boots which had caused all the trouble. Swaine's nose and lips were bleeding so they took him over to the water tap and washed him. Dillon, who stood alone with Peter, brushed his clothes as best he could and fixed his collar and tie.

"You broke his glasses," he said. "There'll be a proper rucky if old Quinny sees him after lunch."

"I don't care about Quinny."

"I do then," Dillon said fervently. "He'll quarter us all in our mother's arms."

They sat with their arms folded while Brother Quinlan, in the high chair at the head of the class, gave religious instruction. Swaine kept his bruised face lowered. Without the glasses it had a bald, maimed look, as though his eyebrows, or a nose, or an eye, were missing. They had exchanged no words since the fight. Peter was aware of the boots. They were a defeat, something to be ashamed of. His mother only thought they would keep out the rain. She didn't understand that it would be better to have wet feet. People did not laugh at you because your feet were wet.

Brother Quinlan was speaking of our relationship to one another, of the boy to his neighbour and of the boy to his God. We communicated with one another, he said, by looks, gestures, speech. But these were surface contacts. They conveyed little of what went on in the mind, and nothing at all of the soul. Inside us, the greatest and the humblest of us, a whole world was locked. Even if we tried we could convey nothing of that interior world, that life which was nourished, as the poet had said, within the brain. In our interior life we stood without friend or ally— alone. In the darkness and silence of that interior and eternal world the immortal soul and its God were at all times face to face. No one else could peer into another's soul, neither our teacher, nor our father or mother, nor even our best friend. But God saw all. Every stray little thought which moved in that inaccessible world was as plain to Him as if it were thrown across the bright screen of a cinema. That was why we must be as careful to discipline our thoughts as our actions. Custody of the eyes, custody of the ears, but above all else custody . . .

Brother Quinlan let the sentence trail away and fixed his eyes on Swaine.

"You—boy," he said in a voice tired but patient. "What are you doing with that handkerchief?"

Swaine's nose had started to bleed again. He said nothing. "Stand up, boy," Brother Quinlan commanded. He had glasses himself, which he wore during class on the tip of his nose. He was a big man too, and his head was bald in front, which made his large forehead appear even more massive. He stared over the glasses at Swaine.

"Come up here," he said, screwing up his eyes, the fact that something was amiss with Swaine's face dawning gradually on him. Swaine came up to him, looking woebegone, still dabbing his nose with the handkerchief. Brother Quinlan contemplated the battered face for some time. He turned to the class.

"Whose handiwork is this?" he asked quietly. "Stand up, the boy responsible for this."

For a while nobody stirred. There was an uneasy stillness. Poker faces looked at the desks in front of them and waited. Peter looked around and saw Dillon gazing at him hopefully. After an unbearable moment feet shuffled and Peter stood up.

"I am sir," he said.

Brother Quinlan told Clancy to take Swaine out to the yard to bathe his nose. Then he spoke to the class about violence, and what was worse, violence to a boy weaker than oneself. That was the resort of the bully and the scoundrel— physical violence——The Fist. At this Brother Quinlan held up his large bunched fist so that all might see it. Then with the other hand he indicated the picture of the Sacred Heart.

Charity and Forbearance, he said, not revenge and intoler-
ance, those were qualities most dear to Our Blessed Lord.

"Are you not ashamed of yourself, Farrell? Do you
think what you have done is a heroic or a creditable thing?"

"No sir."

"Then why did you do it boy?"

Peter made no answer. It was no use making an answer. It was no use saying Swaine had squealed about the
boots being his father's. Swaine's face was badly battered.
But deep inside him Peter felt battered too. Brother Quinlan
couldn't see your soul. He could see Swaine's face, though,
when he fixed his glasses on him properly. Brother Quinlan
took his silence for defiance.

"A blackguardly affair," he pronounced. "A low, cow-
ardly assault. Hold out your hand."

Peter hesitated. There was a limit. He hadn't meant not
to learn the Poetry and it wasn't his fault about the boots.

"He's been licked already, sir," Dillon said. "Mr.
O'Rourke gave him ten."

"Mr. O'Rourke is a discerning man," said Brother
Quinlan, "but he doesn't seem to have given him half
enough. Think of the state of that poor boy who has just
gone out."

Peter could think of nothing to say. He tried hard to
word his defence but it was useless. There were no words
there. Reluctantly he presented his hand. It was mud-
stained. Brother Quinlan looked at it with distaste. Then he
proceeded to beat hell out of him, and charity and forbearance into him, in the same way as Mr. O'Rourke earlier
had hammered in patriotism and respect for Irish History.

It was raining again when he was going home. Usually
there were three or four to go home with him, but this afternoon he went alone. He did not want them with him. He
passed some shops and walked by the first small suburban
gardens, with their sodden gravel paths and dripping gates.
On the canal bridge a boy passed him pushing fuel in a

pram. His feet were bare. The mud had splashed upwards in thick streaks to his knees. Peter kept his left hand under his coat. There was a blister on the ball of the thumb which ached now like a burn. Brother Quinlan did that. He probably didn't aim to hit the thumb as Mr. O'Rourke always did, but his sight was so bad he had a rotten shot. The boots had got looser than they were earlier. He realized this when he saw Clancy with three or four others passing on the other side of the road. When Clancy waved and called to him, he backed automatically until he felt the parapet against his back.

"Hey, Farrell," they called. Then one of them, his head forward, his behind stuck out, began to waddle with grotesque movements up the road. The rest yelled to call Peter's attention. They indicated the mime. Come back if you like, they shouted. Peter waited until they had gone. Then he turned moodily down the bank of the canal. He walked with a stiff ungainly dignity, his mind not yet quite made up. Under the bridge the water was deep and narrow, and a raw wind which moaned in the high arch whipped coldly at his face. It might rain to-morrow and his shoes wouldn't be mended. If his mother thought the boots were all right God knows when his shoes would be mended. After a moment of indecision he took off the boots and dropped them, first one—and then the other, into the water.

There would be hell to pay when he came home without them. But there would be hell to pay anyway when Swaine's father sent around the note to say he had broken young Swaine's glasses. Like the time he broke the Cassidys' window. Half regretfully he stared at the silty water. He could see his father rising from the table to reach for the belt which hung behind the door. The outlook was frightening; but it was better to walk in your bare feet. It was better to walk without shoes and barefooted than to walk without dignity. He took off his stockings and stuffed them into his pocket. His heart sank as he felt the cold wet mud of the path on his bare feet.

GEORGE BERNARD SHAW

The Miraculous Revenge

❅

I arrived in Dublin on the evening of the 5th of August, and
drove to the residence of my uncle, the Cardinal Archbishop. He is, like most of my family, deficient in feeling,
and consequently cold to me personally. He lives in a dingy
house, with a side-long view of the portico of his cathedral
from the front windows, and of a monster national school
from the back. My uncle maintains no retinue. The people
believe that he is waited upon by angels. When I knocked
at the door, an old woman, his only servant, opened it, and
informed me that her master was then officiating in the cathedral, and that he had directed her to prepare dinner for
me in his absence. An unpleasant smell of salt fish made me
ask her what the dinner consisted of. She assured me that
she had cooked all that could be permitted in His Holiness's
house on a Friday. On my asking her further why on a Friday, she replied that Friday was a fast day. I bade her tell
His Holiness that I had hoped to have the pleasure of calling

From Short Stories, Scraps, and Shavings, London, 1933. First published
in *Time A Monthly Magazine*, London, 1885.

on him shortly, and drove to a hotel in Sackville Street, where I engaged apartments and dined.

After dinner I resumed my eternal search—I know not for what; it drives me to and fro like another Cain. I sought in the streets without success. I went to the theatre. The music was execrable, the scenery poor. I had seen the play a month before in London, with the same beautiful artist in the chief part. Two years had passed since, seeing her for the first time, I had hoped that she, perhaps, might be the long-sought mystery. It had proved otherwise. On this night I looked at her and listened to her for the sake of that bygone hope, and applauded her generously when the curtain fell. But I went out lonely still. When I had supped at a restaurant, I returned to my hotel, and tried to read. In vain. The sound of feet in the corridors as the other occupants of the hotel went to bed distracted my attention from my book. Suddenly it occurred to me that I had never quite understood my uncle's character. He, father to a great flock of poor and ignorant Irish; an austere and saintly man, to whom livers of hopeless lives daily appealed for help heavenward; who was reputed never to have sent away a troubled peasant without relieving him of his burden by sharing it; whose knees were worn less by the altar steps than by the tears and embraces of the guilty and wretched: he had refused to humour my light extravagances, or to find time to talk with me of books, flowers, and music. Had I not been mad to expect it? Now that I needed sympathy myself, I did him justice. I desired to be with a true-hearted man, and to mingle my tears with his.

I looked at my watch. It was nearly an hour past midnight. In the corridor the lights were out, except one jet at the end. I threw a cloak upon my shoulders, put on a Spanish hat, and left my apartment, listening to the echoes of my measured steps retreating through the deserted passages. A strange sight arrested me on the landing of the grand staircase. Through an open door I saw the moonlight shining through the windows of a saloon in which some entertainment had recently taken place. I looked at my watch again.

It was but one o'clock; and yet the guests had departed. I entered the room, my boots ringing loudly on the waxed boards. On a chair lay a child's clock and a broken toy. The entertainment had been a children's party. I stood for a time looking at the shadow of my cloaked figure upon the floor, and at the disordered decorations, ghostly in the white light. Then I saw that there was a grand piano, still open, in the middle of the room. My fingers throbbed as I sat down before it, and expressed all that I felt in a grand hymn which seemed to thrill the cold stillness of the shadows into a deep hum of approbation, and to people the radiance of the moon with angels. Soon there was a stir without too, as if the rapture was spreading abroad. I took up the chant triumphantly with my voice, and the empty saloon resounded as though to the thunder of an orchestra.

"Hallo, sir!" "Confound you, sir—" "Do you suppose that this—" "What the deuce—?"

I turned, and silence followed. Six men, partially dressed, and with dishevelled hair, stood regarding me angrily. They all carried candles. One of them had a bootjack, which he held like a truncheon. Another, the foremost, had a pistol. The night porter was behind trembling.

"Sir," said the man with the revolver, coarsely, "may I ask whether you are mad, that you disturb people at this hour with such an unearthly noise?"

"Is it possible that you dislike it?" I replied, courteously.

"Dislike it!" said he, stamping with rage. "Why—damn everything—do you suppose we were enjoying it?"

"Take care. He's mad," whispered the man with the bootjack.

I began to laugh. Evidently they did think me mad. Unaccustomed to my habits, and ignorant of music as they probably were, the mistake, however absurd, was not unnatural. I rose. They came closer to one another; and the night porter ran away.

"Gentlemen," I said, "I am sorry for you. Had you lain still and listened, we should all have been the better and happier. But what you have done, you cannot undo. Kindly inform the night porter that I am gone to visit my uncle, the Cardinal Archbishop. Adieu!"

I strode past them, and left them whispering among themselves. Some minutes later I knocked at the door of the Cardinal's house. Presently a window on the first floor was opened; and the moonbeams fell on a grey head, with a black cap that seemed ashy pale against the unfathomable gloom of the shadow beneath the stone sill.

"Who are you?"

"I am Zeno Legge."

"What do you want at this hour?"

The question wounded me. "My dear uncle," I exclaimed, "I know you do not intend it, but you make me feel unwelcome. Come down and let me in, I beg."

"Go to your hotel," he said sternly. "I will see you in the morning. Goodnight." He disappeared and closed the window.

I felt that if I let this rebuff pass, I should not feel kindly towards my uncle in the morning, nor, indeed, at any future time. I therefore plied the knocker with my right hand, and kept the bell ringing with my left until I heard the door-chain rattle within. The Cardinal's expression was grave nearly to moroseness as he confronted me on the threshold.

"Uncle," I cried, grasping his hand, "do not reproach me. Your door is never shut against the wretched. I am wretched. Let us sit up all night and talk."

"You may thank my position and not my charity for your admission, Zeno," he said. "For the sake of the neighbours, I had rather you played the fool in my study than upon my doorstep at this hour. Walk upstairs quietly, if you please. My housekeeper is a hard-working woman: the little sleep she allows herself must not be disturbed."

"You have a noble heart, uncle. I shall creep like a mouse."

"This is my study," he said, as we entered an ill-furnished den on the second floor. "The only refreshment I can offer you, if you desire any, is a bunch of raisins. The doctors have forbidden you to touch stimulants, I believe."

"By heaven—!" He raised his finger. "Pardon me: I was wrong to swear. But I had totally forgotten the doctors. At dinner I had a bottle of *Grave*."

"Humph! You have no business to be travelling alone. Your mother promised me that Bushy should come over here with you."

"Pshaw! Bushy is not a man of feeling. Besides, he is a coward. He refused to come with me because I purchased a revolver."

"He should have taken the revolver from you, and kept to his post."

"Why will you persist in treating me like a child, uncle? I am very impressionable, I grant you; but I have gone round the world alone, and do not need to be dry-nursed through a tour in Ireland."

"What do you intend to do during your stay here?"

I had no plans; and instead of answering I shrugged my shoulders and looked round the apartment. There was a statuette of the Virgin upon my uncle's desk. I looked at its face, as he was wont to look in the midst of his labours. I saw there eternal peace. The air became luminous with an infinite network of the jewelled rings of Paradise descending in roseate clouds upon us.

"Uncle," I said, bursting into the sweetest tears I had ever shed, "my wanderings are over. I will enter the Church, if you will help me. Let us read together the third part of *Faust*; for I understand it at last."

"Hush, man," he said, half rising with an expression of alarm. "Control yourself."

"Do not let my tears mislead you. I am calm and strong. Quick, let us have Goethe:

> *Das Unbeschreibliche,*
> *Hier ist gethan;*
> *Das Ewig-Weibliche,*
> *Zieht uns hinan."*

"Come, come. Dry your eyes and be quiet. I have no library here."

"But I have—in my portmanteau at the hotel," I said, rising. "Let me go for it, I will return in fifteen minutes."

"The devil is in you, I believe. Cannot—"

I interrupted him with a shout of laughter. "Cardinal," I said noisily, "you have become profane; and a profane priest is always the best of good fellows. Let us have some wine; and I will sing you a German beer song."

"Heaven forgive me if I do you wrong," he said; "but I believe God has laid the expiation of some sin on your unhappy head. Will you favor me with your attention for a while? I have something to say to you, and I have also to get some sleep before my hour for rising, which is half-past five."

"My usual hour for retiring—when I retire at all. But proceed. My fault is not inattention, but over-susceptibility."

"Well, then, I want you to go to Wicklow. My reasons—"

"No matter what they may be," said I, rising again. "It is enough that you desire me to go. I shall start forthwith."

"Zeno! will you sit down and listen to me?"

I sank upon my chair reluctantly. "Ardor is a crime in your eyes, even when it is shown in your service," I said. "May I turn down the light?"

"Why?"

"To bring on my sombre mood, in which I am able to listen with tireless patience."

"I will turn it down myself. Will that do?"

I thanked him, and composed myself to listen in the shadow. My eyes, I felt, glittered. I was like Poe's raven.

"Now for my reasons for sending you to Wicklow. First, for your own sake. If you stay in town, or in any place where excitement can be obtained by any means, you will be in Swift's Hospital in a week. You must live in the country, under the eye of one upon whom I can depend. And you must have something to do to keep you out of mischief, and away from your music and painting and poetry, which, Sir John Richards writes to me, are dangerous for you in your present morbid state. Second, because I can entrust you with a task which, in the hands of a sensible man, might bring discredit on the Church. In short, I want you to investigate a miracle."

He looked attentively at me. I sat like a statue.

"You understand me?" he said.

"Nevermore," I replied, hoarsely. "Pardon me," I added, amused at the trick my imagination had played me, "I understand you perfectly. Proceed."

"I hope you do. Well, four miles distant from the town of Wicklow is a village called Four Mile Water. The resident priest is Father Hickey. You have heard of the miracles at Knock?"

I winked.

"I did not ask you what you think of them, but whether you have heard of them. I see you have. I need not tell you that even a miracle may do more harm than good to the Church in this country, unless it can be proved so thoroughly that her powerful and jealous enemies are silenced by the testimony of followers of their heresy. Therefore, when I saw in a Wexford newspaper last week a description of a strange manifestation of the Divine Power which was said to have taken place at Four Mile Water, I was troubled in my mind about it. So I wrote to Father Hickey, bidding him give me an account of the matter if it were true, and, if not, to denounce from the altar the author of the report, and to contradict it in the paper at once. This is his reply. He says—well, the first part is about Church matters: I need not trouble you with it. He goes on to say—"

"One moment. Is that his own handwriting? It does not look like a man's."

"He suffers from rheumatism in the fingers of his right hand, and his niece, who is an orphan, and lives with him, acts as his amanuensis. Well—"

"Stay. What is her name?"

"Her name? Kate Hickey."

"How old is she?"

"Tush, man, she is only a little girl. If she were old enough to concern you, I should not send you into her way. Have you any more questions to ask about her?"

"None. I can fancy her in a white veil at the rite of confirmation, a type of faith and innocence. Enough of her. What says the Reverend Hickey of the apparitions?"

"They are not apparitions. I will read you what he says. Ahem!

'In reply to your inquiries concerning the late miraculous event in this parish, I have to inform you that I can vouch for its truth, and that I can be confirmed not only by the inhabitants of the place, who are all Catholics, but by every person acquainted with the former situation of the graveyard referred to, including the Protestant Archdeacon of Baltinglas, who spends six weeks annually in the neighbourhood. The newspaper account is incomplete and inaccurate. The following are the facts: About four years ago, a man named Wolfe Tone Fitzgerald settled in this village as a farrier. His antecedents did not transpire, and he had no family. He lived by himself, was very careless of his person; and when in his cups, as he often was, regarded the honor neither of God nor man in his conversation. Indeed if it were not speaking ill of the dead, one might say that he was a dirty, drunken, blasphemous blackguard. Worse again, he was, I fear, an atheist, for he never attended Mass, and gave his Holiness worse language even than he gave the Queen. I should have mentioned that he was a bitter rebel, and boasted that his grandfather had been out in '98, and his father with Smith O'Brien. At last he went by the name of Brimstone Billy, and was held up in the village as the type of all wickedness.

'You are aware that our graveyard, situated on the north side of the water, is famous throughout the

399

country as the burial place of the nuns of St. Ursula, the hermit of Four Mile Water, and many other holy people. No Protestant has ever ventured to enforce his legal right of interment there, though two have died in the parish within my own recollection. Three weeks ago, this Fitzgerald died in a fit brought on by drink, and a great hullabaloo was raised in the village when it became known that he would be buried in the grave-yard. The body had to be watched to prevent its being stolen and buried at the cross-roads. My people were greatly disappointed when they were told I could do nothing to stop the burial, particularly as I of course refused to read any service on the occasion. However, I bade them not interfere; and the interment was effected on the 14th of July, late in the evening, and long after the legal hour. There was no disturbance. Next morning, the graveyard was found moved to the south side of the water, with the one newly-filled grave left behind on the north side; and thus they both remain. The departed saints would not lie with the reprobate. I can testify to it on the oath of a Christian priest; and if this will not satisfy those outside the Church, everyone, as I said before, who remembers where the graveyard was two months ago, can confirm me.

'I respectfully suggest that a thorough investigation into the truth of this miracle be proposed to a com-mittee of Protestant gentlemen. They shall not be asked to accept a single fact on hearsay from my peo-ple. The ordnance maps show where the graveyard was; and anyone can see for himself where it is. I need not tell your Eminence what a rebuke this would be to those enemies of the holy Church that have sought to put a stain on her by discrediting the late wonderful manifestations at Knock Chapel. If they come to Four Mile Water, they need cross-examine no one. They will be asked to believe nothing but their own senses.

     'Awaiting your Eminence's counsel to guide me
further in the matter,

                           'I am, etc.'

    "Well, Zeno," said my uncle, "what do you think of
Father Hickey now?"

    "Uncle, do not ask me. Beneath this roof I desire to
believe everything. The Reverend Hickey has appealed
strongly to my love of legend. Let us admire the poetry of
his narrative and ignore the balance of probability between
a Christian priest telling a lie on his oath and a graveyard swimming across a river in the middle of the night
and forgetting to return."

    "Tom Hickey is not telling a lie, sir. You may take my
word for that. But he may be mistaken."

    "Such a mistake amounts to insanity. It is true that I
myself, awaking suddenly in the depth of night, have
found myself convinced that the position of my bed had
been reversed. But on opening my eyes the illusion ceased.
I fear Mr. Hickey is mad. Your best course is this. Send
down to Four Mile Water a perfectly sane investigator; an
acute observer; one whose perceptive faculties, at once
healthy and subtle, are absolutely unclouded by religious
prejudice. In a word, send me. I will report to you the true
state of affairs in a few days, and you can then make arrangements for transferring Hickey from the altar to the
asylum."

    "Yes, I had intended to send you. You are wonderfully
sharp and you would make a capital detective if you could
only keep your mind to one point. But your chief qualifica-
tion for this business is that you are too crazy to excite the
suspicion of those whom you may have to watch. For the
affair may be a trick. If so, I hope and believe that Hickey
has no hand in it. Still, it is my duty to take every precaution."

    "Cardinal; may I ask whether traces of insanity have
ever appeared in our family?"

"Except in you and in my grandmother, no. She was a Pole; and you resemble her personally. Why do you ask?"

"Because it has often occurred to me that you are, perhaps, a little cracked. Excuse my candour, but a man who has devoted his life to the pursuit of a red hat, who accuses everyone else besides himself of being mad, and who is disposed to listen seriously to a tale of a peripatetic graveyard, can hardly be quite sane. Depend upon it, uncle, you want rest and change. The blood of your Polish grandmother is in your veins."

"I hope I may not be committing a sin in sending a ribald on the Church's affairs," he replied, fervently. "However, we must use the instruments put into our hands. Is it agreed that you go?"

"Had you not delayed me with this story, which I might as well have learned on the spot, I should have been there already."

"There is no occasion for impatience, Zeno. I must first send to Hickey to find a place for you. I shall tell him that you are going to recover your health, as, in fact, you are. And, Zeno, in Heaven's name be discreet. Try to act like a man of sense. Do not dispute with Hickey on matters of religion. Since you are my nephew, you had better not disgrace me."

"I shall become an ardent Catholic, and do you infinite credit, uncle."

"I wish you would, although you would hardly be an acquisition to the Church. And now I must turn you out. It is nearly three o'clock, and I need some sleep. Do you know your way back to your hotel?"

"I need not stir. I can sleep in this chair. Go to bed, and never mind me."

"I shall not close my eyes until you are safely out of the house. Come, rouse yourself, and say goodnight."

The following is a copy of my first report to the Cardinal:

The Miraculous Revenge

Four Mile Water, County Wicklow,
10th August.

My Dear Uncle,

The miracle is genuine. I have affected perfect credulity in order to throw the Hickeys and the countryfolk off their guard with me. I have listened to their method of convincing sceptical strangers. I have examined the ordnance maps, and cross-examined the neighbouring Protestant gentlefolk. I have spent a day upon the ground on each side of the water, and have visited it at midnight. I have considered the upheaval theories, subsidence theories, volcanic theories, and tidal wave theories which the provincial *savants* have suggested. They are all untenable. There is only one scoffer in the district, an Orangeman; and he admits the removal of the cemetery, but says it was dug up and transplanted in the night by a body of men under the command of Father Tom. This also is out of the question. The interment of Brimstone Billy was the first which had taken place for four years; and his is the only grave which bears a trace of recent digging. It is alone on the north bank, and the inhabitants shun it after nightfall. As each passer-by during the day throws a stone upon it, it will soon be marked by a large cairn. The graveyard, with a ruined stone chapel still standing in its midst, is on the south side. You may send down a committee to investigate the matter as soon as you please. There can be no doubt as to the miracle having actually taken place, as recorded by Hickey. As for me, I have grown so accustomed to it that if the county Wicklow were to waltz off with me to Middlesex, I should be quite impatient of any expressions of surprise from my friends in London.

Is not the above a businesslike statement? Away, then, with this stale miracle. If you would see for yourself a miracle which can never pall, a vision of youth and health to be crowned with garlands for ever, come down and see Kate Hickey, whom you suppose to be a little girl. Illusion, my lord cardinal, illusion! She is seventeen, with a bloom and a brogue that would lay your asceticism in ashes at a flash. To her I am an object of wonder, a strange man bred in wicked cities. She is courted by six feet of farming material, chopped off a spare length of coarse humanity by the Almighty, and flung into Wicklow to plough the fields. His name is Phil Langan; and he hates me. I have to consort with him for the sake of Father Tom, whom I entertain vastly by stories of your wild oats sown at Salamanca. I exhausted all my authentic anecdotes the first day; and now I invent gallant escapades with Spanish donnas, in which you figure as a youth of unstable morals. This delights Father Tom infinitely. I feel that I have done you a service by thus casting on the cold sacerdotal abstraction which formerly represented you in Kate's imagination a ray of vivifying passion.

What a country this is! A Hesperidean garden: such skies! Adieu, uncle.

Zeno Legge.

Behold me, then, at Four Mile Water, in love. I had been in love frequently; but not oftener than once a year had I encountered a woman who affected me as seriously as Kate Hickey. She was so shrewd, and yet so flippant! When I spoke of art she yawned. When I deplored the sordidness of the world she laughed, and called me "poor fellow!" When I told her what a treasure of beauty and freshness she had she ridiculed me. When I reproached her with her brutality she became angry, and sneered at me for being what she called a fine gentleman. One sunny afternoon we were standing at the gate of her uncle's house, she looking down the dusty road for the detestable Langan, I watching the spotless azure sky, when she said:

"How soon are you going back to London?"

"I am not going back to London, Miss Hickey. I am not yet tired of Four Mile Water."

"I'm sure Four Mile Water ought to be proud of your approbation."

"You disapprove of my liking it, then? Or is it that you grudge me the happiness I have found there? I think Irish ladies grudge a man a moment's peace."

"I wonder you have ever prevailed on yourself to associate with Irish ladies, since they are so far beneath you."

"Did I say they were beneath me, Miss Hickey? I feel that I have made a deep impression on you."

"Indeed! Yes, you're quite right. I assure you I can't sleep at night for thinking of you, Mr. Legge. It's the best a Christian can do, seeing you think so mighty little of yourself."

"You are triply wrong, Miss Hickey: wrong to be sarcastic with me, wrong to pretend that there is anything unreasonable in my belief that you think of me sometimes, and wrong to discourage the candour with which I always avow that I think constantly of myself."

"Then you had better not speak to me, since I have no manners."

"Again! Did I say you had no manners? The warmest expressions of regard from my mouth seem to reach your ears transformed into insults. Were I to repeat the Litany of the Blessed Virgin, you would retort as though I had been reproaching you. This is because you hate me. You never misunderstand Langan, whom you love."

"I don't know what London manners are, Mr. Legge; but in Ireland gentlemen are expected to mind their own business. How dare you say I love Mr. Langan?"

"Then you do not love him?"

"It is nothing to you whether I love him or not."

"Nothing to me that you hate me and love another?"

"I did not say that I hated you. You are not so very clever yourself at understanding what people say, though you make such a fuss because they don't understand you." Here, as she glanced down the road again, she suddenly looked glad.

"Aha!" I said.

"What do you mean by 'Aha!'?"

"No matter. I will now show you what a man's sympathy is. As you perceived just then, Langan—who is too tall for his age, by-the-bye—is coming to pay you a visit. Well, instead of staying with you, as a jealous woman would, I will withdraw."

"I don't care whether you go or stay, I'm sure. I wonder what you would give to be as fine a man as Mr. Langan."

"All I possess: I swear it! But solely because you admire tall men more than broad views. Mr. Langan may be defined geometrically as length without breadth; altitude without position; a line on the landscape, not a point in it."

"How very clever you are!"

"You do not understand me, I see. Here comes your lover, stepping over the wall like a camel. And here go I, out through the gate like a Christian. Good afternoon, Mr. Langan. I am going because Miss Hickey has something to say to you about me which she would rather not say in my presence. You will excuse me?"

"Oh, I'll excuse you," said he boorishly. I smiled, and went out. Before I was quite out of hearing, Kate whispered vehemently to him, "I *hate* that fellow."

I smiled again; but I had scarcely done so when my spirits fell. I walked hastily away with a coarse threatening sound in my ears like that of the clarionets whose sustained low notes darken the woodland in "Der Freischütz." I found myself presently at the graveyard. It was a barren place, enclosed by a mud wall with a gate to admit funerals, and numerous gaps to admit the peasantry, who made short cuts across it as they went to and fro between Four Mile Water and the market town. The graves were mounds overgrown with grass: there was no keeper; nor were there flowers, railings or any of the conventionalities that make an English graveyard repulsive. A great thornbush, near what was called the grave of the holy sisters, was covered with scraps of cloth and flannel, attached by peasant women who had prayed before it. There were three kneeling there as I entered, for the reputation of the place had been revived of late by the miracle, and a ferry had been established close by, to conduct visitors over the route taken by the graveyard. From where I stood I could see on the opposite bank the heap of stones, perceptibly increased since my last visit, marking the deserted grave of Brimstone Billy. I strained my eyes broodingly at it for some minutes, and then descended the river bank and entered the boat.

"Good evenin' t'your honour," said the ferryman, and set to work to draw the boat hand-over-hand by a rope stretched across the water.

"Good evening. Is your business beginning to fall off yet?"

"Faith, it never was as good as it might ha' been. The people that comes from the south side can see Billy's grave —Lord have mercy on him—across the wather; and they think bad of payin a penny to put a stone over him. It's them that lives tow'rst Dublin that makes the journey. Your honour is the third I've brought from south to north this blessed day."

"When do most people come? In the afternoon, I suppose?"

"All hours, sur, except afther dusk. There isn't a sowl in the counthry ud come within sight of that grave wanst the sun goes down."

"And you! Do you stay here all night by yourself?"

"The holy heavens forbid! Is it me stay here all night? No, your honour; I tether the boat at siven o'hlyock, and lave Brimstone Billy—God forgimme!—to take care of it t'll mornin."

"It will be stolen some night, I'm afraid."

"Arra, who'd dar come next or near it, let alone stale it? Faith, I'd think twice before lookin at it meself in the dark. God bless your honour, and gran'che long life."

I had given him sixpence. I went to the reprobate's grave and stood at the foot of it, looking at the sky, gorgeous with the descent of the sun. To my English eyes, accustomed to giant trees, broad lawns, and stately mansions, the landscape was wild and inhospitable. The ferryman was already tugging at the rope on his way back (I had told him I did not intend to return that way), and presently I saw him make the painter fast to the south bank; put on his coat; and trudge homeward. I turned towards the gravè at my feet. Those who had interred Brimstone Billy, working hastily at an unlawful hour, and in fear of molestation by the people, had hardly dug a grave. They had scooped out earth enough to hide their burden, and no more. A stray goat had kicked away a corner of the mound and exposed the coffin. It occurred to me, as I took some of the stones from the cairn, and heaped them so as to repair the breach, that had the miracle been the work of a body of men, they would have moved the one grave instead of the many. Even from a supernatural point of view, it seemed strange that the sinner should have banished the elect, when, by their superior numbers, they might so much more easily have banished him.

It was almost dark when I left the spot. After a walk of half a mile, I recrossed the water by a bridge, and returned to the farmhouse in which I lodged. Here, finding that I had had enough of solitude, I only stayed to take a cup of tea. Then I went to Father Hickey's cottage.

Kate was alone when I entered. She looked up quickly as I opened the door, and turned away disappointed when she recognized me.

"Be generous for once," I said. "I have walked about aimlessly for hours in order to avoid spoiling the beautiful afternoon for you by my presence. When the sun was up I withdrew my shadow from your path. Now that darkness has fallen, shed some light on mine. May I stay half an hour?"

"You may stay as long as you like, of course. My uncle will soon be home. He is clever enough to talk to you."

"What! More sarcasms! Come, Miss Hickey, help me to spend a pleasant evening. It will only cost you a smile.

I am somewhat cast down. Four Mile Water is a paradise;
but without you, it would be a little lonely."

"It must be very lonely for you. I wonder why you
came here."

"Because I heard that the women here were all Zer-
linas, like you, and the men Masettos, like Mr. Phil—where
are you going to?"

"Let me pass, Mr. Legge. I had intended never speaking to you again after the way you went on about Mr.
Langan today; and I wouldn't either, only my uncle made
me promise not to take any notice of you, because you
were—no matter; but I won't listen to you any more on the
subject."

"Do not go. I swear never to mention his name again.
I beg your pardon for what I said: you shall have no further cause for complaint. Will you forgive me?"

She sat down, evidently disappointed by my submis-
sion. I took a chair, and placed myself near her. She tapped
the floor impatiently with her foot. I saw that there was not
a movement I could make, not a look, not a tone of my
voice, which did not irritate her.

"You were remarking," I said, "that your uncle desired you to take no notice of me because—"

She closed her lips, and did not answer.

"I fear I have offended you again by my curiosity.
But indeed, I had no idea that he had forbidden you to
tell me the reason."

"He did not forbid me. Since you are so determined to
find out—"

"No, excuse me. I do not wish to know, I am sorry I
asked."

"Indeed! Perhaps you would be sorrier still to be told.
I only made a secret of it out of consideration for you."

"Then your uncle has spoken ill of me behind my
back. If that be so, there is no such thing as a true man in
Ireland. I would not have believed it on the word of any
woman alive save yourself."

"I never said my uncle was a backbiter. Just to show you what he thinks of you, I will tell you, whether you want to know it or not, that he bid me not mind you because you were only a poor mad creature, sent down here by your family to be out of harm's way."

"Oh, Miss Hickey!"

"There now! You have got it out of me; and I wish I had bit my tongue out first. I sometimes think—that I mayn't sin!—that you have a bad angel in you."

"I am glad you told me this," I said gently. "Do not reproach yourself for having done so, I beg. Your uncle has been misled by what he has heard of my family, who are all more or less insane. Far from being mad, I am actually the only rational man named Legge in the three kingdoms. I will prove this to you, and at the same time keep your indiscretion in countenance, by telling you something I ought not to tell you. It is this. I am not here as an invalid or a chance tourist. I am here to investigate the miracle. The Cardinal, a shrewd if somewhat erratic man, selected mine from all the long heads at his disposal to come down here, and find out the truth of Father Hickey's story. Would he have entrusted such a task to a madman, think you?"

"The truth of—who dared to doubt my uncle's word? And so you are a spy, a dirty informer."

I started. The adjective she had used, though probably the commonest expression of contempt in Ireland, is revolting to an Englishman.

"Miss Hickey," I said, "there is in me, as you have said, a bad angel. Do not shock my good angel—who is a person of taste—quite away from my heart, lest the other be left undisputed monarch of it. Hark! The chapel bell is ringing the angelus. Can you, with that sound softening the darkness of the village night, cherish a feeling of spite against one who admires you?"

"You come between me and my prayers," she said hysterically, and began to sob. She had scarcely done so, when

I heard voices without. Then Langan and the priest entered.

"Oh Phil," she cried, running to him, "take me away from him: I can't bear—" I turned towards him, and showed him my dog-tooth in a false smile. He felled me at one stroke, as he might have felled a poplar tree.

"Murdher!" exclaimed the priest. "What are you doin, Phil?"

"He's an informer," sobbed Kate. "He came down here to spy on you, uncle, and to try and show that the blessed miracle was a make-up. I knew it long before he told me, by his insulting ways. He wanted to make love to me."

I rose with difficulty from beneath the table, where I had lain motionless for a moment.

"Sir," I said, "I am somewhat dazed by the recent action of Mr. Langan, whom I beg, the next time he converts himself into a fulling-mill, to do so at the expense of a man more nearly his equal in strength than I. What your niece has told you is partly true. I am indeed the Cardinal's spy; and I have already reported to him that the miracle is a genuine one. A committee of gentlemen will wait on you tomorrow to verify it, at my suggestion. I have thought that the proof might be regarded by them as more complete if you were taken by surprise. Miss Hickey, that I admire all that is admirable in you is but to say that I have a sense of the beautiful. To say that I love you would be mere profanity. Mr. Langan, I have in my pocket a loaded pistol, which I carry from a silly English prejudice against your countrymen. Had I been the Hercules of the ploughtail, and you in my place, I should have been a dead man now. Do not redden; you are safe as far as I am concerned."

"Let me tell you before you leave my house for good," said Father Hickey, who seemed to have become unreasonably angry, "that you should never have crossed my threshold if I had known you were a spy; no, not if your uncle were his Holiness the Pope himself."

Here a frightful thing happened to me. I felt giddy, and put my hand to my head. Three warm drops trickled over it. Instantly I became murderous. My mouth filled with blood, my eyes were blinded with it; I seemed to drown in it. My hand went involuntarily to the pistol. It is my habit to obey my impulses instantaneously. Fortunately the impulse to kill vanished before a sudden perception of how I might miraculously humble the mad vanity in which these foolish people had turned upon me. The blood receded from my ears; and I again heard and saw distinctly.

"And let *me* tell you," Langan was saying, "that if you think yourself handier with cold lead than you are with your fists, I'll exchange shots with you, and welcome, whenever you please. Father Tom's credit is the same to me as my own, and if you say a word against it, you lie."

"His credit is in my hands," I said. "I am the Cardinal's witness. Do you defy me?"

"There is the door," said the priest, holding it open before me. "Until you can undo the visible work of God's hand your testimony can do no harm to me."

"Father Hickey," I replied, "before the sun rises again upon Four Mile Water, I will undo the visible work of God's hand, and bring the pointing finger of the scoffer upon your altar."

I bowed to Kate, and walked out. It was so dark that I could not at first see the garden-gate. Before I found it, I heard through the window Father Hickey's voice, saying, "I wouldn't for ten pound that this had happened, Phil. He's as mad as a march hare. The Cardinal told me so."

I returned to my lodging, and took a cold bath to cleanse the blood from my neck and shoulder. The effect of the blow I had received was so severe, that even after the bath and a light meal I felt giddy and languid. There was an alarum-clock on the mantelpiece. I wound it; set the alarum for half-past twelve; muffled it so that it should not disturb the people in the adjoining room; and went to bed, where I slept soundly for an hour and a quarter.

Then the alarum roused me, and I sprang up before I was thoroughly awake. Had I hesitated, the desire to relapse into perfect sleep would have overpowered me. Although the muscles of my neck were painfully stiff, and my hands unsteady from my nervous disturbance, produced by the interruption of my first slumber, I dressed myself resolutely, and, after taking a draught of cold water, stole out of the house. It was exceedingly dark and I had some difficulty in finding the cow-house, whence I borrowed a spade, and a truck with wheels, ordinarily used for moving sacks of potatoes. These I carried in my hands until I was beyond earshot of the house, when I put the spade on the truck, and wheeled it along the road to the cemetery. When I approached the water, knowing that no one would dare to come thereabout at such an hour, I made greater haste, no longer concerning myself about the rattling of the wheels. Looking across to the opposite bank, I could see a phosphorescent glow, marking the lonely grave of Brimstone Billy. This helped me to find the ferry station, where, after wandering a little and stumbling often, I found the boat, and embarked with my implements. Guided by the rope, I crossed the water without difficulty; landed; made fast the boat; dragged the truck up the bank; and sat down to rest on the cairn at the grave. For nearly a quarter of an hour I sat watching the patches of jack-o'-lantern fire, and collecting my strength for the work before me. Then the distant bell of the chapel clock tolled one. I rose, took the spade, and in about ten minutes uncovered the coffin, which smelt horribly. Keeping to windward of it, and using the spade as a lever, I contrived with great labor to place it on the truck. I wheeled it without accident to the landing-place, where, by placing the shafts of the truck upon the stern of the boat and lifting the foot by main strength, I succeeded in embarking my load after twenty minutes' toil, during which I got covered with clay and perspiration, and several times all but upset the boat. At the southern bank I had less difficulty in getting truck and coffin ashore, and dragging them up to the graveyard.

It was now past two o'clock, and the dawn had begun, so that I had no further trouble from want of light. I wheeled the coffin to a patch of loamy soil which I had noticed in the afternoon near the grave of the holy sisters. I had warmed to my work; my neck no longer pained me; and I began to dig vigorously, soon making a shallow trench, deep enough to hide the coffin with the addition of a mound. The chill pearl-coloured morning had by this time quite dissipated the darkness. I could see, and was myself visible, for miles around. This alarmed me, and made me impatient to finish my task. Nevertheless, I was forced to rest for a moment before placing the coffin in the trench. I wiped my brow and wrists, and again looked about me. The tomb of the holy women, a massive slab supported on four stone spheres, was grey and wet with dew. Near it was the thornbush covered with rags, the newest of which were growing gaudy in the radiance which was stretching up from the coast on the east. It was time to finish my work. I seized the truck; laid it alongside the grave; and gradually prized the coffin off with the spade until it rolled over into the trench with a hollow sound like a drunken remonstrance from the sleeper within. I shovelled the earth round and over it, working as fast as possible. In less than a quarter of an hour it was buried. Ten minutes more sufficed to make the mound symmetrical, and to clear the traces of my work from the adjacent sward. Then I flung down the spade; threw up my arms; and vented a sigh of relief and triumph. But I recoiled as I saw that I was standing on a barren common, covered with furze. No product of man's handiwork was near me except my truck and spade and the grave of Brimstone Billy, now as lonely as before. I turned towards the water. On the opposite bank was the cemetery, with the tomb of the holy women, the thornbush with its rags stirring in the morning breeze, and the broken mud wall. The ruined chapel was there too, not a stone shaken from its crumbling walls, not a sign to show that it and its precinct were less rooted in their place than the eternal hills around.

I looked down at the grave with a pang of compassion for the unfortunate Wolfe Tone Fitzgerald, with whom the blessed would not rest. I was even astonished, though I had worked expressly to this end. But the birds were astir, and the cocks crowing. My landlord was an early riser. I put the spade on the truck again, and hastened back to the farm, where I replaced them in the cowhouse. Then I stole into the house, and took a clean pair of boots, an overcoat, and a silk hat. These, with a change of linen, were sufficient to make my appearance respectable. I went out again, bathed in the Four Mile Water, took a last look at the cemetery, and walked to Wicklow, whence I travelled by the first train to Dublin.

Some months later, at Cairo, I received a packet of Irish newspapers and a leading article, cut from the *Times*, on the subject of the miracle. Father Hickey had suffered the meed of his inhospitable conduct. The committee, arriving at Four Mile Water the day after I left, had found the graveyard exactly where it had formerly stood. Father Hickey, taken by surprise, had attempted to defend himself by a confused statement, which led the committee to declare finally that the miracle was a gross imposture. The *Times*, commenting on this after adducing a number of examples of priestly craft, remarked, "We are glad to learn that the Rev. Mr. Hickey has been permanently relieved of his duties as the parish priest of Four Mile Water by his ecclesiastical superior. It is less gratifying to have to record that it has been found possible to obtain two hundred signatures to a memorial embodying the absurd defense offered to the committee, and expressing unabated confidence in the integrity of Mr. Hickey."

EDWARD SHEEHY

The Black Mare

✳

Michael Fardy Cullen wasn't drunk when he saw the mare. He was just in the cheerful state of a man who's had six pints running on an empty stomach following the sale of two bullocks and a springer for the tidy sum of thirty-seven pounds. Anyhow, he decided afterwards that even if he'd been cold sober it wouldn't have made any difference.

Her coat was black and glossy; she had three white stockings and a white star on her forehead. In spite of the patched and shabby winkers he could see that she had a fine head, small, with lively pointed ears and a greyey velvet muzzle. He loved looking at her, appraising the depth of her chest and the cleanness of her legs and wondering what she was doing here, tied by a rope reins to a ring in the wall behind Sheridan's pub. A little way down the lane stood a gaudy tinkers' caravan from behind which came the sound of snarling, quarrelling voices, a man's and a woman's. Maybe the tinkers owned her; if they did, God help her.

From *The Dublin Magazine*.

He looked at the mare again and saw that the reins had become looped around her off foreleg. He was on the point of setting it to rights when two tinkers came out from behind the caravan followed by an oldish striall of a woman who seemed to be dancing mad with rage at them. When they took no notice of her it only provoked her further. Just as the two were within half a dozen paces of Michael Fardy and the mare she darted to one side, picked up a stone the size of a man's fist and hurled it after them. The pair scattered and ducked, and the stone struck the wall right in front of the mare's nose. The mare snorted in fright; she reared and backed. As she came down the tightened reins tripped her and flung her over on her side. The tinkers ran back towards the caravan leaving the mare as she was with the mouth nearly torn out of her. Michael Fardy with pity for her rushed forward and started tearing at the knot; but it was so hard with the strain of the mare's fall that it wouldn't yield to his fingers. He thought of the clasp-knife in his pocket. He had it in his hand with the blade open when one of the tinkers rushed up with his mouth full of curses asking him did he want to destroy a beautiful bit of rope for the want of a little patience. He shouldered Michael Fardy to one side and started working on the knot himself, saying to the other:

"That'll cool her now, Nailer. She wanted that. She's ruined with idleness and good-feeding—that one is."

"I was afeared she might hurt herself," Michael Fardy said apologetically.

"Devil a fear of that one," the tinker said. He was a short stocky fellow with the small cruel eyes of a pig and a wart on his left eyelid. The tinker called Nailer was tall, lean and foxy.

"She's a fine mare," Michael Fardy said.

"She's all that," the short fellow said, and, with a savage tug on the bit he jerked the mare to her feet.

"That one has breeding," Nailer said.

"I can see that," Michael Fardy said.

"Now's your chance to pick her up cheap," Nailer

said, smiling. His smile was yellow-toothed and without friendliness.

"Yerra, come away out of that, Nailer," the short fellow said. "What'd that poor boy be doing with the finest mare this side of the town of Mallow and she sired by the famous Flying Rocket and the mother of Romping Rosa that won the flapper stakes at the Curragh two years back?"

"What are ye asking for her?" Michael Fardy asked, more out of bravado than anything else.

The short fellow looked straight at him; the eyelid with the wart hung a shade lower than the other giving its owner a look of mocking unbelief.

"Listen here to me, boy," he said, as if he had a secret to confide. "You look to me to be a decent boy so I'll be straight and honest with you, as straight and honest as if you were my own brother. Listen to me now. I'm selling that mare cheap if I can get a buyer for her this day in Castletown. She's nine year old; you can see that for yourself. She was hurt once in the hunting field. There's the scar on her off leg there. But she's as sound on it to-day as ever she was. She'll work under a dray or a trap, plough, harrow or anything you like. She's gentle as a lamb; a child could follow her; ask Nailer there and he'll tell you. And she's selling for ten pound, no more no less. She's selling cheap because I bought her cheap. The man that had her couldn't feed her for the winter and with the gentry in such bad case there's small sale for a classy animal like her. I know a man'd pay three times that for her for a brood mare; but he's in the County Meath and that's a long road. Ten pound, boy, ten pound; and God strike me dead this minute if I'm telling you the word of a lie."

"Show him the action of her," Nailer said, and the short fellow started to trot the mare up and down the lane. She moved well, with an easy and supple grace. Michael Fardy trembled with anxiety as he looked at her. When she came to a standstill again he felt her legs and fetlocks, looked at her teeth, walked around her and looked her over from every angle. He did so more for the effect of the thing than anything else and to gain time. He wanted her, to own her; and ten pounds was cheap. But tinkers could fool you up to your eyes about a horse. Still he couldn't see anything wrong with her.

"I'll give ye eight for her," he said, suddenly forsaking all caution.

The upshot of it all was that Michael Fardy bought the mare for nine pounds with the winkers thrown in, but not the beautiful bit of rope.

II

It was dark night before he topped Mam-a-Casac and the drink he had taken before leaving the town was wearing off. At one moment he felt like a rapparee riding the black mare out on to the hillcrest. The next he was troubled and nervous; troubled when he thought of what old Pats would say; nervous when the mare shuddered in her muscles and curved away, head up and ears cocked, from a white stone that appeared dimly out of the bogland. He was afraid of her, of the proud spirit he was beginning to sense in her. Would she work? Would she go under a cart and haul home their turf from the bog? The fellow with the wart on his eye said she would; but then he was in a hell-sight too great a hurry to get shut of her. She might be doped; it wouldn't be the first time tinkers doped a horse. Even when she slowed down he hardly dared touch her with the crop; but talked to her coaxingly:

"Ho there, girleen! Come on now, girl!"

Nellie was up by the fire waiting for him when he got in. She put by her darning and started blowing the fire under the kettle.

"You're late," she said.

"Yea," he said.

"How was the fair?"

"Good. I got thirty-seven for the three and I bought a

fine mare cheap. You'll see her in the morning. We'll be the envy of them all with her for she's a beautiful beast."

"You had no talk with my father about buying a horse?" she asked.

"Well, what has that to do with it? Don't we need one instead of having to beg the loan of that old garrawn of my brothers every time we want to do a hand's turn? And anyway 'tis none of his business."

"That won't stop his tongue; and you know yourself that if she was the finest out he'd find fault with her, because he had no thought himself of buying a horse."

" 'Tis time he knew who's master in this house then," he shouted. "Didn't we make a settlement? Didn't we? And a generous one too for the bloody old cripple? Has he any complaint to make on that score?"

"But, Michael Fardy," she answered patiently, "we don't want trouble in the house."

"Then let him mind his soul, the old codger, for he's finished minding my business. Let him have what he's entitled to; but I won't be bothered with the vagaries and the contradictions of an old doting amadawn even if he is your father."

He looked belligerently towards the room door and felt a lot better for having spoken his mind. Nellie made him a strong cup of tea and gave it to him with some griddle-bread by the fire. After that they went up to their room, softly so as not to wake the child. Without talk they undressed and got into bed where neither of them slept for a long time; she because of a dull resentment at his not having brought her back any present from the town; he with nursing his anger against his father-in-law and thinking that he'd have to take up a stand with him now or never.

There was hardly light to see when he opened his eyes. Nellie was shaking him roughly, telling him to listen. He heard the heavy thud of hooves. The mare must have got out. She was moving round the house. Lucky she hadn't taken to the road. Even so her heavy restless hoofbeats made him uneasy. Then he remembered that he had forgotten to water her. He got out of bed and started pulling on his clothes.

When he opened the kitchen door he saw her standing on the little grassy hillock on the other side of the boreen. She stood there, noble and strange, surveying the grey, misty valley below her. God, but she was lovely! It frightened him how lovely she was there against the morning sky. She turned, trotted swingingly down the slope, and, nimbly as a cat, leaped the low stone wall to land on all fours in the boreen. "If she sulks," he thought, "there'll be no catching her." But he had no trouble. When he took her by the forelock she came with him willingly to the well where he hauled out two buckets of water for her.

When he got back to the yard there was old Pats at the door, red-nosed and shivering in the rawness of the morning. Usually he had his breakfast in bed and didn't get up until the day was well aired. "Be the holy!" he muttered, stepping forward, screwing up his watery eyes to peer at Michael Fardy and the mare.

"Wisha, good morrow to your honor," he jeered. "Ah, sure," he went on in mock disappointment, "it's only Michael Fardy that's in it and me thinking 'twas some fine gentleman with his hunter. And what'd you be doing with her, Michael Fardy?"

Michael Fardy was too angry to answer. His father-in-law's jeering always gave him that tightening of the throat and an itch in his hands to take the old cripple by the scruff of the neck . . .

"Ah, wisha," old Pats went on, "sure 'tis the beggar on horseback, a proud seat without a prop. Excuse me asking you, sir. But where did you get the mare, sir?"

"I bought her," Michael Fardy said. "Isn't that enough for you?"

"Ah, I see now. So you're thinking of joining the Edenferry hunt and consorting with the gentry."

"You know damn well we want a horse on the farm."

"Aye, indeed."

"And she's a fine mare," Michael Fardy blustered.

"Aye, that she is. And I suppose you've got grazing and stabling for her at the big house down in Edenferry for 'twould be a pity to see a fine beast famished when she'd eaten every bit of grass off the hill. Or maybe you'd liefer spend a handful of sovereigns on a few loads of hay and a couple of barrels of oats and keep her up in the room. But of course you can't expect to be taken for one of the gentry unless you're prepared to lash the money around."

"Look here now, Pats Byrne," Michael Fardy shouted, "I've had enough of your bloody guff. D'you hear me now? She's staying here and she's working on the farm and I'll feed her all right. And that's my say."

"Oh, have your say, boy, have your say. No one'll begrudge you that. And I suppose now you had a trial of her under a cart and saw her working? Sure, you'd hardly buy her without, a sensible boy like you?"

Michael Fardy didn't answer. Nellie came to the door of the house and called out that the breakfast was ready. He left the mare in the haggard and went in after his father-in-law.

III

The news spread like wildfire that Michael Fardy had bought a full-blooded hunter of a mare, and in the course of the day the neighbouring men dropped over on one excuse or another. And each one of them walked into the haggard, circled round the mare, eyeing her all over and each one of them with a smile on his puss as if he knew something bloody funny but wasn't going to give it away. And old Pats went on with his litany, telling every one that came how he had a gentleman for a son-in-law whom nothing would do but a sixteen-hand thoroughbred who'd eat as much as an elephant and demand kinder treatment than a Christian. They had a sheaf of stories of this horse and that horse and how tinkers had fooled men up to the eyes. Michael Fardy knew they thought him a fool. She was a fine mare, they admitted, a grand looking mare. And maybe she'd work. But she was a bit big for the country; the country was too poor to feed the likes of her properly. And if one of them was buying a horse he'd rather a smaller, commoner animal. She'd suit Sam Stockwell, now, down at Edenferry; or a gentleman somewhere who could afford to keep a hunter.

Michael Fardy knew that they were right; but all the talk and all the jeering turned him sour and stubborn. When he looked at them, cringing and mean, and looked at the mare, at the clean beauty of her, he didn't set much store by their talk. But he couldn't keep her just as an ornament so he listened to their advice when they told him to have a couple of the lads around when he put her under the cart for the first time. Frankeen Sugrue and Tim Egan, though they agreed with the others about her being too big and too finely bred for the country, were full of admiration for her. Michael Fardy asked them to give him a hand with her the next day.

The morning was bright with sun, but an ice-cold wind blew down from Knocknagarragh and stripped the first leaves from the ash-trees in the haggard. As Michael Fardy put the winkers on the mare, he nearly prayed to her to take it kindly and put him in the right. He was shivering with fright, even though the mare was as biddable as anyone could ask; but he couldn't rid himself of a feeling that some terrible power lay hidden in those smooth easy muscles. The others were a bit nervous too and trying not to show it as they took the tackling down from the pegs in the cowhouse with quick jerky movements. Old Pats stood over by the kitchen door with a smile under his wispy, yellow mustache; he looked to Michael Fardy as if he was wishing for the worst.

She took kindly enough to the tackling, though she looked insulted by it, like a delicate lady forced to wear the clothes of a servant-girl. They wheeled the cart around her a couple of times to get her used to the jangling of the chains and the sound of the iron-shod wheels on the cobbles. She obeyed the hand on the bit when Michael Fardy backed her in between the shafts. She didn't stir while they linked up the traces and the britchin.

"We'll take her up by the village," he said.

"Yea," Frankeen Sugrue said, "but better lead her a bit till she's used to the feel of the cart."

They took up positions, one on either side of her head. Tim Egan stood the length of the reins behind.

"Come on, girl," Michael Fardy said, urging her forward.

She moved across the yard. 'Twas easy to see that she felt it strange by the way she tried to edge sideways. As they reached the rough patch in front of the door the wheels and the chains made an unmerciful clatter. The mare stopped dead. She didn't look wicked; she just stalled. They urged her and coaxed her but she gave them no heed. Then without warning Tim Egan gave her a touch of the ashplant across the rump. In a second she was like a mad thing. She reared, dragging the reins out of Frankeen's grip and lifting Michael Fardy off the ground. She came down, her hooves crashing hardly an inch from his feet. She dipped her head and flung her heels against the bottom-boards of the cart. The britchin snapped; the wood splintered.

"Mother of God, she'll be the death of them!" Nellie wailed, and young Jem clinging to her skirts set up a howl fit to wake the dead.

"Hold her ye divils," old Pats croaked, dancing around them as the mare plunged forward dragging the three of them across the yard.

"Shut the gate, you bloody idiot!" Michael Fardy yelled to him so savagely that without a word he hobbled across the yard and got the gate closed just in the mare's nose.

The three of them held her head while old Pats unlinked the traces and the britchin on the side it still held. When they got her out from under the cart she stood there shivering in every muscle but with no sign at all of vice or wickedness.

"You won't get no good out of that one," Frankeen Sugrue said and Tim Egan agreed. The pair of them, at any rate, had had enough of her.

IV

In bed that night his delight in her beauty was mixed with feelings of fear and helplessness. If she was a common animal he knew he'd be able to tame her. But she wasn't and there was some power in her that bested him. He felt that he had no right to her. It was like the gnawing bitterness of a hopeless love.

She must have got out of the field during the night because once when he woke in the darkness he could hear her hooves on the cobbles of the yard, halting now, then stamping sharply as if she were restless. With ears strained and heart thumping he listened to her moving about. He was afraid and couldn't understand his fear. There was nothing to keep her, no ditch in the place that could hold her from the roads and still she kept nosing round the house, restlessly, as if she were seeking something. There must have been some good reason for selling her so cheap. Maybe she killed a man; maybe once she tore a man with that fierce mouth of hers; maybe she pounded a man to bloody pulp under quick savage hooves. There was nothing he could do but get rid of her . . . and be the laughing-stock of the place and give old Pats something to jeer about till the day of his death.

Morning came and she was standing in the yard, quiet and contented in the sun. Old Pats wasn't up and while he and Nellie were at their breakfast she came to the door and stood looking into the kitchen. He could hardly believe it was the same animal that was under the cart the day before. He went over and gave her a crust of bread which she munched contentedly. "It must have been the hullabuloo," he thought, "and old Pats shouting, that

frightened her. Maybe if I just try her myself after milking . . ."

He had the idea in his head all the morning. Old Pats
had a touch of his rheumatics and would keep to his bed
for half the day. But he was afraid when he remembered
the wildness of her the day before; and he was ashamed of
his fear. He had bought her and he ought to make the best
of his bargain. Even if he couldn't keep her she might at
least bring home a few loads of turf while she was in the
place. In the end he forced himself to put the winkers on
her, promising himself that he'd give up at the first sign
from her that she was going to take it badly. He got the
collar and hames on her without any trouble; but when
it came to the straddle she was inclined to wheel away
from it. He looped the reins through the staple on the
door-jamb of the cowhouse; but when he picked up the
straddle and tried to throw it across her back she started
with fright, straining wildly on the rein till the door-jamb
shook and pieces of rotten thatch began to fall from the
cowhouse roof. He dropped the straddle; but before he
could take her by the head she had pulled half a ton of
thatch, loose stones and rafters down on top of him.

A cut on the forehead and a few aches in his bones
was all he had as a result of the collapse of the cowhouse;
but old Pats couldn't stop talking about the ruin the mare
was bringing on them all and the curse on his old age of a
son-in-law who was an idiot born, who bought a mad racehorse for good money from a band of tinkers, a lunatic
animal that'd be dear if you got her for nothing. But in
spite of the wreck of the cowhouse, which was easily
mended anyway, Michael Fardy felt easier in his mind. He
couldn't keep her now. He gave in to her once and for all.

He had a fortnight to wait for the fair at Dunsorley
and in the meantime he couldn't meet a neighbour without
being asked how he was getting on with the mare. He
knew they were laughing at him behind his back but he
held his peace and let them think what they liked. He
worked all day digging out the potatoes and pitting them;

opening the drains; mending the fences between his place and Sugrues. When nobody was around he went and looked at the mare, enjoying the beauty generations of breeding had given her. The gentry had made her like that; they had bred her for themselves and she belonged to them. It was the same with their women. They didn't have to care about work, in a woman, a horse or a dog. A poor man couldn't marry one of their daughters; even if she'd have him, she'd eat him up. The poor man could only marry a drudge who was plain and willing. Looking at her made him feel how tied he was to those half-barren, mountainy fields for a life of endless labour, without adventure, without excitement, without anything of grandeur. The people from the towns drove round in their cars and looked at the hills and said how grand it must be to live in a place like Farranroe. But Michael Fardy cursed the hills, cursed the bleak steep face of Knocknagarragh that meant miles of tramping after sheep through the rock and heath. No man should live in a place like it. He should have gone out into the world, to America, to Australia instead of tying himself down to slavery by marrying Nellie Pats Byrne.

He began to hate the black mare and to be impatient for the day of the fair.

v

He was up at four and spent almost an hour combing her and rubbing her down. He put on her the saddle and bridle he had borrowed from his brother, and which, till now, had lain hidden under the hay, and set out for Dunsorley in the chill starlight.

He reached Dunsorley good and early and spent the morning riding the mare through the streets of the town. He saw with a certain amount of pride how the people turned their heads to look after him as he guided her in and out among the tethered horses, carts and groups of men intent on a deal. But it was well after nine o'clock before anyone tried to stop him. He was beginning to feel desperate when he heard a call:

"Hi, you on the black mare!"

He turned. A wizened, bandy-legged little man in knee-breeches and leggings was beckoning him. He was talking to a tall gentleman with a mustache at the rate of a mile a minute. As he came near Michael Fardy heard him saying:

"I'll lay half-a-dollar to a fiver it's her, sir."

"Well then, go ahead, Kelly," the gentleman said.

"Are you selling?" Kelly asked.

"Yea, then," Michael Fardy answered, "if I can get a price." He tried to look surly and unwilling.

"What are you asking?"

"Twenty-five pound," Michael Fardy said coolly.

The little fellow laughed, a thin jeering cackle.

"Have a heart," he said. "Twenty-five shillings'd be more like it. You won't get no twenty-five pound for that broken-down hack."

Michael Fardy looked away, out over the square crowded with horses and carts and people; he looked at the clock on the town hall which said a quarter to ten. He drew gently on the rein and the mare started to turn.

"Hi!" Kelly called, "aren't you in the hell of a hurry?"

"You heard what I said," Michael Fardy said surlily.

The gentleman looked on with an amused smile.

"Bring her over to the fair-field till we see how she moves," Kelly said.

The three of them went to the fair-field and Michael Fardy dismounted. Kelly shortened the stirrups and swung into the saddle. The gentleman and Michael Fardy stood side by side watching while he wheeled her, cantered her and trotted her over the trampled grass. Every eye on the field was turned to watch the fine, gallant mare with Kelly perched like a monkey on her back. The gentleman was delighted with her. You could see that by his face. He didn't have to haggle; Kelly was paid to do that for him. Michael Fardy was sorry now he hadn't asked for more.

By all the laws of dealing he'd have to come down from twenty-five. When Kelly brought the mare back the gentleman patted her neck and she nuzzled his coat. She looked like his already, as if he was born to own her.

"I'll tell you what," Kelly said, "the Major here'll give you fifteen for her. That's a lot more than you're likely to get for her these times for she's a long way past her best."

"Twenty-five," Michael Fardy said, "and I'll stick to it."

In the end, after leading the mare away and being called back, after being offered eighteen and sticking out for twenty-two, he sold her for twenty pounds, as they all knew from the start that he would.

A few hours later he bought a cob, a sturdy sorrel gelding for eleven pounds after trying her out in every way that he knew. He left her in the stable yard and went out to have a look round the town and to buy a few things. In Edward Street he ran into Tom Egan, Frankeen's brother, and Pats Simon Danagher from home. From the amused look on their faces he knew they were thinking about the mare. He asked them in for a drink. In the pub he could feel that they were itching for information but he didn't volunteer any. They talked of this, that and the other and had drunk two rounds of pints before Pats Simon said with a grin:

"Well, Michael Fardy, and did you sell her?"

"The mare, is it? Sure I did," Michael Fardy said.

"And did you get any sort of a price for her?" Tom Egan asked.

"Well," he answered slowly, "if you call a pound and double the money I gave for her a good price, I suppose I did."

"Glory be to God!" Pats Simon said, "look at that now. Aren't you the clever boyo and they all thinking you was fooled up to the eyes."

"Ah sure that was only old Pats. Sure I never thought to keep her; but I knew she was a bargain."

"Begor, you ought to take up dealing," Tom Egan said.

"Two pounds and double your money, be Japers!" Pats Simon said.

They had several rounds and the praise of Michael Fardy grew with every round. They wouldn't be so quick to laugh at him after this, so they wouldn't. And old Pats'd keep his mouth shut. The drink and the praise nearly made him forget his bitterness in realizing that never again in his life would he own anything so beautiful.

JAMES STEPHENS

Schoolfellows

❋

We had been at school together and I remembered him perfectly well, for he had been a clever and prominent boy. He won prizes for being at the top of his class; and prizes for good behaviour; and prizes for games. Whatever prizes were going we knew that he should get them; and, although he was pleasant about it, he knew it himself.

He saw me first, and he shouted and waved his hat, but I had jumped on a tram already in motion. He ran after me for quite a distance; but the trams only stop at regular places, and he could not keep up: he fell behind, and was soon left far behind.

I had intended jumping off to shake his hand; but I thought, so fast did he run, that he would catch up; and then the tram went quicker and quicker; and quite a stream of cars and taxis were in the way; so that when the tram did stop he was out of sight. Also I was in a hurry to get home.

From Etched in Moonlight, New York, The Macmillan Company.

Going home I marvelled for a few moments that he should have run so hard after me. He ran almost—desperately.

"It would strain every ounce of a man's strength to run like that!" I said.

And his eyes had glared as he ran!

"Poor old chap!" I thought. "He must have wanted to speak to me very badly."

Three or four days afterwards I met him again; and we talked together for a while on the footpath. Then, at whose suggestion I do not remember, we moved into the bar of an hotel near by.

We drank several glasses of something; for which, noticing that his hat was crumpled and his coat sleeves shiny, I paid. We spoke of the old days at school and he told me of men whom he had met, but whom I had not heard of for a long time. Such old schoolfellows as I did know of I mentioned, and in every instance he took their addresses down on a piece of paper.

He asked what I was doing and how I was succeeding and where I lived; and this latter information he pencilled also on his piece of paper.

"My memory is getting bad," he said with a smile.

Every few minutes he murmured into our schoolday conversation—

"Whew! Isn't it hot!"

And at other times, laughing a little, apologising a little, he said:

"I am terribly thirsty to-day; it's the heat, I suppose."

I had not noticed that it was particularly hot; but we are as different in our skins as we are in our souls, and one man's heat may be tepid enough to his neighbour.

II

Then I met him frequently. One goes home usually at the same hour and by the same road; and it was on these home-goings and on this beaten track that we met.

Somehow, but by what subtle machinery I cannot recall, we always elbowed one another into a bar; and, as his hat was not getting less crumpled nor his coat less shiny, I paid for whatever liquor was consumed.

One can do anything for a long time without noticing it, and the paying for a few drinks is not likely to weigh on the memory. Still, we end by noticing everything; and perhaps I noticed it the earlier because liquor does not agree with me. I never mentioned that fact to anyone, being slightly ashamed of it, but I knew it very woefully myself by the indigestion which for two or three days followed on even a modest consumption of alcohol.

So it was that setting homeward one evening on the habitual track I turned very deliberately from it; and, with the slightest feeling of irritation, I went homewards by another route: and each night that followed I took this new path.

I did not see him for some weeks, and then one evening he hailed me on the new road. When I turned at the call and saw him running—he was running—I was annoyed, and, as we shook hands, I became aware that it was not so much the liquor I was trying to side-track as my old schoolfellow.

He walked with me for quite a distance; and he talked more volubly than was his wont. He talked excitedly; and his eyes searched the streets ahead as they widened out before our steps, or as they were instantly and largely visible when we turned a corner. A certain malicious feeling was in my mind as we paced together; I thought:

"There is no public-house on this road."

Before we parted he borrowed a half-sovereign from me, saying that he would pay it back in a day or two, but I cheerfully bade adieu to the coin as I handed it over, and thought also that I was bidding a lengthy adieu to him.

"I won't meet him for quite a while," I said to myself; and that proved to be true.

III

Nevertheless, when a fair month had elapsed I did meet him again, and we marched together in a silence which was but sparsely interrupted by speech.

He had apparently prospected my new route, for he informed me that a certain midway side-street was a short cut; and midway in this side-street we found a public-house.

I went into this public-house with the equable pulse of a man who has no true grievance; for I should have been able to provide against a contingency which even the worst equipped prophet might have predicted.

As often as his glass was emptied I saw that it was re-filled; but, and perhaps with a certain ostentation, I re-frained myself from the cup.

Of course, one drink leads to another and the path between each is conversational. My duty it appeared was to supply the drinks, but I thought it just that he should supply the conversation.

I had myself a fund of silence which might have been uncomfortable to a different companion, and against which he was forced to deploy many verbal battalions.

We had now met quite a number of times. He had exhausted our schooldays as a topic; he knew nothing about politics or literature or city scandal, and talk about weather dies of inanition in less than a minute; and yet—he may have groaned at the necessity—there had to be fashioned a conversational bridge which should unite drink to drink, or drinks must cease.

In such a case a man will talk about himself. It is one's last subject; but it is a subject upon which, given the pre-liminary push, one may wax eternally eloquent.

He rehearsed to me a serial tale of unmerited calam-ity, and of hardship by field and flood; of woes against which he had been unable to provide, and against which no man could battle; and of accidents so attuned to the chords of fiction that one knew they had to be true. He

434

had been to rustic-sounding places in England and to Span-ish-sounding places in America; and from each of these places an undefined but complete misfortune had uprooted him and chased him as with a stick. So by devious, circui-tous, unbelievable routes he had come home again.

One cannot be utterly silent unless one is dead, and then possibly one makes a crackle with one's bones; so I spoke:

"You are glad to be home again," I queried.

He was glad; but he was glad dubiously and with res-ervations. Misfortune had his address, and here or else-where could thump a hand upon his shoulder.

His people were not treating him decently, it ap-peared. They had been content to see him return from outlandish latitudes, but since then they had not given him a fair show.

Domestic goblins hinted at, not spoken, but which one sensed to be grisly, half detached themselves from be-tween the drinks. He was not staying with his people. They made him an allowance. You could not call it an al-lowance either: they paid him a weekly sum. Weekly sum was a large way of putting it, for you cannot do much on fifteen shillings a week: that sum per week would hardly pay for, for—

"The drinks," I put in brightly; for one cannot be persistently morose in jovial company.

"I must be off," I said, and I filled the chink of silence which followed on my remark with a waving hand and the bustle of my hasty departure.

IV

Two evenings afterward he met me again.

We did not shake hands; and my salutation was so brief as not really to merit that name.

He fell in beside me and made a number of remarks about the weather; which, if they were as difficult to make as they were to listen to, must have been exceedingly trou-blesome to him. One saw him searching as in bottomless pits for something to say; and he hauled a verbal wisp from these profundities with the labour of one who drags miseries up a mountain.

The man was pitiable, and I pitied him. I went alternately hot and cold. I blushed for him and for myself; for the stones under our feet and for the light clouds that went scudding above our heads; and in another instant I was pale with rage at his shameful, shameless persistence. I thrust my hands into my pockets, because they were no longer hands but fists; and because they tingled and were inclined to jerk without authority from me.

We came to the midway cross-street which as well as being a short cut was the avenue to a public-house; and he dragged slightly at the crossing as I held to my course.

"This is the longest way," he murmured.

"I prefer it," I replied.

After a moment he said:

"You always go home this way."

"I shall go a different way to-morrow," I replied.

"What way?" he enquired timidly.

"I must think that out," said I.

With that I stood and resolutely bade him good-bye. We both moved a pace from each other, and then he turned again, flurriedly, and asked me for the loan of half a crown. He wanted it to get a—a—a—

I gave it to him hurriedly and walked away, prickling with a sensation of weariness and excitement as of one who has been worried by a dog but has managed to get away from it.

Then I did not see him for two days, but of course I knew that I should meet him, and the knowledge was as exasperating as any kind of knowledge could be.

v

It was quite early in the morning; and he was waiting outside my house. He accompanied me to the tram, and on the way asked me for half a crown. I did not give it, and I did not reply to him.

As I was getting on the tram he lowered his demand and asked me urgently for sixpence. I did not answer nor look at him, but got on my tram and rode away in such a condition of nervous fury that I could have assaulted the conductor who asked me to pay my fare.

When I reached home that evening he was still waiting for me; at least, he was there, and he may have hung about all day; or he may have arrived just in time to catch me.

At the sight of him all the irritation which had almost insensibly been adding to and multiplying and storing itself in my mind, fused together into one sole consciousness of rage which not even a language of curses could make explicit enough to suit my need of expression. I swore when I saw him; and I cursed him openly when he came to me with the sly, timid, outfacing bearing, which had become for me his bearing.

He began at once; for all pretence was gone, and all the barriers of reserve and decency were down. He did not care what I thought of him: nor did he heed in the least what I said to him. He did not care about anything except only by any means; by every means; by cajolery, or savagery, or sentimentality, to get or screw or torment some money out of me.

I knew as we stood glaring and panting that to get the few pence he wanted he would have killed me with as little compunction as one would kill a moth which had fluttered into the room; and I knew that with as little pity I could have slaughtered him as he stood there.

He wanted sixpence, and I swore that I would see him dead before I gave it to him. He wanted twopence and I swore I would see him damned before I gave him a penny.

I moved away, but he followed me clawing my sleeve and whining:

"Twopence: you can spare twopence: what is twopence to you? If I had twopence and a fellow asked me for it I'd give it to him: twopence . . ."

I turned and smashed my fist into his face. His head jerked upwards, and he went staggering backwards and fell backwards into the road; as he staggered the blood jetted out of his nose.

He picked himself up and came over to me bloody, and dusty, and cautious, and deprecating, with a smile that was a leer. . . .

"Now will you give me twopence?" he said.

I turned then and I ran from him as if I were running for my life. As I went I could hear him padding behind me, but he was in no condition, and I left him easily behind. And every time I saw him after that I ran.

JAMES STEPHENS

A Rhinoceros, Some Ladies and a Horse

❋

One day, in my first job, a lady fell in love with me. It was quite unreasonable, of course, for I wasn't wonderful: I was small and thin, and I weighed much the same as a largish duck-egg. I didn't fall in love with her, or anything like that. I got under the table, and stayed there until she had to go wherever she had to go to.

I had seen an advertisement—"Smart boy wanted," it said. My legs were the smartest things about me, so I went there on the run. I got the job.

At that time there was nothing on God's earth that I could do, except run. I had no brains, and I had no memory. When I was told to do anything I got into such an enthusiasm about it that I couldn't remember anything else about it. I just ran as hard as I could, and then I ran back, proud and panting. And when they asked me for the whatever-it-was that I had run for, I started, right on the instant, and ran some more.

From *Irish Writing*.

The place I was working at was, amongst other things, a theatrical agency. I used to be sitting in a corner of the office floor, waiting to be told to run somewhere and back. A lady would come in—a music-hall lady that is—and, in about five minutes, howls of joy would start coming from the inner office. Then, peacefully enough, the lady and my two bosses would come out, and the lady always said, "Splits! I can do splits like no one." And one of my bosses would say, "I'm keeping your splits in mind." And the other would add, gallantly,—"No one who ever saw your splits could ever forget 'em."

One of my bosses was thin, and the other one was fat. My fat boss was composed entirely of stomachs. He had three baby-stomachs under his chin: then he had three more descending in even larger englobings nearly to the ground: but, just before reaching the ground, the final stomach bifurcated into a pair of boots. He was very light on these and could bounce about in the neatest way.

He was the fattest thing I had ever seen, except a rhinoceros that I had met in the Zoo the Sunday before I got the job. That rhino was *very* fat, and it had a smell like twenty-five pigs. I was standing outside its palisade, wondering what it could possibly feel like to be a rhinoceros, when two larger boys passed by. Suddenly they caught hold of me, and pushed me through the bars of the palisade. I was very skinny, and in about two seconds I was right inside, and the rhinoceros was looking at me.

It was very fat, but it wasn't fat like stomachs, it was fat like barrels of cement, and when it moved it creaked a lot, like a woman I used to know who creaked like an old bedstead. The rhinoceros swaggled over to me with a bunch of cabbage sticking out of its mouth. It wasn't angry, or anything like that, it just wanted to see who I was. Rhinos are blindish: they mainly see by smelling, and they smell in snorts. This one started at my left shoe, and snorted right up that side of me to my ear. He smelt that very carefully: then he switched over to my right ear, and snorted right down that side of me to my right shoe: then he fell in love with my shoes and began to lick them. I, naturally, wriggled my feet at that, and the big chap was so astonished that he did the strangest step-dance backwards to his pile of cabbages, and began to eat them.

I squeezed myself out of his cage and walked away. In a couple of minutes I saw the two boys. They were very frightened, and they asked me what I had done to the rhinoceros. I answered, a bit grandly, perhaps, that I had seized it in both hands, ripped it limb from limb, and tossed its carcase to the crows. But when they began shouting to people that I had just murdered a rhinoceros I took to my heels, for I didn't want to be arrested and hanged for a murder that I hadn't committed.

Still, a man can't be as fat as a rhinoceros, but my boss was as fat as a man can be. One day a great lady of the halls came in, and was received on the knee. She was very great. Her name was Maudie Darling, or thereabouts. My bosses called her nothing but "Darling," and she called them the same. When the time came for her to arrive the whole building got palpitations of the heart. After waiting a while my thin boss got angry, and said—"Who does the woman think she is? If she isn't here in two twos I'll go down to the entry, and when she does come I'll boot her out." The fat boss said—"She's only two hours late, she'll be here before the week's out."

Within a few minutes there came great clamors from the court-yard. Patriotic cheers, such as Parnell himself never got, were thundering. My bosses ran instantly to the inner office. Then the door opened, and the lady appeared.

She was very wide, and deep, and magnificent. She was dressed in camels and zebras and goats: she had two peacocks in her hat and a rabbit muff in her hand, and she strode among these with prancings.

But when she got right into the room and saw herself being looked at by three men and a boy she became adorably shy: one could see that she had never been looked at before.

"O," said she, with a smile that made three and a half

hearts beat like one, "O," said she, very modestly, "is Mr. Which-of-'em-is-it really in? Please tell him that Little-Miss-Me would be so glad to see and to be—"

Then the inner door opened, and the large lady was surrounded by my fat boss and my thin boss. She crooned to them—"O, you dear boys, you'll never know how much I've thought of you and longed to see you."

That remark left me stupefied. The first day I got to the office I heard that it was the fat boss's birthday, and that he was thirty years of age: and the thin boss didn't look a day younger than the fat one. How the lady could mistake these old men for boys seemed to me the strangest fact that had ever come my way. My own bet was that they'd both die of old age in about a month.

After a while they all came out again. The lady was helpless with laughter: she had to be supported by my two bosses—"O," she cried, "you boys will kill me." And the bosses laughed and laughed, and the fat one said—"Darling, you're a scream," and the thin one said—"Darling, you're a riot."

And then . . . she saw me! I saw her seeing me the very way I had seen the rhinoceros seeing me: I wondered for an instant would she smell me down one leg and up the other. She swept my two bosses right away from her, and she became a kind of queen, very glorious to behold: but sad, startled. She stretched a long, slow arm out and out and out and then she unfolded a long, slow finger, and pointed it at me—"Who is THAT??" she whispered in a strange whisper that could be heard two miles off.

My fat boss was an awful liar—"The cat brought that in," said he.

But the thin boss rebuked him: "No," he said, "it was not the cat. Let me introduce you; darling, this is James. James, this is the darling of the gods."

"And of the pit," said she, sternly.

She looked at me again. Then she sank to her knees and spread out both arms to me—

"Come to my Boozalum, angel," said she in a tender kind of way.

I knew what she meant, and I knew that she didn't know how to pronounce that word. I took a rapid glance at the area indicated. The lady had a boozalum you could graze a cow on. I didn't wait one second, but slid, in one swift, silent slide, under the table. Then she came forward and said a whole lot of poems to me under the table, imploring me, among a lot of odd things, to "come forth, and gild the morning with my eyes," but at last she was reduced to whistling at me with two fingers in her mouth, the way you whistle for a cab.

I learned after she had gone that most of the things she said to me were written by a poet fellow named Spokeshave. They were very complimentary, but I couldn't love a woman who mistook my old bosses for boys, and had a boozalum that it would take an Arab chieftain a week to trot across on a camel.

The thin boss pulled me from under the table by my leg, and said that my way was the proper way to treat a rip, but my fat boss said, very gravely—"James, when a lady invites a gentleman to her boozalum a real gentleman hops there as pronto as possible, and I'll have none but real gentlemen in this office."

"Tell me," he went on, "what made that wad of Turkish Delight fall in love with you?"

"She didn't love me at all, sir," I answered.

"No?" he enquired.

"She was making fun of me," I explained.

"There's something in that," said he seriously, and went back to his office.

I had been expecting to be sacked that day. I was sacked the next day, but that was about a horse.

I had been given three letters to post, and told to run or they'd be too late. So I ran to the post office and round it and back, with, naturally, the three letters in my pocket. As I came to our door a nice, solid, red-faced man rode up on a horse. He thrust the reins into my hand—

"Hold the horse for a minute," said he.

"I can't," I replied, "my boss is waiting for me."

"I'll only be a minute," said he angrily, and he walked off.

Well, there was I, saddled, as it were, with a horse. I looked at it, and it looked at me. Then it blew a pint of soap-suds out of its nose and took another look at me, and then the horse fell in love with me as if he had just found his long-lost foal. He started to lean against me and to woo me with small whinneys, and I responded and replied as best I could—

"Don't move a toe," said I to the horse, "I'll be back in a minute."

He understood exactly what I said, and the only move he made was to swing his head and watch me as I darted up the street. I was less than half a minute away anyhow, and never out of his sight.

Up the street there was a man, and sometimes a woman, with a barrow, thick-piled with cabbages and oranges and apples. As I raced round the barrow I pinched an apple off it at full speed, and in ten seconds I was back at the horse. The good nag had watched every move I made, and when I got back his eyes were wide open, his mouth was wide open, and he had his legs all splayed out so that he couldn't possibly slip. I broke the apple in halves and popped one half into his mouth. He ate it in slow crunches, and then he looked diligently at the other half. I gave him the other half, and, as he ate it, he gurgled with cidery gargles of pure joy. He then swung his head round from me and pointed his nose up the street, right at the apple-barrow.

I raced up the street again, and was back within the half-minute with another apple. The horse had nigh finished the first half of it when a man who had come up said, thoughtfully—

444

"He seems to like apples, bedad!"

"He loves them," said I.

And then, exactly at the speed of lightning, the man became angry, and invented bristles all over himself like a porcupine—

"What the hell do you mean," he hissed, and then he bawled, "by stealing my apples?"

I retreated a bit into the horse—

"I didn't steal your apples," I said.

"You didn't!" he roared, and then he hissed, "I saw you," he hissed.

"I didn't steal them," I explained, "I pinched them."

"Tell me that one again," said he.

"If," said I patiently, "if I took the apples for myself that would be stealing."

"So it would," he agreed.

"But as I took them for the horse that's pinching."

"Be dam, but!" said he. " 'Tis a real argument," he went on, staring at the sky. "Answer me that one," he demanded of himself, and he in a very stupor of intellection. "I give it up," he roared, "you give me back my apples."

I placed the half apple that was left into his hand, and he looked at it as if it was a dead frog—

"What'll I do with that?" he asked earnestly.

"Give it to the horse," said I.

The horse was now prancing at him, and mincing at him, and making love at him. He pushed the half apple into the horse's mouth, and the horse mumbled it and watched him, and chewed it and watched him, and gurgled it and watched him—

"He does like his bit of apple," said the man.

"He likes you too," said I. "I think he loves you."

"It looks like it," he agreed, for the horse was yearning at him, and its eyes were soulful.

"Let's get him another apple," said I, and, without another word, we both pounded back to his barrow and each of us pinched an apple off it. We got one apple into the horse, and were breaking the second one when a woman said gently—

"Nice, kind, Christian gentlemen, feeding dumb animals—with my apples," she yelled suddenly.

The man with me jumped as if he had been hit by a train—

"Mary," said he humbly.

"Joseph," said she in a completely unloving voice.

But the woman transformed herself into nothing else but woman—

"What about my apples?" said she. "How many have we lost?"

"Three," said Joseph.

"Four," said I, "I pinched three and you pinched one."

"That's true," said he. "That's exact, Mary. I only pinched one of our apples."

"You only," she squealed—

And I, hoping to be useful, broke in—

"Joseph," said I, "is the nice lady your boss?"

He halted for a dreadful second, and made up his mind—

"You bet she's my boss," said he, "and she's better than that, for she's the very wife of my bosum."

She turned to me—

"Child of Grace—" said she—

Now, when I was a child, and did something that a woman didn't like she always expostulated in the same way. If I tramped on her foot, or jabbed her in the stomach—the way women have multitudes of feet and stomachs is always astonishing to a child—the remark such a woman made was always the same. She would grab her toe or her stomach, and say—"Childagrace, what the hell are you doing?" After a while I worked it out that Childagrace was one word, and was my name. When any woman in agony yelled Childagrace I ran right up prepared to be punished, and the woman always said tenderly, "What are you yowling about, Childagrace."

"Childagrace," said Mary earnestly, "how's my family to live if you steal our apples? You take my livelihood away from me! Very good, but will you feed and clothe and educate my children in," she continued proudly, "the condition to which they are accustomed?"

I answered that question cautiously—

"How many kids have you, ma'am?" said I.

"We'll leave that alone for a while," she went on. "You owe me two and six for the apples."

"Mary!" said Joseph, in a pained voice.

"And you," she snarled at him, "owe me three shillings. I'll take it out of you in pints." She turned to me—

"What do you do with all the money you get from the office here?"

"I give it to my landlady."

"Does she stick to the lot of it?"

"Oh, no," I answered, "she always gives me back threepence."

"Well, you come and live with me and I'll give you back fourpence."

"All right," said I.

"By gum," said Joseph, enthusiastically, "that'll be fine. We'll go out every night and we won't steal a thing. We'll just pinch legs of beef, and pig's feet, and barrels of beer—"

"Wait now," said Mary. "You stick to your own landlady. I've trouble enough of my own. You needn't pay me the two and six."

"Good for you," said Joseph heartily, and then, to me—

"You just get a wife of your bosum half as kind as the wife of my bosum and you'll be set up for life. Mary," he cried joyfully, "let's go and have a pint on the strength of it."

"You shut up," said she.

"Joseph," I interrupted, "knows how to pronounce that word properly."

"What word?"

"The one he used when he said you were the wife of his what-you-may-call-it."

"I'm not the wife of any man's what-you-may-call-it," said she, indignantly—"Oh, I see what you mean! So he pronounced it well, did he?"

"Yes, ma'am."

She looked at me very sternly—

"How does it come you know about all these kinds of words?"

"Yes," said Joseph, and he was even sterner than she was, "when I was your age I didn't know any bad words."

"You shut up," said she, and continued, "what made you say that to me?"

"A woman came into our office yesterday, and she mispronounced it."

"What did she say now?"

"Oh, she said it all wrong."

"Do you tell me so? We're all friends here: what way did she say it, son?"

"Well, ma'am, she called it boozalum."

"She said it wrong all right," said Joseph, "but 'tis a good, round, fat kind of a word all the same."

"You shut up," said Mary. "Who did she say the word to?"

"She said it to me, ma'am."

"She must have been a rip," said Joseph.

"Was she a rip, now?"

"I don't know, ma'am. I never met a rip."

"You're too young yet," said Joseph, "but you'll meet them later on. I never met a rip myself until I got married —I mean," he added hastily, "that they were all rips except the wife of my what-do-you-call-ems, and that's why I married her."

"I expect you've got a barrel-full of rips in your past," said she bleakly, "you must tell me about some of them tonight." And then, to me, "tell us about the woman," said she.

So I told them all about her, and how she held out her arms to me, and said, "Come to my boozalum, angel."

"What did you do when she shoved out the old arms at you?" said Joseph.

"I got under the table," I answered.

"That's not a bad place at all, but," he continued earnestly, "never get under the bed when there's an old girl chasing you, for that's the worst spot you could pick on. What was the strap's name?"

"Maudie Darling, she called herself."

"You're a blooming lunatic," said Joseph, "she's the loveliest thing in the world, barring," he added hastily, "the wife of my blast-the-bloody-word."

"We saw her last night," said Mary, "at Dan Lowrey's Theatre, and she's just lovely."

"She isn't as nice as you, ma'am," I asserted.

"Do you tell me that now?" said she.

"You are twice as nice as she is, and twenty times nicer."

"There you are," said Joseph, "the very words I said to you last night."

"You shut up," said Mary scornfully, "you were trying to knock a pint out of me! Listen, son," she went on, "we'll take all that back about your landlady. You come and live with me, and I'll give you back sixpence a week out of your wages."

"All right, ma'am," I crowed in a perfectly monstrous joy.

"Mary," said Joseph, in a reluctant voice—

"You shut up," said she.

"He can't come to live with us," said Joseph. "He's a bloody Prodestan," he added sadly.

"Why—" she began—

"He'd keep me and the childer up all night, pinching apples for horses and asses, and reading the Bible, and up to every kind of devilment."

Mary made up her mind quickly—

"You stick to your own landlady," said she, "tell her that I said she was to give you sixpence." She whirled about, "There won't be a thing left on that barrow," said she to Joseph.

"Damn the scrap," said Joseph violently.

"Listen," said Mary to me very earnestly, "am I nicer than Maudie Darling?"

"You are, ma'am," said I.

Mary went down on the road on her knees: she stretched out both arms to me, and said——

"Come to my boozalum, angel."

I looked at her, and I looked at Joseph, and I looked at the horse. Then I turned from them all and ran into the building and into the office. My fat boss met me—

"Here's your five bob," said he. "Get to hell out of here," said he.

And I ran out.

I went to the horse, and leaned my head against the thick end of his neck, and the horse leaned as much of himself against me as he could manage. Then the man who owned the horse came up and climbed into his saddle. He fumbled in his pocket—

"You were too long," said I. "I've been sacked for minding your horse."

"That's too bad," said he: "that's too damn bad," and he tossed me a penny.

I caught it, and lobbed it back into his lap, and I strode down the street the most outraged human being then living in the world.

MAURICE WALSH

Come Back,
My Love

❄

They were a young couple, and six months married, and
they should have been as happy as the day was long; and
the day was long, for it was in the very heart of June—a
slumberous Sunday in June, early in the afternoon, with a
gentle warmth in the sun, and a tenuous haze over the
orange glory of the furze on all the hillsides.

The thatched cottage nestled securely halfway up the
slope at the head of a small valley. A hundred paces below,
a spring bubbled from the limestone roots of the hill into
a miniature pool; and the overflow went singing down the
hollow between clumps of sally and bracken. And far
away, in a deep notch of the mountains, the Atlantic sea
shimmered under the sun.

Maire Dhu—dark-haired Mary—sat on a straw hassock
at the hearthside where the remnants of a peat fire were
deeply smoored in white ashes. She was a long-limbed
young woman, who, later on, would be a veritable ma-

From TAKE YOUR CHOICE, New York, Lippincott.

451

tron and matriarch—nobly busted, placid-eyed, with long strong bones padded in firm flesh. She was knitting placidly and sometimes she smiled softly at a thought of her own.

Manus Boy—yellow Magnus—sat on a rush-bottomed chair at the other side of the fire, his face as solemn and hard as justice, his eyes, unseeing, looking through the open door across the valley, and the rich somber yellow of his eyes matching the golden glory of the furze over there. He was feeling his first touch of discontent, and he was frightened as well as unhappy.

He was a man of no more than middle height, but mighty-shouldered, deep-chested, flat-flanked, with a bush of yellow hair and a lean aquiline face, eagle-eyed. And, for the first time, he felt chained like a chained eagle.

Maire lifted slow blue eyes, and looked at her husband—a long, deep, considering look—and then she smiled wisely as a woman will, but there was a trace of wistfulness in her smile too.

She spoke, as if to herself, in her soft Western voice, "So it has come then."

"What has come then?" There was a quick startle in her husband's voice.

"What my mother told me to look for—sooner than I thought, my sorrow!" Maire's voice half mused.

There was a resonant timbre in Manus' voice and he made it deeper, "A wise man told me one time that a wife's mother is apt to be an interfering woman. I believe it."

"Not my mother," said Maire, and went on in the same quiet strain, as if musing to herself. "She told me that a live man and him married would be feeling the halter in the first year."

"Whatever are you talking about?" Manus wanted to know, though well he knew.

Maire gave him her slow, direct gaze. "You are a live man, Manus Boy, and you were lively, too; a seeing man and a doing man, and your hand on more than one girl. And now you feel tired and bound and spanceled to a strange woman's daughter."

"You are my wife whoever your mother is," said Manus gruffly.

Maire went on equably. "Man that you are, you will have to get over it in your own way, for myself can't help you; but if you don't get over it, that will be God's will, too—or my blame, for I have not yet the power over you."

"Who is to blame you, foolish girl?" Manus chided.

Maire leaned toward the long-thighed tongs. "Leave it be, boy," she said cheerfully enough. "Look! I'll light a furze root from the embers, and we'll make a cup of tea to ourselves. It is a comforting thing, tea, and might restore you for a short while. Will you go down to the spring for a pail of fresh water?"

"I will and welcome," said Manus, promptly on his feet. He picked up the zinc-hooped wooden pail from below the dresser and bent below the lintel into the drowsy sunlight.

"Don't be more than an hour anyway," Maire called after him.

"Five minutes and I'll be back," Manus called over his shoulder.

"Mother o' God, send him back to me—all of him!" prayed Maire, and her voice was no longer equable.

Manus put the pail down on a flat slab close to the water. A circle had been worn on the surface of the slab by the many pails that had rested there over the centuries. He thrust his hands deep into the pockets of his gray flannels, looked down-headed into the crystal pool, and sighed. Gloom was in him and around him. After a while he sat himself on a knee-high boss of rock, and after another while he shook his yellow head and murmured to himself:

"It is true for her; indeed, it is true for her, and damn her mother's eyes! Tied to the one woman all my life! Oh, the times that were, the great times that were—and the times that will never come again, for, bad as I am, there's an honest streak in me. I do, I must love that girl up there, but it is a tame love now, and no wild ecstasy any more. But I'll get used to that, too, and grow sluggishly content. And she will be the mother of my sons, and hold me in one place stagnant as a rain splash in a rut. Never again the loose foot and the woman not kissed before, never again rain on the brae and the wind blowing. Heigh-ho!"

It was then, in the heart of that mood, that a strange, waiting hush came about Manus. The tinkle of the inlet runlet, the sighing song of the streamlet down the valley grew remote as in a dream; no bird sang in these dead hours of the day, the goldfinches no longer flitted from whin to whin. Everything was hushed and waiting.

And then a new sound got through to Manus in his remoteness. It was the sound of someone or something softly splashing the water at the end of the pool not ten feet away. Manus let his eyes drift, and what he saw stilled his heart and changed his mood utterly.

It was as if a wand had touched him; it was as if the solid land of Ireland about him had become unreal; it was as if himself and what his eyes saw were in a dimension of their own in a dream world. He was under a spell, though he did not know it.

What his eyes saw were a pair of shapely small feet, toes spread and lifted, softly churning the water. They were creamy-white feet, pink-toed, and an entrancing blue vein went delicately aslant an instep into the curve of an ankle. The old devil, never far under the surface, lifted head in Manus, and the skilly use of words had not forsaken him. His voice was as vibrant as a bell. "They are made to tread on a man's heart, and the heart wanting more torment."

And a silver, mocking voice made answer, "So it has been said."

"Ay, and an ankle like that I once saw in a dream."

"That dream I made you dream."

454

His hand moved in an upward curve. "And that gentle, slender, flowing line—"

A mellow tinkle of laughter stopped him. "That is as far as you need go, golden man."

"But one could be thinking," said Manus softly.

He lifted eyes then, and was pleased by what he saw.

She was a brown girl and dainty—shining brown in the hair, lustrous brown in the eyes, golden-tanned in neck and breast and slender arms. She was wearing a low-necked, short-sleeved, flowing, diaphanous dress the color of ripe corn, with a wide sash studded with topaz, and her brown hair was held loosely by a wheaten ribbon.

The whole blending of her colors and coloring gave her an extraordinary vividness, a strange, other-world vividness. Her eyes sparkled at him, her mouth smiled at him, showing the tips of small white teeth, and her smile was of heart-stirring sweetness and extraordinary gaiety—a gaiety outside time and space.

Manus smiled back at her, and lifted a sweeping arm in salute.

"Under your feet, Princess."

She crowed delightedly. "Princess! But that is my name. How did you know, golden man?"

"What other name could you have in all the world?" said Manus.

"And your own name, it is Golden?"

"I am known as Manus Boy, which means Yellow Magnus."

"Not yellow! Golden, golden! Golden is your name."

"Whatever you say, Princess," said Manus agreeably.

She, in one deft motion, swung her feet aside out of the water and under the billowing hem of her dress. Then she leaned aside on one brown hand and contemplated Manus seriously. But the seriousness was not genuine.

"You did not live in this place always, Golden?"

"Not always, Princess. That is our—my summer cottage up the slope."

"A good choice for summer."

"Surely," said Manus complacently. "For in this place I meet a princess, and, besides, it is the sweetest valley in all the west."

Again her laughter mocked him.

"No-no! Not the sweetest. The valley where I live— my Queen Mother's valley—is the loveliest of all the valleys."

"It will be some distance away," said Manus politely.

"It is but over there." She lifted a curving arm and pointed a finger southward. "Over that small hill."

Manus knew that over that small hill was a wilderness of stone outcrops in a broken country of moorland spreading twenty miles to the Mountains of Maam. He had hunted over it, and there was no valley in it anywhere.

He made judicious answer, "Where you live, Princess, such a valley would be."

She shook her head at him and grimaced in impish, pretended anger. "You do not believe me. But it is there, there." Again she swung her arm and stabbed a finger. "Up the valley and through the gap, and there is my valley below you." She was impulsive now. "Look! Let me show you. I dare you to let me show you. Come!"

She lifted off the stone lightly as a bird, slipped her feet into flat brown sandals, and flitted to him tiptoe, her hand out. And the two of them, hand in hand, went down the hollow of the little valley by the stream. It was as easy as that.

He never looked back, never looked up toward the house where his young wife waited for her pail of spring water. In his present mood that old tame life was as dim and unsure as a dream remembered.

A bare quarter mile down the valley a gap opened in the slope to the left, and to the draw of her hand he turned in with her. Manus knew that gap. It finished in a steep chorrie of boulders, and he had often been up and over into the wild country beyond.

They came to the face of the chorrie, but did not climb. She drew him to the right along the front of it, where, as he knew, was only a bounding wall of stone. He was wrong, for there was now a narrow opening between chorrie and cliff that he had not noticed before, but that did not surprise him in the least. Through that opening she led him, in and on and up and up, in a half shade, the rock walls towering on either hand, and the sky far overhead.

And then the gorge widened, the walls lowered, and, after one final stiff pinch, they came out into the open at the head of the pass. There the little eager pressure of her palm halted him.

"Look, oh, look!" She was on tiptoe and tugging at his hand. "That is my very own valley where my mother reigns."

"I knew in my heart it was there all the time," said Manus.

"And beautiful?"

"There is no small valley anywhere so beautiful."

The valley that he had forsaken had now no objective reality in his mind, but this new valley was solidly real. It was a big, bowl-shaped green hollow in the hills. The green ran up into brown slopes that rolled over smoothly, and behind rose other slopes a fainter brown, and behind these other slopes turning purple, and behind all the smoky blue ghosts of mountains.

There was a small lake in the flat bottom of the bowl, with a cascade splashing in at one end, and a stream flowing out like a shining ribbon at the other. There were wide demesnes sweeping round the lake, clumped with flowering shrubs, and between the clumps fallow deer and roe deer and gazelles browsed and romped. To the left of the lake was a spread of lawn, emerald green, with a border brilliant with the flowers of summer; and at the back of the lawn on a high terrace stood a long, wide, low, lime-white mansion.

But, most important of all, there were many people on the lawn and about the lake; some were reclining on the grass, some slouching on seats of marble, some strolling with linked arms, many running about at some ball game and many swimming in the lake.

"That is my Queen Mother's great house," said Princess, "and these her people and my dear friends."

"Jealous I might be of one here and there," said Manus.

"Jealous! That is a word I do not know. Is it love?"

"The obverse of the medal, brown darling. But you will have love in this delectable place? It is a subject I could tell you about."

"Yes, yes, yes! Love and more love. In this valley there is nothing but love and gaiety."

"Love is not often gay, but I might be jealous all the same."

She released his hand now and slipped an arm inside his elbow. "Golden, dear," she said, softly persuasive, "you will come down and kiss the Queen's hand and meet my friends?"

"What you want me to do, that I will do," said Manus.

"My dear one," she whispered softly.

So they moved down leisurely over the grassy slopes and between fragrant shrubs, and talked and talked—and it was still afternoon, a land in which it seemed always afternoon.

"Are you a champion, Golden?" she asked him.

"Your champion, Princess."

"But a great champion?"

"There might be one or two greater," said Manus carelessly.

"And you fight other champions?"

"I have used my hands," Manus told her, and that was true.

"And a wrestler?"

"A bit collar-and-elbow in the days of my youth."

"Our champions are great champions, Golden."

"I will challenge them for you, one after the other," said Manus.

"No, no!" There was a serious note in her voice for the first time. "There is one, the greatest in all the valleys—"

"There are other valleys?"

She swung an arm gracefully wide. "Valleys without number, and the greatest champion of all is our champion, Cuchulain."

"There was indeed a great hero of that name."

"He is here now."

"And you love him?"

"There is love always."

"I will take a look at your Cuchulain," said Manus soberly.

"But no!" She was urgent. "He would break you in two with his hands."

He pressed her arm inside his, and nudged her softly with his shoulder. "Same as I could break you with my hands?"

"Your dear, ugly, brown hands! They are round my heart already." There was a thrill in her voice and his blood answered it.

So they moved down to the easier slopes, and were seen coming; and many, crying gay greetings, came flocking to meet them. The maidens came first, skipping and holding hands, and swung in an eager, laughing ring around them. They were all daintily lovely, and of all colorings and shimmerings, but, to Manus' mind, none of them had the extraordinary vividness of his Princess.

The men in richer colors, like a garden of peacocks, came more slowly, bustled through the ring of maidens, and faced the two, thrusting heads forward and grimacing at Princess with a ferocity that Manus recognized as make-believe. Himself they ignored.

But Princess brushed them aside with a quick imperious gesture, and cried, "Children, first my Queen Mother."

The crowd swung in behind, and laughed and chattered and wondered about this soberly clad, deep-chested, yellow-eyed stranger who had a somber gravity that they could not assess. And one whispered to another, "Would this hero have what is called a soul?"

Manus and Princess, still arm in arm, skirted round the lake and came up between flower beds to the wide lawn, where the rest of the company made a curve back of a white marble dais whereon a malachite canopy enclosed a wide throne seat of white marble piled with blue and yellow cushions. And among the cushions sat a great lady, a tiara of gold and jewels in her yellow hair.

A golden, noble, mature woman she was, but not old. Indeed, in that valley Manus never met an old man or an aging woman. Nor did he meet any children.

Princess still holding his arm, Manus mounted the steps of the dais slowly and gravely, and Princess cried out eagerly, "Queen Mother Fand, I present my new champion, Golden."

Queen Mother bent her fine head and smiled slowly. "Your new champion is welcome here, little one." Her voice was low-pitched where all the other voices were high and even shrill. And Manus noticed, too, that she was a quiet woman, and grave, and that behind her slate-blue eyes was something that might be melancholy, as if she half knew something precious and would never know the other half. She reached him a slow hand at the end of a molded arm, and Manus took the coolness of it in his finger tips and bent his lips to it.

And Princess made exultant little boast, "All by myself I found him, Queen Mother."

"You found him when the mood was on him and the gate open, my daughter," said the woman wisely. "He is a quiet man, your champion."

"But he can speak, and his words have a hidden meaning."

"You may find out that meaning if you hold him long enough."

Princess threw up her hands joyously, and cried, "I will keep him forever and ever and ever."

"That has been tried before," said the woman, a sad

mockery in her voice. "Go now to your friends and rivals!"

There is no need to go into details. The slow afternoon passed into evening, and evening into gloaming, but at no time did darkness come. Manus, Princess ever at his side, strolled here and there and talked to this one and that one; he looked on at the games and wrestling, and make-believe fighting, and once he swam in the lake, outpacing Princess and most of the others. When he came out of the water he found that his gray flannels had disappeared, and in their place were a gorgeous silken tunic and trews of Venetian red, with a corn-colored sash studded with topaz. It was Princess' own sash to show whose champion he was. After some hesitation he donned his splendors, and was not even ashamed.

Sometime in the evening Princess whispered to him, a shade of doubt in her voice, "It is the custom, Golden, for a new champion to show his skill. What are you skilled in besides love?"

From what he had seen, the young men were deft at wrestling, but merely playful at boxing, which was his own game. They were tall enough and active but not durable looking, and he felt that a solid right hook might knock any one of them into the middle of next week.

"You will choose a wrestler for your poor champion," he told her.

"That I will do," she said eagerly, "for I will not have you hurt." She put her hand over her heart and frowned. "There is a strange feeling here when I think of it. You will let me choose, Golden, please? You have a devil in your eyes."

Holding his hand, she hopped lightly, skirts awhirl, onto a marble bench, and he stepped firmly up to her side. He was not a tall man, but her brown head was only level with his shoulder.

She clapped her hands and gave a clear, ringing halloo; and the young people came thronging as if knowing what was afoot. She reached a hand so that the back of it touched Manus' breast, and the silver of her voice carried far, "This is now my champion, Golden, and he challenges one of you to wrestle!"

A mighty shout drowned her voice, and the youths pressed forward, hands up, faces fierce, but gaiety in every eye.

"Try me! Try me! Try me!"

Princess' flat-handed, imperious gesture brought silence, and she looked them over to choose a victim. Manus' voice was in her ear, his arm across her shoulder, "Is the hero Cuchulain amongst them?"

"No, no, not Cuchulain," and again her hand came to her heart.

"That is he standing apart?"

"Yes, but he would break you in his hands, that hero. Look, Golden, dear!" And her voice was urgent, "If you are shamed I cannot stand the pain, and I might not have life in me any more."

Manus was not heeding her. He had his eye on this Cuchulain for some time. A man in purple and red, he stood behind the crowd, feet wide-planted, hands on hips and black head forward; a quiet man—dark in the hair, cleanly pallid in face, blue-black in the eyes, not any taller than Manus, but wide as a door.

Manus found a dominance rise in him, not for the first time. He patted Princess' shoulder.

"Your champion chooses the best always, and after that works down to his own level. Stay and see!"

He moved aside her hands that would clutch him and took a long stride off the bench. And Princess stood there forlornly, a constriction about her heart that her hands could not ease.

Manus strode straight at the press and shoved through. Something in the carriage of his head, some other-world savagery in his eyes made these young men move hastily aside to give him room. And there he was, yellow head thrown back and yellow eyes half-hooded, face to face with Cuchulain. For the first time there was a hush.

Cuchulain smiled gravely, but Manus was brusque.

"Are you that Cuchulain who was once the Hound of Ulster?"

"What I once was I do not know," said Cuchulain, heavy-voiced, "but what I am now is well known."

"The champion of all the valleys?"

"That is what I am."

"Or the second best?"

"You would dispute it?" Cuchulain smiled again, but a spark lit behind the black eyes. "I warn you that sometimes I lose my temper and am rougher than is permitted. You will forgive me."

"I might be rough, too," said Manus, "and I will not ask anyone to forgive me."

He thrust his right hand out low and his left high. Cuchulain did the same, and forthwith the two champions grappled. Slowly, link by link, they took the strain, testing each other's strength before trying any feints or clips. And there Manus got the surprise of his life.

Cuchulain was indeed strong, weightily strong, but, somehow, there was no pith in him, no explosive energy of body or soul to oppose the electric explosiveness of a man. He strained heavily, eyes hot and hotter, but Manus held him glued to the ground.

"Let us try it this way," said Manus. He loosed a spurt of energy, swung Cuchulain in half circle, and brought him down on spread feet; and in turn he took Cuchulain's sluggish swing and came down poised. And so at it they went, in half swings, three-quarter swings, full swings, Manus gradually increasing the tempo, so that the young people, crying shrilly, had to scatter and get out from under.

And then, with a sudden resistant wrench, Manus brought that bearlike dance to a dead stop, and Cuchulain's legs buckled and he went down on his knees. But Manus brought him upright again, patted his shoulder and let him go.

"Show you a trick or two sometime, brother," Manus said, and walked away.

Everyone there knew that there was a new champion amongst them, and everyone cheered mightily, forgetting the defeated. But Manus walked on to where Princess waited on her bench, her eyes glistening with something that might be moisture. He lifted arms to her, and she came down into them, and she knew that she was being kissed—for the first time. Her heart would not let her speak.

What is the use of going on? It was evening now, the evening that never darkened, and there was feasting in the white palace, where rose-pink silken curtains moved in the soft air and countless mirrors made endless crystal vistas. Thereafter there was music making on harps and thin-sounding pipes, and arabesque-like dancing, and poetry reciting and song making and song singing, and more feasting and dancing and singing. And Manus sang the one song he wanted to sing, an old passionate song, in his flexible baritone voice:

> "For you I thirst, O Strange Woman's
>   Daughter!
> Give me strong wine of Love, not cool
>   spring water,
> Not pallid joy—red love and its sorrow,
> For my heart you hold in your hands'
>   hollow."

He sang that song for one only, and that one knew.

Need it be said? Manus did not go home that night. He did not even remember that he had any home to go to. And after that night he did not want to go anywhere.

He stayed a week, he stayed a month, he stayed a year. He stayed. And his brown Princess was always with him, and always loving him; and her Queen Mother looked on and smiled sadly.

It was sometime in the seventh year that the change of mood came over Manus. Make-believe gaiety, make-believe fighting began to weary him, and he began to move about by himself on the northern slopes of the valley, avoiding even Princess, in whose company there was a spell no longer. The scene, the people, the spiral of fevered pleasure seeking were losing a sense of reality; and some inner vision was seeing a clean and wholesome world starkly etched under an evening sun. And there was a dark woman—

Princess noted his mood from the very beginning; she saw it bud and burgeon and bloom, and keep on blooming, and a new pain grew and grew in her. But she did not importune him, and some new desolate mood in herself would not let her do what she could do to hold him. She just followed him about at a distance, a woebegone small princess, no longer shimmering with vividness, gay never again.

Came the day when Manus, heavy with gloom, sticky with the soft warmth no longer salubrious, plunged into the lake, battled sullenly against the clinging waters, and came out unrefreshed. He reached for his Venetian reds. They were not there. There, instead, were the gray flannels that he had not seen or thought about for seven years. The roughish texture of them was pleasant to the feel, and the very stiffness of them, compared with silk, was oddly comforting and manly.

Again and heavy-footed he plodded up the northern slopes, where no longer as he well knew, was there a gap leading anywhere—anywhere he wanted to be. Gay voices called after him to join in a game of hurling, but to him they were only voices that were calling in a dream.

Princess watched him go, and herself went to where her Queen Mother sat, as usual, amongst her cushions; and that wise woman moved her fine blond head from side to side.

"So it has come, little one," she murmured sadly.

"And what now, Queen Mother?"

"If you want your Golden he can be held."

"I want him."

"There are spells—"

"And spells?"

"And more and more spells."

"And when he wakes one time, any time, will he want to stay with me for myself, myself only?"

Queen Mother again moved her head slowly. "There is a tie that no spell can kill forever. Listen, little one! You have the one chance that few get in all the valleys, but the pain is too great. Once, long ago, I, too, had that chance. I let my lover go, but you, his daughter, I could not forsake even to win a soul. I know only the half life, but I know all the pain, and that pain I will not let you suffer. I will make a spell."

Princess threw her head up, and her voice was anguished, "No, no, no! I am used to pain, and I will have no spells."

She turned away, and she, too, moved northward, her feet unsure and her eyes blinded.

Manus sat on a shelf of stone close up to the northern rim of the valley, his arms folded firmly across his breast. And he was thinking:

This is not life; it is only an image of life. Effort is useless, for effort leads nowhere, and all motion returns on one spiral. It is maybe some subtle form of hell. No, not hell. It is life without a soul, and I will have no more of it though I am held here forever. I threw my life away in a blind and selfish hour, the only life worth living. With manhood on, you choose your road and hold by it. Take a wife and cleave to her, and to hell with romantic urges. Work and beget and rear and teach and toil. Leave hostages to fortune; let love renew itself as it will; and let one die unafraid. Oh, love that I threw away in a dark hour. Oh, my dark love.

A whisper, that he did not know was a whisper, came out of the air, "And she was beautiful?"

"That is only a word," he whispered back. "She had black hair and blue eyes, a generous mouth, and a white nape to her neck. No, not white! White is the color of dread. A smooth and fragrant ivory! And when I used

466

move my hand up from her neck through her hair, her hair used crackle and crisp between my fingers, and the waves of it reached my throat."

"And she had the thing we call a soul?"

"Shining through in day and dark."

"Ayeh me! there is no soul in this valley or in any valley. It is what we seek, and we do not know what it is. My Queen Mother knows, and she tells a story that once in a hundred years one of us wins a soul through a great pain and great sacrifice, and that one is seen no more, ever. I held you as long as I could, Golden."

"You held me a long time."

"Not against your will?"

"Not against my will."

"And I will not hold you against your will now. Pain I know, and if I must know more, I will know it. Come!"

He found himself on his feet, her left hand holding his right as of yore. Head down, he went where she drew him. He found himself in a gap of the hills going downward; he found himself in shade between high stone walls, he found himself through the gut, and a clean cool live air in his face. And there was a final whisper, "You are back now, Golden, and I go, where I do not know. All I know is that I will never see you again, never, never, never."

After a while he had grace enough to lift his head and turn round. Princess was not there, and there was no longer a gap between the chorrie and the cliff.

"And that is the end of that," he said in his throat, and there was neither sorrow nor regret in him.

He went out of the side gap then, and into his own valley, and up by the course of the runlet. He went slow-footed, heart down, head down, not daring to lift his head for fear of what he might see—ruined thatched, gaping windows, broken walls.

So in time he came to the little pool of spring water, and sat him down on the boss of stone where he had sat seven years before. He looked through the shimmering translucency of the water, and went deep into the recesses of his own mind.

It was again a sun-hazed summer afternoon, and stillness was over all that land. The birds were not yet singing, though goldfinches flitted from whin to whin; and the tinkle of running water was in a remote dimension of its own.

After a time Manus sighed deeply, drew in a long breath and stiffened his shoulders. His voice was sad, but not forlorn, "Seven years is a long time, but it is by, and there is nothing I can do about it. I threw the living life away, but there is great life in me still. If it be so willed, and the one woman remains to me still, I will seek her out at the world's end, and put my hands under her feet, and cherish her, and strive for her and her children, so that life shall be always eager and always calling. And if that is not given me, as God made me, I will face whatever life there is."

He shook his head, fiercely resolute, looked about him and stared.

"That is a strange thing," he said. "It looks like our water pail, but our pail will be worn into staves these many days."

A zinc-hooped wooden pail did, indeed, rest on the flag where many a pail had worn a ring. It was a good new pail and there were traces of moisture in the bottom of it.

Manus held his breath, and, for the first time, looked up the slope. Then he exhaled shortly. For the cottage was still there, nestling securely into the breast of the hill. It had not changed at all. The small four-paned windows shone; the walls were still blue-white; the door was still open to the summer air; and the rough-cast chimney out of the brown thatch sent up a thin ribbon of smoke, as if some housewife were burning furze roots to boil a kettle.

Manus smiled, and some of the old dare-devil was back in his smile. He got to his feet.

"Whatever woman is in that house," said he, "she will be having use for a pail of spring water. Very well so! A

468

pail of spring water she shall have, and let it be a good beginning to set my feet on the seeking road."

Firmly, then, he scooped the pail full, and faced the upward path steadily, shelf above shelf amongst the furze and bracken. He stood in the open doorway, and his heart hollowed out, and he drew thin air into a tightened throat.

Maire, his young wife, sat there at the fireside on her hassock. She was placidly knitting, and a last furze root was burning down into white ash. She half turned and smiled her slow smile.

"You took a long time to bring me my pail of water," she said in her quiet, soft voice.

His voice might have broken if he had not kept it vibrating deeply in his throat.

"But in the end I brought it. Was it a long time indeed?"

"A full hour anyway."

"I thought it was longer," said Manus evenly.

"No. You were sitting on the stone hunched over, and brooding to yourself. I thought you were asleep."

"Asleep and dreaming. But at end—in one hour or in seven years—I had only one desire in all the world."

Something in his voice, in his eyes made her heart shake her.

"Yes, Manus?" she said softly.

His voice thickened. "I only wanted to come back to you and put my hands under your feet."

Her heart turned completely over, and her blue eyes were drowned in the glow of his yellow ones.

"Manus Boy, Manus Boy! You are back to me."

"Till time and tides are done, one woman."

He put the pail down at the fireside. He ran his hand from the soft cream of her neck into her black hair, and it crisped and crinkled between his fingers. He bent his cheek to hers and whispered, "Let us not boil the kettle for a small while yet."

And she turned her mouth to his.

But what of the fairy Princess? Was she only the vision of an hour to show a man the definite road he must take? It could be. Yet there is a tradition in that countryside of a sad and lonesome small song that comes out of the hillside in the gloaming of a June evening. Words have been put to that song, and here are a few of them:

When I see the plover rising
Or the curlew wheeling,
Then I hope my mortal lover
Back to me is stealing.

It is not easy to win a soul.

OSCAR WILDE

The Happy Prince

❄

High above the city, on a tall column, stood the statue of the Happy Prince. He was gilded all over with thin leaves of fine gold, for eyes he had two bright sapphires, and a large red ruby glowed on his sword-hilt.

He was very much admired indeed. "He is as beautiful as a weathercock," remarked one of the Town Councillors who wished to gain a reputation for having artistic tastes; "only not quite so useful," he added, fearing lest people should think him unpractical, which he really was not.

"Why can't you be like the Happy Prince?" asked a sensible mother of her little boy who was crying for the moon. "The Happy Prince never dreams of crying for anything."

"I am glad there is some one in the world who is quite happy," muttered a disappointed man as he gazed at the wonderful statue.

From The Happy Prince and Other Tales, London.

"He looks just like an angel," said the Charity Children as they came out of the cathedral in their bright scarlet cloaks and their clean white pinafores.

"How do you know?" said the Mathematical Master, "you have never seen one."

"Ah! but we have, in our dreams," answered the children; and the Mathematical Master frowned and looked very severe, for he did not approve of children dreaming.

One night there flew over the city a little Swallow. His friends had gone away to Egypt six weeks before, but he had stayed behind, for he was in love with the most beautiful Reed. He had met her early in the spring as he was flying down the river after a big yellow moth, and had been so attracted by her slender waist that he had stopped to talk to her.

"Shall I love you?" said the Swallow, who liked to come to the point at once, and the Reed made him a low bow. So he flew round and round her, touching the water with his wings, and making silver ripples. This was his courtship, and it lasted all through the summer.

"It is a ridiculous attachment," twittered the other Swallows; "she has no money, and far too many relations"; and indeed the river was quite full of Reeds. Then, when the autumn came they all flew away.

After they had gone he felt lonely, and began to tire of his lady-love. "She has no conversation," he said, "and I am afraid that she is a coquette, for she is always flirting with the wind." And certainly, whenever the wind blew, the Reed made the most graceful curtseys. "I admit that she is domestic," he continued, "but I love travelling, and my wife, consequently, should love travelling also."

"Will you come away with me?" he said finally to her, but the Reed shook her head, she was so attached to her home.

"You have been trifling with me," he cried. "I am off to the Pyramids. Good-bye!" and he flew away.

All day long he flew, and at night-time he arrived at

the city. "Where shall I put up?" he said; "I hope the town has made preparations."

Then he saw the statue on the tall column.

"I will put up there," he cried; "it is a fine position, with plenty of fresh air." So he alighted just between the feet of the Happy Prince.

"I have a golden bedroom," he said softly to himself as he looked round, and he prepared to go to sleep; but just as he was putting his head under his wing a large drop of water fell on him. "What a curious thing!" he cried; "there is not a single cloud in the sky, the stars are quite clear and bright, and yet it is raining. The climate in the north of Europe is really dreadful. The Reed used to like the rain, but that was merely her selfishness."

Then another drop fell.

"What is the use of a statue if it cannot keep the rain off?" he said; "I must look for a good chimney-pot," and he determined to fly away.

But before he had opened his wings, a third drop fell, and he looked up, and saw——Ah! what did he see?

The eyes of the Happy Prince were filled with tears, and tears were running down his golden cheeks. His face was so beautiful in the moonlight that the little Swallow was filled with pity.

"Who are you?" he said.

"I am the Happy Prince."

"Why are you weeping then?" asked the Swallow; "you have quite drenched me."

"When I was alive and had a human heart," answered the statue, "I did not know what tears were, for I lived in the Palace of Sans-Souci, where sorrow is not allowed to enter. In the daytime I played with my companions in the garden, and in the evening I led the dance in the Great Hall. Round the garden ran a very lofty wall, but I never cared to ask what lay beyond it, everything about me was so beautiful. My courtiers called me the Happy Prince, and happy indeed I was, if pleasure be happiness. So I lived, and so I died. And now that I am dead they have set me up here so high that I can see all the ugliness and all the misery of my city, and though my heart is made of lead yet I cannot choose but weep."

"What! is he not solid gold?" said the Swallow to himself. He was too polite to make any personal remarks out loud.

"Far away," continued the statue in a low musical voice, "far away in a little street there is a poor house. One of the windows is open, and through it I can see a woman seated at a table. Her face is thin and worn, and she has coarse, red hands, all pricked by the needle, for she is a seamstress. She is embroidering passion-flowers on a satin gown for the loveliest of the Queen's maids-of-honour to wear at the next Court-ball. In a bed in the corner of the room her little boy is lying ill. He has a fever, and is asking for oranges. His mother has nothing to give him but river water, so he is crying. Swallow, Swallow, little Swallow, will you not bring her the ruby out of my sword-hilt? My feet are fastened to this pedestal and I cannot move."

"I am waited for in Egypt," said the Swallow. "My friends are flying up and down the Nile, and talking to the large lotus-flowers. Soon they will go to sleep in the tomb of the great King. The King is there himself in his painted coffin. He is wrapped in yellow linen, and embalmed with spices. Round his neck is a chain of pale green jade, and his hands are like withered leaves."

"Swallow, Swallow, little Swallow," said the Prince, "will you not stay with me for one night, and be my messenger? The boy is so thirsty, and the mother so sad."

"I don't think I like boys," answered the Swallow. "Last summer, when I was staying on the river, there were two rude boys, the miller's sons, who were always throwing stones at me. They never hit me, of course; we swallows fly far too well for that, and besides, I come of a family famous for its agility; but still, it was a mark of disrespect."

But the Happy Prince looked so sad that the little

Swallow was sorry. "It is very cold here," he said; "but I will stay with you for one night, and be your messenger."

"Thank you, little Swallow," said the Prince.

So the Swallow picked out the great ruby from the Prince's sword, and flew away with it in his beak over the roofs of the town.

He passed by the cathedral tower, where the white marble angels were sculptured. He passed by the palace and heard the sound of dancing. A beautiful girl came out on the balcony with her lover. "How wonderful the stars are," he said to her, "and how wonderful is the power of love!"

"I hope my dress will be ready in time for the State-ball," she answered; "I have ordered passion-flowers to be embroidered on it; but the seamstresses are so lazy."

He passed over the river, and saw the lanterns hanging to the masts of the ships. He passed over the Ghetto, and saw the old Jews bargaining with each other, and weighing out money in copper scales. At last he came to the poor house and looked in. The boy was tossing feverishly on his bed, and the mother had fallen asleep, she was so tired. In he hopped, and laid the great ruby on the table beside the woman's thimble. Then he flew gently round the bed, fanning the boy's forehead with his wings. "How cool I feel!" said the boy, "I must be getting better"; and he sank into a delicious slumber.

Then the Swallow flew back to the Happy Prince, and told him what he had done. "It is curious," he remarked, "but I feel quite warm now, although it is so cold."

"That is because you have done a good action," said the Prince. And the little Swallow began to think, and then he fell asleep. Thinking always made him sleepy.

When day broke he flew down to the river and had a bath. "What a remarkable phenomenon!" said the Professor of Ornithology as he was passing over the bridge. "A swallow in winter!" And he wrote a long letter about it to the local newspaper. Every one quoted it, it was full of so many words that they could not understand.

"To-night I go to Egypt," said the Swallow, and he was in high spirits at the prospect. He visited all the public monuments, and sat a long time on top of the church steeple. Wherever he went the Sparrows chirruped, and said to each other, "What a distinguished stranger!" so he enjoyed himself very much.

When the moon rose he flew back to the Happy Prince. "Have you any commissions for Egypt?" he cried; "I am just starting."

"Swallow, Swallow, little Swallow," said the Prince, "will you not stay with me one night longer?"

"I am waited for in Egypt," answered the Swallow. "To-morrow my friends will fly up to the Second Cataract. The river-horse couches there among the bulrushes, and on a great granite throne sits the God Memnon. All night long he watches the stars, and when the morning star shines he utters one cry of joy, and then he is silent. At noon the yellow lions come down to the water's edge to drink. They have eyes like green beryls, and their roar is louder than the roar of the cataract."

"Swallow, Swallow, little Swallow," said the Prince, "far away across the city I see a young man in a garret. He is leaning over a desk covered with papers, and in a tumbler by his side there is a bunch of withered violets. His hair is brown and crisp, and his lips are red as a pomegranate, and he has large and dreamy eyes. He is trying to finish a play for the Director of the Theater, but he is too cold to write any more. There is no fire in the grate, and hunger has made him faint."

"I will wait with you one night longer," said the Swallow, who really had a good heart. "Shall I take him another ruby?"

"Alas! I have no ruby now," said the Prince; "my eyes are all that I have left. They are made of rare sapphires, which were brought out of India a thousand years ago. Pluck out one of them and take it to him. He will sell it to the jeweller, and buy firewood, and finish his play."

"Dear Prince," said the Swallow, "I cannot do that"; and he began to weep.

"Swallow, Swallow, little Swallow," said the Prince, "do as I command you."

So the Swallow plucked out the Prince's eye, and flew away to the student's garret. It was easy enough to get in, as there was a hole in the roof. Through this he darted, and came into the room. The young man had his head buried in his hands, so he did not hear the flutter of the bird's wings, and when he looked up he found the beautiful sapphire lying on the withered violets.

"I am beginning to be appreciated," he cried; "this is from some great admirer. Now I can finish my play," and he looked quite happy.

The next day the Swallow flew down to the harbor. He sat on the mast of a large vessel and watched the sailors hauling big chests out of the hold with ropes. "Heave a-hoy!" they shouted as each chest came up. "I am going to Egypt!" cried the Swallow, but nobody minded, and when the moon rose he flew back to the Happy Prince.

"I am come to bid you good-bye," he cried.

"Swallow, Swallow, little Swallow," said the Prince, "will you not stay with me one night longer?"

"It is winter," answered the Swallow, "and the chill snow will soon be here. In Egypt the sun is warm on the green palm-trees, and the crocodiles lie in the mud and look lazily about them. My companions are building a nest in the Temple of Baalbec, and the pink and white doves are watching them, and cooing to each other. Dear Prince, I must leave you, but I will never forget you, and next spring I will bring you back two beautiful jewels in place of those you have given away. The ruby shall be redder than a red rose, and the sapphire shall be as blue as the great sea."

"In the square below," said the Happy Prince, "there stands a little match-girl. She has let her matches fall in the gutter, and they are all spoiled. Her father will beat her if she does not bring home some money, and she is crying. She has no shoes or stockings, and her little head is bare. Pluck out my other eye, and give it to her, and her father will not beat her."

"I will stay with you one night longer," said the Swallow, "but I cannot pluck out your eye. You would be quite blind then."

"Swallow, Swallow, little Swallow," said the Prince, "do as I command you."

So he plucked out the Prince's other eye, and darted down with it. He swooped past the match-girl, and slipped the jewel into the palm of her hand. "What a lovely bit of glass!" cried the little girl; and she ran home, laughing.

Then the Swallow came back to the Prince. "You are blind now," he said, "so I will stay with you always."

"No, little Swallow," said the poor prince, "you must go away to Egypt."

"I will stay with you always," said the Swallow, and he slept at the Prince's feet.

All the next day he sat on the Prince's shoulder, and told him stories of what he had seen in strange lands. He told him of the red ibises, who stand in long rows on the banks of the Nile, and catch goldfish in their beaks; of the Sphinx, who is as old as the world itself, and lives in the desert, and knows everything; of the merchants, who walk slowly by the side of their camels and carry amber beads in their hands; of the King of the Mountains of the Moon, who is as black as ebony, and worships a large crystal; of the great green snake that sleeps in a palm-tree, and has twenty priests to feed it with honey-cakes; and of the pygmies who sail over a big lake on large flat leaves, and are always at war with the butterflies.

"Dear little Swallow," said the Prince, "you tell me of marvellous things, but more marvellous than anything is the suffering of men and of women. There is no Mystery so great as Misery. Fly over my city, little Swallow, and tell me what you see there."

So the Swallow flew over the great city, and saw the rich making merry in their beautiful houses, while the beggars were sitting at the gates. He flew into dark lanes, and saw the white faces of starving children looking out listlessly at the black streets. Under the archway of a bridge two little boys were lying in one another's arms to try and keep themselves warm. "How hungry we are!" they said. "You must not lie here," shouted the watchman, and they wandered out into the rain.

Then he flew back and told the Prince what he had seen.

"I am covered with fine gold," said the Prince, "you must take it off, leaf by leaf, and give it to my poor; the living always think that gold can make them happy."

Leaf after leaf of the fine gold the Swallow picked off, till the Happy Prince looked quite dull and grey. Leaf after leaf of the fine gold he brought to the poor, and the children's faces grew rosier, and they laughed and played games in the street. "We have bread now!" they cried.

Then the snow came, and after the snow came the frost. The streets looked as if they were made of silver, they were so bright and glistening; long icicles like crystal daggers hung down from the eaves of the houses, everybody went about in furs, and the little boys wore scarlet caps and skated on the ice.

The poor little Swallow grew colder and colder, but he would not leave the Prince, he loved him too well. He picked up crumbs outside the baker's door when the baker was not looking, and tried to keep himself warm by flapping his wings.

But at last he knew that he was going to die. He had just enough strength to fly up to the Prince's shoulder once more. "Good-bye, dear Prince!" he murmured, "will you let me kiss your hand?"

"I am glad that you are going to Egypt at last, little Swallow," said the Prince, "you have stayed too long here; but you must kiss me on the lips, for I love you."

"It is not to Egypt that I am going," said the Swallow. "I am going to the House of Death. Death is the brother of Sleep, is he not?"

And he kissed the Happy Prince on the lips, and fell down dead at his feet.

At that moment a curious crack sounded inside the statue, as if something had broken. The fact is that the leaden heart had snapped right in two. It certainly was a dreadfully hard frost.

Early the next morning the Mayor was walking in the square below in company with the Town Councillors. As they passed the column he looked up at the statue: "Dear me! how shabby the Happy Prince looks!" he said.

"How shabby, indeed!" cried the Town Councillors, who always agreed with the Mayor: and they went up to look at it.

"The ruby has fallen out of his sword, his eyes are gone, and he is golden no longer," said the Mayor; "in fact, he is little better than a beggar!"

"Little better than a beggar," said the Town Councillors.

"And here is actually a dead bird at his feet!" continued the Mayor. "We must really issue a proclamation that birds are not to be allowed to die here." And the Town Clerk made a note of the suggestion.

So they pulled down the statue of the Happy Prince. "As he is no longer beautiful he is no longer useful," said the Art Professor at the University.

Then they melted the statue in a furnace, and the Mayor held a meeting of the Corporation to decide what was to be done with the metal. "We must have another statue, of course," he said, "and it shall be a statue of myself."

"Of myself," said each of the Town Councillors, and they quarrelled. When I last heard of them they were quarrelling still.

"What a strange thing!" said the overseer of the workmen at the foundry. "This broken lead heart will not melt in the furnace. We must throw it away." So they threw it on a dust-heap where the dead Swallow was also lying.

"Bring me the two most precious things in the city," said God to one of His Angels; and the Angel brought Him the leaden heart and the dead bird.

"You have rightly chosen," said God, "for in my garden of Paradise this little bird shall sing for evermore, and in my city of gold the Happy Prince shall praise Me."

WILLIAM BUTLER YEATS

Red Hanrahan

✽

Hanrahan, the hedge schoolmaster, a tall, strong, red-haired young man, came into the barn where some of the men of the village were sitting on Samhain Eve. It had been a dwelling-house, and when the man that owned it had built a better one, he had put the two rooms together, and kept it for a place to store one thing or another. There was a fire on the old hearth, and there were dip candles stuck in bottles, and there was a black quart bottle upon some boards that had been put across two barrels to make a table. Most of the men were sitting beside the fire, and one of them was singing a long wandering song, about a Munster man and a Connaught man that were quarrelling about their two provinces.

Hanrahan went to the man of the house and said, "I got your message"; but when he had said that, he stopped, for an old mountainy man that had a shirt and trousers of unbleached flannel, and that was sitting by himself near

From STORIES OF RED HANRAHAN, New York, The Macmillan Company.

the door, was looking at him, and moving an old pack of cards about in his hands and muttering. "Don't mind him," said the man of the house; "he is only some stranger came in awhile ago, and we bade him welcome, it being Samhain night, but I think he is not in his right wits. Listen to him now and you will hear what he is saying."

They listened then, and they could hear the old man muttering to himself as he turned the cards, "Spades and Diamonds, Courage and Power; Clubs and Hearts, Knowledge and Pleasure."

"That is the kind of talk he has been going on with for the last hour," said the man of the house, and Hanrahan turned his eyes from the old man as if he did not like to be looking at him.

"I got your message," Hanrahan said then; "he is in the barn with his three first cousins from Gilchreist," the messenger said, "and there are some of the neighbours with them."

"It is my cousin over there is wanting to see you," said the man of the house, and he called over a young frieze-coated man, who was listening to the song, and said, "This is Red Hanrahan you have the message for."

"It is a kind message, indeed," said the young man, "for it comes from your sweetheart, Mary Lavelle."

"How would you get a message from her, and what do you know of her?"

"I don't know her, indeed, but I was in Loughrea yesterday, and a neighbour of hers that had some dealings with me was saying that she bade him send you word, if he met anyone from this side in the market, that her mother has died from her, and if you have a mind yet to join with herself, she is willing to keep her word to you."

"I will go to her indeed," said Hanrahan.

"And she bade you make no delay, for if she has not a man in the house before the month is out, it is likely the little bit of land will be given to another."

When Hanrahan heard that, he rose up from the bench he had sat down on. "I will make no delay indeed," he said, "there is a full moon, and if I get as far as Gilchreist to-night, I will reach to her before the setting of the sun to-morrow."

When the others heard that, they began to laugh at him for being in such haste to go to his sweetheart, and one asked him if he would leave his school in the old limekiln, where he was giving the children such good learning. But he said the children would be glad enough in the morning to find the place empty, and no one to keep them at their task; and as for his school he could set it up again in any place, having as he had his little inkpot hanging from his neck by a chain, and his big Virgil and his primer in the skirt of his coat.

Some of them asked him to drink a glass before he went, and a young man caught hold of his coat, and said he must not leave them without singing the song he had made in praise of Venus and of Mary Lavelle. He drank a glass of whiskey, but he said he would not stop but would set out on his journey.

"There's time enough, Red Hanrahan," said the man of the house. "It will be time enough for you to give up sport when you are after your marriage, and it might be a long time before we will see you again."

"I will not stop," said Hanrahan; "my mind would be on the roads all the time, bringing me to the woman that sent for me, and she lonesome and watching till I come."

Some of the others came about him, pressing him that had been such a pleasant comrade, so full of songs and every kind of trick and fun, not to leave them till the night would be over, but he refused them all, and shook them off, and went to the door. But as he put his foot over the threshold, the strange old man stood up and put his hand that was thin and withered like a bird's claw on Hanrahan's hand, and said: "It is not Hanrahan, the learned man and the great songmaker, that should go out from a gathering like this, on a Samhain night. And stop here, now," he said, "and play a hand with me; and here is

484

an old pack of cards has done its work many a night before this, and old as it is, there has been much of the riches of the world lost and won over it."

One of the young men said, "It isn't much of the riches of the world has stopped with yourself, old man," and he looked at the old man's bare feet, and they all laughed. But Hanrahan did not laugh, but he sat down very quietly, without a word. Then one of them said, "So you will stop with us after all, Hanrahan"; and the old man said: "He will stop indeed, did you not hear me asking him?"

They all looked at the old man then as if wondering where he came from. "It is far I am come," he said, "through France I have come, and through Spain, and by Lough Greine of the hidden mouth, and none has refused me anything." And then he was silent and nobody liked to question him, and they began to play. There were six men at the boards playing, and the others were looking on behind. They played two or three games for nothing, and then the old man took a fourpenny bit, worn very thin and smooth, out from his pocket, and he called to the rest to put something on the game. Then they all put down something on the boards, and little as it was it looked much, from the way it was shoved from one to another, first one man winning it and then his neighbour. And sometimes the luck would go against a man and he would have nothing left, and then one or another would lend him something, and he would pay it again out of his winnings, for neither good nor bad luck stopped long with anyone.

And once Hanrahan said as a man would say in a dream, "It is time for me to be going the road"; but just then a good card came to him, and he played it out, and all the money began to come to him. And once he thought of Mary Lavelle, and he sighed; and that time his luck went from him, and he forgot her again.

But at last the luck went to the old man and it stayed with him, and all they had flowed into him, and he began to laugh little laughs to himself, and to sing over and over to himself, "Spades and Diamonds, Courage and Power," and so on, as if it was a verse of a song.

And after a while anyone looking at the men, and seeing the way their bodies were rocking to and fro, and the way they kept their eyes on the old man's hands, would think they had drink taken, or that the whole story they had in the world was put on the cards; but that was not so, for the quart bottle had not been disturbed since the game began, and was nearly full yet, and all that was on the game was a few sixpenny bits and shillings, and maybe a handful of coppers.

"You are good men to win and good men to lose," said the old man, "you have play in your hearts." He began then to shuffle the cards and to mix them, very quick and fast, till at last they could not see them to be cards at all, but you would think him to be making rings of fire in the air, as little lads would make them with whirling a lighted stick; and after that it seemed to them that all the room was dark, and they could see nothing but his hands and the cards.

And all in a minute a hare made a leap out from between his hands, and whether it was one of the cards that took that shape, or whether it was made out of nothing in the palms of his hands, nobody knew, but there it was running on the floor of the barn, as quick as any hare that ever lived.

Some looked at the hare, but more kept their eyes on the old man, and while they were looking at him a hound made a leap out between his hands, the same way as the hare did, and after that another hound and another, till there was a whole pack of them following the hare round and round the barn.

The players were all standing up now, with their backs to the boards, shrinking from the hounds, and nearly deafened with the noise of their yelping, but as quick as the hounds were they could not overtake the hare, but it went round, till at the last it seemed as if a blast of wind burst open the barn door, and the hare doubled and made a leap over the boards where the men had been playing, and went out of the door and away through the night, and the hounds over the boards and through the door after it.

Then the old man called out, "Follow the hounds, follow the hounds, and it is a great hunt you will see to-night," and he went out after them. But used as the men were to go hunting after hares, and ready as they were for any sport, they were in dread to go out into the night, and it was only Hanrahan that rose up and that said, "I will follow, I will follow on."

"You had best stop here, Hanrahan," the young man that was nearest him said, "for you might be going into some great danger." But Hanrahan said, "I will see fair play, I will see fair play," and he went stumbling out of the door like a man in a dream, and the door shut after him as he went.

He thought he saw the old man in front of him, but it was only his own shadow that the full moon cast on the road before him, but he could hear the hounds crying after the hare over the wide green fields of Granagh, and he followed them very fast, for there was nothing to stop him; and after a while he came to smaller fields that had little walls of loose stones around them, and he threw the stones down as he crossed them, and did not wait to put them up again; and he passed by the place where the river goes under ground at Ballylee, and he could hear the hounds going before him up towards the head of the river. Soon he found it harder to run, for it was uphill he was go-ing, and clouds came over the moon, and it was hard for him to see his way, and once he left the path to take a short cut, but his foot slipped into a boghole and he had to come back to it. And how long he was going he did not know, or what way he went, but at last he was up on the bare moun-tain, with nothing but the rough heather about him, and he could neither hear the hounds nor any other thing. But their cry began to come to him again, at first far off and then very near, and when it came quite close to him, it went up all of a sudden into the air, and there was the sound of hunting over his head; then it went away northward till he could hear nothing more at all. "That's not fair," he said, "that's not fair." And he could walk no longer, but sat down on the heather where he was, in the heart of Slieve Echtge, for all the strength had gone from him, with the dint of the long journey he had made.

And after a while he took notice that there was a door close to him, and a light coming from it, and he wondered that being so close to him he had not seen it before. And he rose up, and tired as he was he went in at the door, and although it was night time outside, it was daylight he found within. And presently he met with an old man that had been gathering summer thyme and yellow flag-flowers, and it seemed as if all the sweet smells of the summer were with them. And the old man said: "It is a long time you have been coming to us, Hanrahan the learned man and the great songmaker."

And with that he brought him into a very big shining house, and every grand thing Hanrahan had ever heard of, and every color he had ever seen, were in it. There was a high place at the end of the house, and on it there was sitting in a high chair a woman, the most beautiful the world ever saw, having a long pale face and flowers about it, but she had the tired look of one that had been long waiting. And there was sitting on the step below her chair four grey old women, and the one of them was holding a great cauldron in her lap; and another a great stone on her knees, and heavy as it was it seemed light to her; and another of them had a very long spear that was made of pointed wood; and the last of them had a sword that was without a scabbard.

Hanrahan stood looking at them for a long time, but none of them spoke any word to him or looked at him at all. And he had it in his mind to ask who that woman in the chair was, that was like a queen, and what she was waiting for; but ready as he was with his tongue and afraid of no person, he was in dread now to speak to so beautiful a woman, and in so grand a place. And then he thought to ask what were the four things the four grey old women were holding like great treasures, but he could not think of the right words to bring out.

Then the first of the old women rose up, holding the cauldron between her two hands, and she said, "Pleasure," and Hanrahan said no word. Then the second old woman rose up with the stone in her hands, and she said, "Power"; and the third old woman rose up with the spear in her hand, and she said, "Courage"; and the last of the old women rose up having the sword in her hands, and she said, "Knowledge." And everyone, after she had spoken, waited as if for Hanrahan to question her, but he said nothing at all. And then the four old women went out of the door, bringing their four treasures with them, and as they went out one of them said, "He has no wish for us"; and another said, "He is weak, he is weak"; and another said, "He is afraid"; and the last said, "His wits are gone from him." And then they all said, "Echtge, daughter of the Silver Hand, must stay in her sleep. It is a pity, it is a great pity."

And then the woman that was like a queen gave a very sad sigh, and it seemed to Hanrahan as if the sigh had the sound in it of hidden streams; and if the place he was in had been ten times grander and more shining than it was, he could not have hindered sleep from coming on him; and he staggered like a drunken man and lay down there and then.

When Hanrahan awoke, the sun was shining on his face, but there was white frost on the grass around him, and there was ice on the edge of the stream he was lying by, and that goes running on through Daire-caol and Druim-da-rod. He knew by the shape of the hills and by the shining of Lough Greine in the distance that he was upon one of the hills of Slieve Echtge, but he was not sure how he came there; for all that had happened in the barn had gone from him, and all of his journey but the soreness of his feet and the stiffness in his bones.

It was a year after that, there were men of the village of Cappaghtagle sitting by the fire in a house on the roadside, and Red Hanrahan that was now very thin and worn and his hair very long and wild, came to the half-door and asked leave to come in and rest himself; and they bid him welcome because it was Samhain night. He sat down with them, and they gave him a glass of whiskey out of a quart bottle; and they saw the little inkpot hanging about his neck, and knew he was a scholar, and asked for stories about the Greeks.

He took the Virgil out of the big pocket of his coat, but the cover was very black and swollen with the wet, and the page when he opened it was very yellow, but that was no great matter, for he looked at it like a man that had never learned to read. Some young man that was there began to laugh at him then, and to ask why did he carry so heavy a book with him when he was not able to read it.

It vexed Hanrahan to hear that, and he put the Virgil back in his pocket and asked if they had a pack of cards among them, for cards were better than books. When they brought out the cards he took them and began to shuffle them, and while he was shuffling them something seemed to come into his mind, and he put his hand to his face like one that is trying to remember, and he said: "Was I ever here before, or where was I on a night like this?" and then of a sudden he stood up and let the cards fall to the floor, and he said, "Who was it brought me a message from Mary Lavelle?"

"We never saw you before now, and we never heard of Mary Lavelle," said the man of the house. "And who is she," he said, "and what is it you are talking about?"

"It was this night a year ago, I was in a barn, and there were men playing cards, and there was money on the table, they were pushing it from one to another here and there—and I got a message, and I was going out of the door to look for my sweetheart that wanted me, Mary Lavelle."

And then Hanrahan called out very loud: "Where have I been since then? Where was I for the whole year?"

"It is hard to say where you might have been in that time," said the oldest of the men, "or what part of the world you may have travelled; and it is like enough you have the dust of many roads on your feet; for there are many go wandering and forgetting like that," he said, "when once they have been given the touch."

"That is true," said another of the men. "I knew a woman went wandering like that through the length of seven years; she came back after, and she told her friends she had often been glad enough to eat the food that was put in the pig's trough. And it is best for you to go to the priest now," he said, "and let him take off you whatever may have been put upon you."

"It is to my sweetheart I will go, to Mary Lavelle," said Hanrahan; "it is too long I have delayed, how do I know what might have happened her in the length of a year?"

He was going out of the door then, but they all told him it was best for him to stop the night, and to get strength for the journey; and indeed he wanted that, for he was very weak, and when they gave him food he eat it like a man that had never seen food before, and one of them said, "He is eating as if he had trodden on the hungry grass." It was in the white light of the morning he set out, and the time seemed long to him till he could get to Mary Lavelle's house. But when he came to it, he found the door broken, and the thatch dropping from the roof, and no living person to be seen. And when he asked the neighbours what had happened her, all they could say was that she had been put out of the house, and had married some laboring man, and they had gone looking for work to London or Liverpool or some big place. And whether she found a worse place or a better he never knew, but anyway he never met with her or with news of her again.

Where There Is Nothing, There Is God

※

Abbot Malathgeneus, Brother Dove, Brother Bald Fox, Brother Peter, Brother Patrick, Brother Bittern, Brother Fair-Brows sat about the fire, one mending lines to lay in the river for eels, one fashioning a snare for birds, one mending the broken handle of a spade, one writing in a large book, and one hammering at the corner of a gold box that was to hold the book; and among the rushes at their feet lay the scholars, who would one day be Brothers. One of these, a child of eight or nine years, called Olioll, lay upon his back looking up through the hole in the roof, through which the smoke went, and watching the stars appearing and disappearing in the smoke. He turned presently to the Brother who wrote in the big book, and whose duty was to teach the children, and said, "Brother Dove, to what are the stars fastened?" The Brother, pleased to find so much curiosity in the stupidest of his scholars, laid down the pen and said, "There are nine crystalline

From STORIES OF RED HANRAHAN, New York, The Macmillan Company.

492

spheres, and on the first the Moon is fastened, on the second the planet Mercury, on the third the planet Venus, on the fourth the Sun, on the fifth the planet Mars, on the sixth the planet Jupiter, on the seventh the planet Saturn; these are the wandering stars; and on the eighth are fastened the fixed stars; but the ninth sphere is a sphere made out of the First Substance."

"What is beyond that?" said the child.

"There is nothing beyond that; there is God."

And then the child's eyes strayed to the gold box, and he said, "Why has Brother Peter put a great ruby on the side of his box?"

"The ruby is a symbol of the love of God."

"Why is the ruby a symbol of the love of God?"

"Because it is red, like fire, and fire burns up everything, and where there is nothing, there is God."

The child sank into silence, but presently sat up and said, "There is somebody outside."

"No," replied the Brother. "It is only the wolves; I have heard them moving about in the snow for some time. They are growing very wild, now that the winter drives them from the mountains. They broke into a fold last night and carried off many sheep, and if we are not careful they will devour everything."

"No, it is the footstep of a man, for it is heavy; but I can hear the footsteps of the wolves also."

He had no sooner done speaking than somebody rapped three times.

"I will go and open, for he must be very cold."

"Do not open, for it may be a man-wolf, and he may devour us all."

But the boy had already drawn the bolt, and all the faces, most of them a little pale, turned towards the slowly-opening door.

"He has beads and a cross, he cannot be a man-wolf," said the child, as a man with the snow heavy on his long, ragged beard, and on his matted hair, that fell over his shoulders and nearly to his waist, and upon the tattered cloak that but half-covered his withered brown body, came in and looked slowly from face to face. Standing some way from the fire, and with eyes that had rested at last upon the Abbot Malathgeneus, he said, "O blessed abbot, let me come to the fire and warm myself; that I may not die of the cold and anger the Lord with a wilful martyrdom."

"Come to the fire," said the abbot. "It is a pitiful thing surely that any for whom Christ has died should be as poor as you."

The man sat over the fire, and Olioll took away his now dripping cloak and laid meat and bread and wine before him; but he would eat only of the bread, and he put away the wine, asking for water. When his beard and hair had begun to dry and his limbs had ceased to shiver, he spoke again.

"Set me to some labor, the hardest there is, for I am the poorest of God's poor."

Then the Brothers discussed together what work they could put him to, and at first to little purpose, for there was no labour that had not found its labourer; but at last one remembered that Father Bald Fox, whose business it was to turn the great quern in the quern-house, for he was too stupid for anything else, was getting old; and so he could go to the quern-house in the morning.

The cold passed away, and the spring grew to summer, and the quern was never idle, nor was it turned with grudging labour, for when any passed the beggar was heard singing as he drove the handle round. The last reason for gloom passed from the brotherhood, for Olioll, who had always been stupid and unteachable, grew clever, and this was the more miraculous because it had come of a sudden. One day he had been even duller than usual, and was beaten and told to know his lesson better in future or be sent into a lower class among little boys who would make a joke of him. He had gone out in tears, and when he came the next day, although his stupidity had so long been the byword of the school, he knew his lesson so well that he passed to the head of the class, and from that day was the best of scholars. At first Brother Dove thought this was an answer to his own prayers and grew proud; but when many far more fervid prayers for more important things had failed, he convinced himself that the child was trafficking with bards, or druids, or witches, and resolved to follow and watch. He had told his thought to the abbot, who told him to come to him the moment he hit the truth; and the next day, which was a Sunday, he stood in the path when the abbot and the Brothers were coming from vespers, and took the abbot by the sleeve and said, "The beggar is of the greatest of saints and of the workers of miracle. I followed Olioll but now, and when he came to the little wood by the quern-house I knew by the path broken in the under-wood and by the foot-marks in the muddy places that he had gone that way many times. I hid behind a bush where the path doubled upon itself at a sloping place, and under-stood by the tears in his eyes that his stupidity was too old and his wisdom too new to save him from terror of the rod. When he was in the quern-house I went to the window and looked in, and the birds came down and perched upon my head and my shoulders, for they are not timid in that holy place; and a wolf passed by, his right side shaking my habit, his left the leaves of a bush. Olioll opened his book and turned to the page I had told him to learn, and began to cry, and the beggar sat beside him and comforted him until he fell asleep. When his sleep was of the deepest the beggar knelt down and prayed aloud, and said, 'O Thou Who dwellest beyond the stars, show forth Thy power as at the beginning, and let knowledge sent from Thee awaken in his mind, wherein is nothing from the world'; and then a light broke out of the air and I smelt the breath of roses. I stirred a little, and the beggar turned and saw me, and, bending low, said, 'O Brother Dove, if I have done wrong, forgive me, and I will do penance. It was my pity moved me'; but I was afraid and I ran away, and did not stop running until I came here."

Then all the Brothers began talking together, one saying it was such and such a saint, and one that it was not he but another; and one that it was none of these, for they were still in their brotherhoods, but that it was such and such a one; and the talk was near to quarrelling, for each had begun to claim so great a saint for his native province. At last the abbot said, "He is none that you have named, for at Easter I had greeting from all, and each was in his brotherhood; but he is Aengus the Walker to Nowhere. Ten years ago he went into the forest that he might labour only with song to the Lord; but the fame of his holiness brought many thousands to his cell, so that a little pride clung to a soul from which all else had been driven. Nine years ago he dressed himself in rags, and from that day nobody has seen him, unless, indeed, it be true that he has been seen living among the wolves on the mountains and eating the grass of the fields. Let us go to him and bow down before him; for at last, after long seeking, he has found the nothing that is God."

Notes on the Authors

PAUL VINCENT CARROLL was born July 10, 1900, at Blackrock near Dundalk. A schoolteacher and a playwright of first rank, he is best known in America for his plays, *Shadow and Substance* and *The White Steed*, both of which had successful Broadway runs.

DESMOND CLARKE was born in 1907. His short stories have appeared in the *Manchester Guardian, New Writing, Dublin Magazine, The Bell, Irish Writing,* and elsewhere. Some of his stories have been listed by Martha Foley among the best for the years 1949, 1950, 1951. He has written a life of Thomas Prior which was published in 1951, and has recently completed a life of Arthur Dobbs, Governor of North Carolina (1754-1766). He is Librarian of the Royal Dublin Society and Editor of the *Journal of the Library Association of Ireland.*

JOHN COLLIER "Collector of demons, connoisseur of jinn, and an old acquaintance of the devil himself," as the *Saturday Review* described him, was born in London, England, in 1901. He lives there now. His knowledge of Ireland derives from a visit to that land, plus the reading of innumerable books.

DANIEL CORKERY was born in 1878 in Cork City and has spent his life there as a schoolmaster and Gaelic teacher. He has written a novel, four selections of short stories and two critical works. Three plays were produced at the Abbey. His influence on younger Irish writers, especially O'Connor and O'Faolain, has been considerable.

ERIC CROSS was born in Ireland in 1905, the son of an English father and Irish mother. Professionally a research chemist specializing in food and "organotherapy," his hobbies include writing short stories, broadcasting from Radio Eireann and touring Ireland from his home in County Mayo.

LORD DUNSANY Edward John Moreton Drax Plunkett has produced some sixty volumes of novels, short stories, poetry and plays. Born July 24, 1878, he was educated at Eton and Sandhurst, served with the Coldstream Guard in the Boer War and was wounded in World War I. He spends his time between Dunsany Castle, Co. Meath; Kent, England, and the west coast of the United States searching for the "lost times and vanished regimes" that haunt his imaginative stories.

ST. JOHN ERVINE's stories, plays, and novels are generally considered excellent expressions of the Ulster mind, if a bit on the aggressive side. A member of the Irish Academy of letters, he has had plays produced at the Abbey, which he managed for a time, and written a powerful novel, "Mrs. Martin's Man," depicting Ulster types. He lives in Devon.

NOTES ON THE AUTHORS

PADRAIC FALLON was born in Athenry, Galway, in 1906. He is a customs official at Wexford, where he writes excellent poetry and an occasional story for the *Dublin Magazine* and other periodicals.

ARNOLD HILL writes of the same middle-class Belfast individuals that engage St. John Ervine. Born in Belfast in 1918, he has had stories published in various English and Irish periodicals and plays produced by the B.B.C. and other broadcasting companies. Like most Irish writers, he is "working on a novel."

DAVID HOGAN (Frank Gallagher) A veteran of Ireland's war of independence has served long terms of imprisonment, engaged in protracted hunger strikes, (the shortest 3 days, the longest 41 days) been an official of the first Dail Eireann and founder-editor of the *Irish Press*. He has written a history of these events and called it *Four Glorious Years*. He has also written *Days of Fear* the journal of a hunger strike.

JAMES JOYCE was born in Dublin, February 2, 1882, and died at Zürich, Switzerland, January 13, 1941. His influence on modern literature is very great indeed, and his stature seems to be gaining with the years.

PATRICK KAVANAGH was born on a farm in Co. Monaghan in 1905. He has published an autobiography, *The Green Fool*, a novel, *Tarry Flynn*, and some fine poetry in a slim volume called *A Soul for Sale*. He lives in Dublin, where he has become something of a legend.

MARY LAVIN lives in Co. Meath on a farm. She was born in Boston, Mass., in 1912, but was raised and educated in Ireland, where she was graduated from the National University, Dublin. She has published several books of short stories and two novels.

DONAGH MacDONAGH was born in Dublin in 1912, son of the 1916 poet Thomas MacDonagh. Educated at University College, Dublin, he is a barrister who writes as a hobby. Two volumes of verse and a verse play, *Happy As Larry*, have been published.

MICHAEL MacGRIAN is the pen name of C.A.M. West of Anglesey, N. Wales. He was born in 1910 "in the sweet County Down." In 1930, he visited the U.S. and Canada for five years, served another five with the RAF as Pathfinder Navigator. In 1946, he won a Rockefeller Award in literature and moved with his family to Wales. He has written a number of stories and is working on a novel.

MICHAEL McLAVERTY was born in Co. Monaghan in 1907 and was educated at St. Malachy's College in the city of Belfast. He has lived there ever since and teaches school. His novels (six to date) have enjoyed increasing popularity in America. *The Game Cock*, a collection of short stories, achieved great critical acclaim when published here in 1947.

BRYAN MacMAHON first made a hit with his book of stories, *The Lion Tamer*, published here in 1949. It was followed by a successful novel, *Children of the Rainbow*, 1952. He was born in Listowel, Co. Kerry, and now teaches school there. A second book of stories, *The Red Petticoat*, was published in 1955.

GEORGE MOORE was born in 1852 in Co. Mayo, spent much of his adult life in London, where he died in 1933. He spent the years 1901-1910 in Dublin, however, and there wrote his book of short stories, *The Untilled Field*. He is best known for his three-volume history of the Literary Revival, *Hail and Farewell*, and for his somewhat ostentatious conversation to Protestantism.

VAL MULKERNS (Mrs. Maurice Kennedy) was born in Dublin and educated at the Dominican College there. She has taught school and written a successful novel, *A Time Outworn*, which Frank O'Connor has praised as "the most interesting and significant to have come out of Ireland in 25 years." She now lives in Dublin and is working on a second novel.

498

BRIAN O'NOLAN is better known by his two pseudonyms, Flann O'Brien (author of *At Swim-Two-Birds*) and Myles na gCopaleen (columnist of the *Irish Times*). He was born in Strabane, Co. Tyrone, in 1912, studied in Berlin and holds a degree of M.A. from the National University, Dublin. He is equally at home in Irish and English. Married and lives in Dublin.

PADRAIC O CONAIRE our only Gaelic author, was born in 1882 in Galway City. Educated by the Christian Brothers, he taught Gaelic classes in London. Two books of stories and sketches have been translated into English. He died in Dublin in 1928. A statue, subscribed for by Gaels the world over, was unveiled in Galway in 1935.

FRANK O'CONNOR (Michael O'Donovan), Ireland's best-known contemporary writer, has had six selections of his stories published here. Born in Cork City in 1903, he has taken part in "The Troubles," been a librarian, a director of the Abbey Theatre, translated various poems from the Gaelic, written several novels and a travel book and is presently living in the United States, where he has been giving courses in the short story at various universities.

SEAN O'FAOLAIN was born in Dublin in 1900, and raised in Cork. He was graduated from University College, Dublin. He has done his stint with the I.R.A., taught school, edited *The Bell*, is perhaps Ireland's most prolific writer. Three novels, five full-length biographies, three travel books, three volumes of short stories plus a book on writing, a study of the Irish temperament and a collection of translations from the Irish have appeared to date. He has studied at Harvard and given a series of graduate lectures at Princeton.

LIAM O'FLAHERTY was born in the Aran Islands in 1897 and early studied for the priesthood. After a short time at University College, Dublin, he joined the Irish Guards and spent six months in France, returning shellshocked to Ireland, where he has lived, off and on, ever since. He has written 14 novels, the best of which are *The Informer* and *Famine*. His various shorty-story selections have been combed and a volume of the best of them, *The Stories of Liam O'Flaherty*, was published in 1955 by Devin-Adair.

SEUMAS O'KELLY was born in Galway. His first book of stories was published in 1906. It was followed by three others and by a novel, *The Lady of Deer Park*. Several of his plays were produced at the Abbey. He died prematurely in 1918.

JIM PHELAN is a tramp by profession, in the tradition of Jack London and Jim Tully. About 35 years ago, he "took to the road and quite suddenly felt at peace and at home." He has published a book of tramp stories and another of Irish stories, as well as two books of autobiographical sketches. Born in Ireland, he presently lives in England.

JAMES PLUNKETT (Kelly) was born in Dublin. He was educated by the Christian Brothers, is a trade union official and plays the viola professionally. His first book of short stories, *The Trusting and the Maimed*, was published in 1955 by Devin-Adair. He is married and has three children. His trip to Russia in 1955 created a sensation in Dublin.

GEORGE BERNARD SHAW published the altogether remarkable story (remarkable that Shaw should have written it) included here, in 1885. Born in Dublin in 1856, Shaw died in London in 1950. He was a charter member of the Irish Academy and one of the great playwrights of all time.

EDWARD SHEEHY was born in Tralee, Co. Kerry, some forty years ago and holds an M.A. degree from the National University. He has contributed stories to different magazines, taught school and presently lives in Co. Wicklow with his artist-wife and two children.

NOTES ON THE AUTHORS

JAMES STEPHENS was born in Dublin in 1881. He died in London in 1950. A novel, *The Crock of Gold*, has become a classic. His collected poetry was recently reissued by Macmillan. He died before completing his autobiography, from which "A Rhinoceros, Some Ladies and a Horse" is taken.

MAURICE WALSH was born May 2, 1879, in County Kerry on a farm. He became a customs officer and traveled widely through the British Isles. His *Saturday Evening Post* stories became very popular in the U.S. He has published some 14 novels, served as president of the Irish P.E.N. and now lives outside Dublin. He has three sons and two grandsons.

OSCAR FINGAL O'FLAHERTIE WILLS WILDE was born in Dublin on October 16, 1854, and died in Paris on November 30, 1900. He was buried in the cemetery of Père Lachaise. In 1951, St. John Ervine published *Oscar Wilde: A Present Day Appraisal*. The *Complete Works* have recently been made available through Dutton & Company; also *The Epigrams of Oscar Wilde* (John Day) and the autobiography of Wilde's son, Vyvyan Holland.

WILLIAM BUTLER YEATS was born near Dublin, June 13, 1865, and died Jan. 28, 1939, while visiting in France. His genius is universally recognized and his reputation increases with the years.